Dimension X

OTHER BOOKS BY DAMON KNIGHT

DIMENSION X

FIVE SCIENCE FICTION NOVELLAS
COMPILED BY
DAMON KNIGHT

SIMON AND SCHUSTER
NEW YORK

ACKNOWLEDGMENTS

"The Man Who Sold the Moon," by Robert A. Heinlein, copyright 1949 by Robert A. Heinlein; reprinted from *The Man Who Sold the Moon* by permission of the author and Lurton Blassingame.

"The Marching Morons," by C. M. Kornbluth, copyright 1951 by Galaxy Publishing Corp.; reprinted from *Galaxy* by permission of Robert P. Mills, Ltd.

"Fiddler's Green," by Richard McKenna, copyright © 1967 by Damon Knight; reprinted from *Orbit 2* by permission of Mrs. Eva McKenna.

"The Saliva Tree," by Brian Aldiss, copyright © 1965 by Mercury Press, Inc.; reprinted from *The Magazine of Fantasy and Science Fiction* by permission of the author and Scott Meredith Literary Agency, Inc.

"The Ugly Little Boy," by Isaac Asimov, copyright © 1958 by Galaxy Publishing Corp.; reprinted from *Galaxy* by permission of the author.

First Printing

SBN 671-65129-3 Trade
SBN 671-65128-5 Library
Library of Congress Catalog Card Number: 71-122940
Manufactured in the United States of America

CONTENTS

1694805

The Man Who Sold the Moon

The Man Who Sold the Moon

ROBERT A. HEINLEIN

In 1949, when this story was first published, a flight to the Moon was science fiction—or, as most people still called it, "pseudoscience." In 1969, as I write, it is journalism. The curious thing is that Heinlein's account does not suffer by contrast with the "real" events as they actually happen. His fiction is so circumstantial, so believable, and so self-consistent that it has a reality of its own.

"The Man Who Sold the Moon" is the story of a man obsessed by a private vision. Ordinary people can't cope with him because they are limited by prudence and common sense. They fear him, admire him in spite of themselves, and in the end bring him down; but it is his vision, not theirs, that shapes the world they will have to live in. All this is precisely observed, profoundly true, even though it "never happened": it is true in the sense that the story of Moses and the Promised Land is true.

$\mathbf{Y}$ou've got to be a believer!"

George Strong snorted at his partner's declaration. "Delos, why don't you give up? You've been singing this tune for years. Maybe someday men will get to the Moon, though I doubt it. In any case, you and I will never live to see it. The loss of the power satellite washes the matter up for our generation."

D. D. Harriman grunted. "We won't see it if we sit on our fat behinds and don't do anything to make it happen. But we can make it happen."

"Question number one: how? Question number two: why?"

" 'Why?' The man asks 'why.' George, isn't there anything in your soul but discounts and dividends? Didn't you ever sit with a girl on a soft summer night and stare up at the Moon and wonder what was there?"

"Yeah, I did once. I caught a cold."

Harriman asked the Almighty why he had been delivered into the hands of the Philistines. He then turned back to his partner. "I could tell you why, the real 'why,' but you wouldn't understand me. You want to know why in terms of cash, don't you? You want to know how Harriman & Strong and Harriman Enterprises can show a profit, don't you?"

"Yes," admitted Strong, "and don't give me any guff about tourist trade and fabulous lunar jewels. I've had it."

"You ask me to show figures on a brand-new type of enterprise, knowing I can't. It's like asking the Wright brothers at Kitty Hawk to estimate how much money Curtiss-Wright Corporation would someday make out of building airplanes. I'll put it another way. You didn't want us to go into plastic houses, did you? If you had had your way we would still be back in Kansas City, subdividing cow pastures and showing rentals."

Strong shrugged.

"How much has New World Homes made to date?"

Strong looked absentminded while exercising the talent he brought to the partnership. "Uh . . . $172,946,004.62, after taxes, to the end of the last fiscal year. The running estimate to date is—"

"Never mind. What was our share in the take?"

"Well, uh, the partnership, exclusive of the piece you took personally and then sold to me later, has benefited from New World Homes during the same period by $13,010,437.20, ahead of personal taxes. Delos, this double taxation has got to

stop. Penalizing thrift is a sure way to run this country straight
into—"

"Forget it, forget it! How much have we made out of Sky-
blast Freight and Antipodes Transways?"

Strong told him.

"And yet I had to threaten you with bodily harm to get you
to put up a dime to buy control of the injector patent. You said
rockets were a passing fad."

"We were lucky," objected Strong. "You had no way of
knowing that there would be a big uranium strike in Australia.
Without it, the Skyways group would have left us in the red.
For that matter New World Homes would have failed, too, if
the roadtowns hadn't come along and given us a market out
from under local building codes."

"Nuts on both points. Fast transportation will pay; it always
has. As for New World, when ten million families need new
houses and we can sell 'em cheap, they'll buy. They won't let
building codes stop them, not permanently. We gambled on a
certainty. Think back, George: what ventures have we lost
money on and what ones have paid off? Every one of my crack-
brain ideas has made money, hasn't it? And the only times
we've lost our ante was on conservative, blue-chip investments."

"But we've made money on some conservative deals, too,"
protested Strong.

"Not enough to pay for your yacht. Be fair about it, George;
the Andes Development Company, the integrating pantograph
patent, every one of my wildcat schemes I've had to drag you
into—and every one of them paid."

"I've had to sweat blood to make them pay," Strong
grumbled.

"That's why we are partners. I get a wildcat by the tail; you
harness him and put him to work. Now we go to the Moon—
and you'll make it pay."

"Speak for yourself. I'm not going to the Moon."

"I am."

"Hummph! Delos, granting that we have gotten rich by spec-ulating on your hunches, it's a steel-clad fact that if you keep on gambling you lose your shirt. There's an old saw about the pitcher that went once too often to the well."

"Damn it, George—I'm going to the Moon! If you won't back me up, let's liquidate and I'll do it alone."

Strong drummed on his desk top. "Now, Delos, nobody said anything about not backing you up."

"Fish or cut bait. Now is the opportunity and my mind's made up. I'm going to be the Man in the Moon."

"Well . . . let's get going. We'll be late to the meeting."

As they left their joint office, Strong, always penny con-scious, was careful to switch off the light. Harriman had seen him do so a thousand times; this time he commented. "George, how about a light switch that turns off automatically when you leave a room?"

"Hmm—but suppose someone were left in the room?"

"Well . . . hitch it to stay on only when someone was *in* the room—key the switch to the human body's heat radiation, maybe."

"Too expensive and too complicated."

"Needn't be. I'll turn the idea over to Ferguson to fiddle with. It should be no larger than the present light switch and cheap enough so that the power saved in a year will pay for it."

"How would it work?" asked Strong.

"How should I know? I'm no engineer; that's for Ferguson and the other educated laddies."

Strong objected, "It's no good commercially. Switching off a light when you leave a room is a matter of temperament. I've got it; you haven't. If a man hasn't got it, you can't interest him in such a switch."

"You can if power continues to be rationed. There is a power shortage now; and there will be a bigger one."

"Just temporary. This meeting will straighten it out."

"George, there is nothing in this world so permanent as a temporary emergency. The switch will sell."

Strong took out a notebook and stylus. "I'll call Ferguson in about it tomorrow."

Harriman forgot the matter, never to think of it again. They had reached the roof; he waved to a taxi, then turned to Strong. "How much could we realize if we unloaded our holdings in Roadways and in Belt Transport Corporation—yes, and in New World Homes?"

"Huh? Have you gone crazy?"

"Probably. But I'm going to need all the cash you can shake loose for me. Roadways and Belt Transport are no good anyhow; we should have unloaded earlier."

"You *are* crazy! It's the one really conservative venture you've sponsored."

"But it wasn't conservative when I sponsored it. Believe me, George, roadtowns are on their way out. They are growing moribund, just as the railroads did. In a hundred years there won't be a one left on the continent. What's the formula for making money, George?"

"Buy low and sell high."

"That's only half of it . . . *your* half. We've got to guess which way things are moving, give them a boost, and see that we are cut in on the ground floor. Liquidate that stuff, George; I'll need money to operate." The taxi landed; they got in and took off.

The taxi delivered them to the roof of the Hemisphere Power Building; they went to the power syndicate's board room, as far below ground as the landing platform was above—in those days, despite years of peace, tycoons habitually came to rest at spots relatively immune to atom bombs. The room did not seem like a bomb shelter; it appeared to be a chamber in a luxurious penthouse, for a "view window" back of the chairman's end of the table looked out high above the city, in convincing, live stereo, relayed from the roof.

The other directors were there before them. Dixon nodded as they came in, glanced at his watch finger and said, "Well, gentlemen, our bad boy is here, we may as well begin." He took the chairman's seat and rapped for order.

"The minutes of the last meeting are on your pads as usual. Signal when ready." Harriman glanced at the summary before him and at once flipped a switch on the tabletop; a small green light flashed on at his place. Most of the directors did the same.

"Who's holding up the procession?" inquired Harriman, looking around. "Oh—you, George. Get a move on."

"I like to check the figures," his partner answered testily, then flipped his own switch. A larger green light showed in front of Chairman Dixon, who then pressed a button; a transparency, sticking an inch or two above the tabletop in front of him, lit up with the word RECORDING.

"Operations report," said Dixon and touched another switch. A female voice came out from nowhere. Harriman followed the report from the next sheet of paper at his place. Thirteen Curie-type power piles were now in operation, up five from the last meeting. The Susquehanna and Charleston piles had taken over the load previously borrowed from Atlantic Roadcity and the roadways of that city were now up to normal speed. It was expected that the Chicago-Angeles road could be restored to speed during the next fortnight. Power would continue to be rationed, but the crisis was over.

All very interesting but of no direct interest to Harriman. The power crisis that had been caused by the explosion of the power satellite was being satisfactorily met—very good, but Harriman's interest in it lay in the fact that the cause of interplanetary travel had thereby received a setback from which it might not recover.

When the Harper-Erickson isotopic artificial fuels had been developed three years before it had seemed that, in addition to solving the dilemma of an impossibly dangerous power source which was also utterly necessary to the economic life of the continent, an easy means had been found to achieve interplanetary travel.

The Arizona power pile had been installed in one of the largest of the Antipodes rockets, the rocket powered with isotopic fuel created in the power pile itself, and the whole thing was placed in an orbit around the Earth. A much smaller rocket had shuttled between satellite and Earth, carrying supplies to the staff of the power pile, bringing back synthetic radioactive fuel for the power-hungry technology of Earth.

As a director of the power syndicate Harriman had backed the power satellite—with a private ax to grind: he expected to power a Moon ship with fuel manufactured in the power satellite and thus to achieve the first trip to the Moon almost at once. He had not even attempted to stir the Department of Defense out of its sleep; he wanted no government subsidy—the job was a cinch; anybody could do it—and Harriman *would* do it. He had the ship; shortly he would have the fuel.

The ship had been a freighter of his own Antipodes line, her chem-fuel motors replaced, her wings removed. She still waited, ready for fuel—the recommissioned *Santa Maria,* née *City of Brisbane.*

But the fuel was slow in coming. Fuel had to be earmarked for the shuttle rocket; the power needs of a rationed continent came next—and those needs grew faster than the power satellite could turn out fuel. Far from being ready to supply him for a "useless" Moon trip, the syndicate had seized on the safe but less efficient low-temperature uranium salts and heavy water, Curie-type power piles as a means of using uranium directly to meet the ever growing need for power rather than build and launch more satellites.

Unfortunately the Curie piles did not provide the fierce star-interior conditions necessary to breeding the isotopic fuels needed for an atom-powered rocket. Harriman had reluctantly come around to the notion that he would have to use political pressure to squeeze the necessary priority for the fuels he wanted for the *Santa Maria*.

Then the power satellite had blown up.

Harriman was stirred out of his brown study by Dixon's voice. "The operations report seems satisfactory, gentlemen. If there is no objection, it will be recorded as accepted. You will note that in the next ninety days we will be back up to the power level which existed before we were forced to close down the Arizona pile."

"But with no provision for future needs," pointed out Harriman. "There have been a lot of babies born while we have been sitting here."

"Is that an objection to accepting the report, D. D.?"

"No."

"Very well. Now the public relations report—let me call attention to the first item, gentlemen. The vice-president in charge recommends a schedule of annuities, benefits, scholarships and so forth for dependents of the staff of the power satellite and of the pilot of the *Charon:* see appendix 'C.' "

A director across from Harriman—Phineas Morgan, chairman of the food trust, Cuisine, Incorporated—protested, "What is this, Ed? Too bad they were killed of course, but we paid them sky-high wages and carried their insurance to boot. Why the charity?"

Harriman grunted. "Pay it—I so move. It's peanuts. 'Do not bind the mouths of the kine who tread the grain.' "

"I wouldn't call better than nine hundred thousand 'peanuts,' " protested Morgan.

"Just a minute, gentlemen—" It was the vice-president in charge of public relations, himself a director. "If you'll look at the breakdown, Mr. Morgan, you will see that eighty-five percent of the appropriation will be used to publicize the gifts."

Morgan squinted at the figures. "Oh—why didn't you say so? Well, I suppose the gifts can be considered unavoidable overhead, but it's a bad precedent."

"Without them we have nothing to publicize."

"Yes, but—"

Dixon rapped smartly. "Mr. Harriman has moved acceptance. Please signal your desires." The tally board glowed green; even Morgan, after hesitation, okayed the allotment. "We have a related item next," said Dixon. "A Mrs.—uh, Garfield, through her attorneys, alleges that we are responsible for the congenital crippled condition of her fourth child. The putative facts are that her child was being born just as the satellite exploded and that Mrs. Garfield was then on the meridian underneath the satellite. She wants the court to award her half a million."

Morgan looked at Harriman. "Delos, I suppose that *you* will say to settle out of court."

"Don't be silly. We fight it."

Dixon looked around, surprised. "Why, D. D.? It's my guess we could settle for ten or fifteen thousand—and that was what I was about to recommend. I'm surprised that the legal department referred it to publicity."

"It's obvious why; it's loaded with high explosive. But we should fight, regardless of bad publicity. It's not like the last case; Mrs. Garfield and her brat are not our people. And any dumb fool knows you can't mark a baby by radioactivity at birth; you have to get at the germ plasm of the previous generation at least. In the third place, if we let this get by, we'll be sued for every double-yolked egg that's laid from now on. This calls for an open allotment for defense and not one damned cent for compromise."

"It might be very expensive," observed Dixon.

"It'll be more expensive not to fight. If we have to, we should buy the judge."

The public relations chief whispered to Dixon, then an-

nounced, "I support Mr. Harriman's view. That's my department's recommendation."

It was approved. "The next item," Dixon went on, "is a
whole sheaf of suits arising out of slowing down the roadcities
to divert power during the crisis. They allege loss of business,
loss of time, loss of this and that, but they are all based on the
same issue. The most touchy, perhaps, is a stockholder's suit
which claims that Roadways and this company are so inter-
locked that the decision to divert the power was not done in the
interests of the stockholders of Roadways. Delos, this is your
pidgin; want to speak on it?"

"Forget it."

"Why?"

"Those are shotgun suits. This corporation is not responsible;
I saw to it that Roadways volunteered to sell the power because
I anticipated this. And the directorates don't interlock; not on
paper, they don't. That's why dummies were born. Forget it—
for every suit you've got there, Roadways has a dozen. We'll
beat them."

"What makes you so sure?"

"Well—" Harriman lounged back and hung a knee over the
arm of his chair. "A good many years ago I was a Western
Union messenger boy. While waiting around the office I read
everything I could lay hands on, including the contract on the
back of the telegram forms. Remember those? They used to
come in big pads of yellow paper; by writing a message on the
face of the form you accepted the contract in the fine print on
the back—only most people didn't realize that. Do you know
what that contract obligated the company to do?"

"Send a telegram, I suppose."

"It didn't promise a darn thing. The company offered to *attempt* to deliver the message, by camel caravan or snail back,
or some equally streamlined method, if convenient, but in event
of failure, the company was not responsible. I read that fine
print until I knew it by heart. It was the loveliest piece of prose

I had ever seen. Since then all my contracts have been worded on the same principle. Anybody who sues Roadways will find that Roadways can't be sued on the element of time, because time is not of the essence. In the event of complete nonperformance—which hasn't happened yet—Roadways is financially responsible only for freight charges or the price of the personal transportation tickets. So forget it."

Morgan sat up. "D. D., suppose I decided to run up to my country place tonight, by the roadway, and there was a failure of some sort so that I didn't get there until tomorrow? You mean to say Roadways is not liable?"

Harriman grinned. "Roadways is not liable even if you starve to death on the trip. Better use your copter." He turned back to Dixon. "I move that we stall these suits and let Roadways carry the ball for us."

"The regular agenda being completed," Dixon announced later, "time is allotted for our colleague, Mr. Harriman, to speak on a subject of his own choosing. He has not listed a subject in advance, but we will listen until it is your pleasure to adjourn."

Morgan looked sourly at Harriman. "I move we adjourn."

Harriman grinned. "For two cents I'd second that and let you die of curiosity." The motion failed for want of a second. Harriman stood up.

"Mr. Chairman, friends—" he then looked at Morgan "—and associates. As you know, I am interested in space travel."

Dixon looked at him sharply. "Not that again, Delos! If I weren't in the chair, I'd move to adjourn myself."

" 'That again,' " agreed Harriman. "Now and forever. Hear me out. Three years ago, when we were crowded into moving the Arizona power pile out into space, it looked as if we had a bonus in the shape of interplanetary travel. Some of you here joined with me in forming Spaceways, Incorporated, for experimentation, exploration—and exploitation.

"Space was conquered; rockets that could establish orbits around the globe could be modified to get to the Moon—and from there, anywhere! It was just a matter of doing it. The problems remaining were financial—and political.

"In fact, the real engineering problems of space travel have been solved since World War II. Conquering space has long been a matter of money and politics. But it did seem that the Harper-Erickson process, with its concomitant of a round-the-globe rocket and a practical economical rocket fuel, had at last made it a very present thing, so close indeed that I did not object when the early allotments of fuel from the satellite were earmarked for industrial power."

He looked around. "I shouldn't have kept quiet. I should have squawked and brought pressure and made a hairy nuisance of myself until you allotted fuel to get rid of me. For now we have missed our best chance. The satellite is gone; the source of fuel is gone. Even the shuttle rocket is gone. We are back where we were in 1950. Therefore—"

He paused again. "Therefore—I propose that we build a spaceship and send it to the Moon!"

Dixon broke the silence. "Delos, have you come unzipped? You just said that it was no longer possible. Now you say to build one."

"I didn't say it was impossible; I said we had missed our best chance. The time is overripe for space travel. This globe grows more crowded every day. In spite of technical advances the daily food intake on this planet is lower than it was thirty years ago—and we get 46 new babies every minute, 65,000 every day, 25,000,000 every year. Our race is about to burst forth to the planets; if we've got the initiative God promised an oyster we will help it along!

"Yes, we missed our best chance—but the engineering details can be solved. The real question is who's going to foot the bill? That is why I address you gentlemen, for right here in this room is the financial capital of this planet."

Morgan stood up. "Mr. Chairman, if all *company* business is finished, I ask to be excused."

Dixon nodded. Harriman said, "So long, Phineas. Don't let me keep you. Now, as I was saying, it's a money problem and here is where the money is. I move we finance a trip to the Moon."

The proposal produced no special excitement; these men knew Harriman. Presently Dixon said, "Is there a second to D. D.'s proposal?"

"Just a minute, Mr. Chairman—" It was Jack Entenza, president of Two-Continents Amusement Corporation. "I want to ask Delos some questions." He turned to Harriman. "D. D., you know I strung along when you set up Spaceways. It seemed like a cheap venture and possibly profitable in educational and scientific values—I never did fall for space liners plying between planets; that's fantastic. I don't mind playing along with your dreams to a moderate extent, but how do you propose to get to the Moon? As you say, you are fresh out of fuel."

Harriman was still grinning. "Don't kid me, Jack, I know why you came along. You weren't interested in science; you've never contributed a dime to science. You expected a monopoly on pix and television for your chain. Well, you'll get 'em, if you stick with me—otherwise I'll sign up 'Recreations, Unlimited'; they'll pay just to have you in the eye."

Entenza looked at him suspiciously. "What will it cost me?"

"Your other shirt, your eyeteeth, and your wife's wedding ring—unless 'Recreations' will pay more."

"Damn you, Delos, you're crookeder than a dog's hind leg."

"From you, Jack, that's a compliment. We'll do business. Now as to how I'm going to get to the Moon, that's a silly question. There's not a man in here who can cope with anything more complicated in the way of machinery than a knife and fork. You can't tell a left-handed monkey wrench from a reaction engine, yet you ask me for blueprints of a spaceship.

"Well, I'll tell you how I'll get to the Moon. I'll hire the proper brain boys, give them everything they want, see to it that they have all the money they can use, sweet talk them into long hours—then stand back and watch them produce. I'll run it like the Manhattan Project—most of you remember the A-bomb job; shucks, some of you can remember the Mississippi Bubble. The chap that headed up the Manhattan Project didn't know a neutron from Uncle George—but he got results. They solved that trick *four ways*. That's why I'm not worried about fuel; we'll get a fuel. We'll get several fuels."

Dixon said, "Suppose it works? Seems to me you're asking us to bankrupt the company for an exploit with no real value, aside from pure science, and a one-shot entertainment exploitation. I'm not against you—I wouldn't mind putting in ten, fifteen thousand to support a worthy venture—but I can't see the thing as a business proposition."

Harriman leaned on his fingertips and stared down the long table. "Ten or fifteen thousand gumdrops! Dan, I mean to get into you for a couple of megabucks *at least*—and before we're through you'll be hollering for more stock. This is the greatest real estate venture since the Pope carved up the New World. Don't ask me what we'll make a profit on; I can't itemize the assets—but I can lump them. The assets are a planet—a *whole planet,* Dan, that's never been touched. And more planets beyond it. If we can't figure out ways to swindle a few fast bucks out of a sweet setup like that then you and I had better both go on relief. It's like having Manhattan Island offered to you for twenty-four dollars and a case of whiskey."

Dixon grunted. "You make it sound like the chance of a lifetime."

"Chance of a lifetime, nuts! This is the greatest chance in all history. It's raining soup; grab yourself a bucket."

Next to Entenza sat Gaston P. Jones, director of Trans-America and half a dozen other banks, one of the richest men in the room. He carefully removed two inches of cigar ash, then said dryly, "Mr. Harriman, I will sell you all of my interest in the Moon, present and future, for fifty cents."

Harriman looked delighted. "Sold!"

Entenza had been pulling at his lower lip and listening with a brooding expression on his face. Now he spoke up. "Just a minute, Mr. Jones—I'll give you a dollar for it."

"Dollar fifty," answered Harriman.

"Two dollars," Entenza answered slowly.

"Five!"

They edged each other up. At ten dollars Entenza let Harriman have it and sat back, still looking thoughtful. Harriman looked happily around. "Which one of you thieves is a lawyer?" he demanded. The remark was rhetorical; out of seventeen directors the normal percentage—eleven, to be exact—were lawyers. "Hey, Tony," he continued, "draw me up an instrument right *now* that will tie down this transaction so that it couldn't be broken before the Throne of God. All of Mr. Jones' interests, rights, title, natural interest, future interests, interests held directly or through ownership of stock, presently held or to be acquired, and so forth and so forth. Put lots of Latin in it. The idea is that every interest in the Moon that Mr. Jones now has or may acquire is mine—for a ten spot, cash in hand paid." Harriman slapped a bill down on the table. "That right, Mr. Jones?"

Jones smiled briefly. "That's right, young fellow." He pocketed the bill. "I'll frame this for my grandchildren—to show them how easy it is to make money." Entenza's eyes darted from Jones to Harriman.

"Good!" said Harriman. "Gentlemen, Mr. Jones has set a market price for one human being's interest in our satellite. With around three billion persons on this globe that sets a price on the Moon of thirty billion dollars." He hauled out a wad of money. "Any more suckers? I'm buying every share that's offered, ten bucks a copy."

"I'll pay twenty!" Entenza rapped out.

Harriman looked at him sorrowfully. "Jack—don't do that! We're on the same team. Let's take the shares together, at ten."

Dixon pounded for order. "Gentlemen, please conduct such transactions after the meeting is adjourned. Is there a second to Mr. Harriman's motion?"

Gaston Jones said, "I owe it to Mr. Harriman to second his motion, without prejudice. Let's get on with a vote."

No one objected; the vote was taken. It went eleven to three against Harriman—Harriman, Strong, and Entenza for; all others against. Harriman popped up before anyone could move to adjourn and said, "I expected that. My real purpose is this: since the company is no longer interested in space travel, will it do me the courtesy of selling me what I may need of patents, processes, facilities, and so forth now held by the company but relating to space travel and not relating to the production of power on this planet? Our brief honeymoon with the power satellite built up a backlog; I want to use it. Nothing formal— just a vote that it is the policy of the company to assist me in any way not inconsistent with the primary interests of the company. How about it, gentlemen? It'll get me out of your hair."

Jones studied his cigar again. "I see no reason why we should not accommodate him, gentlemen . . . and I speak as the perfect disinterested party."

"I think we can do it, Delos," agreed Dixon, "only we won't sell you anything, we'll *lend* it to you. Then, if you happen to hit the jackpot, the company still retains an interest. Has anyone any objection?" he said to the room at large.

There was none; the matter was recorded as company policy and the meeting was adjourned. Harriman stopped to whisper with Entenza and, finally, to make an appointment. Gaston Jones stood near the door, speaking privately with Chairman Dixon. He beckoned to Strong, Harriman's partner. "George, may I ask a personal question?"

"I don't guarantee to answer. Go ahead."

"You've always struck me as a levelheaded man. Tell me—

why do you string along with Harriman? Why, the man's mad as a hatter."

Strong looked sheepish. "I ought to deny that, he's my friend . . . but I can't. But doggone it! every time Delos has a wild hunch, it turns out to be the real thing. I hate to string along—it makes me nervous—but I've learned to trust his hunches rather than another man's sworn financial report."

Jones cocked one brow. "The Midas touch, eh?"

"You could call it that."

"Well, remember what happened to King Midas—in the long run. Good day, gentlemen."

Harriman had left Entenza; Strong joined him. Dixon stood staring at them, his face very thoughtful.

<h1 style="text-align:center">2</h1>

Harriman's home had been built at the time when everyone who could was decentralizing and going underground. Above ground there was a perfect little Cape Cod cottage—the clapboards of which concealed armor plate—and most delightful, skillfully landscaped grounds; below ground there was four or five times as much floor space, immune to anything but a direct hit and possessing an independent air supply with reserves for one thousand hours. During the Crazy Years the conventional wall surrounding the grounds had been replaced by a wall which looked the same but which would stop anything short of a broaching tank—nor were the gates weak points; their gadgets were as personally loyal as a well-trained dog.

Despite its fortresslike character the house was comfortable. It was also very expensive to keep up.

Harriman did not mind the expense; Charlotte liked the house and it gave her something to do. When they were first married she had lived uncomplainingly in a cramped flat over a grocery store; if Charlotte now liked to play house in a castle, Harriman did not mind.

But he was again starting a shoestring venture; the few thousand per month of ready cash represented by the household expenses might, at some point in the game, mean the difference between success and the sheriff's bailiffs. That night at dinner, after the servants fetched the coffee and port, he took up the matter.

"My dear, I've been wondering how you would like a few months in Florida."

His wife stared at him. "Florida? Delos, is your mind wandering? Florida is unbearable at this time of the year."

"Switzerland, then. Pick your own spot. Take a real vacation, as long as you like."

"Delos, you are up to something."

Harriman sighed. Being "up to something" was the unnameable and unforgivable crime for which any American male could be indicted, tried, convicted, and sentenced in one breath. He wondered how things had gotten rigged so that the male half of the race must always behave to suit feminine rules and feminine logic, like a snotty-nosed schoolboy in front of a stern teacher.

"In a way, perhaps. We've both agreed that this house is a bit of a white elephant. I was thinking of closing it, possibly even of disposing of the land—it's worth more now than when we bought it. Then, when we get around to it, we could build something more modern and a little less like a bombproof."

Mrs. Harriman was temporarily diverted. "Well, I *have* thought it might be nice to build another place, Delos—say a little chalet tucked away in the mountains, nothing ostentatious, not more than two servants, or three. But we won't close this place until it's built, Delos—after all, one must live somewhere."

"I was not thinking of building right away," he answered cautiously.

"Why not? We're not getting any younger, Delos; if we are to enjoy the good things of life we had better not make delays. You needn't worry about it; I'll manage everything."

Harriman turned over in his mind the possibility of letting her build to keep her busy. If he earmarked the cash for her "little chalet," she would live in a hotel nearby wherever she decided to build it—and he could sell this monstrosity they were sitting in. With the nearest roadcity now less than ten miles away, the land should bring more than Charlotte's new house would cost and he would be rid of the monthly drain on his pocketbook.

"Perhaps you are right," he agreed. "But suppose you do build at once; you won't be living here; you'll be supervising every detail of the new place. I say we should unload this place; it's eating its head off in taxes, upkeep, and running expenses."

She shook her head. "Utterly out of the question, Delos. This is my home."

He ground out an almost unsmoked cigar. "I'm sorry, Charlotte, but you can't have it both ways. If you build, you can't stay here. If you stay here, we'll close these below-ground catacombs, fire about a dozen of the parasites I keep stumbling over, and live in the cottage on the surface. I'm cutting expenses."

"Discharge the servants? Delos, if you think that I will undertake to make a home for you without a proper staff, you can just—"

"Stop it." He stood up and threw his napkin down. "It doesn't take a squad of servants to make a home. When we were first married you had *no* servants—and you washed and ironed my shirts in the bargain. But we had a home then. This place is owned by that staff you speak of. Well, we're getting rid of them, all but the cook and a handyman."

She did not seem to hear him. "Delos! sit down and behave yourself. Now what's all this about cutting expenses? Are you in some sort of trouble? Are you? Answer me!"

He sat down wearily and answered, "Does a man have to be in trouble to want to cut out unnecessary expenses?"

"In your case, yes. Now what is it? Don't try to evade me."

"Now see here, Charlotte, we agreed a long time ago that I would keep business matters in the office. As for the house, we simply don't need a house this size. It isn't as if we had a passel of kids to fill up—"

"*Oh!* Blaming me for *that* again!"

"Now see here, Charlotte," he wearily began again, "I never did blame you and I'm not blaming you now. All I ever did was suggest that we both see a doctor and find out what the trouble was that we didn't have any kids. And for twenty years you've been making me pay for that one remark. But that's all over and done with now; I was simply making the point that two people don't fill up twenty-two rooms. I'll pay a reasonable price for a new house, if you want it, and give you an ample household allowance." He started to say how much, then decided not to. "Or you can close this place and live in the cottage above. It's just that we are going to quit squandering money—for a while."

She grabbed the last phrase. " 'For a while.' What's going on, Delos? What are *you* going to squander money on?" When he did not answer she went on, "Very well, if you won't tell me, I'll call George. He will tell me."

"Don't do that, Charlotte. I'm warning you. I'll—"

"You'll what!" She studied his face. "I don't need to talk to George; I can tell by looking at you. You've got the same look on your face you had when you came home and told me that you had sunk all our money in those crazy rockets."

"Charlotte, that's not fair. Skyways paid off. It's made us a mint of money."

"That's beside the point. I know why you're acting so strangely; you've got that old trip-to-the-Moon madness again. Well, I won't stand for it, do you hear? I'll stop you; I don't have to put up with it. I'm going right down in the morning and see Mr. Kamens and find out what has to be done to make you behave yourself." The cords of her neck jerked as she spoke.

He waited, gathering his temper before going on. "Charlotte, you have no real cause for complaint. No matter what happens to me, your future is taken care of."

"Do you think I want to be a widow?"

He looked thoughtfully at her. "I wonder."

"Why—why, you heartless *beast.*" She stood up. "We'll say no more about it; do you mind?" She left without waiting for an answer.

His "man" was waiting for him when he got to his room. Jenkins got up hastily and started drawing Harriman's bath. "Beat it," Harriman grunted. "I can undress myself."

"You require nothing more tonight, sir?"

"Nothing. But don't go unless you feel like it. Sit down and pour yourself a drink. Ed, how long you been married?"

"Don't mind if I do." The servant helped himself. "Twenty-three years, come May, sir."

"How's it been, if you don't mind me asking?"

"Not bad. Of course there have been times—"

"I know what you mean. Ed, if you weren't working for me, what would you be doing?"

"Well, the wife and I have talked many times of opening a little restaurant, nothing pretentious, but good. A place where a gentleman could enjoy a quiet meal of good food."

"Stag, eh?"

"No, not entirely, sir—but there would be a parlor for gentlemen only. Not even waitresses; I'd tend that room myself."

"Better look around for locations, Ed. You're practically in business."

3

Strong entered their joint offices the next morning at a precise nine o'clock, as usual. He was startled to find Harriman there before him. For Harriman to fail to show up at all meant nothing; for him to beat the clerks in was significant.

Harriman was busy with a terrestrial globe and a book—the

current Nautical Almanac, Strong observed. Harriman barely glanced up. "Morning, George. Say, who've we got a line to in Brazil?"

"Why?"

"I need some trained seals who speak Portuguese, that's why. And some who speak Spanish, too. Not to mention three or four dozen scattered around in this country. I've come across something very, very interesting. Look here . . . according to these tables the Moon only swings about twenty-eight, just short of twenty-nine degrees north and south of the equator." He held a pencil against the globe and spun it. "Like that. That suggest anything?"

"No. Except that you're getting pencil marks on a sixty dollar globe."

"And you an old real estate operator! What does a man own when he buys a parcel of land?"

"That depends on the deed. Usually mineral rights and other subsurface rights are—"

"Never mind that. Suppose he buys the works, without splitting the rights; how far down does he own? How far up does he own?"

"Well, he owns a wedge down to the center of the Earth. That was settled in the slant-drilling and offset oil lease cases. Theoretically he used to own the space above the land, too, out indefinitely, but that was modified by a series of cases after the commercial airlines came in—and a good thing for us, too, or we would have to pay tolls every time one of our rockets took off for Australia."

"No, no, no, George! you didn't read those cases right. Right of passage was established—but *ownership* of the space above the land remained unchanged. And even right of passage was not absolute; you can build a thousand-foot tower on your own land right where airplanes, or rockets, or whatever, have been in the habit of passing and the ships will thereafter have to go above it, with no kickback on you. Remember how we had to lease the air south of Hughes Field to insure that our approach wasn't built up?"

Strong looked thoughtful. "Yes. I see your point. The ancient principle of land ownership remains undisturbed—down to the center of the Earth, up to infinity. But what of it? It's a purely theoretical matter. You're not planning to pay tolls to operate those spaceships you're always talking about, are you?" He grudged a smile at his own wit.

"Not on your tintype. Another matter entirely. George—*who owns the Moon?*"

Strong's jaw dropped, literally. "Delos, you're joking."

"I am not. I'll ask you again: if basic law says that a man owns the wedge of sky above his farm out to infinity, *who owns the Moon?* Take a look at this globe and tell me."

Strong looked. "But it can't mean anything, Delos. Earth laws wouldn't apply to the Moon."

"They apply here and that's where I am worrying about it. The Moon stays constantly over a slice of Earth bounded by latitude twenty-nine north and the same distance south; if one man owned all that belt of Earth—it's roughly the tropical zone —then he'd own the Moon, too, wouldn't he? By all the theories of real property ownership that our courts pay any attention to. And, by direct derivation, according to the sort of logic that lawyers like, the various owners of that belt of land have title—good vendable title—to the Moon somehow lodged collectively in them. The fact that the distribution of the title is a little vague wouldn't bother a lawyer; they grow fat on just such distributed titles every time a will is probated."

"It's fantastic!"

"George, when are you going to learn that 'fantastic' is a notion that doesn't bother a lawyer?"

"You're not planning to try to buy the entire tropical zone— that's what you would have to do."

"No," Harriman said slowly, "but it might not be a bad idea to buy right, title and interest in the Moon, as it may appear, from each of the sovereign countries in that belt. If I thought I could keep it quiet and not run the market up, I might try it. You can buy a thing awful cheap from a man if he thinks it's worthless and wants to sell before you regain your senses.

"But that's not the plan," he went on. "George, I want corporations—local corporations—in every one of those countries. I want the legislature of each of those countries to grant franchises to its local corporation for lunar exploration, exploitation, et cetera, and the right to claim lunar soil on behalf of the country—with fee simple, naturally, being handed on a silver platter to the patriotic corporation that thought up the idea. And I want all this done quietly, so that the bribes won't go too high. We'll own the corporations, of course, which is why I need a flock of trained seals. There is going to be one hell of a fight one of these days over who owns the Moon; I want the deck stacked so that we win no matter how the cards are dealt."

"It will be ridiculously expensive, Delos. And you don't even know that you will ever get to the Moon, much less that it will be worth anything after you get there."

"We'll get there! It'll be more expensive not to establish these claims. Anyhow it need not be very expensive; the proper use of bribe money is a homeopathic art—you use it as a catalyst. Back in the middle of the last century four men went from California to Washington with forty thousand dollars; it was all they had. A few weeks later they were broke—but Congress had awarded them a billion dollars' worth of railroad right of way. The trick is not to run up the market."

Strong shook his head. "Your title wouldn't be any good anyhow. The Moon doesn't stay in one place; it passes *over* owned land certainly—but so does a migrating goose."

"And nobody has title to a migrating bird. I get your point—but the Moon *always* stays over that one belt. If you move a boulder in your garden, do you lose title to it? Is it still real estate? Do the title laws still stand? This is like that group of real estate cases involving wandering islands in the Mississippi,

George—the land moved as the river cut new channels, *but somebody always owned it.* In this case I plan to see to it that we are the 'somebody.' "

Strong puckered his brow. "I seem to recall that some of those island-and-riparian cases were decided one way and some another."

"We'll pick the decisions that suit us. That's why lawyers' wives have mink coats. Come on, George; let's get busy."

"On what?"

"Raising the money."

"Oh." Strong looked relieved. "I thought you were planning to use *our* money."

"I am. But it won't be nearly enough. We'll use our money for the senior financing to get things moving; in the meantime we've got to work out ways to keep the money rolling in." He pressed a switch at his desk; the face of Saul Kamens, their legal chief of staff, sprang out at him. "Hey, Saul, can you slide in for a powwow?"

"Whatever it is, just tell them 'no,' " answered the attorney. "I'll fix it."

"Good. Now come on in—they're moving Hell and I've got an option on the first ten loads."

Kamens showed up in his own good time. Some minutes later Harriman had explained his notion for claiming the Moon ahead of setting foot on it. "Besides those dummy corporations," he went on, "we need an agency that can receive contributions without having to admit any financial interest on the part of the contributor—like the National Geographic Society."

Kamens shook his head. "You can't buy the National Geographic Society."

"Damn it, who said we were going to? We'll set up our own."

"That's what I started to say."

"Good. As I see it, we need at least one tax-free, nonprofit corporation headed up by the right people—we'll hang on to voting control, of course. We'll probably need more than one;

we'll set them up as we need them. And we've got to have at least one new ordinary corporation, *not* tax free—but it won't show a profit until we are ready. The idea is to let the nonprofit corporations have all of the prestige and all of the publicity— and the other gets all of the profits, if and when. We swap assets around between corporations, always for perfectly valid reasons, so that the nonprofit corporations pay the expenses as we go along. Come to think about it, we had better have at least two ordinary corporations, so that we can let one of them go through bankruptcy if we find it necessary to shake out the water. That's the general sketch. Get busy and fix it up so that it's legal, will you?"

Kamens said, "You know, Delos, it would be a lot more honest if you did it at the point of a gun."

"A lawyer talks to me of honesty! Never mind, Saul; I'm not actually going to cheat anyone—"

"Hmmph!"

"—and I'm just going to make a trip to the Moon. That's what everybody will be paying for; that's what they'll get. Now fix it up so that it's legal, that's a good boy."

"I'm reminded of something the elder Vanderbilt's lawyer said to the old man under similar circumstances: 'It's beautiful the way it is; why spoil it by making it legal?' Okay, brother gonoph, I'll rig your trap. Anything else?"

"Sure. Stick around, you might have some ideas. George, ask Montgomery to come in, will you?" Montgomery, Harriman's publicity chief, had two virtues in his employer's eyes: he was personally loyal to Harriman, and, secondly, he was quite capable of planning a campaign to convince the public that Lady Godiva wore a Caresse-brand girdle during her famous ride . . . or that Hercules attributed his strength to Crunchies for breakfast.

He arrived with a large portfolio under his arm. "Glad you sent for me, Chief. Get a load of this—" He spread the folder open on Harriman's desk and began displaying sketches and layouts. "Kinsky's work—is that boy hot!"

Harriman closed the portfolio. "What outfit is it for?"

"Huh? New World Homes."

"I don't want to see it; we're dumping New World Homes. Wait a minute—don't start to bawl. Have the boys go through with it; I want the price kept up while we unload. But open your ears to another matter." He rapidly explained the new enterprise.

Presently Montgomery was nodding. "When do we start and how much do we spend?"

"Right away and spend what you need to. Don't get chicken about expenses; this is the biggest thing we've ever tackled." Strong flinched; Harriman went on, "Have insomnia over it to-night; see me tomorrow and we'll kick it around."

"Wait a sec, Chief. How are you going to sew up all those franchises from the, uh—the Moon states, those countries the Moon passes over, while a big publicity campaign is going on about a trip to the Moon and how big a thing it is for every-body? Aren't you about to paint yourself into a corner?"

"Do I look stupid? We'll get the franchises *before* you hand out so much as a filler—*you'll* get 'em, you and Kamens. That's your first job."

"Hmmm. . . ." Montgomery chewed a thumbnail. "Well, all right—I can see some angles. How soon do we have to sew it up?"

"I give you six weeks. Otherwise just mail your resignation in, written on the skin off your back."

"I'll write it right now, if you'll help me by holding a mirror."

"Damn it, Monty, I know you can't do it in six weeks. But make it fast; we can't take a cent in to keep the thing going until you sew up those franchises. If you dillydally, we'll all starve—and we won't get to the Moon, either."

Strong said, "D. D., why fiddle with these trick claims from

a bunch of moth-eaten tropical countries? If you are dead set
on going to the Moon, let's call Ferguson in and get on with
the matter."

"I like your direct approach, George," Harriman said, frown-
ing. "Mmmm . . . back about 1845 or '46 an eager-beaver
American army officer captured California. You know what the
State Department did?"

"No."

"They made him hand it back. Seems he hadn't touched second base, or something. So they had to go to the trouble of cap-
turing it all over again a few months later. Now I don't want
that to happen to us. It's not enough just to set foot on the
Moon and claim it; we've got to validate that claim in terrestrial
courts—or we're in for a peck of trouble. Eh, Saul?"

Kamens nodded. "Remember what happened to Columbus."

"Exactly. We aren't going to let ourselves be rooked the way
Columbus was."

Montgomery spat out some thumbnail. "But, Chief—you
know damn well those banana-state claims won't be worth two
cents after I do tie them up. Why not get a franchise right from
the UN and settle the matter? I'd as lief tackle that as tackle
two dozen cockeyed legislatures. In fact I've got an angle already—we work it through the Security Council and—"

"Keep working on that angle; we'll use it later. You don't appreciate the full mechanics of the scheme, Monty. Of course
those claims are worth nothing—except nuisance value. But
their nuisance value is all-important. Listen: we get to the
Moon, or appear about to. Every one of those countries puts up
a squawk; we goose them into it through the dummy corporations they have enfranchised. Where do they squawk? To the
UN, of course. Now the big countries on this globe, the rich and
important ones, are all in the northern temperate zone. They
see what the claims are based on and they take a frenzied look
at the globe. Sure enough, the Moon does not pass over a one
of them. The biggest country of all—Russia—doesn't own a

spadeful of dirt south of twenty-nine north. So they reject all the claims.

"Or do they?" Harriman went on. "The U. S. balks. *The Moon passes over Florida and the southern part of Texas.* Washington is in a tizzy. Should they back up the tropical countries and support the traditional theory of land title or should they throw their weight to the idea that the Moon belongs to everyone? Or should the United States try to claim the whole thing, seeing as how it was Americans who actually got there first?

"At this point we creep out from under cover. It seems that the Moon ship was owned and the expenses paid by a nonprofit corporation chartered by the UN itself—"

"Hold it," interrupted Strong. "I didn't know that the UN could create corporations?"

"You'll find it can," his partner answered. "How about it, Saul?" Kamens nodded. "Anyway," Harriman continued, "I've already got the corporation. I had it set up several years ago. It can do most anything of an educational or scientific nature —and, brother, that covers a lot of ground! Back to the point— this corporation, this creature of the UN, asks its parent to declare the lunar colony autonomous territory, under the protection of the UN. We won't ask for outright membership at first because we want to keep it simple—"

"Simple, he calls it!" said Montgomery.

"Simple. This new colony will be a de facto sovereign state, holding title to the entire Moon, and—listen closely!—capable of buying, selling, passing laws, issuing title to land, setting up monopolies, collecting tariffs, et cetera without end. *And we own it!*

"The reason we get all this is because the major states in the UN can't think up a claim that sounds as legal as the claim made by the tropical states, they can't agree among themselves as to how to split up the swag if they were to attempt brute force and the other major states aren't willing to see the United

States claim the whole thing. They'll take the easy way out of their dilemma by appearing to retain title in the UN itself. The real title, the title controlling all economic and legal matters, will revert to us. Now do you see my point, Monty?"

Montgomery grinned. "Damned if I know if it's necessary, Chief, but I love it. It's beautiful."

"Well, I don't think so," Strong grumbled. "Delos, I've seen you rig some complicated deals—some of them so devious that they turned even my stomach—but this one is the worst yet. I think you've been carried away by the pleasure you get out of cooking up involved deals in which somebody gets double crossed."

Harriman puffed hard on his cigar before answering. "I don't give a damn, George. Call it chicanery, call it anything you want to. *I'm going to the Moon!* If I have to manipulate a million people to accomplish it, I'll do it."

"But it's not necessary to do it this way."

"Well, how would you do it?"

"Me? I'd set up a straightforward corporation. I'd get a resolution in Congress making my corporation the chosen instrument of the United States—"

"Bribery?"

"Not necessarily. Influence and pressure ought to be enough. Then I would set about raising the money and make the trip."

"And the United States would then own the Moon?"

"Naturally," Strong answered a little stiffly.

Harriman got up and began pacing. "You don't see it, George, you don't see it. The Moon was not meant to be owned by a single country, even the United States."

"It was meant to be owned by *you*, I suppose."

"Well, if I own it—for a short while—I won't misuse it and I'll take care that others don't. Damnation, nationalism should stop at the stratosphere. Can you see what would happen if the United States lays claim to the Moon? The other nations won't recognize the claim. It will become a permanent bone of con-

tention in the Security Council—just when we were beginning
to get straightened out to the point where a man could do business planning without having his elbow jogged by a war every
few years. The other nations—quite rightfully—will be scared
to death of the United States. They will be able to look up in
the sky any night and see the main atom-bomb rocket base of
the United States staring down the backs of their necks. Are
they going to hold still for it? No, sirree—they are going to try
to clip off a piece of the Moon for their own national use. The
Moon is too big to hold, all at once. There will be other bases
established there and presently there will be the Goddamnedest
war this planet has ever seen—and we'll be to blame.

"No, it's got to be an arrangement that everybody will hold
still for—and that's why we've got to plan it, think of all the
angles, and be devious about it until we are in a position to
make it work.

"Anyhow, George, if we claim it in the name of the United
States, do you know where we will be, as businessmen?"

"In the driver's seat," answered Strong.

"In a pig's eye! We'll be dealt right out of the game. The Department of National Defense will say, 'Thank you, Mr. Harriman. Thank you, Mr. Strong. We are taking over in the interests of national security; you can go home now.' And that's just
what we would have to do—go home and wait for the next
atom war.

"I'm not going to do it, George. I'm not going to let the brass
hats muscle in. I'm going to set up a lunar colony and then
nurse it along until it is big enough to stand on its own feet.
I'm telling you—all of you!—this is the biggest thing for the
human race since the discovery of fire. Handled right, it can
mean a new and braver world. Handle it wrong and it's a one-
way ticket to Armageddon. It's coming, it's coming soon,
whether we touch it or not. But I plan to be the Man in the
Moon myself—and give it my personal attention to see that it's
handled right."

He paused. Strong said, "Through with your sermon, Delos?"

"No, I'm not," Harriman denied testily. "You don't see this thing the right way. Do you know what we may find up there?" He swung his arm in an arc toward the ceiling. *"People!"*

"On the *Moon?"* said Kamens.

"Why not on the Moon?" whispered Montgomery to Strong.

"No, not on the Moon—at least I'd be amazed if we dug down and found anybody under that airless shell. The Moon has had its day; I was speaking of the other planets—Mars and Venus and the satellites of Jupiter. Even maybe out at the stars themselves. Suppose we do find people? Think what it will mean to us. We've been alone, all alone, the only intelligent race in the only world we know. We haven't even been able to talk with dogs or apes. Any answers we got we had to think up by ourselves, like deserted orphans. But suppose we find *people,* intelligent people, who have done some thinking in their own way. *We wouldn't be alone any more!* We could look up at the stars and never be afraid again."

He finished, seeming a little tired and even a little ashamed of his outburst, like a man surprised in a private act. He stood facing them, searching their faces.

"Gee whiz, Chief," said Montgomery, "I can use that. How about it?"

"Think you can remember it?"

"Don't need to—I flipped on your 'silent steno.' "

"Well, damn your eyes!"

"We'll put it on video—in a play, I think."

Harriman smiled almost boyishly. "I've never acted, but if you think it'll do any good, I'm game."

"Oh, no, not you, Chief," Montgomery answered in horrified tones. "You're not the type. I'll use Basil Wilkes-Booth, I think. With his organlike voice and that beautiful archangel face, he'll really send 'em."

Harriman glanced down at his paunch and said gruffly,

"Okay—back to business. Now about money. In the first place we can go after straight donations to one of the nonprofit corporations, just like endowments for colleges. Hit the upper brackets, where tax deductions really matter. How much do you think we can raise that way?"

"Very little," Strong opined. "That cow is about milked dry."

"It's never milked dry, as long as there are rich men around who would rather make gifts than pay taxes. How much will a man pay to have a crater on the Moon named after him?"

"I thought they all had names?" remarked the lawyer.

"Lots of them don't—and we have the whole back face that's not touched yet. We won't try to put down an estimate today; we'll just list it. Monty, I want an angle to squeeze dimes out of the school kids, too. Forty million school kids at a dime a head is four million dollars—we can use that."

"Why stop at a dime?" asked Monty. "If you get a kid really interested he'll scrape together a dollar."

"Yes, but what do we offer him for it? Aside from the honor of taking part in a noble venture and so forth?"

"Mmmm. . . ." Montgomery used up more thumbnail. "Suppose we go after both the dimes and the dollars. For a dime he gets a card saying that he's a member of the Moonbeam club—"

"No, the 'Junior Spacemen.' "

"Okay, the Moonbeams will be girls—and don't forget to rope the Boy Scouts and the Girl Scouts into it, too. We give each kid a card; when he kicks in another dime, we punch it. When he's punched out a dollar, we give him a certificate, suitable for framing, with his name and some process engraving, and on the back a picture of the Moon."

"On the *front*," answered Harriman. "Do it in one print job; it's cheaper and it'll look better. We give him something else, too, a steel-clad guarantee that his name will be on the rolls of the Junior Pioneers of the Moon, which same will be placed in a monument to be erected on the Moon at the landing site of the first Moon ship—in microfilm, of course; we have to watch weight."

"Fine!" agreed Montgomery. "Want to swap jobs, Chief? When he gets up to ten dollars we give him a genuine, solid gold-plated shooting star pin and he's a senior Pioneer, with the right to vote or something or other. And his name goes *outside* of the monument—microengraved on a platinum strip."

Strong looked as if he had bitten a lemon. "What happens when he reaches a hundred dollars?" he asked.

"Why, then," Montgomery answered happily, "we give him another card and he can start over. Don't worry about it, Mr. Strong—if any kid goes that high, he'll have his reward. Probably we will take him on an inspection tour of the ship before it takes off and give him, absolutely free, a picture of himself standing in front of it, with the pilot's own signature signed across the bottom by some female clerk."

"Chiseling from kids. Bah!"

"Not at all," answered Montgomery in hurt tones. "Intangibles are the most honest merchandise anyone can sell. They are always worth whatever you are willing to pay for them and they never wear out. You can take them to your grave untarnished."

"Hmmmph!"

Harriman listened to this, smiling and saying nothing. Kamens cleared his throat. "If you two ghouls are through cannibalizing the youth of the land, I've another idea."

"Spill it."

"George, you collect stamps, don't you?"

"Yes."

"How much would a cover be worth which had been to the Moon and been cancelled there?"

"Huh? But you couldn't, you know."

"I think we could get our Moon ship declared a legal post

office substation without too much trouble. What would it be worth?"

"Uh, that depends on how rare they are."

"There must be some optimum number which will fetch a maximum return. Can you estimate it?"

Strong got a faraway look in his eye, then took out an old-fashioned pencil and commenced to figure.

Harriman went on. "Saul, my minor success in buying a share in the Moon from Jones went to my head. How about selling building lots on the Moon?"

"Let's keep this serious, Delos. You can't do that until you've landed there."

"I am serious. I know you are thinking of that ruling back in the forties that such land would have to be staked out and accurately described. I want to sell land on the Moon. You figure out a way to make it legal. I'll sell the whole Moon, if I can— surface rights, mineral rights, anything."

"Suppose they want to occupy it?"

"Fine. The more the merrier. I'd like to point out, too, that we'll be in a position to assess taxes on what we have sold. If they don't use it and won't pay taxes, it reverts to us. Now you figure out how to offer it, without going to jail. You may have to advertise it abroad, then plan to peddle it personally in this country, like Irish Sweepstakes tickets."

Kamens looked thoughtful. "We could incorporate the land company in Panama and advertise by video and radio from Mexico. Do you really think you can sell the stuff?"

"You can sell snowballs in Greenland," put in Montgomery. "It's a matter of promotion."

Harriman added, "Did you ever read about the Florida land boom, Saul? People bought lots they had never seen and sold them at tripled prices without ever having laid eyes on them. Sometimes a parcel would change hands a dozen times before anyone got around to finding out that the stuff was ten-foot deep in water. We can offer bargains better than that—an acre, a guaranteed dry acre with plenty of sunshine, for maybe ten dollars—or a thousand acres at a dollar an acre. Who's going to turn down a bargain like that? Particularly after the rumor gets around that the Moon is believed to be loaded with uranium?"

"Is it?"

"How should I know? When the boom sags a little we will announce the selected location of Luna City—and it will just happen to work out that the land around the site is still available for sale. Don't worry, Saul, if it's real estate, George and I can sell it. Why, down in the Ozarks, where the land stands on edge, we used to sell both sides of the same acre." Harriman looked thoughtful. "I think we'll reserve mineral rights—there just might actually be uranium there!"

Kamens chuckled. "Delos, you are a kid at heart. Just a great big, overgrown, lovable—juvenile delinquent."

Strong straightened up. "I make it half a million," he said.

"Half a million what?" asked Harriman.

"For the cancelled philatelic covers, of course. That's what we were talking about. Five thousand is my best estimate of the number that could be placed with serious collectors and with dealers. Even then we will have to discount them to a syndicate and hold back until the ship is built and the trip looks like a probability."

"Okay," agreed Harriman. "You handle it. I'll just note that we can tap you for an extra half million toward the end."

"Don't I get a commission?" asked Kamens. "I thought of it."

"You get a rising vote of thanks—and ten acres on the Moon. Now what other sources of revenue can we hit?"

"Don't you plan to sell stocks?" asked Kamens.

"I was coming to that. Of course—but no preferred stock; we don't want to be forced through a reorganization. Participating common, nonvoting—"

"Sounds like another banana-state corporation to me."

"Naturally—but I want some of it on the New York Exchange, and you'll have to work that out with the Securities Exchange Commission somehow. Not too much of it—that's our showcase and we'll have to keep it active and moving up."

"Wouldn't you rather I swam the Hellespont?"

"Don't be like that, Saul. It beats chasing ambulances, doesn't it?"

"I'm not sure."

"Well, that's what I want you—wups!" The screen on Harriman's desk had come to life. A girl said, "Mr. Harriman, Mr. Dixon is here. He has no appointment but he says that you want to see him."

"I thought I had that thing shut off," muttered Harriman, then pressed his key and said, "Okay, show him in."

"Very well, sir—oh, Mr. Harriman, Mr. Entenza came in just this second."

"Send them both in." Harriman disconnected and turned back to his associates. "Zip your lips, gang, and hold on to your wallets."

"Look who's talking," said Kamens.

Dixon came in with Entenza behind him. He sat down, looked around, started to speak, then checked himself. He looked around again, especially at Entenza.

"Go ahead, Dan," Harriman encouraged him. "'Tain't nobody here at all but just us chickens."

Dixon made up his mind. "I've decided to come in with you, D. D.," he announced. "As an act of faith I went to the trouble of getting this." He took a formal-looking instrument from his pocket and displayed it. It was a sale of lunar rights, from Phineas Morgan to Dixon, phrased in exactly the same fashion as that which Jones had granted to Harriman.

Entenza looked startled, then dipped into his own inner coat pocket. Out came three more sales contracts of the same sort, each from a director of the power syndicate. Harriman cocked an eyebrow at them. "Jack sees you and raises you two, Dan. You want to call?"

Dixon smiled ruefully. "I can just see him." He added two more to the pile, grinned and offered his hand to Entenza.

"Looks like a standoff." Harriman decided to say nothing just yet about seven telestated contracts now locked in his desk —after going to bed the night before he had been quite busy on the phone almost till midnight. "Jack, how much did you pay for those things?"

"Standish held out for a thousand; the others were cheap."

"Damn it, I warned you not to run the price up. Standish will gossip. How about you, Dan?"

"I got them at satisfactory prices."

"So you won't talk, eh? Never mind—gentlemen, how serious are you about this? How much money did you bring?"

Entenza looked to Dixon, who answered, "How much does it take?"

"How much can you raise?" demanded Harriman.

Dixon shrugged. "We're getting no place. Let's use figures. A hundred thousand."

Harriman sniffed. "I take it what you really want is to reserve a seat on the first regularly scheduled Moon ship. I'll sell it to you at that price."

"Let's quit sparring, Delos. How much?"

Harriman's face remained calm but he thought furiously. He was caught short, with too little information—he had not even talked figures with his chief engineer as yet. Confound it! why had he left that phone hooked in? "Dan, as I warned you, it will cost you at least a million just to sit down in this game."

"So I thought. How much will it take to *stay* in the game?"

"All you've got."

"Don't be silly, Delos. I've got more than you have."

Harriman lit a cigar, his only sign of agitation. "Suppose you match us, dollar for dollar."

"For which I get two shares?"

"Okay, okay, you chuck in a buck whenever each of us does —share and share alike. But I run things."

"You run the operations," agreed Dixon. "Very well, I'll put up a million now and match you as necessary. You have no objection to me having my own auditor, of course."

"When have I ever cheated you, Dan?"

"Never and there is no need to start."

"Have it your own way—but be damned sure you send a man who can keep his mouth shut."

"He'll keep quiet. I keep his heart in a jar in my safe."

Harriman was thinking about the extent of Dixon's assets. "We just might let you buy in with a second share later, Dan. This operation will be expensive."

Dixon fitted his fingertips carefully together. "We'll meet that question when we come to it. I don't believe in letting an enterprise fold up for lack of capital."

"Good." Harriman turned to Entenza. "You heard what Dan had to say, Jack. Do you like the terms?"

Entenza's forehead was covered with sweat. "I can't raise a million that fast."

"That's all right, Jack. We don't need it this morning. Your note is good; you can take your time liquidating."

"But you said a million is just the beginning. I can't match you indefinitely; you've got to place a limit on it. I've got my family to consider."

"No annuities, Jack? No monies transferred in an irrevocable trust?"

"That's not the point. You'll be able to squeeze me—freeze me out."

Harriman waited for Dixon to say something. Dixon finally said, "We wouldn't squeeze you, Jack—as long as you could prove you had converted every asset you hold. We would let you stay in on a pro rata basis."

Harriman nodded. "That's right, Jack." He was thinking that

any shrinkage in Entenza's share would give himself and Strong a clear voting majority.

Strong had been thinking of something of the same nature, for he spoke up suddenly, "I don't like this. Four equal partners —we can be deadlocked too easily."

Dixon shrugged. "I refuse to worry about it. I am in this because I am betting that Delos can manage to make it profitable."

"We'll get to the Moon, Dan!"

"I didn't say that. I am betting that you will show a profit whether we get to the Moon or not. Yesterday evening I spent looking over the public records of several of your companies; they were very interesting. I suggest we resolve any possible deadlock by giving the Director—that's you, Delos—the power to settle ties. Satisfactory, Entenza?"

"Oh, sure!"

Harriman was worried but tried not to show it. He did not trust Dixon, even bearing gifts. He stood up suddenly. "I've got to run, gentlemen. I leave you to Mr. Strong and Mr. Kamens. Come along, Monty." Kamens, he was sure, would not spill anything prematurely, even to nominal full partners. As for Strong—George, he knew, had not even let his left hand know how many fingers there were on his right.

He dismissed Montgomery outside the door of the partners' personal office and went across the hall. Andrew Ferguson, chief engineer of Harriman Enterprises, looked up as he came in. "Howdy, Boss. Say, Mr. Strong gave me an interesting idea for a light switch this morning. It did not seem practical at first but—"

"Skip it. Let one of the boys have it and forget it. You know the line we are on now."

"There have been rumors," Ferguson answered cautiously.

"Fire the man that brought you the rumor. No—send him on a special mission to Tibet and keep him there until we are through. Well, let's get on with it. I want you to build a Moon ship as quickly as possible."

Ferguson threw one leg over the arm of his chair, took out a penknife and began grooming his nails. "You say that like it was an order to build a privy."

"Why not? There have been theoretically adequate fuels since way back in '49. You get together the team to design it and the gang to build it; you build it—I pay the bills. What could be simpler?"

Ferguson stared at the ceiling. " 'Adequate fuels—' " he repeated dreamily.

"So I said. The figures show that hydrogen and oxygen are enough to get a step rocket to the Moon and back—it's just a matter of proper design."

" 'Proper design,' he says," Ferguson went on in the same gentle voice, then suddenly swung around, jabbed the knife into the scarred desk top and bellowed, "What do you know about proper design? Where do I get the steels? What do I use for a throat liner? How in the hell do I burn enough tons of your crazy mix per second to keep from wasting all my power breaking loose? How can I get a decent mass ratio with a step rocket? Why in the hell didn't you let me build a proper ship when we had the fuel?"

Harriman waited for him to quiet down, then said, "What do we do about it, Andy?"

"Hmmm. . . . I was thinking about it as I lay abed last night—and my old lady is sore as hell at you; I had to finish the night on the couch. In the first place, Mr. Harriman, the proper way to tackle this is to get a research appropriation from the Department of National Defense. Then you—"

"Damn it, Andy, you stick to engineering and let me handle the political and financial end of it. I don't want your advice."

"Damn it, Delos, don't go off half cocked. This *is* engineering I'm talking about. The government owns a whole mass of former art about rocketry—all classified. Without a government contract you can't even get a peek at it."

"It can't amount to very much. What can a government rocket do that a Skyways rocket can't do? You told me yourself that Federal rocketry no longer amounted to anything."

Ferguson looked supercilious. "I am afraid I can't explain it in lay terms. You will have to take it for granted that we need those government research reports. There's no sense in spending thousands of dollars in doing work that has already been done."

"Spend the thousands."

"Maybe millions."

"Spend the millions. Don't be afraid to spend money. Andy, I don't want this to be a military job." He considered elaborating to the engineer the involved politics back of his decision, thought better of it. "How bad do you actually need that government stuff? Can't you get the same results by hiring engineers who used to work for the government? Or even hire them away from the government right now?"

Ferguson pursed his lips. "If you insist on hampering me, how can you expect me to get results?"

"I am not hampering you. I am telling you that this is not a government project. If you won't attempt to cope with it on those terms, let me know now, so that I can find somebody who will."

Ferguson started playing mumblety-peg on his desk top. When he got to "noses"—and missed—he said quietly, "I mind a boy who used to work for the government at White Sands. He was a very smart lad indeed—design chief of section."

"You mean he might head up your team?"

"That was the notion."

"What's his name? Where is he? Who's he working for?"

"Well, as it happened, when the government closed down White Sands, it seemed a shame to me that a good boy should be out of a job, so I placed him with Skyways. He's maintenance chief engineer out on the Coast."

"Maintenance? What a hell of a job for a creative man! But you mean he's working for us now? Get him on the screen. No —call the Coast and have them send him here in a special rocket; we'll all have lunch together."

"As it happens," Ferguson said quietly, "I got up last night and called him—that's what annoyed the Missus. He's waiting outside. Coster—Bob Coster."

A slow grin spread over Harriman's face. "Andy! You black-hearted old scoundrel, why did you pretend to balk?"

"I wasn't pretending. I like it here, Mr. Harriman. Just as long as you don't interfere, I'll do my job. Now my notion is this: we'll make young Coster chief engineer of the project and give him his head. I won't joggle his elbow; I'll just read the reports. Then you leave him alone, d'you hear me? Nothing makes a good technical man angrier than to have some incompetent nitwit with a checkbook telling him how to do his job."

"Suits. And I don't want a penny-pinching old fool slowing him down, either. Mind you don't interfere with him, either, or I'll jerk the rug out from under you. Do we understand each other?"

"I think we do."

"Then get him in here."

Apparently Ferguson's concept of a "lad" was about age thirty-five, for such Harriman judged Coster to be. He was tall, lean, and quietly eager. Harriman braced him immediately, after shaking hands, with, "Bob, can you build a rocket that will go to the Moon?"

Coster took it without blinking. "Do you have a source of X-fuel?" he countered, giving the rocket man's usual shorthand for the isotope fuel formerly produced by the power satellite.

"No."

Coster remained perfectly quiet for several seconds, then answered, "I can put an unmanned messenger rocket on the face of the Moon."

"Not good enough. I want it to go there, land, and come

back. Whether it lands here under power or by atmosphere braking is unimportant."

It appeared that Coster never answered promptly; Harriman had the fancy that he could hear wheels turning over in the man's head. "That would be a very expensive job."

"Who asked you how much it would cost? Can you do it?"

"I could try."

"Try, hell. Do you think you can do it? Would you bet your shirt on it? Would you be willing to risk your neck in the attempt? If you don't believe in yourself, man, you'll always lose."

"How much will *you* risk, sir? I told you this would be expensive—and I doubt if you have any idea how expensive."

"And I told you not to worry about money. Spend what you need; it's my job to pay the bills. Can you do it?"

"I can do it. I'll let you know later how much it will cost and how long it will take."

"Good. Start getting your team together. Where are we going to do this, Andy?" he added, turning to Ferguson. "Australia?"

"No." It was Coster who answered. "It can't be Australia; I want a mountain catapult. That will save us one step-combination."

"How big a mountain?" asked Harriman. "Will Pikes Peak do?"

"It ought to be in the Andes," objected Ferguson. "The mountains are taller and closer to the equator. After all, we own facilities there—or the Andes Development Company does."

"Do as you like, Bob," Harriman told Coster. "I would prefer Pikes Peak, but it's up to you." He was thinking that there were tremendous business advantages to locating Earth's spaceport number 1 inside the United States—and he could visualize the advertising advantage of having Moon ships blast off from the top of Pikes Peak, in plain view of everyone for hundreds of miles to the East.

"I'll let you know."

"Now about salary. Forget whatever it was we were paying you; how much do you want?"

Coster actually gestured, waving the subject away. "I'll work for coffee and cakes."

"Don't be silly."

"Let me finish. Coffee and cakes and one other thing: I get to make the trip."

Harriman blinked. "Well, I can understand that," he said slowly. "In the meantime I'll put you on a drawing account." He added, "Better calculate for a three-man ship, unless you are a pilot."

"I'm not."

"Three men, then. You see, I'm going along, too."

4

"A good thing you decided to come in, Dan," Harriman was saying, "or you would find yourself out of a job. I'm going to put an awful crimp in the power company before I'm through with this."

Dixon buttered a roll. "Really? How?"

"We'll set up high-temperature piles, like the Arizona job, just like the one that blew up, around the corner on the far face of the Moon. We'll remote-control them; if one explodes it won't matter. And I'll breed more X-fuel in a week than the company turned out in three months. Nothing personal about it; it's just that I want a source of fuel for interplanetary liners. If we can't get good stuff here, we'll have to make it on the Moon."

"Interesting. But where do you propose to get the uranium for six piles? The last I heard the Atomic Energy Commission had the prospective supply earmarked twenty years ahead."

"Uranium? Don't be silly; we'll get it on the Moon."

"On the Moon? Is there uranium on the Moon?"

"Didn't you know? I thought that was why you decided to join up with me."

"No, I didn't know," Dixon said deliberately. "What proof have you?"

"Me? I'm no scientist, but it's a well-understood fact. Spectroscopy, or something. Catch one of the professors. But don't go showing too much interest; we aren't ready to show our hand." Harriman stood up. "I've got to run, or I'll miss the shuttle for Rotterdam. Thanks for the lunch." He grabbed his hat and left.

Harriman stood up. "Suit yourself, Mynheer van der Velde. I'm giving you and your colleagues a chance to hedge your bets. Your geologists all agree that diamonds result from volcanic action. What do you think we will find *there?*" He dropped a large photograph of the Moon on the Hollander's desk.

The diamond merchant looked impassively at the pictured planet, pockmarked by a thousand giant craters. "If you get there, Mr. Harriman."

Harriman swept up the picture. "We'll get there. And we'll find diamonds—though I would be the first to admit that it may be twenty years or even forty before there is a big enough strike to matter. I've come to you because I believe that the worst villain in our social body is the man who introduces a major new economic factor without planning his innovation in such a way as to permit peaceful adjustment. I don't like panics. But all I can do is warn you. Good day."

"Sit down, Mr. Harriman. I'm always confused when a man explains how he is going to do *me* good. Suppose you tell me instead how this is going to do *you* good? Then we can discuss how to protect the world market against a sudden influx of diamonds from the Moon."

Harriman sat down.

Harriman liked the Low Countries. He was delighted to locate a dog-drawn milk cart whose young master wore real wooden shoes; he happily took pictures and tipped the child heavily, unaware that the setup was arranged for tourists. He visited several other diamond merchants but without speaking of the Moon. Among other purchases he found a brooch for Charlotte—a peace offering.

Then he took a taxi to London, planted a story with the representatives of the diamond syndicate there, arranged with his London solicitors to be insured by Lloyd's of London, through a dummy, *against* a successful Moon flight, and called his home office. He listened to numerous reports, especially those concerning Montgomery, and found that Montgomery was in New Delhi. He called him there, spoke with him at length, then hurried to the port just in time to catch his ship. He was in Colorado the next morning.

At Peterson Field, east of Colorado Springs, he had trouble getting through the gate, even though it was now his domain, under lease. Of course he could have called Coster and gotten it straightened out at once, but he wanted to look around before seeing Coster. Fortunately the head guard knew him by sight; he got in and wandered around for an hour or more, a tri-colored badge pinned to his coat to give him freedom.

The machine shop was moderately busy, so was the foundry . . . but most of the shops were almost deserted. Harriman left the shops, went into the main engineering building. The drafting room and the loft were fairly active, as was the computation section. But there were unoccupied desks in the structures group and a churchlike quiet in the metals group and in the adjoining metallurgical laboratory. He was about to cross over into the chemicals and materials annex when Coster suddenly showed up.

"Mr. Harriman! I just heard you were here."

"Spies everywhere," remarked Harriman. "I didn't want to disturb you."

"Not at all. Let's go up to my office."

Settled there a few moments later, Harriman asked, "Well—how's it going?"

Coster frowned. "All right, I guess."

Harriman noted that the engineer's desk baskets were piled high with papers which spilled over onto the desk. Before Harriman could answer, Coster's desk phone lit up and a feminine voice said sweetly, "Mr. Coster—Mr. Morgenstern is calling."

"Tell him I'm busy."

After a short wait the girl answered in a troubled voice, "He says he's just got to speak to you, sir."

Coster looked annoyed. "Excuse me a moment, Mr. Harriman—Okay, put him on."

The girl was replaced by a man who said, "Oh, there you are —what was the holdup? Look, Chief, we're in a jam about these trucks. Every one of them that we leased needs an overhaul and now it turns out that the White Fleet company won't do anything about it—they're sticking to the fine print in the contract. Now the way I see it, we'd do better to cancel the contract and do business with Peak City Transport. They have a scheme that looks good to me. They guarantee to—"

"Take care of it," snapped Coster. "You made the contract and you have authority to cancel. You know that."

"Yes, but Chief, I figured this would be something you would want to pass on personally. It involves policy and—"

"Take care of it! I don't give a damn what you do as long as we have transportation when we need it." He switched off.

"Who is that man?" inquired Harriman.

"Who? Oh, that's Morgenstern, Claude Morgenstern."

"Not his name—what does he do?"

"He's one of my assistants—buildings, grounds, and transportation."

"Fire him!"

Coster looked stubborn. Before he could answer, a secretary came in and stood insistently at his elbow with a sheaf of papers. He frowned, initialed them, and sent her out.

"Oh, I don't mean that as an order," Harriman added, "but I do mean it as serious advice. I won't give orders in your backyard, but will you listen to a few minutes of advice?"

"Naturally," Coster agreed stiffly.

"Mmm . . . this your first job as top boss?"

Coster hesitated, then admitted it.

"I hired you on Ferguson's belief that you were the engineer most likely to build a successful Moon ship. I've had no reason to change my mind. But top administration ain't engineering, and maybe I can show you a few tricks there, if you'll let me." He waited. "I'm not criticizing," he added. "Top bossing is like sex; until you've had it, you don't know about it." Harriman had the mental reservation that if the boy would not take advice, he would suddenly be out of a job, whether Ferguson liked it or not.

Coster drummed on his desk. "I don't know what's wrong and that's a fact. It seems as if I can't turn anything over to anybody and have it done properly. I feel as if I were swimming in quicksand."

"Done much engineering lately?"

"I try to." Coster waved at another desk in the corner. "I work there, late at night."

"That's no good. I hired you as an engineer. Bob, this setup is all wrong. The joint ought to be jumping—and it's not. Your office ought to be quiet as a grave. Instead your office is jumping and the plant looks like a graveyard."

Coster buried his face in his hands, then looked up. "I know it. I know what needs to be done—but every time I try to tackle a technical problem some bloody fool wants me to make a decision about trucks—or telephones—or some damn thing. I'm sorry, Mr. Harriman. I thought I could do it."

Harriman said very gently, "Don't let it throw you, Bob. You haven't had much sleep lately, have you? Tell you what—we'll put over a fast one on Ferguson. I'll take that desk you're at for a few days and build you a setup to protect you against such things. I want that brain of yours thinking about reaction vectors and fuel efficiencies and design stresses, not about contracts for trucks." Harriman stepped to the door, looked around the outer office and spotted a man who might or might not be the office's chief clerk. "Hey, you! C'mere."

The man looked startled, got up, came to the door and said, "Yes?"

"I want that desk in the corner and all the stuff that's on it moved to an empty office on this floor, right away."

The clerk raised his eyebrows. "And who are you, if I may ask?"

"Goddamn it—"

"Do as he tells you, Weber," Coster put in.

"I want it done inside of twenty minutes," added Harriman. "Jump!"

He turned back to Coster's other desk, punched the phone, and presently was speaking to the main offices of Skyways. "Jim, is your boy Jock Berkeley around? Put him on leave and send him to me, at Peterson Field, right away, special trip. I want the ship he comes in to raise ground ten minutes after we sign off. Send his gear after him." Harriman listened for a moment, then answered, "No, your organization won't fall apart if you lose Jock—or, if it does, maybe we've been paying the wrong man the top salary . . . okay, okay, you're entitled to one swift kick at my tail the next time you catch up with me, but send Jock. So long."

He supervised getting Coster and his other desk moved into another office, saw to it that the phone in the new office was disconnected, and, as an afterthought, had a couch moved in there, too. "We'll install a projector and a drafting machine and bookcases and other junk like that tonight," he told Coster. "Just make a list of anything you need—to work on *engineering*. And call me if you want anything." He went back to the nominal chief engineer's office and got happily to work trying to figure where the organization stood and what was wrong with it.

Some four hours later he took Berkeley in to meet Coster. The chief engineer was asleep at his desk, head cradled on his arms. Harriman started to back out, but Coster roused. "Oh! Sorry," he said, blushing, "I must have dozed off."

"That's why I brought you the couch," said Harriman. "It's more restful. Bob, meet Jock Berkeley. He's your new slave. You remain chief engineer and top, undisputed boss. Jock is Lord High Everything Else. From now on you've got absolutely nothing to worry about—except for the little detail of building a Moon ship."

They shook hands. "Just one thing I ask, Mr. Coster," Berkeley said seriously; "bypass me all you want to—you'll have to run the technical show—but for God's sake record it so I'll know what's going on. I'm going to have a switch placed on your desk that will operate a sealed recorder at my desk."

"Fine!" Coster was looking, Harriman thought, younger already.

"And if you want something that is not technical, don't do it yourself. Just flip a switch and whistle; it'll get done!" Berkeley glanced at Harriman. "The Boss says he wants to talk with you about the real job. I'll leave you and get busy." He left.

Harriman sat down; Coster followed suit and said, "Whew!"

"Feel better?"

"I like the looks of that fellow Berkeley."

"That's good; he's your twin brother from now on. Stop worrying; I've used him before. You'll think you're living in a well-run hospital. By the way, where do you live?"

"At a boardinghouse in the Springs."

"That's ridiculous. And you don't even have a place here to sleep?" Harriman reached over to Coster's desk, got through to Berkeley. "Jock—get a suite for Mr. Coster at the Broadmoor, under a phony name."

"Right."

"And have this stretch along here adjacent to his office fitted out as an apartment."

"Right. Tonight."

"Now, Bob, about the Moon ship. Where do we stand?"

They spent the next two hours contentedly running over the details of the problem, as Coster had laid them out. Admittedly very little work had been done since the field was leased, but Coster had accomplished considerable theoretical work and computation before he had gotten swamped in administrative details. Harriman, though no engineer and certainly not a mathematician outside the primitive arithmetic of money, had for so long devoured everything he could find about space travel that he was able to follow most of what Coster showed him.

"I don't see anything here about your mountain catapult," he said presently.

Coster looked vexed. "Oh, that! Mr. Harriman, I spoke too quickly."

"Huh? How come? I've had Montgomery's boys drawing up beautiful pictures of what things will look like when we are running regular trips. I intend to make Colorado Springs the spaceport capital of the world. We hold the franchise of the old cog railroad now; what's the hitch?"

"Well, it's both time and money."

"Forget money. That's my pidgin."

"Time then. I still think an electric gun is the best way to get the initial acceleration for a chem-powered ship. Like this—" He began to sketch rapidly. "It enables you to omit the first step-rocket stage, which is bigger than all the others put together and is terribly inefficient, as it has such a poor mass ratio. But what do you have to do to get it? You can't build a tower, not a tower a couple of miles high, strong enough to take the thrusts—not this year, anyway. So you have to use a mountain. Pikes Peak is as good as any; it's accessible, at least.

"But what do you have to do to use it? First, a tunnel in through the side, from Manitou to just under the peak, and big enough to take the loaded ship—"

"Lower it down from the top," suggested Harriman.

Coster answered, "I thought of that. Elevators two miles high for loaded spaceships aren't exactly built out of string; in fact they aren't built out of any available materials. It's possible to gimmick the catapult itself so that the accelerating coils can be reversed and timed differently to do the job, but believe me, Mr. Harriman, it will throw you into other engineering problems quite as great . . . such as a giant railroad up to the top of the ship. And it still leaves you with the shaft of the catapult itself to be dug. It can't be as small as the ship, not like a gun barrel for a bullet. It's got to be considerably larger; you don't compress a column of air two miles high with impunity. Oh, a mountain catapult could be built, but it might take ten years— or longer."

"Then forget it. We'll build it for the future but not for this flight. No, wait—how about a *surface* catapult. We scoot up the side of the mountain and curve it up at the end?"

"Quite frankly, I think something like that is what will eventually be used. But, as of today, it just creates new problems. Even if we could devise an electric gun in which you could make that last curve—we can't, at present—the ship would have to be designed for terrific side stresses and all the additional weight would be parasitic so far as our main purpose is concerned, the design of a rocket ship."

"Well, Bob, what *is* your solution?"

Coster frowned. "Go back to what we know how to do— build a step rocket."

5

"Monty—"

"Yeah, Chief?"

"Have you ever heard this song?" Harriman hummed, *"The Moon belongs to everyone; the best things in life are free—"* then sang it, badly off key.

"Can't say as I ever have."

"It was before your time. I want it dug out again. I want it revived, plugged until Hell wouldn't have it, and on everybody's lips."

"Okay." Montgomery took out his memorandum pad. "When do you want it to reach its top?"

Harriman considered. "In, say, about three months. Then I want the first phrase picked up and used in advertising slogans."

"A cinch."

"How are things in Florida, Monty?"

"I thought we were going to have to buy the whole damned legislature until we got the rumor spread around that Los Angeles had contracted to have a City-Limits-of-Los-Angeles sign planted on the Moon for publicity pix. Then they came around."

"Good." Harriman pondered. "You know, that's not a bad idea. How much do you think the Chamber of Commerce of Los Angeles would pay for such a picture?"

Montgomery made another note. "I'll look into it."

"I suppose you are about ready to crank up Texas, now that Florida is loaded?"

"Most any time now. We're spreading a few snide rumors first."

Headline from Dallas-Fort Worth *Banner:*

THE MOON BELONGS TO TEXAS!!!

"—and that's all for tonight, kiddies. Don't forget to send in those box tops, or reasonable facsimiles. Remember—first prize is a thousand-acre ranch on the Moon itself, free and clear; the second prize is a six-foot scale model of the actual Moon ship, and there are fifty, count them, fifty third prizes, each a saddle-trained Shetland pony. Your hundred-word composition 'Why I want to go to the Moon' will be judged for sincerity and originality, not on literary merit. Send those box tops to Uncle Taffy, Box 214, Juarez, Old Mexico."

Harriman was shown into the office of the president of the Moka-Coka Company ("Only a Moke is truly a coke"—"Drink the Cola drink with the Lift"). He paused at the door, some twenty feet from the president's desk, and quickly pinned a two-inch-wide button to his lapel.

Patterson Griggs looked up. "Well, this is really an honor, D. D. Do come in and—" The soft-drink executive stopped suddenly, his expression changed. "What are you doing wearing *that?*" he snapped. "Trying to annoy me?"

"That" was the two-inch disc; Harriman unpinned it and put it in his pocket. It was a celluloid advertising pin, in plain yellow; printed on it in black, almost covering it, was a simple 6 +, the trademark of Moka-Coka's only serious rival.

"No," answered Harriman, "though I don't blame you for being irritated. I see half the school kids in the country wearing these silly buttons. But I came to give you a friendly tip, not to annoy you."

"What do you mean?"

"When I paused at your door that pin on my lapel was just the size—to you, standing at your desk—that the full Moon looks when you are standing in your garden, looking up at it. You didn't have any trouble reading what was on the pin, did you? I know you didn't; you yelled at me before either one of us stirred."

"What about it?"

"How would you feel—and what would the effect be on your sales—if there was 'six-plus' written across the face of the Moon instead of just on a school kid's sweater?"

Griggs thought about it, then said, "D. D., don't make poor jokes. I've had a bad day."

"I'm not joking. As you have probably heard around the Street, I'm behind this Moon trip venture. Between ourselves, Pat, it's quite an expensive undertaking, even for me. A few days ago a man came to me—you'll pardon me if I don't men-

tion names? You can figure it out. Anyhow, this man represented a client who wanted to buy the advertising concession
for the Moon. He knew we weren't sure of success, but he said
his client would take the risk.

"At first I couldn't figure out what he was talking about; he
set me straight. Then I thought he was kidding. Then I was
shocked. Look at this—" Harriman took out a large sheet of
paper and spread it on Griggs' desk. "You see the equipment is
set up anywhere near the center of the Moon, as we see it.
Eighteen pyrotechnics rockets shoot out in eighteen directions,
like the spokes of a wheel, but to carefully calculated distances.
They hit and the bombs they carry go off, spreading finely divided carbon black for calculated distances. There's no air on
the Moon, you know, Pat—a fine powder will throw just as
easily as a javelin. Here's your result." He turned the paper
over; on the back there was a picture of the Moon, printed
lightly. Overlying it, in black, heavy print was: 6 +

"So it *is* that outfit—those poisoners!"

"No, no, I didn't say so! But it illustrates the point; six-plus
is only two symbols; it can be spread large enough to be read on
the face of the Moon."

Griggs stared at the horrid advertisement. "I don't believe it
will work!"

"A reliable pyrotechnics firm has guaranteed that it will—
provided I can deliver their equipment to the spot. After all,
Pat, it doesn't take much of a pyrotechnics rocket to go a long
distance on the Moon. Why, you could throw a baseball a
couple of miles yourself—low gravity, you know."

"People would never stand for it. It's sacrilege!"

Harriman looked sad. "I wish you were right. But they stand
for skywriting—and video commercials."

Griggs chewed his lip. "Well, I don't see why you come to me
with it," he exploded. "You know damn well the name of my
product won't go on the face of the Moon. The letters would be
too small to be read."

Harriman nodded. "That's exactly why I came to you. Pat, this isn't just a business venture to me; it's my heart and soul. It just made me sick to think of somebody actually wanting to use the face of the Moon for advertising. As you say, it's sacrilege. But somehow, these jackals found out I was pressed for cash. They came to me when they knew I would have to listen.

"I put them off. I promised them an answer on Thursday. Then I went home and lay awake about it. After a while I thought of you."

"Me?"

"You. You and your company. After all, you've got a good product and you need legitimate advertising for it. It occurred to me that there are more ways to use the Moon in advertising than by defacing it. Now just suppose that your company bought the same concession, but with the public-spirited promise of never letting it be used. Suppose you featured that fact in your ads? Suppose you ran pictures of a boy and girl, sitting out under the Moon, sharing a bottle of Moke? Suppose Moke was the only soft drink carried on the first trip to the Moon? But I don't have to tell you how to do it." He glanced at his watch finger. "I've got to run and I don't want to rush you. If you want to do business, just leave word at my office by noon tomorrow and I'll have our man Montgomery get in touch with your advertising chief."

The head of the big newspaper chain kept him waiting the minimum time reserved for tycoons and cabinet members. Again Harriman stopped at the threshold of a large office and fixed a disc to his lapel.

"Howdy, Delos," the publisher said, "how's the traffic in green cheese today?" He then caught sight of the button and frowned. "If that is a joke, it is in poor taste."

Harriman pocketed the disc; it displayed not 6 +, but the hammer and sickle.

"No," he said, "it's not a joke; it's a nightmare. Colonel, you and I are among the few people in this country who realize that Communism is still a menace."

Sometime later they were talking as chummily as if the Colonel's chain had not obstructed the Moon venture since its inception. The publisher waved a cigar at his desk. "How did you come by those plans? Steal them?"

"They were copied," Harriman answered with narrow truth. "But they aren't important. The important thing is to get there first; we can't risk having an enemy rocket base on the Moon. For years I've had a recurrent nightmare of waking up and seeing headlines that the Russians had landed on the Moon and declared the Lunar Soviet—say thirteen men and two female scientists—and had petitioned for entrance into the U.S.S.R.—and that the petition had, of course, been graciously granted by the Supreme Soviet. I used to wake up and tremble. I don't know that they would actually go through with painting a hammer and sickle on the face of the Moon, but it's consistent with their psychology. Look at those enormous posters they are always hanging up."

The publisher bit down hard on his cigar. "We'll see what we can work out. Is there any way you can speed up your takeoff?"

6

"Mr. Harriman?"

"Yes?"

"That Mr. LeCroix is here again."

"Tell him I can't see him."

"Yes, sir—uh, Mr. Harriman, he did not mention it the other day but he says he is a rocket pilot."

"Damn it, send him around to Skyways. I don't hire pilots."

A man's face crowded into the screen, displacing Harriman's reception secretary. "Mr. Harriman—I'm Leslie LeCroix, relief pilot of the *Charon*."

"I don't care if you are the Angel Gab— Did you say *Charon?*"

"I said *Charon*. And I've got to talk to you."

"Come in."

Harriman greeted his visitor, offered him tobacco, then looked him over with interest. The *Charon,* shuttle rocket to the lost power satellite, had been the nearest thing to a spaceship the world had yet seen. Its pilot, lost in the same explosion that had destroyed the satellite and the *Charon,* had been the first, in a way, of the coming breed of spacemen.

Harriman wondered how it had escaped his attention that the *Charon* had alternating pilots. He had known it, of course—but somehow he had forgotten to take the fact into account. He had written off the power satellite, its shuttle rocket and everything about it, ceased to think about them. He now looked at LeCroix with curiosity.

He saw a small, neat man with a thin, intelligent face, and the big, competent hands of a jockey. LeCroix returned his inspection without embarrassment. He seemed calm and utterly sure of himself.

"Well, Captain LeCroix?"

"You are building a Moon ship."

"Who says so?"

"A Moon ship is being built. The boys all say you are behind it."

"Yes?"

"I want to pilot it."

"Why should you?"

"I'm the best man for it."

Harriman paused to let out a cloud of tobacco smoke. "If you can prove that, the billet is yours."

"It's a deal." LeCroix stood up. "I'll leave my name and address outside."

"Wait a minute. I said 'if.' Let's talk. I'm going along on this trip myself; I want to know more about you before I trust my neck to you."

They discussed Moon flight, interplanetary travel, rocketry, what they might find on the Moon. Gradually Harriman warmed up, as he found another spirit so like his own, so obsessed with the Wonderful Dream. Subconsciously he had already accepted LeCroix; the conversation began to assume that it would be a joint venture.

After a long time Harriman said, "This is fun, Les, but I've got to do a few chores yet today, or none of us will get to the Moon. You go on out to Peterson Field and get acquainted with Bob Coster—I'll call him. If the pair of you can manage to get along, we'll talk contract." He scribbled a chit and handed it to LeCroix. "Give this to Miss Perkins as you go out and she'll put you on the payroll."

"That can wait."

"Man's got to eat."

LeCroix accepted it but did not leave. "There's one thing I don't understand, Mr. Harriman."

"Huh?"

"Why are you planning on a chemically powered ship? Not that I object; I'll herd her. But why do it the hard way? I know you had the *City of Brisbane* refitted for X-fuel—"

Harriman stared at him. "Are you off your nut, Les? You're asking why pigs don't have wings—there isn't any X-fuel and there won't be any more until we make some ourselves—on the Moon."

"Who told you that?"

"What do you mean?"

"The way I heard it, the Atomic Energy Commission allocated X-fuel, under treaty, to several other countries—and some of them weren't prepared to make use of it. But they got it just the same. What happened to it?"

"Oh, *that!* Sure, Les, several of the little outfits in Central America and South America were cut in for a slice of pie for political reasons, even though they had no way to eat it. A good thing, too—we bought it back and used it to ease the immediate power shortage." Harriman frowned. "You're right, though. I should have grabbed some of the stuff then."

"Are you *sure* it's all gone?"

"Why, of course, I'm— No, I'm not. I'll look into it. G'bye."

His contacts were able to account for every pound of X-fuel in short order—save for Costa Rica's allotment. That nation had declined to sell back its supply because its power plant, suitable for X-fuel, had been almost finished at the time of the disaster. Another inquiry disclosed that the power plant had never been finished.

Montgomery was even then in Managua; Nicaragua had had a change in administration and Montgomery was making certain that the special position of the local Moon corporation was protected. Harriman sent him a coded message to proceed to San José, locate X-fuel, buy it and ship it back—at any cost. He then went to see the chairman of the Atomic Energy Commission.

That official was apparently glad to see him and anxious to be affable. Harriman got around to explaining that he wanted a license to do experimental work in isotopes—X-fuel, to be precise.

"This should be brought up through the usual channels, Mr. Harriman."

"It will be. This is a preliminary inquiry. I want to know your reactions."

"After all, I am not the only commissioner . . . and we almost always follow the recommendations of our technical branch."

"Don't fence with me, Carl. You know darn well you control a working majority. Off the record, what do you say?"

"Well, D. D.—off the record—you can't get any X-fuel, so why get a license?"

"Let me worry about that."

"Mmmm . . . we weren't required by law to follow every millicurie of X-fuel, since it isn't classed as potentially suitable for mass weapons. Just the same, we knew what happened to it. There's none available."

Harriman kept quiet.

"In the second place, you can have an X-fuel license, if you wish—for any purpose but rocket fuel."

"Why the restriction?"

"You are building a Moon ship, aren't you?"

"Me?"

"Don't *you* fence with *me,* D. D. It's my business to know things. You can't use X-fuel for rockets, even if you can find it —which you can't." The chairman went to a vault back of his desk and returned with a quarto volume, which he laid in front of Harriman. It was titled: *Theoretical Investigation into the Stability of Several Radioisotopic Fuels—With Notes on the* Charon-*Power-Satellite Disaster.* The cover had a serial number and was stamped: SECRET.

Harriman pushed it away. "I've got no business looking at that—and I wouldn't understand it if I did."

The chairman grinned. "Very well, I'll tell you what's in it. I'm deliberately tying your hands, D. D., by trusting you with a defense secret—"

"I won't have it, I tell you!"

"Don't try to power a spaceship with X-fuel, D. D. It's a lovely fuel—but it may go off like a firecracker anywhere out in space. That report tells why."

"Confound it, we ran the *Charon* for nearly three years!"

"You were lucky. It is the official—but utterly confidential— opinion of the government that the *Charon* set off the power satellite, rather than the satellite setting off the *Charon.* We had thought it was the other way around at first, and of course it could have been, but there was the disturbing matter of the radar records. It seemed as if the ship had gone up a split second before the satellite. So we made an intensive theoretical investigation. X-fuel is too dangerous for rockets."

"That's ridiculous! For every pound burned in the *Charon* there were at least a hundred pounds used in power plants on the surface. How come *they* didn't explode?"

"It's a matter of shielding. A rocket necessarily uses less shielding than a stationary plant, but the worst feature is that it operates out in space. The disaster is presumed to have been triggered by primary cosmic radiation. If you like, I'll call in one of the mathematical physicists to elucidate."

Harriman shook his head. "You know I don't speak the language." He considered. "I suppose that's all there is to it?"

"I'm afraid so. I'm really sorry." Harriman got up to leave. "Uh, one more thing, D. D.—you weren't thinking of approaching any of my subordinate colleagues, were you?"

"Of course not. Why should I?"

"I'm glad to hear it. You know, Mr. Harriman, some of our staff may not be the most brilliant scientists in the world—it's very hard to keep a first-class scientist happy in the conditions of government service. But there is one thing I am sure of: all of them are utterly incorruptible. Knowing that, I would take it as a personal affront if anyone tried to influence one of my people—a very personal affront."

"So?"

"Yes. By the way, I used to box light-heavyweight in college. I've kept it up."

"Hmmm . . . well, I never went to college. But I play a fair game of poker." Harriman suddenly grinned. "I won't tamper with your boys, Carl. It would be too much like offering a bribe to a starving man. Well, so long."

When Harriman got back to his office he called in one of his confidential clerks. "Take another coded message to Mr. Montgomery. Tell him to ship the stuff to Panama City, rather than to the States." He started to dictate another message to Coster, intending to tell him to stop work on the *Pioneer,* whose skeleton was already reaching skyward on the Colorado prairie, and shift to the *Santa Maria,* formerly the *City of Brisbane.*

He thought better of it. Takeoff would have to be outside the United States; with the Atomic Energy Commission acting stuffy, it would not do to try to move the *Santa Maria:* it would give the show away.

Nor could she be moved without refitting her for chem-powered flight. No, he would have another ship of the *Brisbane* class taken out of service and sent to Panama, and the power plant of the *Santa Maria* could be disassembled and shipped there, too. Coster could have the new ship ready in six weeks, maybe sooner . . . and he, Coster, and LeCroix would start for the Moon!

The devil with worries over primary cosmic rays! The *Charon* operated for three years, didn't she? They would make the trip, they would prove it could be done, then, if safer fuels were needed, there would be the incentive to dig them out. The important thing was to do it, make the trip. If Columbus had waited for decent ships, we'd all still be in Europe. A man had to take some chances or he never got anywhere.

Contentedly he started drafting the messages that would get the new scheme under way.

He was interrupted by a secretary. "Mr. Harriman, Mr. Montgomery wants to speak to you."

"Eh? Has he gotten my code already?"

"I don't know, sir."

"Well, put him on."

Montgomery had not received the second message. But he had news for Harriman: Costa Rica had sold all its X-fuel to the English Ministry of Power, soon after the disaster. There was not an ounce of it left, neither in Costa Rica, nor in England.

Harriman sat and moped for several minutes after Montgomery had cleared the screen. Then he called Coster. "Bob? Is LeCroix there?"

"Right here—we were about to go out to dinner together. Here he is, now."

"Howdy, Les. Les, that was a good brain storm of yours, but it didn't work. Somebody stole the baby."

"Eh? Oh, I get you. I'm sorry."

"Don't ever waste time being sorry. We'll go ahead as originally planned. We'll get there!"

"Sure we will."

7

From the June issue of *Popular Technics* magazine: "URANIUM PROSPECTING ON THE MOON—a Fact Article about a soon-to-come Major Industry."

From *Holiday:* "Honeymoon on the Moon—A Discussion of the Miracle Resort that your children will enjoy, as told to our travel editor."

From the *American Sunday Magazine:* "DIAMONDS ON THE MOON?—A World-Famous Scientist Shows Why Diamonds Must Be Common as Pebbles in the Lunar Craters."

"Of course, Clem, I don't know anything about electronics, but here is the way it was explained to me. You can hold the beam of a television broadcast down to a degree or so these days, can't you?"

"Yes—if you use a big enough reflector."

"You'll have plenty of elbowroom. Now Earth covers a space two degrees wide, as seen from the Moon. Sure, it's quite a distance away, but you'd have no power losses and absolutely perfect and unchanging conditions for transmission. Once you made your setup, it wouldn't be any more expensive than broadcasting from the top of a mountain here, and a darned sight less expensive than keeping copters in the air from coast to coast, the way you're having to do now."

"It's a fantastic scheme, Delos."

"What's fantastic about it? Getting to the Moon is my worry, not yours. Once we are there, there's going to be television back to Earth, you can bet your shirt on that. It's a natural setup for line-of-sight transmission. If you aren't interested, I'll have to find someone who is."

"I didn't say I wasn't interested."

"Well, make up your mind. Here's another thing, Clem—I don't want to go sticking my nose into your business, but haven't you had a certain amount of trouble since you lost the use of the power satellite as a relay station?"

"You know the answer; don't needle me. Expenses have gone out of sight without any improvement in revenue."

"That wasn't quite what I meant. How about censorship?"

The television executive threw up his hands. "Don't say that word! How anybody expects a man to stay in business with every two-bit wowser in the country claiming a veto over what we can say and can't say and what we can show and what we can't show—it's enough to make you throw up. The whole principle is wrong; it's like demanding that grown men live on skim milk because the baby can't eat steak. If I were able to lay my hands on those confounded, prurient-minded, slimy—"

"Easy! Easy!" Harriman interrupted. "Did it ever occur to you that there is absolutely no way to interfere with a telecast from the Moon—and that boards of censorship on Earth won't have jurisdiction in any case?"

"What? Say that again."

" 'LIFE goes to the Moon.' Time-Life Inc. is proud to announce that arrangements have been completed to bring *Life*'s readers a personally conducted tour of the first trip to our satellite. In place of the usual weekly feature 'LIFE

Goes to a Party' there will commence, immediately after the return of the first successful—"

"ASSURANCE FOR THE NEW AGE"

(An excerpt from an advertisement of the North Atlantic Mutual Insurance and Liability Company)

"—the same looking-to-the-future that protected our policyholders after the Chicago Fire, after the San Francisco Fire, after every disaster since the War of 1812, now reaches out to insure you from unexpected loss *even on the Moon*—"

"THE UNBOUNDED FRONTIERS OF TECHNOLOGY"

"When the Moon ship *Pioneer* climbs skyward on a ladder of flame, twenty-seven essential devices in her 'innard's will be powered by especially engineered DELTA batteries—"

"Mr. Harriman, could you come out to the field?"

"What's up, Bob?"

"Trouble," Coster answered briefly.

"What sort of trouble?"

Coster hesitated. "I'd rather not talk about it by screen. If you can't come, maybe Les and I had better come there."

"I'll be there this evening."

When Harriman got there he saw that LeCroix's impassive face concealed bitterness, Coster looked stubborn and defensive. He waited until the three were alone in Coster's workroom before he spoke. "Let's have it, boys."

LeCroix looked at Coster. The engineer chewed his lip and said, "Mr. Harriman, you know the stages this design has been through."

"More or less."

"We had to give up the catapult idea. Then we had this—" Coster rummaged on his desk, pulled out a perspective treatment of a four-step rocket, large but rather graceful. "Theoretically it was a possibility; practically it cut things too fine. By the time the stress group boys and the auxiliary group and the control group got through adding things we were forced to come to this—" He hauled out another sketch; it was basically like the first, but squatter, almost pyramidal. "We added a fifth stage as a ring around the fourth stage. We even managed to save some weight by using most of the auxiliary and control equipment for the fourth stage to control the fifth stage. And it still had enough sectional density to punch through the atmosphere with no important drag, even if it was clumsy."

Harriman nodded. "You know, Bob, we're going to have to get away from the step rocket idea before we set up a scheduled run to the Moon."

"I don't see how you can avoid it with chem-powered rockets."

"If you had a decent catapult you could put a single-stage chem-powered rocket into an orbit around the Earth, couldn't you?"

"Sure."

"That's what we'll do. Then it will refuel in that orbit."

"The old space-station setup. I suppose that makes sense—in fact I know it does. Only the ship wouldn't refuel and continue on to the Moon. The economical thing would be to have special ships that never landed anywhere make the jump from there to another fueling station around the Moon. Then—"

LeCroix displayed a most unusual impatience. "All that doesn't mean anything now. Get on with the story, Bob."

"Right," agreed Harriman.

"Well, this model should have done it. And, damn it, it still should do it."

Harriman looked puzzled. "But, Bob, that's the approved design, isn't it? That's what you've got two-thirds built right out there on the field."

"Yes." Coster looked stricken. "But it won't do it. It won't work."

"Why not?"

"Because I've had to add in too much dead weight, that's why. Mr. Harriman, you aren't an engineer; you've no idea how fast the performance falls off when you have to clutter up a ship with anything but fuel and power plant. Take the landing arrangements for the fifth-stage power ring. You use that stage for a minute and a half, then you throw it away. But you don't dare take a chance of it falling on Wichita or Kansas City. We have to include a parachute sequence. Even then we have to plan on tracking it by radar and cutting the shrouds by radio control when it's over empty countryside and not too high. That means more weight, besides the parachute. By the time we are through, we don't get a net addition of a mile a second out of that stage. It's not enough."

Harriman stirred in his chair. "Looks like we made a mistake in trying to launch it from the States. Suppose we took off from someplace unpopulated, say the Brazil coast, and let the booster stages fall in the Atlantic; how much would that save you?"

Coster looked off in the distance, then took out a slide rule. "Might work."

"How much of a chore will it be to move the ship, at this stage?"

"Well . . . it would have to be disassembled completely; nothing less would do. I can't give you a cost estimate offhand, but it would be expensive."

"How long would it take?"

"Hmm . . . shucks, Mr. Harriman, I can't answer offhand. Two years—eighteen months, with luck. We'd have to prepare a site. We'd have to build shops."

Harriman thought about it, although he knew the answer in his heart. His shoestring, big as it was, was stretched to the danger point. He couldn't keep up the promotion, on talk alone, for another two years; he *had* to have a successful flight and soon —or the whole jerry-built financial structure would burst. "No good, Bob."

"I was afraid of that. Well, I tried to add still a sixth stage."
He held up another sketch. "You see that monstrosity? I reached
the point of diminishing returns. The final effective velocity is
actually less with this abortion than with the five-step job."

"Does that mean you are whipped, Bob? You can't build a
Moon ship?"

"No, I—"

LeCroix said suddenly, "Clear out Kansas."

"Eh?" asked Harriman.

"Clear everybody out of Kansas and Eastern Colorado. Let
the fifth and fourth sections fall anywhere in that area. The
third section falls in the Atlantic; the second section goes into a
permanent orbit—and the ship itself goes on to the Moon. You
could do it if you didn't have to waste weight on the para-
chuting of the fifth and fourth sections. Ask Bob."

"So? How about it, Bob?"

"That's what I said before. It was the parasitic penalties that
whipped us. The basic design is all right."

"Hmmm . . . somebody hand me an atlas." Harriman
looked up Kansas and Colorado, did some rough figuring. He
stared off into space, looking surprisingly, for the moment, as
Coster did when the engineer was thinking about his own work.
Finally he said, "It won't work."

"Why not?"

"Money. I told you not to worry about money—for the ship.
But it would cost upward of six or seven million dollars to evac-
uate that area even for a day. We'd have to settle nuisance suits
out of hand; we couldn't wait. And there would be a few die-
hards who just couldn't move anyhow."

LeCroix said savagely, "If the crazy fools won't move, let
them take their chances."

"I know how you feel, Les. But this project is too big to hide
and too big to move. Unless we protect the bystanders we'll be
shut down by court order and force. I can't buy all the judges
in two states. Some of them wouldn't be for sale."

"It was a nice try, Les," consoled Coster.

"I thought it might be an answer for all of us," the pilot answered.

Harriman said, "You were starting to mention another solution, Bob?"

Coster looked embarrassed. "You know the plans for the ship itself—a three-man job, space and supplies for three."

"Yes. What are you driving at?"

"It doesn't have to be three men. Split the first step into two parts, cut the ship down to the bare minimum for one man and jettison the remainder. That's the only way I see to make this basic design work." He got out another sketch. "See? One man and supplies for less than a week. No airlock—the pilot stays in his pressure suit. No galley. No bunks. The bare minimum to keep one man alive for a maximum of two hundred hours. It will work."

"It will work," repeated LeCroix, looking at Coster.

Harriman looked at the sketch with an odd, sick feeling at his stomach. Yes, no doubt it would work—and for the purposes of the promotion it did not matter whether one man or three went to the Moon and returned. Just to do it was enough; he was dead certain that one successful flight would cause money to roll in so that there would be capital to develop to the point of practical, passenger-carrying ships.

The Wright brothers had started with less.

"If that is what I have to put up with, I suppose I have to," he said slowly.

Coster looked relieved. "Fine! But there is one more hitch. You know the conditions under which I agreed to tackle this job—I was to go along. Now Les here waves a contract under my nose and says *he* has to be the pilot."

"It's not just that," LeCroix countered. "You're no pilot, Bob. You'll kill yourself and ruin the whole enterprise, just through bullheaded stubbornness."

"I'll learn to fly it. After all, I designed it. Look here, Mr.

Harriman, I hate to let you in for a suit—Les says he will sue—
but my contract antedates his. I intend to enforce it."

"Don't listen to him, Mr. Harriman. Let him do the suing.
I'll fly that ship and bring her back. He'll wreck it."

"Either I go or I don't build the ship," Coster said flatly.

Harriman motioned both of them to keep quiet. "Easy, easy,
both of you. You can both sue me if it gives you any pleasure.
Bob, don't talk nonsense; at this stage I can hire other engineers
to finish the job. You tell me it has to be just one man."

"That's right."

"You're looking at him."

They both stared.

"Shut your jaws," Harriman snapped. "What's funny about
that? You both knew I meant to go. You don't think I went to
all this trouble just to give you two a ride to the Moon, do you?
I intend to go. What's wrong with me as a pilot? I'm in good
health, my eyesight is all right, I'm still smart enough to learn
what I have to learn. If I have to drive my own buggy, I'll do it.
I won't step aside for anybody, not anybody, d'you hear me?"

Coster got his breath first. "Boss, you don't know what you
are saying."

Two hours later they were still wrangling. Most of the time
Harriman had stubbornly sat still, refusing to answer their arguments. At last he went out of the room for a few minutes, on
the usual pretext. When he came back in he said, "Bob, what
do you weigh?"

"Me? A little over two hundred."

"Close to two twenty, I'd judge. Les, what do you weigh?"

"One twenty-six."

"Bob, design the ship for a net load of one hundred and
twenty-six pounds."

"Huh? Now wait a minute, Mr. Harriman—"

"*Shut up!* If I can't learn to be a pilot in six weeks, neither
can you."

"But I've got the mathematics and the basic knowledge to—"

"Shut up I said! Les has spent as long learning his profession as you have learning yours. Can he become an engineer in six weeks? Then what gave you the conceit to think that you can learn his job in that time? I'm not going to have you wrecking my ship to satisfy your swollen ego. Anyhow, you gave out the real key to it when you were discussing the design. The real limiting factor is the actual weight of the passenger or passengers, isn't it? Everything—*everything* works in proportion to that one mass. Right?"

"Yes, but—"

"Right or wrong?"

"Well . . . yes, that's right. I just wanted—"

"The smaller man can live on less water, he breathes less air, he occupies less space. Les goes." Harriman walked over and put a hand on Coster's shoulder. "Don't take it hard, son. It can't be any worse on you than it is on me. This trip has got to succeed—and that means you and I have got to give up the honor of being the first man on the Moon. But I promise you this: we'll go on the second trip, we'll go with Les as our private chauffeur. It will be the first of a lot of passenger trips. Look, Bob—you can be a big man in this game, if you'll play along now. How would you like to be chief engineer of the first lunar colony?"

Coster managed to grin. "It might not be so bad."

"You'd like it. Living on the Moon will be an engineering problem; you and I have talked about it. How'd you like to put your theories to work? Build the first city? Build the big observatory we'll found there? Look around and know that you were the man who had done it?"

Coster was definitely adjusting himself to it. "You make it sound good. Say, what will *you* be doing."

"Me? Well, maybe I'll be the first mayor of Luna City." It was a new thought to him; he savored it. "The Honorable Delos

David Harriman, Mayor of Luna City. Say, I like that! You know, I've never held any sort of public office; I've just owned things." He looked around. "Everything settled?"

"I guess so," Coster said slowly. Suddenly he stuck his hand out at LeCroix. "You fly her, Les; I'll build her."

LeCroix grabbed his hand. "It's a deal. And you and the Boss get busy and start making plans for the next job—big enough for all of us."

"Right!"

Harriman put his hand on top of theirs. "That's the way I like to hear you talk. We'll stick together and we'll found Luna City together."

"I think we ought to call it 'Harriman,' " LeCroix said seriously.

"Nope, I've thought of it as Luna City ever since I was a kid; Luna City it's going to be. Maybe we'll put Harriman Square in the middle of it," he added.

"I'll mark it that way in the plans," agreed Coster.

Harriman left at once. Despite the solution he was terribly depressed and did not want his two colleagues to see it. It had been a Pyrrhic victory; he had saved the enterprise but he felt like an animal who has gnawed off his own leg to escape a trap.

8

Strong was alone in the offices of the partnership when he got a call from Dixon. "George, I was looking for D. D. Is he there?"

"No, he's back in Washington—something about clearances. I expect him back soon."

"Hmmm . . . . Entenza and I want to see him. We're coming over."

They arrived shortly. Entenza was quite evidently very much worked up over something; Dixon looked sleekly impassive as usual. After greetings Dixon waited a moment, then said, "Jack, you had some business to transact, didn't you?"

Entenza jumped, then snatched a draft from his pocket. "Oh, yes! George, I'm not going to have to prorate after all. Here's my payment to bring my share up to full payment to date."

Strong accepted it. "I know that Delos will be pleased." He tucked it in a drawer.

"Well," said Dixon sharply, "aren't you going to receipt for it?"

"If Jack wants a receipt. The canceled draft will serve." However, Strong wrote out a receipt without further comment; Entenza accepted it.

They waited a while. Presently Dixon said, "George, you're in this pretty deep, aren't you?"

"Possibly."

"Want to hedge your bets?"

"How?"

"Well, candidly, I want to protect myself. Want to sell me half of one percent of your share?"

Strong thought about it. In fact he was worried—worried sick. The presence of Dixon's auditor had forced them to keep on a cash basis—and only Strong knew how close to the line that had forced the partners.

"Why do you want it?"

"Oh, I wouldn't use it to interfere with Delos' operations. He's our man; we're backing him. But I would feel a lot safer if I had the right to call a halt if he tried to commit us to something we couldn't pay for. You know Delos; he's an incurable optimist. We ought to have some sort of a brake on him."

Strong thought about it. The thing that hurt him was that he agreed with everything Dixon said; he had stood by and watched while Delos dissipated two fortunes, painfully built up through the years. D. D. no longer seemed to care. Why, only this morning he had refused even to look at a report on the H&S automatic household switch—after dumping it on Strong.

Dixon leaned forward. "Name a price, George. I'll be generous."

Strong squared his stooped shoulders. "I'll sell—"

"Good!"

"—if Delos okays it. Not otherwise."

Dixon muttered something. Entenza snorted. The conversation might have gone acrimoniously further had not Harriman walked in.

No one said anything about the proposal to Strong. Strong inquired about the trip; Harriman pressed a thumb and finger together. "All in the groove! But it gets more expensive to do business in Washington every day." He turned to the others. "How's tricks? Any special meaning to the assemblage? Are we in executive session?"

Dixon turned to Entenza. "Tell him, Jack."

Entenza faced Harriman. "What do you mean by selling television rights?"

Harriman cocked a brow. "And why not?"

"Because you promised them to me, that's why. That's the original agreement; I've got it in writing."

"Better take another look at the agreement, Jack. And don't go off half-cocked. You have the exploitation rights for radio, television, and other amusement and special feature ventures in connection with the first trip to the Moon. You've still got 'em. Including broadcasts from the ship, provided we are able to make any." He decided that this was not a good time to mention that weight considerations had already made the latter impossible; the *Pioneer* would carry no electronic equipment of any sort not needed in astrogation. "What I sold was the franchise to erect a television station on the Moon, later. By the way, it wasn't even an exclusive franchise, although Clem Haggerty thinks it is. If you want to buy one yourself, we can accommodate you."

"*Buy* it! Why, you—"

"Wups! Or you can have it free, if you can get Dixon and

George to agree that you are entitled to it. I won't be a tight-wad. Anything else?"

Dixon cut in. "Just where do we stand now, Delos?"

"Gentlemen, you can take it for granted that the *Pioneer* will leave on schedule—next Wednesday. And now, if you will excuse me, I'm on my way to Peterson Field."

After he had left, his three associates sat in silence for some time, Entenza muttering to himself, Dixon apparently thinking, and Strong just waiting. Presently Dixon said, "How about that fractional share, George?"

"You didn't see fit to mention it to Delos."

"I see." Dixon carefully deposited an ash. "He's a strange man, isn't he?"

Strong shifted around. "Yes."

"How long have you known him?"

"Let me see—he came to work for me in—"

"*He* worked for *you?*"

"For several months. Then we set up our first company." Strong thought back about it. "I suppose he had a power complex, even then."

"No," Dixon said carefully. "No, I wouldn't call it a power complex. It's more of a Messiah complex."

Entenza looked up. "He's a crooked son of a bitch, that's what he is!"

Strong looked at him mildly. "I'd rather you wouldn't talk about him that way. I'd really rather you wouldn't."

"Stow it, Jack," ordered Dixon. "You might force George to take a poke at you. One of the odd things about him," went on Dixon, "is that he seems to be able to inspire an almost feudal loyalty. Take yourself. I know you are cleaned out, George— yet you won't let me rescue you. That goes beyond logic; it's personal."

Strong nodded. "He's an odd man. Sometimes I think he's the last of the Robber Barons."

Dixon shook his head. "Not the last. The last of them opened

up the American West. He's the first of the *new* Robber Barons
—and you and I won't see the end of it. Do you ever read
Carlyle?"

Strong nodded again. "I see what you mean, the 'Hero' theory, but I don't necessarily agree with it."

"There's something to it, though," Dixon answered. "Truth-
fully, I don't think Delos knows what he is doing. He's setting
up a new imperialism. There'll be hell to pay before it's
cleaned up." He stood up. "Maybe we should have waited.
Maybe we should have balked him—*if* we could have. Well,
it's done. We're on the merry-go-round and we can't get off. I
hope we enjoy the ride. Come on, Jack."

9

The Colorado Prairie was growing dusky. The Sun was behind the peak and the broad white face of Luna, full and round,
was rising in the east. In the middle of Peterson Field the *Pioneer* thrust toward the sky. A barbed-wire fence, a thousand
yards from its base in all directions, held back the crowds. Just
inside the barrier, guards patrolled restlessly. More guards cir-
culated through the crowd. Inside the fence, close to it, trucks
and trailers for camera, sound, and television equipment were
parked and, at the far ends of cables, remote-control pickups
were located both near and far from the ship on all sides. There
were other trucks near the ship and a stir of organized activity.

Harriman waited in Coster's office; Coster himself was out
on the field, and Dixon and Entenza had a room to themselves.
LeCroix, still in a drugged sleep, was in the bedroom of Coster's on-the-job living quarters.

There was a stir and a challenge outside the door. Harriman
opened it a crack. "If that's another reporter, tell him 'no.' Send
him to Mr. Montgomery across the way. Captain LeCroix will
grant no unauthorized interviews."

"Delos! Let me in."

"Oh—you, George. Come in. We've been hounded to death."

Strong came in and handed Harriman a large and heavy handbag. "Here it is."

"Here is what?"

"The canceled covers for the philatelic syndicate. You forgot them. That's half a million dollars, Delos," he complained. "If I hadn't noticed them in your coat locker we'd have been in the soup."

Harriman composed his features. "George, you're a brick, that's what you are."

"Shall I put them in the ship myself?" Strong said anxiously.

"Huh? No, no. Les will handle them." He glanced at his watch. "We're about to waken him. I'll take charge of the covers." He took the bag and added, "Don't come in now. You'll have a chance to say goodbye on the field."

Harriman went next door, shut the door behind him, waited for the nurse to give the sleeping pilot a counteracting stimulant by injection, then chased her out. When he turned around the pilot was sitting up, rubbing his eyes. "How do you feel, Les?"

"Fine. So this is it."

"Yup. And we're all rooting for you, boy. Look, you've got to go out and face them in a couple of minutes. Everything is ready—but I've got a couple of things I've got to say to you."

"Yes?"

"See this bag?" Harriman rapidly explained what it was and what it signified.

LeCroix looked dismayed. "But I *can't* take it, Delos. It's all figured to the last ounce."

"Who said you were going to take it? Of course you can't; it must weigh sixty, seventy pounds. I just plain forgot it. Now here's what we do: for the time being I'll just hide it in here—" Harriman stuffed the bag far back into a clothes closet. "When you land, I'll be right on your tail. Then we pull a sleight-of-hand trick and you fetch it out of the ship."

LeCroix shook his head ruefully. "Delos, you beat me. Well, I'm in no mood to argue."

"I'm glad you're not; otherwise I'd go to jail for a measly half million dollars. We've already spent that money. Anyhow, it doesn't matter," he went on. "Nobody but you and me will know it—and the stamp collectors will get their money's worth." He looked at the younger man as if anxious for his approval.

"Okay, okay," LeCroix answered. "Why should I care what happens to a stamp collector—tonight? Let's get going."

"One more thing," said Harriman and took out a small cloth bag. "This you take with you—and the weight *has* been figured in. I saw to it. Now here is what you do with it." He gave detailed and very earnest instructions.

LeCroix was puzzled. "Do I hear you straight? I let it be found—then I tell the exact truth about what happened?"

"That's right."

"Okay." LeCroix zipped the little bag into a pocket of his coveralls. "Let's get out to the field. H-hour minus twenty-one minutes already."

Strong joined Harriman in the control blockhouse after LeCroix had gone up inside the ship. "Did they get aboard?" he demanded anxiously. "LeCroix wasn't carrying anything."

"Oh, sure," said Harriman. "I sent them ahead. Better take your place. The ready flare has already gone up."

Dixon, Entenza, the Governor of Colorado, the Vice-President of the United States, and a round dozen of VIP's were already seated at periscopes, mounted in slits, on a balcony above the control level. Strong and Harriman climbed a ladder and took the two remaining chairs.

Harriman began to sweat and realized he was trembling. Through his periscope out in front he could see the ship; from below he could hear Coster's voice, nervously checking departure station reports. Muted through a speaker by him was a running commentary of one of the newscasters reporting the show. Harriman himself was the—well, the admiral, he decided—of the operation, but there was nothing more he could do but wait, watch, and try to pray.

A second flare arched up in the sky, burst into red and green. Five minutes.

The seconds oozed away. At minus two minutes Harriman realized that he could not stand to watch through a tiny slit; he had to be outside, take part in it himself—he had to. He climbed down, hurried to the exit of the blockhouse. Coster glanced around, looked startled, but did not try to stop him; Coster could not leave his post no matter what happened. Harriman elbowed the guard aside and went outdoors.

To the east the ship towered skyward, her slender pyramid sharp black against the full Moon. He waited.

And waited.

What had gone wrong? There had remained less than two minutes when he had come out; he was sure of that—yet there she stood, silent, dark, unmoving. There was not a sound, save the distant ululation of sirens warning the spectators behind the distant fence. Harriman felt his own heart stop, his breath dry up in his throat. Something had failed. Failure.

A single flare rocket burst from the top of the blockhouse; a flame licked at the base of the ship.

It spread, there was a pad of white fire around the base. Slowly, almost lumberingly, the *Pioneer* lifted, seemed to hover for a moment, balanced on a pillar of fire—then reached for the sky with acceleration so great that she was above him almost at once, overhead at the zenith, a dazzling circle of flame. So quickly was she above, rather than out in front, that it seemed as if she were arching back over him and must surely fall on him. Instinctively and futilely he threw a hand in front of his face.

The sound reached him.

Not as sound—it was a white noise, a roar in all frequencies, sonic, subsonic, supersonic, so incredibly loaded with energy that it struck him in the chest. He heard it with his teeth and with his bones as well as with his ears. He crouched his knees, bracing against it.

Following the sound at the snail's pace of a hurricane came the backwash of the splash. It ripped at his clothing, tore his breath from his lips. He stumbled blindly back, trying to reach the lee of the concrete building, was knocked down.

He picked himself up coughing and strangling and remembered to look at the sky. Straight overhead was a dwindling star. Then it was gone.

He went into the blockhouse.

The room was a babble of high-tension, purposeful confusion. Harriman's ears, still ringing, heard a speaker blare, "Spot One! Spot One to Blockhouse! Step five loose on schedule—ship and step five showing separate blips—" and Coster's voice, high and angry, cutting in with, "Get Track One! Have they picked up step five yet? Are they tracking it?"

In the background the news commentator was still blowing his top. "A great day, folks, a great day! The mighty *Pioneer,* climbing like an angel of the Lord, flaming sword at hand, is even now on her glorious way to our sister planet. Most of you have seen her departure on your screens; I wish you could have seen it as I did, arching up into the evening sky, bearing her precious load of—"

"Shut that damn thing off!" ordered Coster, then to the visitors on the observation platform, "And pipe down up there! Quiet!"

The Vice-President of the United States jerked his head around, closed his mouth. He remembered to smile. The other VIP's shut up, then resumed again in muted whispers. A girl's voice cut through the silence, "Track One to Blockhouse—step five tracking high, plus two." There was a stir in the corner. There a large canvas hood shielded a heavy sheet of Plexiglas from direct light. The sheet was mounted vertically and was edge-lighted; it displayed a coordinate map of Colorado and Kansas in fine white lines; the cities and towns glowed red. Unevacuated farms were tiny warning dots of red light.

A man behind the transparent map touched it with a grease pencil; the reported location of step five shone out. In front of the map screen a youngish man sat quietly in a chair, a pear-shaped switch in his hand, his thumb lightly resting on the button. He was a bombardier, borrowed from the Air Forces; when he pressed the switch, a radio-controlled circuit in step five should cause the shrouds of step five's landing chute to be cut and let it plummet to Earth. He was working from radar reports alone with no fancy computing bombsight to think for him. He was working almost by instinct—or, rather, by the accumulated subconscious knowledge of his trade, integrating in his brain the meager data spread before him, deciding where the tons of step five would land if he were to press his switch at any particular instant. He seemed unworried.

"Spot One to Blockhouse!" came a man's voice again. "Step four free on schedule," and almost immediately following, a deeper voice echoed, "Track Two, tracking step four, instantaneous altitude nine-five-one miles, predicted vector."

No one paid any attention to Harriman.

Under the hood the observed trajectory of step five grew in shining dots of grease, near to, but not on, the dotted line of its predicted path. Reaching out from each location dot was drawn a line at right angles, the reported altitude for that location.

The quiet man watching the display suddenly pressed down hard on his switch. He then stood up, stretched, and said, "Anybody got a cigarette?" "Track Two!" he was answered. "Step four—first impact prediction—forty miles west of Charleston, South Carolina."

"Repeat!" yelled Coster.

The speaker blared out again without pause, "Correction, correction—forty miles east, repeat *east*."

Coster sighed. The sigh was cut short by a report: "Spot One to Blockhouse—step three free, minus five seconds," and a talker at Coster's control desk called out, "Mr. Coster, *Mister Coster*—Palomar Observatory wants to talk to you."

"Tell 'em to go—no, tell 'em to wait." Immediately another voice cut in with, "Track One, auxiliary range Fox—Step One about to strike near Dodge City, Kansas."

"How near!"

There was no answer. Presently the voice of Track One proper said, "Impact reported approximately fifteen miles southwest of Dodge City."

"Casualties?"

Spot One broke in before Track One could answer, "Step two free, step two free—the ship is now on its own."

"Mr. Coster—*please, Mr. Coster—*"

And a totally new voice: "Spot Two to Blockhouse—we are now tracking the ship. Stand by for reported distances and bearings. Stand by—"

"Track Two to Blockhouse—step four will definitely land in Atlantic, estimated point of impact oh-five-seven miles east of Charleston bearing oh-nine-three. I will repeat—"

Coster looked around irritably. "Isn't there any drinking water anywhere in this dump?"

"Mr. Coster, please—Palomar says they've just *got* to talk to you."

Harriman eased over to the door and stepped out. He suddenly felt very much let down, utterly weary, and depressed.

The field looked strange without the ship. He had watched it grow; now suddenly it was gone. The Moon, still rising, seemed oblivious—and space travel was as remote a dream as it had been in his boyhood.

There were several tiny figures prowling around the flash apron where the ship had stood—souvenir hunters, he thought contemptuously. Someone came up to him in the gloom. "Mr. Harriman?"

"Eh?"

"Hopkins—with the A.P. How about a statement?"

"Uh? No, no comment. I'm bushed."

"Oh, now, just a word. How does it feel to have backed the first successful Moon flight—if it is successful."

"It will be successful." He thought a moment, then squared his tired shoulders and said, "Tell them that this is the beginning of the human race's greatest era. Tell them that every one of them will have a chance to follow in Captain LeCroix's footsteps, seek out new planets, wrest a home for themselves in new lands. Tell them that this means new frontiers, a shot in the arm for prosperity. It means—" He ran down. "That's all tonight. I'm whipped, son. Leave me alone, will you?"

Presently Coster came out, followed by the VIP's. Harriman went up to Coster. "Everything all right?"

"Sure. Why shouldn't it be? Track Three followed him out to the limit of range—all in the groove." Coster added, "Step five killed a cow when it grounded."

"Forget it—we'll have steak for breakfast." Harriman then had to make conversation with the Governor and the Vice-President, had to escort them out to their ship. Dixon and Entenza left together, less formally; at last Coster and Harriman were alone save for subordinates too junior to constitute a strain and for guards to protect them from the crowds. "Where you headed, Bob?"

"Up to the Broadmoor and about a week's sleep. How about you?"

"If you don't mind, I'll doss down in your apartment."

"Help yourself. Sleepy pills in the bathroom."

"I won't need them." They had a drink together in Coster's quarters, talked aimlessly, then Coster ordered a copter cab and went to the hotel. Harriman went to bed, got up, read a day-old copy of the Denver *Post* filled with pictures of the *Pioneer,* finally gave up and took two of Coster's sleeping capsules.

10

Someone was shaking him. "Mr. Harriman! Wake up—Mr. Coster is on the screen."

"Huh? Wazza? Oh, all right." He got up and padded to the phone. Coster was looking tousleheaded and excited. "Hey, Boss—*he made it!*"

"Huh? What do you mean?"

"Palomar just called me. They saw his mark and now they've spotted the ship itself. He—"

"Wait a minute, Bob. Slow up. He *can't* be there yet. He just left last night."

Coster looked disconcerted. "What's the matter, Mr. Harriman? Don't you feel well? He left Wednesday."

Vaguely, Harriman began to be oriented. No, the takeoff had not been the night before—fuzzily he recalled a drive up into the mountains, a day spent dozing in the sun, some sort of a party at which he had drunk too much. What day was today? He didn't know. If LeCroix had landed on the Moon, then— never mind. "It's all right, Bob—I was half asleep. I guess I dreamed the takeoff all over again. Now tell me the news, slowly."

Coster started over. "LeCroix has landed, just west of Archimedes crater. They can see his ship, from Palomar. Say that was a great stunt you thought up, marking the spot with carbon black. Les must have covered two acres with it. They say it shines out like a billboard, through the Big Eye."

"Maybe we ought to run down and have a look. No—later," he amended. "We'll be busy."

"I don't see what more we can do, Mr. Harriman. We've got twelve of our best ballistic computers calculating possible routes for you now."

Harriman started to tell the man to put on another twelve, switched off the screen instead. He was still at Peterson Field, with one of Skyways' best stratoships waiting for him outside, waiting to take him to whatever point on the globe LeCroix might ground. LeCroix was in the upper stratosphere, had been there for more than twenty-four hours. The pilot was slowly, cautiously wearing out his terminal velocity, dissipating the incredible kinetic energy as shock wave and radiant heat.

They had tracked him by radar around the globe and around again—and again . . . yet there was no way of knowing just where and what sort of landing the pilot would choose to risk. Harriman listened to the running radar reports and cursed the fact that they had elected to save the weight of radio equipment.

The radar figures started coming closer together. The voice broke off and started again: "He's in his landing glide!"

"Tell the field to get ready!" shouted Harriman. He held his breath and waited. After endless seconds another voice cut in with, "The Moon ship is now landing. It will ground somewhere west of Chihuahua in Old Mexico."

Harriman started for the door at a run.

Coached by radio en route, Harriman's pilot spotted the *Pioneer* incredibly small against the desert sand. He put his own ship quite close to it, in a beautiful landing. Harriman was fumbling at the cabin door before the ship was fairly stopped.

LeCroix was sitting on the ground, resting his back against a skid of his ship and enjoying the shade of its stubby triangular wings. A paisano sheepherder stood facing him, openmouthed. As Harriman trotted out and lumbered toward him LeCroix stood up, flipped a cigarette butt away and said, "Hi, Boss!"

"Les!" The older man threw his arms around the younger. "It's good to see you, boy."

"It's good to see *you*. Pedro here doesn't speak my language." LeCroix glanced around; there was no one else nearby but the pilot of Harriman's ship. "Where's the gang? Where's Bob?"

"I didn't wait. They'll surely be along in a few minutes—hey, there they come now!" It was another stratoship, plunging in to a landing. Harriman turned to his pilot. "Bill—go over and meet them."

"Huh? They'll come, never fear."

"Do as I say."

"You're the doctor." The pilot trudged through the sand, his back expressing disapproval. LeCroix looked puzzled. "Quick, Les—help me with this."

"This" was the five thousand canceled envelopes which were supposed to have been to the Moon. They got them out of Harriman's stratoship and into the Moon ship, there to be stowed in an empty food locker, while their actions were still shielded from the later arrivals by the bulk of the stratoship.

"Whew!" said Harriman. "That was close. Half a million dollars. We need it, Les."

"Sure, but look, Mr. Harriman, the di—"

"Sssh! The others are coming. How about the other business? Ready with your act?"

"Yes. But I was trying to tell you—"

"Quiet!"

It was not their colleagues; it was a shipload of reporters, cameramen, mike men, commentators, technicians. They swarmed over them.

Harriman waved to them jauntily. "Help yourselves, boys. Get a lot of pictures. Climb through the ship. Make yourselves at home. Look at anything you want to. But go easy on Captain LeCroix—he's tired."

Another ship had landed, this time with Coster, Dixon and Strong. Entenza showed up in his own chartered ship and began bossing the TV, pix, and radiomen, in the course of which he almost had a fight with an unauthorized camera crew. A large copter transport grounded and spilled out nearly a platoon of khaki-clad Mexican troops. From somewhere—out of the sand apparently—several dozen native peasants showed up. Harriman broke away from reporters, held a quick and expensive discussion with the captain of the local troops and a degree of order was restored in time to save the *Pioneer* from being picked to pieces.

"Just let that be!" It was LeCroix's voice, from inside the *Pioneer*. Harriman waited and listened. "None of your business!" the pilot's voice went on, rising higher, "and put them back!"

Harriman pushed his way to the door of the ship. "What's the trouble, Les?"

Inside the cramped cabin, hardly large enough for a TV booth, three men stood—LeCroix and two reporters. All three men looked angry. "What's the trouble, Les?" Harriman repeated.

LeCroix was holding a small cloth bag which appeared to be empty. Scattered on the pilot's acceleration rest between him and the reporters were several small, dully brilliant stones. A reporter held one such stone up to the light.

"These guys were poking their noses into things that didn't concern them," LeCroix said angrily.

The reporter looked at the stone and said, "You told us to look at what we liked, didn't you, Mr. Harriman?"

"Yes."

"Your pilot here—" he jerked a thumb at LeCroix "—apparently didn't expect us to find these. He had them hidden in the pads of his chair."

"What of it?"

"They're diamonds."

"What makes you think so?"

"They're diamonds all right."

Harriman stopped and unwrapped a cigar. Presently he said, "Those diamonds were where you found them because I put them there."

A flashlight went off behind Harriman; a voice said, "Hold the rock up higher, Jeff."

The reporter called Jeff obliged, then said, "That seems an odd thing to do, Mr. Harriman."

"I was interested in the effect of outer space radiations on raw diamonds. On my orders Captain LeCroix placed that sack of diamonds in the ship."

Jeff whistled thoughtfully. "You know, Mr. Harriman, if you did not have that explanation, I'd think LeCroix had found the rocks on the Moon and was trying to hold out on you."

"Print that and you will be sued for libel. I have every confidence in Captain LeCroix. Now give me the diamonds."

Jeff's eyebrows went up. "But not confidence enough in him to let him keep them, maybe?"

"Give me the stones. Then get out."

Harriman got LeCroix away from the reporters as quickly as possible and into Harriman's own ship. "That's all for now," he told the news and pictures people. "See us at Peterson Field."

Once the ship raised ground he turned to LeCroix. "You did a beautiful job, Les."

"That reporter named Jeff must be sort of confused."

"Eh? Oh, *that*. No, I mean the flight. You did it. You're head man on this planet."

LeCroix shrugged it off. "Bob built a good ship. It was a cinch. Now about those diamonds—"

"Forget the diamonds. You've done your part. We placed those rocks in the ship; now we tell everybody we did—truthful as can be. It's not our fault if they don't believe us."

"But Mr. Harriman—"

"What?"

LeCroix unzipped a pocket in his coveralls, hauled out a soiled handkerchief, knotted into a bag. He untied it—and spilled into Harriman's hands many more diamonds than had been displayed in the ship—larger, finer diamonds.

Harriman stared at them. He began to chuckle.

Presently he shoved them back at LeCroix. "Keep them."

"I figure they belong to all of us."

"Well, keep them for us, then. And keep your mouth shut about them. No, wait." He picked out two large stones. "I'll have rings made from these two, one for you, one for me. But keep your mouth shut, or they won't be worth anything, except as curiosities."

It was quite true, he thought. Long ago the diamond syndicate had realized that diamonds in plentiful supply were worth little more than glass, except for industrial uses. Earth had more than enough for that, more than enough for jewels. If Moon diamonds were literally "common as pebbles" then they were just that—pebbles.

Not worth the expense of bringing them to earth.

But now take uranium. If that were plentiful—

Harriman sat back and indulged in daydreaming.

Presently LeCroix said softly, "You know, Boss, it's wonderful there."

"Eh? Where?"

"Why, on the Moon of course. I'm going back. I'm going back just as soon as I can. We've got to get busy on the new ship."

"Sure, sure! And this time we'll build one big enough for all of us. This time I go, too!"

"You bet."

"Les—" The older man spoke almost diffidently. "What does it look like when you look back and see the Earth?"

"Huh? It looks like—It looks—" LeCroix stopped. "Hell's bells, Boss, there isn't any way to tell you. It's wonderful, that's all. The sky is black and—well, wait until you see the pictures I took. Better yet, wait and see it yourself."

Harriman nodded. "But it's hard to wait."

11

FIELDS OF DIAMONDS ON THE MOON!!!
BILLIONAIRE BACKER DENIES DIAMOND STORY

Says Jewels Taken into Space for Science Reasons
MOON DIAMONDS: HOAX OR FACT?

—but consider this, friends of the invisible audience: why would anyone take diamonds *to* the moon? Every ounce of that ship and its cargo was calculated; diamonds would not be taken along without reason. Many scientific authorities have pronounced Mr. Harriman's professed reason an absurdity. It is easy to guess that diamonds might be taken along for the purpose of "salting" the Moon, so to speak, with earthly jewels, with the intention of convincing us that diamonds exist on the Moon—but Mr. Harriman, his pilot Captain LeCroix, and everyone connected with the enterprise have sworn from the beginning that the diamonds *did not* come from the Moon. But it is an absolute certainty that the diamonds were in the space ship when it landed. Cut it how you will; this reporter is going to try to buy some lunar diamond mining stock—

Strong was, as usual, already in the office when Harriman came in. Before the partners could speak, the screen called out, "Mr. Harriman, Rotterdam calling."

"Tell them to go plant a tulip."

"Mr. van der Velde is waiting, Mr. Harriman."

"Okay."

Harriman let the Hollander talk, then said, "Mr. van der Velde, the statements attributed to me are absolutely correct. I put those diamonds the reporters saw into the ship before it took off. They were mined right here on Earth. In fact I bought them when I came over to see you; I can prove it."

"But Mr. Harriman—"

"Suit yourself. There may be more diamonds on the Moon than you can run and jump over. I don't guarantee it. But I do guarantee that those diamonds the newspapers are talking about came from Earth."

"Mr. Harriman, why would you send diamonds to the Moon? Perhaps you intended to fool us, no?"

"Have it your own way. But I've said all along that those diamonds came from Earth. Now see here: you took an option— an option on an option, so to speak. If you want to make the second payment on that option and keep it in force, the deadline is nine o'clock Thursday, New York time, as specified in the contract. Make up your mind."

He switched off and found his partner looking at him sourly. "What's eating you?"

"I wondered about those diamonds, too, Delos. So I've been looking through the weight schedule of the *Pioneer*."

"Didn't know you were interested in engineering."

"I can read figures."

"Well, you found it, didn't you? Schedule F-17-c, two ounces, allocated to me personally."

"I found it. It sticks out like a sore thumb. But I didn't find something else."

Harriman felt a cold chill in his stomach. "What?"

"I didn't find a schedule for the canceled covers." Strong stared at him.

"It must be there. Let me see that weight schedule."

"It's not there, Delos. You know, I thought it was funny when you insisted on going to meet Captain LeCroix by yourself. What happened, Delos? Did you sneak them aboard?" He continued to stare while Harriman fidgeted. "We've put over some sharp business deals—but this will be the first time that anyone can say that the firm of Harriman and Strong has cheated."

"Damn it, George—I would cheat, lie, steal, beg, bribe—do *anything* to accomplish what we have accomplished."

Harriman got up and paced the room. "We *had* to have that money, or the ship would never have taken off. We're cleaned out. You know that, don't you?"

Strong nodded. "But those covers should have gone to the Moon. That's what we contracted to do."

"Damn it, I just forgot it. Then it was too late to figure the weight in. But it doesn't matter. I figured that if the trip was a failure, if LeCroix cracked up, nobody would know or care that the covers hadn't gone. And I knew if he made it, it wouldn't matter; we'd have plenty of money. And we will, George, we will!"

"We've got to pay the money back."

"Now? Give me time, George. Everybody concerned is happy the way it is. Wait until we recover our stake; then I'll buy every one of those covers back—out of my own pocket. That's a promise."

Strong continued to sit. Harriman stopped in front of him. "I ask you, George, is it worthwhile to wreck an enterprise of this size for a purely theoretical point?"

Strong sighed and said, "When the time comes, use the firm's money."

"That's the spirit! But I'll use my own, I promise you."

"No, the firm's money. If we're in it together, we're in it together."

"Okay, if that's the way you want it."

Harriman turned back to his desk. Neither of the two partners had anything to say for a long while. Presently Dixon and Entenza were announced.

"Well, Jack," said Harriman. "Feel better now?"

"No thanks to you. I had to fight for what I did put on the air—and some of it was pirated as it was. Delos, there should have been a television pickup in the ship."

"Don't fret about it. As I told you, we couldn't spare the weight this time. But there will be the next trip, and the next. Your concession is going to be worth a pile of money."

Dixon cleared his throat. "That's what we came to see you about, Delos. What are your plans?"

"Plans? We go right ahead. Les and Coster and I make the next trip. We set up a permanent base. Maybe Coster stays behind. The third trip we send a real colony—nuclear engineers, miners, hydroponics experts, communications engineers. We'll found Luna City, first city on another planet."

Dixon looked thoughtful. "And when does this begin to pay off?"

"What do you mean by 'pay off'? Do you want your capital back, or do you want to begin to see some return on your investment? I can cut it either way."

Entenza was about to say that he wanted his investment back; Dixon cut in first. "Profits, naturally. The investment is already made."

"Fine!"

"But I don't see how you expect profits. Certainly, LeCroix made the trip and got back safely. There is honor for all of us. But where are the royalties?"

"Give the crop time to ripen, Dan. Do I look worried? What are our assets?" Harriman ticked them off on his fingers. "Royalties on pictures, television, radio—"

"Those things go to Jack."

"Take a look at the agreement. He has the concession, but he pays the firm—that's all of us—for them."

Dixon said, "Shut up, Jack!" before Entenza could speak, then added, "What else? That won't pull us out of the red."

"Endorsements galore. Monty's boys are working on that. Royalties from the greatest best seller yet—I've got a ghostwriter and a stenographer following LeCroix around this very minute. A franchise for the first and only space line—"

"From whom?"

"We'll get it. Kamens and Montgomery are in Paris now, working on it. I'm joining them this afternoon. And we'll tie down that franchise with a franchise from *the other end,* just as soon as we can get a permanent colony there, no matter how small. It will be the autonomous state of Luna, under the protection of the United Nations—and no ship will land or take off in its territory without its permission. Besides that we'll have the right to franchise a dozen other companies for various purposes—and tax them, too—just as soon as we set up the Municipal Corporation of the City of Luna under the laws of the

State of Luna. We'll sell everything but vacuum—we'll even sell vacuum, for experimental purposes. And don't forget—we'll still have a big chunk of real estate, sovereign title in us—as a state—and not yet sold. The Moon is *big.*"

"Your ideas are rather big, too, Delos," Dixon said dryly. "But what actually happens next?"

"First we get title confirmed by the UN. The Security Council is now in secret session; the Assembly meets tonight. Things will be popping; that's why I've got to be there. When the United Nations decides—as it will—that its own nonprofit corporation has the only real claim to the Moon, then I get busy. The poor little weak nonprofit corporation is going to grant a number of things to some real honest-to-God corporations with hair on their chests—in return for help in setting up a physics research lab, an astronomical observatory, a lunography institute and some other perfectly proper nonprofit enterprises. That's our interim pitch until we get a permanent colony with its own laws. Then we—"

Dixon gestured impatiently. "Never mind the legal shenanigans, Delos. I've known you long enough to know that you can figure out such angles. What do we actually have to *do* next?"

"Huh? We've got to build another ship, a bigger one. Not actually bigger, but effectively bigger. Coster has started the design of a surface catapult—it will reach from Manitou Springs to the top of Pikes Peak. With it we can put a ship in free orbit around the Earth. Then we'll use such a ship to fuel more ships —it amounts to a space station, like the power station. It adds up to a way to get there on chemical power without having to throw away nine-tenths of your ship to do it."

"Sounds expensive."

"It will be. But don't worry; we've got a couple of dozen piddling little things to keep the money coming in while we get set up on a commercial basis, then we sell stock. We sold stock before; now we'll sell a thousand dollars' worth where we sold ten before."

"And you think that will carry you through until the enterprise as a whole is on a paying basis? Face it, Delos, the thing as a whole doesn't pay off until you have ships plying between here and the Moon on a paying basis, figured in freight and passenger charges. That means customers, with cash. What is there on the Moon to ship—and who pays for it?"

"Dan, don't you believe there will be? If not, why are you here?"

"I believe in it, Delos—or I believe in you. But what's your time schedule? What's your budget? What's your prospective commodity? And please don't mention diamonds; I think I understand that caper."

Harriman chewed his cigar for a few moments. "There's one valuable commodity we'll start shipping at once."

"What?"

"Knowledge."

Entenza snorted. Strong looked puzzled. Dixon nodded. "I'll buy that. Knowledge is always worth something—to the man who knows how to exploit it. And I'll agree that the Moon is a place to find new knowledge. I'll assume that you can make the next trip pay off. What's your budget and your timetable for that?"

Harriman did not answer. Strong searched his face closely. To him Harriman's poker face was as revealing as large print— he decided that his partner had been crowded into a corner. He waited, nervous but ready to back Harriman's play.

Dixon went on. "From the way you describe it, Delos, I judge that you don't have money enough for your next step— and you don't know where you will get it. I believe in you, Delos—and I told you at the start that I did not believe in letting a new business die of anemia. I'm ready to buy in with a fifth share."

Harriman stared. "Look," he said bluntly, "you own Jack's share now, don't you?"

"I wouldn't say that."

"You vote it. It sticks out all over."

Entenza said, "That's not true. I'm independent. I—"

"Jack, you're a damn liar," Harriman said dispassionately. "Dan, you've got fifty percent now. Under the present rules I decide deadlocks, which gives me control as long as George sticks by me. If we sell you another share, you vote three-fifths —and are boss. Is that the deal you are looking for?"

"Delos, as I told you, I have confidence in you."

"But you'd feel happier with the whip hand. Well, I won't do it. I'll let space travel—*real* space travel, with established runs —wait another twenty years before I'll turn loose. I'll let us all go broke and let us live on glory before I'll turn loose. You'll have to think up another scheme."

Dixon said nothing. Harriman got up and began to pace. He stopped in front of Dixon. "Dan, if you really understood what this is all about, I'd let you have control. But you don't. You see this as just another way to money and to power. I'm perfectly willing to let you vultures get rich—but I keep control. I'm going to see this thing developed, not milked. The human race is heading out to the stars—and this adventure is going to present new problems compared with which atomic power was a kid's toy. The race is about as prepared for it as an innocent virgin is prepared for sex. Unless the whole matter is handled carefully, it will be bitched up. *You'll* bitch it up, Dan, if I let you have the deciding vote in it—because you don't understand it."

He caught his breath and went on, "Take safety for instance. Do you know *why* I let LeCroix take that ship out instead of taking it myself? Do you think I was afraid? No! I wanted it to come back—*safely*. I didn't want space travel getting another setback. Do you know why we have to have a monopoly, for a few years at least? Because every so-and-so and his brother is going to want to build a Moon ship, now that they know it can be done. Remember the first days of ocean flying? After Lindbergh did it, every so-called pilot who could lay hands on a crate took off for some over-water point. Some of them even took their kids along. And most of them landed in the drink. Airplanes got a reputation for being dangerous. A few years after that the airlines got so hungry for quick money in a highly competitive field that you couldn't pick up a paper without seeing headlines about another airliner crash.

"That's not going to happen to space travel! I'm not going to let it happen. Space ships are too big and too expensive; if they get a reputation for being unsafe as well, we might as well have stayed in bed. I run things."

He stopped. Dixon waited and then said, "I said I believed in you, Delos. How much money do you need?"

"Eh? On what terms?"

"Your note."

"My note? Did you say *my note?*"

"I'd want security, of course."

Harriman swore. "I knew there was a hitch in it. Dan, you know damn well everything I've got is tied up in this venture."

"You have insurance. You have quite a lot of insurance, I know."

"Yes, but that's all made out to my wife."

"I seem to have heard you say something about that sort of thing to Jack Entenza," Dixon said. "Come, now—if I know your tax-happy sort, you have at least one irrevocable trust, or paid-up annuities, or something, to keep Mrs. Harriman out of the poorhouse."

Harriman thought fiercely about it. "When's the call date on this note?"

"In the sweet bye and bye. I want a no-bankruptcy clause, of course."

"Why? Such a clause has no legal validity."

"It would be valid with *you,* wouldn't it?"

"Mmm . . . yes. Yes, it would."

"Then get out your policies and see how big a note you can write."

Harriman looked at him, turned abruptly and went to his safe. He came back with quite a stack of long, stiff folders. They added them up together; it was an amazingly large sum—for those days. Dixon then consulted a memorandum taken from his pocket and said, "One seems to be missing—a rather large one. A North Atlantic Mutual policy, I think."

Harriman glared at him. "Damn you, am I going to have to fire every confidential clerk in my force?"

"No," Dixon said mildly, "I don't get my information from your staff."

Harriman went back to the safe, got the policy and added it to the pile. Strong spoke up. "Do you want mine, Mr. Dixon?"

"No," answered Dixon, "that won't be necessary." He started stuffing the policies in his pocket. "I'll keep these, Delos, and attend to keeping up the premiums. I'll bill you of course. You can send the note and the change-of-beneficiary forms to my office. Here's your draft." He took out another slip of paper; it was the draft—already made out in the amount of the policies.

Harriman looked at it. "Sometimes," he said slowly, "I wonder who's kidding who?" He tossed the draft over to Strong. "Okay, George, take care of it. I'm off to Paris, boys. Wish me luck." He strode out as jauntily as a fox terrier.

Strong looked from the closed door to Dixon, then at the note. "I ought to tear this thing up!"

"Don't do it," advised Dixon. "You see, I really do believe in him." He added, "Ever read Carl Sandburg, George?"

"I'm not much of a reader."

"Try him sometime. He tells a story about a man who started a rumor that they had struck oil in Hell. Pretty soon everybody has left for Hell, to get in on the boom. The man who started the rumor watches them all go, then scratches his head and says to himself that there just *might* be something in it, after all. So he left for Hell, too."

Strong waited, finally said, "I don't get the point."

"The point is that I just want to be ready to protect myself if necessary, George—and so should you. Delos might begin believing his own rumors. Diamonds! Come, Jack."

12

The ensuing months were as busy as the period before the flight of the *Pioneer* (now honorably retired to the Smithsonian Institution). One engineering staff and great gangs of men were working on the catapult; two more staffs were busy with two new ships; the *Mayflower,* and the *Colonial;* a third ship was on the drafting tables. Ferguson was chief engineer for all of this; Coster, still buffered by Jock Berkeley, was engineering consultant, working where and as he chose. Colorado Springs was a boom town; the Denver-Trinidad roadcity settlements spread out at the Springs until they surrounded Peterson Field.

Harriman was as busy as a cat with two tails. The constantly expanding exploitation and promotion took eight full days a week of his time, but, by working Kamens and Montgomery almost to ulcers and by doing without sleep himself, he created frequent opportunities to run out to Colorado and talk things over with Coster.

Luna City, it was decided, would be founded on the very next trip. The *Mayflower* was planned for a payload not only of seven passengers, but with air, water and food to carry four of them over to the next trip; they would live in an aluminum Quonset-type hut, sealed, pressurized, and buried under the loose soil of Luna until—and assuming—they were succored.

The choice of the four extra passengers gave rise to another contest, another publicity exploitation—and more sale of stock. Harriman insisted that they be two married couples, over the united objections of scientific organizations everywhere. He gave in only to the extent of agreeing that there was no objection to all four being scientists, providing they constituted two married couples. This gave rise to several hasty marriages—and some divorces, after the choices were announced.

The *Mayflower* was the maximum size that calculations showed would be capable of getting into a free orbit around the Earth from the boost of the catapult, plus the blast of her own engines. Before she took off, four other ships, quite as large, would precede her. But they were not space ships; they were mere tankers—nameless. The most finicky of ballistic calculations, the most precise of launchings, would place them in the same orbit at the same spot. There the *Mayflower* would rendezvous and accept their remaining fuel.

This was the trickiest part of the entire project. If the four tankers could be placed close enough together, LeCroix, using a tiny maneuvering reserve, could bring his new ship to them. If not—well, it gets very lonely out in space.

Serious thought was given to placing pilots in the tankers and accepting as a penalty the use of enough fuel from one tanker to permit a getaway boat, a lifeboat with wings, to decelerate, reach the atmosphere and brake to a landing. Coster found a cheaper way.

A radar pilot, whose ancestor was the proximity fuse and whose immediate parents could be found in the homing devices of guided missiles, was given the task of bringing the tankers together. The first tanker would not be so equipped, but the second tanker through its robot would smell out the first and home on it with a pint-sized rocket engine, using the smallest of vectors to bring them together. The third would home on the first two and the fourth on the group.

LeCroix should have no trouble—if the scheme worked.

13

Strong wanted to show Harriman the sales reports on the H&S automatic household switch; Harriman brushed them aside.

Strong shoved them back under his nose. "You'd better start taking an interest in such things, Delos. *Somebody* around this office had better start seeing to it that some money comes in—some money that belongs to us, personally—or you'll be selling apples on a street corner."

Harriman leaned back and clasped his hands back of his head. "George, how can you talk that way on a day like this? Is there no poetry in your soul? Didn't you hear what I said when I came in? *The rendezvous worked.* Tankers one and two are as close together as Siamese twins. We'll be leaving within the week."

"That's as may be. Business has to go on."

"You keep it going; I've got a date. When did Dixon say he would be over?"

"He's due now."

"Good!" Harriman bit the end off a cigar and went on, "You know, George, I'm not sorry I didn't get to make the first trip. Now I've still got it to do. I'm as expectant as a bridegroom—and as happy." He started to hum.

Dixon came in without Entenza, a situation that had obtained since the day Dixon had dropped the pretense that he controlled only one share. He shook hands. "You heard the news, Dan?"

"George told me."

"This is it—or almost. A week from now, more or less, I'll be on the Moon. I can hardly believe it."

Dixon sat down silently. Harriman went on. "Aren't you even going to congratulate me? Man, this is a great day!"

Dixon said, "D. D., why are you going?"

"Huh? Don't ask foolish questions. This is what I have been working toward."

"It's not a foolish question. I asked why *you* were going. The four colonists have an obvious reason, and each is a selected specialist observer as well. LeCroix is the pilot. Coster is the man who is designing the permanent colony. But why are *you* going? What's your function?"

"My function? Why, I'm the guy who runs things. Shucks,

I'm going to run for mayor when I get there. Have a cigar, friend—the name's Harriman. Don't forget to vote." He grinned.

Dixon did not smile. "I did not know you planned on staying."

Harriman looked sheepish. "Well, that's still up in the air. If we get the shelter built in a hurry, we may save enough in the way of supplies to let me sort of lay over until the next trip. You wouldn't begrudge me that, would you?"

Dixon looked him in the eye. "Delos, I can't let you go at all."

Harriman was too startled to talk at first. At last he managed to say, "Don't joke, Dan. I'm going. You can't stop me. Nothing on Earth can stop me."

Dixon shook his head. "I can't permit it, Delos. I've got too much sunk in this. If you go and anything happens to you, I lose it all."

"That's silly. You and George would just carry on, that's all."

"Ask George."

Strong had nothing to say. He did not seem anxious to meet Harriman's eyes. Dixon went on. "Don't try to kid your way out of it, Delos. This venture is you and you are this venture. If you get killed, the whole thing folds up. I don't say space travel folds up; I think you've already given that a boost that will carry it along even with lesser men in your shoes. But as for this venture—our company—it will fold up. George and I will have to liquidate at about half a cent on the dollar. It would take sale of patent rights to get that much. The tangible assets aren't worth anything."

"Damn it, it's the intangibles we sell. You knew that all along."

"You are the intangible asset, Delos. You are the goose that lays the golden eggs. I want you to stick around until you've laid them. You must not risk your neck in space flight until you have this thing on a profit-making basis, so that any competent manager, such as George or myself, thereafter can keep it solvent. I mean it, Delos. I've got too much in it to see you risk it in a joyride."

Harriman stood up and pressed his fingers down on the edge of his desk. He was breathing hard. "You can't stop me!" he said slowly and forcefully. "You knew all along that I meant to go. You can't stop me now. Not all the forces of Heaven or Hell can stop me."

Dixon answered quietly, "I'm sorry, Delos. But I can stop you and I will. I can tie up that ship out there."

"Try it! I own as many lawyers as you do—and better ones!"

"I think you will find that you are not as popular in American courts as you once were—not since the United States found out it didn't own the Moon after all."

"Try it, I tell you. I'll break you and I'll take your shares away from you, too."

"Easy, Delos! I've no doubt you have some scheme whereby you could milk the basic company right away from George and me if you decided to. But it won't be necessary. Nor will it be necessary to tie up the ship. I want that flight to take place as much as you do. But you won't be on it, because you will decide not to go."

"I will, eh? Do I look crazy from where you sit?"

"No, on the contrary."

"Then why won't I go?"

"Because of your note that I hold. I want to collect it."

"What? There's no due date."

"No. But I want to be sure to collect it."

"Why, you dumb fool, if I get killed you collect it sooner than ever."

"Do I? You are mistaken, Delos. If you are killed—on a flight to the Moon—I collect nothing. I know; I've checked with every one of the companies underwriting you. Most of them have escape clauses covering experimental vehicles that date back to early aviation. In any case all of them will cancel and fight it out in court if you set foot inside that ship."

"You put them up to this!"

"Calm down, Delos. You'll be bursting a blood vessel. Certainly I queried them, but I was legitimately looking after my own interests. I don't want to collect on that note—not now, not by your death. I want you to pay it back out of your own earnings, by staying here and nursing this company through till it's stable."

Harriman chucked his cigar, almost unsmoked and badly chewed, at a wastebasket. He missed. "I don't give a hoot if you lose on it. If you hadn't stirred them up, they'd have paid without a quiver."

"But it did dig up a weak point in your plans, Delos. If space travel is to be a success, insurance will have to reach out and cover the insured anywhere."

"Damn it, one of them does now—N. A. Mutual."

"I've seen their ad and I've looked over what they claim to offer. It's just window dressing, with the usual escape clause. No, insurance will have to be revamped, all sorts of insurance."

Harriman looked thoughtful. "I'll look into it. George, call Kamens. Maybe we'll have to float our own company."

"Never mind Kamens," objected Dixon. "The point is you can't go on this trip. You have too many details of that sort to watch and plan for and nurse along."

Harriman looked back at him. "You haven't gotten it through your head, Dan, that *I'm going!* Tie up the ship if you can. If you put sheriffs around it, I'll have goons there to toss them aside."

Dixon looked pained. "I hate to mention this point, Delos, but I am afraid you will be stopped even if I drop dead."

"How?"

"Your wife."

"What's she got to do with it?"

"She's ready to sue for separate maintenance right now—she's found out about this insurance thing. When she hears about this present plan, she'll force you into court and force an accounting of your assets."

"You put her up to it!"

Dixon hesitated. He knew that Entenza had spilled the beans to Mrs. Harriman—maliciously. Yet there seemed no point in adding to a personal feud. "She's bright enough to have done some investigating on her own account. I won't deny I've talked to her—but she sent for me."

"I'll fight both of you!" Harriman stomped to a window, stood looking out—it was a real window; he liked to look at the sky.

Dixon came over and put a hand on his shoulder, saying softly, "Don't take it this way, Delos. Nobody's trying to keep you from your dream. But you can't go just yet; you can't let us down. We've stuck with you this far; you owe it to us to stick with us until it's done."

Harriman did not answer; Dixon went on. "If you don't feel any loyalty toward me, how about George? He's stuck with you *against* me, when it hurt him, when he thought you were ruining him—and you surely were, unless you finish this job. How about George, Delos? Are you going to let him down, too?"

Harriman swung around, ignoring Dixon and facing Strong. "What about it, George? Do you think I should stay behind?"

Strong rubbed his hands and chewed his lip. Finally he looked up. "It's all right with me, Delos. You do what you think is best."

Harriman stood looking at him for a long moment, his face working as if he were going to cry. Then he said huskily, "Okay, you bastards. Okay. I'll stay behind."

14

It was one of those glorious evenings so common in the Pikes Peak region, after a day in which the sky has been well scrubbed by thunderstorms. The track of the catapult crawled in a straight line up the face of the mountain, whole shoulders having been carved away to permit it. At the temporary spaceport, still raw from construction, Harriman, in company with visiting notables, was saying goodbye to the passengers and crew of the *Mayflower*.

The crowds came right up to the rail of the catapult. There was no need to keep them back from the ship; the jets would not blast until she was high over the peak. Only the ship itself was guarded, the ship and the gleaming rails.

Dixon and Strong, together for company and mutual support, hung back at the edge of the area roped off for passengers and officials. They watched Harriman jollying those about to leave: "Goodbye, Doctor. Keep an eye on him, Janet. Don't let him go looking for Moon Maidens." They saw him engage Coster in private conversation, then clap the younger man on the back.

"Keeps his chin up, doesn't he?" whispered Dixon.

"Maybe we should have let him go," answered Strong.

"Eh? Nonsense! We've got to have him. Anyway, his place in history is secure."

"He doesn't care about history," Strong answered seriously, "he just wants to go to the Moon."

"Well, confound it—he can go to the Moon . . . as soon as he gets his job done. After all, it's his job. He made it."

"I know."

Harriman turned around, saw them, started toward them. They shut up. "Don't duck," he said jovially. "It's all right. I'll go on the next trip. By then I plan to have it running itself. You'll see." He turned back toward the *Mayflower*. "Quite a sight, isn't she?"

The outer door was closed; ready lights winked along the track and from the control tower. A siren sounded.

Harriman moved a step or two closer.

"There she goes!"

It was a shout from the whole crowd. The great ship started

slowly, softly up the track, gathered speed, and shot toward the distant peak. She was already tiny by the time she curved up the face and burst into the sky.

She hung there a split second, then a plume of light exploded from her tail. Her jets had fired.

Then she was a shining light in the sky, a ball of flame, then —nothing. She was gone, upward and outward, to her rendezvous with her tankers.

The crowd had pushed to the west end of the platform as the ship swarmed up the mountain. Harriman had stayed where he was, nor had Dixon and Strong followed the crowd. The three were alone, Harriman most alone, for he did not seem aware that the others were near him. He was watching the sky.

Strong was watching him. Presently Strong barely whispered to Dixon, "Do you read the Bible?"

"Some."

"He looks as Moses must have looked, when he gazed out over the Promised Land."

Harriman dropped his eyes from the sky and saw them. "You guys still here?" he said. "Come on—there's work to be done."

The Marching Morons

The Marching Morons

C. M. KORNBLUTH

The late C. M. Kornbluth, who died when he was thirty-five, was one of the most prolific and talented writers this field has produced. In this story he examines a proposition that I believe in myself—that, all things considered, the Stupids are more dangerous than the Crazies.

Some things had not changed. A potter's wheel was still a potter's wheel and clay was still clay. Efim Hawkins had built his shop near Goose Lake, which had a narrow band of good fat clay and a narrow beach of white sand. He fired three bottle-nosed kilns with willow charcoal from the wood lot. The wood lot was also useful for long walks while the kilns were cooling; if he let himself stay within sight of them, he would open them prematurely, impatient to see how some new shape or glaze had come through the fire, and—*ping!*—the new shape or glaze would be good for nothing but the shard pile back of his slip tanks.

A business conference was in full swing in his shop, a modest cube of brick, tile-roofed, as the Chicago-Los Angeles "rocket" thundered overhead—very noisy, very swept back, very fiery jets, shaped as sleekly swift-looking as an airborne barracuda.

The buyer from Marshall Fields was turning over a black-glazed one-liter carafe, nodding approval with his massive, handsome head. "This is real pretty," he told Hawkins and his own secretary, Gomez-Laplace. "This has got lots of what ya call real est'etic principles. Yeah, it is real pretty."

"How much?" the secretary asked the potter.

"Seven-fifty in dozen lots," said Hawkins. "I ran up fifteen dozen last month."

"They are real est'etic," repeated the buyer from Fields. "I will take them all."

"I don't think we can do that, doctor," said the secretary. "They'd cost us $1,350. That would leave only $532 in our quarter's budget. And we still have to run down to East Liverpool to pick up some cheap dinner sets."

"Dinner sets?" asked the buyer, his big face full of wonder.

"Dinner sets. The department's been out of them for two months now. Mr. Garvy-Seabright got pretty nasty about it yesterday. Remember?"

"Garvy-Seabright, that meat-headed bluenose," the buyer said contemptuously. "He don't know nothin' about est'etics. Why for don't he lemme run my own department?" His eye fell on a stray copy of *Whambozambo Comix* and he sat down with it. An occasional deep chuckle or grunt of surprise escaped him as he turned the pages.

Uninterrupted, the potter and the buyer's secretary quickly closed a deal for two dozen of the liter carafes. "I wish we could take more," said the secretary, "but you heard what I told him. We've had to turn away customers for ordinary dinnerware because he shot the last quarter's budget on some Mexican piggy banks some equally enthusiastic importer stuck him with. The fifth floor is packed solid with them."

"I'll bet they look mighty est'etic."

"They're painted with purple cacti."

The potter shuddered and caressed the glaze of the sample carafe.

The buyer looked up and rumbled, "Ain't you dummies through yakkin' yet? What good's a seckertary for if'n he don't take the burden of *de*-tail off'n my back, harh?"

"We're all through, doctor. Are you ready to go?"

The buyer grunted peevishly, dropped *Whambozambo Comix* on the floor and led the way out of the building and down the log corduroy road to the highway. His car was waiting on the concrete. It was, like all contemporary cars, too low slung to get over the logs. He climbed down into the car and started the motor with a tremendous sparkle and roar.

"Gomez-Laplace," called out the potter under cover of the noise, "did anything come of the radiation program they were working on the last time I was on duty at the Pole?"

"The same old fallacy," said the secretary gloomily. "It stopped us on mutation, it stopped us on culling, it stopped us on segregation, and now it's stopped us on hypnosis."

"Well, I'm scheduled back to the grind in nine days. Time for another firing right now. I've got a new luster to try . . ."

"I'll miss you. I shall be 'vacationing'—running the drafting room of the New Century Engineering Corporation in Denver. They're going to put up a two-hundred-story office building, and naturally somebody's got to be on hand."

"Naturally," said Hawkins with a sour smile.

There was an ear-piercingly sweet blast as the buyer leaned on the horn button. Also, a yard-tall jet of what looked like flame spurted up from the car's radiator cap; the car's power plant was a gas turbine and had no radiator.

"I'm coming, doctor," said the secretary dispiritedly. He climbed down into the car and it whooshed off with much flame and noise.

The potter, depressed, wandered back up the corduroy road and contemplated his cooling kilns. The rustling wind in the boughs was obscuring the creak and mutter of the shrinking refractory brick. Hawkins wondered about the number two kiln— a reduction fire on a load of lusterware mugs. Had the clay chinking excluded the air? Had it been a properly smoky blaze? Would it do any harm if he just took one close—?

Common sense took Hawkins by the scruff of the neck and

yanked him over to the tool shed. He got out his pick and resolutely set off on a prospecting jaunt to a hummocky field that
might yield some oxides. He was especially low on coppers.

The long walk left him sweating hard, with his lust for a peek
into the kiln quiet in his breast. He swung his pick almost at
random into one of the hummocks; it clanged on a stone which
he excavated. A largely obliterated inscription said:

ERSITY OF CHIC
OGICAL LABO
ELOVED MEMORY OF
KILLED IN ACT

The potter swore mildly. He had hoped the field would turn
out to be a cemetery, preferably a once-fashionable cemetery
full of once-massive bronze caskets moldered into oxides of tin
and copper.

Well, hell, maybe there was some around anyway.

He headed lackadaisically for the second largest hillock and
sliced into it with his pick. There was a stone to undercut and
topple into a trench, and then the potter was very glad he'd stuck
at it. His nostrils were filled with the bitter smell and the dirt
was tinged with the exciting blue of copper salts. The pick went
clang!

Hawkins, puffing, pried up a stainless steel plate that was
quite badly stained and was also marked with incised letters.
It seemed to have pulled loose from rotting bronze; there were
rivets on the back that brought up flakes of green patina. The
potter wiped off the surface dirt with his sleeve, turned it to
catch the sunlight obliquely and read:

HONEST JOHN BARLOW
Honest John, famed in university annals, represents a
challenge which medical science has not yet answered: re-

vival of a human being accidentally thrown into a state of suspended animation.

In 1988 Mr. Barlow, a leading Evanston real estate dealer, visited his dentist for treatment of an impacted wisdom tooth. His dentist requested and received permission to use the experimental anesthetic Cycloparadimethanol-B-7, developed at the University.

After administration of the anesthetic, the dentist resorted to his drill. By freakish mischance, a short circuit in his machine delivered 220 volts of 60-cycle current into the patient. (In a damage suit instituted by Mrs. Barlow against the dentist, the University and the makers of the drill, a jury found for the defendants.) Mr. Barlow never got up from the dentist's chair and was assumed to have died of poisoning, electrocution or both.

Morticians preparing him for embalming discovered, however, that their subject was—though certainly not living—just as certainly not dead. The University was notified and a series of exhaustive tests was begun, including attempts to duplicate the trance state on volunteers. After a bad run of seven cases which ended fatally, the attempts were abandoned.

Honest John was long an exhibit at the University museum and livened many a football game as mascot of the University's Blue Crushers. The bounds of taste were overstepped, however, when a pledge to Sigma Delta Chi was ordered in '03 to "kidnap" Honest John from his loosely guarded glass museum case and introduce him into the Rachel Swanson Memorial Girls' Gymnasium shower room.

On May 22, 2003, the University Board of Regents issued the following order: "By unanimous vote, it is directed that the remains of Honest John Barlow be removed from the University museum and conveyed to the University's Lieutenant James Scott III Memorial Biological Laboratories and there be securely locked in a specially prepared vault. It is further directed that all possible measures for the preservation of these remains be taken by the Laboratory administration and that access to these remains be denied to all persons except qualified scholars authorized in writing by the Board. The Board reluctantly takes this action in view of recent notices and photographs in the nation's press which, to say the least, reflect but small credit upon the University."

It was far from his field, but Hawkins understood what had happened—an early and accidental blundering onto the bare bones of the Levantman shock anesthesia, which had since been replaced by other methods. To bring subjects out of Levantman shock, you let them have a squirt of simple saline in the trigeminal nerve. Interesting. And now about that bronze—

He heaved the pick into the rotting green salts, expecting no resistance, and almost fractured his wrist. *Something* down there was *solid*. He began to flake off the oxides.

A half hour of work brought him down to phosphor bronze, a huge casting of the almost incorruptible metal. It had weakened structurally over the centuries; he could fit the point of his pick under a corroded boss and pry off great creaking and grumbling striae of the stuff.

Hawkins wished he had an archaeologist with him but didn't dream of returning to his shop and calling one to take over the find. He was an all-around man: by choice, and in his free time, an artist in clay and glaze; by necessity, an automotive, electronics and atomic engineer who could also swing a project in traffic control, individual and group psychology, architecture or tool design. He didn't yell for a specialist every time something out of his line came up; there were so few with so much to do . . .

He trenched around his find, discovering that it was a great brick-shaped bronze mass with an excitingly hollow sound. A long strip of moldering metal from one of the long vertical faces pulled away, exposing red rust that went *whoosh* and was sucked into the interior of the mass.

It had been de-aired, thought Hawkins, and there must have been an inner jacket of glass which had crystallized through the centuries and quietly crumbled at the first clang of his pick. He didn't know what a vacuum would do to a subject of Levantman shock, but he had hopes, nor did he quite understand what a real estate dealer was, but it might have something to do with pottery. And *anything* might have a bearing on Topic Number One.

He flung his pick out of the trench, climbed out and set off at a dog-trot for his shop. A little rummaging turned up a hypo and there was a plastic container of salt in the kitchen.

Back at his dig, he chipped for another half hour to expose the juncture of lid and body. The hinges were hopeless; he smashed them off.

Hawkins extended the telescopic handle of the pick for the best leverage, fitted its point into a deep pit, set its built-in fulcrum, and heaved. Five more heaves and he could see, inside the vault, what looked like a dusty marble statue. Ten more and he could see that it was the naked body of Honest John Barlow, Evanston real estate dealer, uncorrupted by time.

The potter found the apex of the trigeminal nerve with his needle's point and gave him 60 cc.

In an hour Barlow's chest began to pump.

In another hour, he rasped, "Did it work?"

"Did it!" muttered Hawkins.

Barlow opened his eyes and stirred, looked down, turned his hands before his eyes—

"I'll sue!" he screamed. "My clothes! My fingernails!" A horrid suspicion came over his face and he clapped his hands to his hairless scalp. "My hair!" he wailed. "I'll sue you for every penny you've got! That release won't mean a damned thing in court—I didn't sign away my hair and clothes and fingernails!"

"They'll grow back," said Hawkins casually. "Also your epidermis. Those parts of you weren't alive, you know, so they weren't preserved like the rest of you. I'm afraid the clothes are gone, though."

"What is this—the University hospital?" demanded Barlow. "I want a phone. No, you phone. Tell my wife I'm all right and tell Sam Immerman—he's my lawyer—to get over here right away. Greenleaf 7-4022. Ow!" He had tried to sit up, and a portion of his pink skin rubbed against the inner surface of the casket, which was powdered by the ancient crystallized glass. "What the hell did you guys do, boil me alive? Oh, you're going to pay for this!"

"You're all right," said Hawkins, wishing now he had a reference book to clear up several obscure terms. "Your epidermis will start growing immediately. You're not in the hospital. Look here."

He handed Barlow the stainless steel plate that had labeled the casket. After a suspicious glance, the man started to read. Finishing, he laid the plate carefully on the edge of the vault and was silent for a spell.

"Poor Verna," he said at last. "It doesn't say whether she was stuck with the court costs. Do you happen to know—"

"No," said the potter. "All I know is what was on the plate, and how to revive you. The dentist accidentally gave you a dose of what we call Levantman shock anesthesia. We haven't used it for centuries; it was powerful, but too dangerous."

"Centuries . . ." brooded the man. "Centuries . . . I'll bet Sam swindled her out of her eyeteeth. Poor Verna. How long ago was it? What year is this?"

Hawkins shrugged. "We call it 7-B-936. That's no help to you. It takes a long time for these metals to oxidize."

"Like that movie," Barlow muttered. "Who would have thought it? Poor Verna!" He blubbered and sniffled, reminding Hawkins powerfully of the fact that he had been found under a flat rock.

Almost angrily, the potter demanded, "How many children did you have?"

"None yet," sniffed Barlow. "My first wife didn't want them. But Verna wants one—wanted one—but we're going to wait until—we *were* going to wait until—"

"Of course," said the potter, feeling a savage desire to tell him off, blast him to hell and gone for his work. But he choked it down. There was The Problem to think of; there was always The Problem to think of, and this poor blubberer might unexpectedly supply a clue. Hawkins would have to pass him on.

"Come along," Hawkins said. "My time is short."

Barlow looked up, outraged. "How can you be so unfeeling? I'm a human being like—"

The Los Angeles-Chicago "rocket" thundered overhead and Barlow broke off in mid-complaint. "Beautiful!" he breathed, following it with his eyes. "Beautiful!"

He climbed out of the vault, too interested to be pained by its roughness against his infantile skin. "After all," he said briskly, "this should have its sunny side. I never was much for reading, but this is just like one of those stories. And I ought to make some money out of it, shouldn't I?" He gave Hawkins a shrewd glance.

"You want money?" asked the potter. "Here." He handed over a fistful of change and bills. "You'd better put my shoes on. It'll be about a quarter mile. Oh, and you're—uh, modest?— yes, that was the word. Here." Hawkins gave him his pants, but Barlow was excitedly counting the money.

"Eighty-five, eighty-six—and it's dollars, too! I thought it'd be credits or whatever they call them. 'E Pluribus Unum' and 'Liberty'—just different faces. Say, is there a catch to this? Are these real, genuine, honest twenty-two-cent dollars like we had or just wallpaper?"

"They're quite all right, I assure you," said the potter. "I wish you'd come along. I'm in a hurry."

The man babbled as they stumped toward the shop. "Where

are we going—The Council of Scientists, the World Coordinator
or something like that?"

"Who? Oh, no. We call them 'President' and 'Congress.' No,
that wouldn't do any good at all. I'm just taking you to see some
people."

"I ought to make plenty out of this. *Plenty!* I could write
books. Get some smart young fellow to put it into words for me
and I'll bet I could turn out a best seller. What's the setup on
things like that?"

"It's about like that. Smart young fellows. But there aren't any
best sellers any more. People don't read much nowadays. We'll
find something equally profitable for you to do."

Back in the shop, Hawkins gave Barlow a suit of clothes, deposited him in the waiting room and called Central in Chicago.
"Take him away," he pleaded. "I have time for one more firing
and he blathers and blathers. I haven't told him anything. Perhaps we should just turn him loose and let him find his own
level, but there's a chance—"

"The Problem," agreed Central. "Yes, there's a chance."

The potter delighted Barlow by making him a cup of coffee
with a cube that not only dissolved in cold water but heated the
water to boiling point. Killing time, Hawkins chatted about the
"rocket" Barlow had admired and had to haul himself up short;
he had almost told the real estate man what its top speed really
was—almost, indeed, revealed that it was not a rocket.

He regretted, too, that he had so casually handed Barlow a
couple of hundred dollars. The man seemed obsessed with fear
that they were worthless since Hawkins refused to take a note or
I.O.U. or even a definite promise of repayment. But Hawkins
couldn't go into details, and was very glad when a stranger arrived from Central.

"Tinny-Peete, from Algeciras," the stranger told him swiftly
as the two of them met at the door. "Psychist for Poprob. Pol-
assigned special overtake Barlow."

"Thank Heaven," said Hawkins. "Barlow," he told the man

from the past, "this is Tinny-Peete. He's going to take care of you and help you make lots of money."

The psychist stayed for a cup of the coffee whose preparation had delighted Barlow, and then conducted the real estate man down the corduroy road to his car, leaving the potter to speculate on whether he could at last crack his kilns.

Hawkins, abruptly dismissing Barlow and the Problem, happily picked the chinking from around the door of the number two kiln, prying it open a trifle. A blast of heat and the heady, smoky scent of the reduction fire delighted him. He peered and saw a corner of a shelf glowing cherry red, becoming obscured by wavering black areas as it lost heat through the opened door. He slipped a charred wood paddle under a mug on the shelf and pulled it out as a sample, the hairs on the back of his hand curling and scorching. The mug crackled and pinged and Hawkins sighed happily.

The bismuth resinate luster had fired to perfection, a haunting film of silvery-black metal with strange bluish lights in it as it turned before the eyes, and the Problem of Population seemed very far away to Hawkins then.

Barlow and Tinny-Peete arrived at the concrete highway where the psychist's car was parked in a safety bay.

"What—a—*boat!*" gasped the man from the past.

"Boat? No, that's my car."

Barlow surveyed it with awe. Swept-back lines, deep-drawn compound curves, kilograms of chrome. He ran his hands over the door—or was it the door?—in a futile search for a handle, and asked respectfully, "How fast does it go?"

The psychist gave him a keen look and said slowly, "Two hundred and fifty. You can tell by the speedometer."

"Wow! My old Chevvy could hit a hundred on a straightaway, but you're out of my class, mister!"

Tinny-Peete somehow got a huge, low door open and Barlow descended three steps into immense cushions, floundering over to the right. He was too fascinated to pay serious attention to his flayed dermis. The dashboard was a lovely wilderness of dials, plugs, indicators, lights, scales and switches.

The psychist climbed down into the driver's seat and did something with his feet. The motor started like lighting a blowtorch as big as a silo. Wallowing around in the cushions, Barlow saw through a rear-view mirror a tremendous exhaust filled with brilliant white sparkles.

"Do you like it?" yelled the psychist.

"It's terrific!" Barlow yelled back. "It's—"

He was shut up as the car pulled out from the bay into the road with a great *voo-ooo-ooom!* A gale roared past Barlow's head, though the windows seemed to be closed; the impression of speed was terrific. He located the speedometer on the dashboard and saw it climb past 90, 100, 150, 200.

"Fast enough for me," yelled the psychist, noting that Barlow's face fell in response. "Radio?"

He passed over a surprisingly light object like a football helmet, with no trailing wires, and pointed to a row of buttons. Barlow put on the helmet, glad to have the roar of air stilled, and pushed a pushbutton. It lit up satisfyingly, and Barlow settled back even farther for a sample of the brave new world's supermodern taste in ingenious entertainment.

"TAKE IT AND STICK IT!" a voice roared in his ears.

He snatched off the helmet and gave the psychist an injured look. Tinny-Peete grinned and turned a dial associated with the pushbutton layout. The man from the past donned the helmet again and found the voice had lowered to normal.

"The show of shows! The supershow! The super-duper show! The quiz of quizzes! *Take It and Stick It!*"

There were shrieks of laughter in the background.

"Here we got the contes-tants all ready to go. You know how we work it. I hand a contes-tant a triangle-shaped cutout and like that down the line. Now we got these here boards, they got cutout places the same shape as the triangles and things, only they're all different shapes, and the first contes-tant that sticks the cutouts into the board, he wins.

"Now I'm gonna innaview the first contes-tant. Right here, honey. What's your name?"

"Name? Uh—"

"Hoddaya like that, folks? She don't remember her name! Hah? *Would you buy that for a quarter?*" The question was spoken with arch significance, and the audience shrieked, howled and whistled its appreciation.

It was dull listening when you didn't know the punch lines and catch lines. Barlow pushed another button, with his free hand ready at the volume control.

"—latest from Washington. It's about Senator Hull-Mendoza. He is still attacking the Bureau of Fisheries. The North Cali-fornia Syndicalist says he got affidavits that John Kingsley-Schultz is a bluenose from way back. He didn't publistat the affydavits, but he says they say that Kingsley-Schultz was saw at bluenose meetings in Oregon State College and later at Flor-ida University. Kingsley-Schultz says he gotta confess he did major in fly casting at Oregon and got his Ph.D. in game-fish at Florida.

"And here is a quote from Kingsley-Schultz: 'Hull-Mendoza don't know what he's talking about. He should drop dead.' Un-quote. Hull-Mendoza says he won't publistat the affydavits to pertect his sources. He says they was sworn by three former em-ployes of the Bureau which was fired for in-competence and in-com-pat-ibility by Kingsley-Schultz.

"Elsewhere they was the usual run of traffic accidents. A three-way pileup of cars on Route 66 going outta Chicago took twelve lives. The Chicago-Los Angeles morning rocket crashed and exploded in the Mo-have—Mo-javvy—whatever-you-call-it Desert. All the 94 people aboard got killed. A Civil Aeronautics Authority investigator on the scene says that the pilot was buzz-ing herds of sheep and didn't pull out in time.

"Hey! Here's a hot one from New York! A diesel tug run wild in the harbor while the crew was below and shoved in the port bow of the luck-shury liner S. S. *Placentia*. It says the ship filled and sank taking the lives of an es-ti-mated 180 passengers and 50 crew members. Six divers was sent down to study the wreckage, but they died, too, when their suits turned out to be fulla little holes.

"And here is a bulletin I just got from Denver. It seems—"

Barlow took off the headset uncomprehendingly. "He seemed so callous," he yelled at the driver. "I was listening to a news-cast—"

Tinny-Peete shook his head and pointed at his ears. The roar of air was deafening. Barlow frowned baffledly and stared out of the window.

A glowing sign said:

MOOGS!
WOULD YOU BUY IT
FOR A QUARTER?

He didn't know what Moogs was or were; the illustration showed an incredibly proportioned girl, 99.9 percent naked, writhing passionately in animated full color.

The roadside jingle was still with him, but with a new feature. Radar or something spotted the car and alerted the lines of the jingle. Each in turn sped along a roadside track, even with the car, so it could be read before the next line was alerted.

IF THERE'S A GIRL
YOU WANT TO GET
DEFLOCCULIZE
UNROMANTIC SWEAT.
"A*R*M*P*I*T*T*O"

Another animated job, in two panels, the familiar "Before and After." The first said, "Just Any Cigar?" and was illustrated with a two-person domestic tragedy of a wife holding her nose while her coarse and red-faced husband puffed a slimy-looking rope. The second panel glowed, "Or a VUELTA ABAJO?" and was illustrated with—

Barlow blushed and looked at his feet until they had passed the sign.

"Coming into Chicago!" bawled Tinny-Peete.

Other cars were showing up, all of them dreamboats.

Watching them, Barlow began to wonder if he knew what a kilometer was, exactly. They seemed to be traveling so slowly, if you ignored the roaring air past your ears and didn't let the speedy lines of the dreamboats fool you. He would have sworn they were really crawling along at twenty-five, with occasional spurts up to thirty. How much was a kilometer, anyway?

The city loomed ahead, and it was just what it ought to be: towering skyscrapers, overhead ramps, landing platforms for helicopters—

He clutched at the cushions. Those two copters. They were going to—they were going to—they—

He didn't see what happened because their apparent collision courses took them behind a giant building.

Screamingly sweet blasts of sound surrounded them as they stopped for a red light. "What the hell is going on here?" said Barlow in a shrill, frightened voice, because the braking time was just about zero, and he wasn't hurled against the dashboard. "Who's kidding who?"

"Why, what's the matter?" demanded the driver.

The light changed to green and he started the pickup. Barlow stiffened as he realized that the rush of air past his ears began just a brief, unreal split second before the car was actually moving. He grabbed for the door handle on his side.

The city grew on them slowly: scattered buildings, denser buildings, taller buildings, and a red light ahead. The car rolled to a stop in zero braking time, the rush of air cut off an instant after it stopped, and Barlow was out of the car and running frenziedly down a sidewalk one instant after that.

They'll track me down, he thought, panting. *It's a secret police thing. They'll get you—mind-reading machines, television eyes everywhere, afraid you'll tell their slaves about freedom and stuff. They don't let anybody cross them, like that story I once read.*

Winded, he slowed to a walk and congratulated himself that he had guts enough not to turn around. That was what they always watched for. Walking, he was just another business-suited back among hundreds. He would be safe, he would be safe—

A hand gripped his shoulder and words tumbled from a large, coarse, handsome face thrust close to his: "Wassamatta bumpinninna people likeya owna sidewalk gotta miner slamya inna mushya bassar!" It was neither the mad potter nor the mad driver.

"Excuse me," said Barlow. "What did you say?"

"Oh, yeah?" yelled the stranger dangerously, and waited for an answer.

Barlow, with the feeling that he had somehow been suckered into the short end of an intricate land-title deal, heard himself reply belligerently, "Yeah!"

The stranger let go of his shoulder and snarled, "Oh, yeah?"

"Yeah!" said Barlow, yanking his jacket back into shape.

"Aaah!" snarled the stranger, with more contempt and disgust than ferocity. He added an obscenity current in Barlow's time, a standard but physiologically impossible directive, and strutted off hulking his shoulders and balling his fists.

Barlow walked on, trembling. Evidently he had handled it well enough. He stopped at a red light while the long, low dreamboats roared before him and pedestrians in the sidewalk flow with him threaded their ways through the stream of cars. Brakes screamed, fenders clanged and dented, hoarse cries flew back and forth between drivers and walkers. He leaped backward frantically as one car swerved over an arc of sidewalk to miss another.

The signal changed to green; the cars kept on coming for about thirty seconds and then dwindled to an occasional light runner. Barlow crossed warily and leaned against a vending machine, blowing big breaths.

Look natural, he told himself. *Do something normal. Buy something from the machine.* He fumbled out some change, got a newspaper for a dime, a handkerchief for a quarter and a candy bar for another quarter.

The faint chocolate smell made him ravenous suddenly. He clawed at the glassy wrapper printed *"Crigglies"* quite futilely for a few seconds, and then it divided neatly by itself. The bar made three good bites, and he bought two more and gobbled them down.

Thirsty, he drew a carbonated orange drink in another one of the glassy wrappers from the machine for another dime. When he fumbled with it, it divided neatly and spilled all over his knees. Barlow decided he had been there long enough and walked on.

The shop windows were—shop windows. People still wore and bought clothes, still smoked and bought tobacco, still ate and bought food. And they still went to the movies, he saw with pleased surprise as he passed and then returned to a glittering place whose sign said it was THE BIJOU.

The place seemed to be showing a triple feature, *Babies Are Terrible, Don't Have Children,* and *The Canali Kid.*

It was irresistible; he paid a dollar and went in.

He caught the tail end of *The Canali Kid* in three-dimensional, full-color, full-scent production. It appeared to be an interplanetary saga winding up with a chase scene and a reconciliation between estranged hero and heroine. *Babies Are Terrible* and *Don't Have Children* were fantastic arguments against parenthood—the grotesquely exaggerated dangers of painfully graphic childbirth, vicious children, old parents beaten and starved by their sadistic offspring. The audience, Barlow astoundedly noted, was placidly chomping sweets and showing no particular signs of revulsion.

The *Coming Attractions* drove him into the lobby. The fanfares were shattering, the blazing colors blinding, and the added scents stomach heaving.

When his eyes again became accustomed to the moderate lighting of the lobby, he groped his way to a bench and opened the newspaper he had bought. It turned out to be *The Racing Sheet,* which afflicted him with a crushing sense of loss. The familiar boxed index in the lower-left-hand corner of the front page showed almost unbearably that Churchill Downs and Empire City were still in business—

Blinking back tears, he turned to the Past Performance at Churchill. They weren't using abbreviations any more, and the pages because of that were single-column instead of double. But it was all the same—or was it?

He squinted at the first race, a three-quarter-mile maiden claimer for thirteen hundred dollars. Incredibly, the track record was two minutes, ten and three-fifths seconds. Any beetle in his time could have knocked off the three-quarter in one-fifteen. It was the same for the other distances, much worse for route events.

What the hell had happened to everything?

He studied the form of a five-year-old brown mare in the second and couldn't make head or tail of it. She'd won and lost and placed and showed and lost and placed without rhyme or reason. She looked like a front runner for a couple of races and then she looked like a no-good pig and then she looked like a mudder but the next time it rained she wasn't and then she was a stayer and then she was a pig again. In a good five-thousand-dollar allowances event, too!

Barlow looked at the other entries and it slowly dawned on him that they were all like the five-year-old brown mare. Not a single damned horse running had even the slightest trace of class.

Somebody sat down beside him and said, "That's the story."

Barlow whirled to his feet and saw it was Tinny-Peete, his driver.

"I was in doubts about telling you," said the psychist, "but I see you have some growing suspicions of the truth. Please don't get excited. It's all right, I tell you."

"So you've got me," said Barlow.

"*Got* you?"

"Don't pretend. I can put two and two together. You're the secret police. You and the rest of the aristocrats live in luxury on the sweat of these oppressed slaves. You're afraid of me because you have to keep them ignorant."

There was a bellow of bright laughter from the psychist that got them blank looks from other patrons of the lobby. The laughter didn't sound at all sinister.

"Let's get out of here," said Tinny-Peete, still chuckling. "You couldn't possibly have it more wrong." He engaged Barlow's arm and led him to the street. "The actual truth is that the millions of workers live in luxury on the sweat of the handful of aristocrats. I shall probably die before my time of overwork unless—" He gave Barlow a speculative look. "You may be able to help us."

"I know that gag," sneered Barlow. "I made money in my time and to make money you have to get people on your side. Go ahead and shoot me if you want, but you're not going to make a fool out of me."

"You nasty little ingrate!" snapped the psychist, with a kaleidoscopic change of mood. "This damned mess is all your fault and the fault of people like you! Now come along and no more of your nonsense."

He yanked Barlow into an office building lobby and an elevator that, disconcertingly, went *whoosh* loudly as it rose. The real estate man's knees were wobbly as the psychist pushed him from the elevator, down a corridor and into an office.

A hawk-faced man rose from a plain chair as the door closed

behind them. After an angry look at Barlow, he asked the psychist, "Was I called from the Pole to inspect this—this—?"

"Unget updandered. I've deeprobed etfind quasichance exhim Poprobattackline," said the psychist soothingly.

"Doubt," grunted the hawk-faced man.

"Try," suggested Tinny-Peete.

"Very well. Mr. Barlow, I understand you and your lamented had no children."

"What of it?"

"This of it. You were a blind, selfish stupid ass to tolerate economic and social conditions which penalized childbearing by the prudent and foresighted. You made us what we are today, and I want you to know that we are far from satisfied. Damnfool rockets! Damn-fool automobiles! Damn-fool cities with overhead ramps!"

"As far as I can see," said Barlow, "you're running down the best features of your time. Are you crazy?"

"The rockets aren't rockets. They're turbojets—good turbojets, but the fancy shell around them makes for a bad drag. The automobiles have a top speed of one hundred kilometers per hour—a kilometer is, if I recall my paleolinguistics, three-fifths of a mile—and the speedometers are all rigged accordingly so the drivers will think they're going two hundred and fifty. The cities are ridiculous, expensive, unsanitary, wasteful conglomerations of people who'd be better off and more productive if they were spread over the countryside.

"We need the rockets and trick speedometers and cities because, while you and your kind were being prudent and foresighted and not having children, the migrant workers, slum dwellers and tenant farmers were shiftlessly and shortsightedly having children—breeding, breeding. My God, how they bred!"

"Wait a minute," objected Barlow. "There were lots of people in our crowd who had two or three children."

"The attrition of accidents, illness, wars and such took care of that. Your intelligence was bred out. It is gone. Children that

should have been born never were. The just-average, they'll-get-
along majority took over the population. The average IQ now
is 45."

"But that's far in the future—"

"So are you," grunted the hawk-faced man sourly.

"But who are *you* people?"

"Just people—real people. Some generations ago, the geneti-
cists realized at last that nobody was going to pay any attention
to what they said, so they abandoned words for deeds. Specifi-
cally, they formed and recruited for a closed corporation intended to maintain and improve the breed. We are their descendants, about three million of us. There are five billion of the
others, so we are their slaves.

"During the past couple of years I've designed a skyscraper,
kept Billings Memorial Hospital here in Chicago running,
headed off war with Mexico and directed traffic at LaGuardia
Field in New York."

"I don't understand! Why don't you let them go to hell in
their own way?"

The man grimaced. "We tried it once for three months. We
holed up at the South Pole and waited. They didn't notice it.
Some drafting room people were missing, some chief nurses
didn't show up, minor government people on the nonpolicy level
couldn't be located. It didn't seem to matter.

"In a week there was hunger. In two weeks there were famine
and plague, in three weeks war and anarchy. We called off the
experiment; it took us most of the next generation to get things
squared away again."

"But why *didn't* you let them kill each other off?"

"Five billion corpses mean about five hundred million tons
of rotting flesh."

Barlow had another idea. "Why don't you sterilize them?"

"Two and one-half billion operations is a lot of operations.
Because they breed continuously, the job would never be done."

"I see. Like the marching Chinese!"

"Who the devil are they?"

"It was a—uh—paradox of my time. Somebody figured out that if all the Chinese in the world were to line up four abreast, I think it was, and start marching past a given point, they'd never stop because of the babies that would be born and grow up before they passed the point."

"That's right. Only instead of 'a given point,' make it 'the largest conceivable number of operating rooms that we could build and staff.' There could never be enough."

"Say!" said Barlow. "Those movies about babies—was that your propaganda?"

"It was. It doesn't seem to mean a thing to them. We have abandoned the idea of attempting propaganda contrary to a biological drive."

"So if you work *with* a biological drive—?"

"I know of none which is consistent with inhibition of fertility."

Barlow's face went poker blank, the result of years of careful discipline. "You don't, huh? You're the great brains and you can't think of any?"

"Why, no," said the psychist innocently. "Can you?"

"That depends. I sold ten thousand acres of Siberian tundra— through a dummy firm, of course—after the partition of Russia. The buyers thought they were getting improved building lots on the outskirts of Kiev. I'd say that was a lot tougher than this job."

"How so?" asked the hawk-faced man.

"Those were normal, suspicious customers and these are morons, born suckers. You just figure out a con they'll fall for; they won't know enough to do any smart checking."

The psychist and the hawk-faced man had also had training; they kept themselves from looking with sudden hope at each other.

"You seem to have something in mind," said the psychist.

Barlow's poker face went blanker still. "Maybe I have. I haven't heard any offer yet."

"There's the satisfaction of knowing that you've prevented Earth's resources from being so plundered," the hawk-faced man pointed out, "that the race will soon become extinct."

"I don't know that," Barlow said bluntly. "All I have is your word."

"If you really have a method, I don't think any price would be too great," the psychist offered.

"Money," said Barlow.

"All you want."

"More than you want," the hawk-faced man corrected.

"Prestige," added Barlow. "Plenty of publicity. My picture and my name in the papers and over TV every day, statues to me, parks and cities and streets and other things named after me. A whole chapter in the history books."

The psychist made a facial sign to the hawk-faced man that meant, "Oh, brother!"

The hawk-faced man signaled back, "Steady, boy!"

"It's not too much to ask," the psychist agreed.

Barlow, sensing a seller's market, said, "Power!"

"Power?" the hawk-faced man repeated puzzledly. "Your own hydro station or nuclear pile?"

"I mean a world dictatorship with me as dictator!"

"Well, now—" said the psychist, but the hawk-faced man interrupted, "It would take a special emergency act of Congress but the situation warrants it. I think that can be guaranteed."

"Could you give us some indication of your plan?" the psychist asked.

"Ever hear of lemmings?"

"No."

"They are—were, I guess, since you haven't heard of them—little animals in Norway, and every few years they'd swarm to the coast and swim out to sea until they drowned. I figure on putting some lemming urge into the population."

"How?"

"I'll save that till I get the right signatures on the deal."

The hawk-faced man said, "I'd like to work with you on it, Barlow. My name's Ryan-Ngana." He put out his hand.

Barlow looked closely at the hand, then at the man's face. "Ryan what?"

"Ngana."

"That sounds like an African name."

"It is. My mother's father was a Watusi."

Barlow didn't take the hand. "I thought you looked pretty dark. I don't want to hurt your feelings, but I don't think I'd be at my best working with you. There must be somebody else just as well qualified, I'm sure."

The psychist made a facial sign to Ryan-Ngana that meant, "Steady *yourself,* boy!"

"Very well," Ryan-Ngana told Barlow. "We'll see what arrangement can be made."

"It's not that I'm prejudiced, you understand. Some of my best friends—"

"Mr. Barlow, don't give it another thought. Anybody who could pick on the lemming analogy is going to be useful to us."

And so he would, thought Ryan-Ngana, alone in the office after Tinny-Peete had taken Barlow up to the helicopter stage. So he would. Poprob had exhausted every rational attempt and the new Poprobattacklines would have to be irrational or subrational. This creature from the past with his lemming legends and his improved building lots would be a fountain of precious vicious self-interest.

Ryan-Ngana sighed and stretched. He had to go and run the San Francisco subway. Summoned early from the Pole to study Barlow, he'd left unfinished a nice little theorem. Between interruptions, he was slowly constructing an n-dimensional geometry whose foundations and superstructure owed no debt whatsoever to intuition.

Upstairs, waiting for a helicopter, Barlow was explaining to Tinny-Peete that he had nothing against Negroes, and Tinny-Peete wished he had some of Ryan-Ngana's imperturbability and humor for the ordeal.

The helicopter took them to International Airport where, Tinny-Peete explained, Barlow would leave for the Pole.

The man from the past wasn't sure he'd like a dreary waste of ice and cold.

"It's all right," said the psychist. "A civilized layout. Warm, pleasant. You'll be able to work more efficiently there. All the facts at your fingertips, a good secretary—"

"I'll need a pretty big staff," said Barlow, who had learned from thousands of deals never to take the first offer.

"I meant a private, confidential one," said Tinny-Peete readily, "but you can have as many as you want. You'll naturally have top-primary-top priority if you really have a workable plan."

"Let's not forget this dictatorship angle," said Barlow.

He didn't know that the psychist would just as readily have promised him deification to get him happily on the "rocket" for the Pole. Tinny-Peete had no wish to be torn limb from limb; he knew very well that it would end that way if the population learned from this anachronism that there was a small elite which considered itself head, shoulders, trunk and groin above the rest. The fact that this assumption was perfectly true and the fact that the elite was condemned by its superiority to a life of the most grinding toil would not be considered; the difference would.

The psychist finally put Barlow aboard the "rocket" with some thirty people—real people—headed for the Pole.

Barlow was airsick all the way because of a posthypnotic suggestion Tinny-Peete had planted in him. One idea was to make him as averse as possible to a return trip, and another idea was to spare the other passengers from his aggressive, talkative company.

Barlow during the first day at the Pole was reminded of his first day in the Army. It was the same now-where-the-hell-are-

we-going-to-put-*you?* business until he took a firm line with
them. Then instead of acting like supply sergeants they acted
like hotel clerks.

It was a wonderful, wonderfully calculated buildup, and one
that he failed to suspect. After all, in his time a visitor from the
past would have been lionized.

At day's end he reclined in a snug underground billet with the
sixty-mile gales roaring yards overhead and tried to put two and
two together.

It was like old times, he thought—like a coup in real estate
where you had the competition by the throat, like a fifty-percent
rent boost when you knew damned well there was no place for
the tenants to move, like smiling when you read over the breakfast orange juice that the city council had decided to build a
school on the ground you had acquired by a deal with the city
council. And it was simple. He would just sell tundra building
lots to eagerly suicidal lemmings, and that was absolutely all
there was to solving The Problem that had these double-domes
spinning.

They'd have to work out most of the details, naturally, but
what the hell, that was what subordinates were for. He'd need
specialists in advertising, engineering, communications—did
they know anything about hypnotism? That might be helpful. If
not, there'd have to be a lot of bribery done, but he'd make sure
—damned sure—there were unlimited funds.

Just selling building lots to lemmings . . .

He wished, as he fell asleep, that poor Verna could have been
in on this. It was his biggest, most stupendous deal. Verna—that
sharp shyster Sam Immerman must have swindled her . . .

It began the next day with people coming to visit him. He
knew the approach. They merely wanted to be helpful to their
illustrious visitor from the past and would he help fill them in
about his era, which unfortunately was somewhat obscure his-
torically, and what did he think could be done about The Prob-

lem? He told them he was too old to be roped any more, and they wouldn't get any information out of him until he got a letter of intent from at least the Polar President and a session of the Polar Congress empowered to make him dictator.

He got the letter and the session. He presented his program, was asked whether his conscience didn't revolt at its callousness, explained succinctly that a deal was a deal and anybody who wasn't smart enough to protect himself didn't deserve protection —"Caveat emptor," he threw in for scholarship, and had to translate it to "Let the buyer beware." He didn't, he stated, give a damn about either the morons or their intelligent slaves; he'd told them his price and that was all he was interested in.

Would they meet it or wouldn't they?

The Polar President offered to resign in his favor, with certain temporary emergency powers that the Polar Congress would vote him if he thought them necessary. Barlow demanded the title of World Dictator, complete control of world finances, salary to be decided by himself, and the publicity campaign and historical writeup to begin at once.

"As for the emergency powers," he added, "they are neither to be temporary nor limited."

Somebody wanted the floor to discuss the matter, with the declared hope that perhaps Barlow would modify his demands.

"You've got the proposition," Barlow said. "I'm not knocking off even ten percent."

"But what if the Congress refuses, sir?" the President asked.

"Then you can stay up here at the Pole and try to work it out yourselves. I'll get what I want from the morons. A shrewd operator like me doesn't have to compromise; I haven't got a single competitor in this whole cockeyed moronic era."

Congress waived debate and voted by show of hands. Barlow won unanimously.

"You don't know how close you came to losing me," he said in his first official address to the joint Houses. "I'm not the boy to haggle; either I get what I ask, or I go elsewhere. The first thing I want is to see designs for a new palace for me—nothing *un*ostentatious, either—and your best painters and sculptors to start working on my portraits and statues. Meanwhile, I'll get my staff together."

He dismissed the Polar President and the Polar Congress, telling them that he'd let them know when the next meeting would be.

A week later, the program started with North America the first target.

Mrs. Garvy was resting after dinner before the ordeal of turning on the dishwasher. The TV, of course, was on and it said, "Oooh!"—long, shuddery and ecstatic, the cue for the *Parfum Assault Criminale* spot commercial. "Girls," said the announcer hoarsely, "do you want your man? It's easy to get him—easy as a trip to Venus."

"Huh?" said Mrs. Garvy.

"Wassamatter?" snorted her husband, starting out of a doze.

"Ja hear that?"

"Wha'?"

"He said 'easy like a trip to Venus.' "

"So?"

"Well, I thought ya couldn't get to Venus. I thought they just had that one rocket thing that crashed on the Moon."

"Aah, women don't keep up with the news," said Garvy righteously, subsiding again.

"Oh," said his wife uncertainly.

And the next day, on *Henry's Other Mistress,* there was a new character who had just breezed in: Buzz Rentshaw, Master Rocket Pilot of the Venus run. On *Henry's Other Mistress,* "the broadcast drama about you and your neighbors, *folksy* people, *ordinary* people, *real* people!" Mrs. Garvy listened with amazement over a cooling cup of coffee as Buzz made hay of her hazy convictions.

MONA: Darling, it's so good to see you again!

BUZZ: You don't know how I've missed you on that dreary Venus run.

SOUND: *Venetian blind run down, key turned in lock.*

MONA: Was it *very* dull, dearest?

BUZZ: Let's not talk about my humdrum job, darling. Let's talk about us.

SOUND: *Creaking bed.*

Well, the program was back to normal at last. That evening Mrs. Garvy tried to ask again whether her husband was sure about those rockets, but he was dozing right through *Take It and Stick It,* so she watched the screen and forgot the puzzle.

She was still rocking with laughter at the gag line, "Would you buy it for a quarter?" when the commercial went on for the detergent powder she always faithfully loaded her dishwasher with on the first of every month.

The announcer displayed mountains of suds from a tiny piece of the stuff and coyly added, "Of course, Cleano don't lay around for you to pick up like the soap root on Venus, but it's pretty cheap and it's almost pretty near just as good. So for us plain folks who ain't lucky enough to live up there on Venus, Cleano is the real cleaning stuff!"

Then the chorus went into their "Cleano-is-the-stuff" jingle, but Mrs. Garvy didn't hear it. She was a stubborn woman, but it occurred to her that she was very sick indeed. She didn't want to worry her husband. The next day she quietly made an appointment with her family freud.

In the waiting room she picked up a fresh new copy of *Readers Pablum* and put it down with a faint palpitation. The lead article, according to the table of contents on the cover, was titled "The Most Memorable Venusian I Ever Met."

"The freud will see you now," said the nurse, and Mrs. Garvy tottered into his office.

His traditional glasses and whiskers were reassuring. She choked out the ritual, "Freud, forgive me, for I have neuroses."

He chanted the antiphonal, "Tut, my dear girl, what seems to be the trouble?"

"I got like a hole in the head," she quavered. "I seem to forget all kinds of things. Things like everybody seems to know and I don't."

"Well, that happens to everybody occasionally, my dear. I suggest a vacation on Venus."

The freud stared, openmouthed, at the empty chair. His nurse came in and demanded, "Hey, you see how she scrammed? What was the matter with *her?*"

He took off his glasses and whiskers meditatively. "You can search me. I told her she should maybe try a vacation on Venus." A momentary bafflement came into his face and he dug through his desk drawers until he found a copy of the four-color, profusely illustrated journal of his profession. It had come that morning and he had lip-read it, though looking mostly at the pictures. He leafed to the article "Advantages of the Planet Venus in Rest Cures."

"It's right there," he said.

The nurse looked. "It sure is," she agreed. "Why shouldn't it be?"

"The trouble with these here neurotics," decided the freud, "is that they all the time got to fight reality. Show in the next twitch."

He put on his glasses and whiskers again and forgot Mrs. Garvy and her strange behavior.

"Freud, forgive me, for I have neuroses."

"Tut, my dear girl, what seems to be the trouble?"

Like many cures of mental disorders, Mrs. Garvy's was achieved largely by self-treatment. She disciplined herself sternly out of the crazy notion that there had been only one rocket ship and that one a failure. She could join without wincing, eventually, in any conversation on the desirability of Venus as a place to retire, on its fabulous floral profusion. Finally she went to Venus.

All her friends were trying to book passage with the Evening Star Travel and Real Estate Corporation, but naturally the demand was crushing. She considered herself lucky to get a seat at last for the two-week summer cruise. The spaceship took off from a place called Los Alamos, New Mexico. It looked just like all the spaceships on television and in the picture magazines but was more comfortable than you would expect.

Mrs. Garvy was delighted with the fifty or so fellow-passengers assembled before takeoff. They were from all over the country and she had a distinct impression that they were on the brainy side. The captain, a tall, hawk-faced, impressive fellow named Ryan Something-or-other, welcomed them aboard and trusted that their trip would be a memorable one. He regretted that there would be nothing to see because, "due to the meteorite season," the ports would be dogged down. It was disappointing, yet reassuring that the line was taking no chances.

There was the expected momentary discomfort at takeoff and then two monotonous days of droning travel through space to be whiled away in the lounge at cards or craps. The landing was a routine bump and the voyagers were issued tablets to swallow to immunize them against any minor ailments.

When the tablets took effect, the lock was opened, and Venus was theirs.

It looked much like a tropical island on Earth, except for a blanket of cloud overhead. But it had a heady, otherworldly quality that was intoxicating and glamorous.

The ten days of the vacation were suffused with a hazy magic. The soap root, as advertised, was free and sudsy. The fruits, mostly tropical varieties transplanted from Earth, were delightful. The simple shelters provided by the travel company were more than adequate for the balmy days and nights.

It was with sincere regret that the voyagers filed again into the ship and swallowed more tablets doled out to counteract and sterilize any Venus illnesses they might unwittingly communicate to Earth.

Vacationing was one thing. Power politics was another.

At the Pole, a small man was in a soundproof room, his face deathly pale and his body limp in a straight chair.

In the American Senate Chamber, Senator Hull-Mendoza (Synd., N. Cal.) was saying, "Mr. President and gentlemen, I would be remiss in my duty as a legislature if'n I didn't bring to the attention of the au-gust body I see here a perilous situation which is fraught with peril. As is well known to members of this au-gust body, the perfection of space flight has brought with it a situation I can only describe as fraught with peril. Mr. President and gentlemen, now that swift American rockets now traverse the trackless void of space between this planet and our nearest planetarial neighbor in space—and, gentlemen, I refer to Venus, the star of dawn, the brightest jewel in fair Vulcan's diadome—now, I say, I want to inquire what steps are being taken to colonize Venus with a vanguard of patriotic citizens like those minutemen of yore.

"Mr. President and gentlemen! There are in this world nations, envious nations—I do not name Mexico—who by fair means or foul may seek to wrest from Columbia's grasp the torch of freedom of space; nations whose low living standards and innate depravity give them an unfair advantage over the citizens of our fair republic.

"This is my program: I suggest that a city of more than 100,-000 population be selected by lot. The citizens of the fortunate city are to be awarded choice lands on Venus free and clear, to have and to hold and convey to their descendants. And the national government shall provide free transportation to Venus for these citizens. And this program shall continue, city by city, until there has been deposited on Venus a sufficient vanguard of citizens to protect our manifest rights in that planet.

"Objections will be raised, for carping critics we have always with us. They will say there isn't enough steel. They will call it a cheap giveaway. I say there *is* enough steel for *one* city's population to be transferred to Venus, and that is all that is needed. For when the time comes for the second city to be transferred, the first, emptied city can be wrecked for the needed steel! And is it a giveaway? Yes! It is the most glorious giveaway in the history of mankind! Mr. President and gentlemen, there is no time to waste—Venus must be American!"

Black-Kupperman, at the Pole, opened his eyes and said feebly, "The style was a little uneven. Do you think anybody'll notice?"

"You did fine, boy; just fine," Barlow reassured him.

Hull-Mendoza's bill became law.

Drafting machines at the South Pole were busy around the clock and the Pittsburgh steel mills spewed millions of plates into the Los Alamos spaceport of the Evening Star Travel and Real Estate Corporation. It was going to be Los Angeles, for logistic reasons, and the three most accomplished psychokineticists went to Washington and mingled in the crowd at the drawing to make certain that the Los Angeles capsule slithered into the fingers of the blindfolded Senator.

Los Angeles loved the idea and a forest of spaceships began to blossom in the desert. They weren't very good spaceships, but they didn't have to be.

A team at the Pole worked at Barlow's direction on a mail setup. There would have to be letters to and from Venus to keep the slightest taint of suspicion from arising. Luckily Barlow remembered that the problem had been solved once before —by Hitler. Relatives of persons incinerated in the furnaces of Lublin or Majdanek continued to get cheery postal cards.

The Los Angeles flight went off on schedule, under tremendous press, newsreel and television coverage. The world cheered the gallant Angelenos who were setting off on their patriotic voyage to the land of milk and honey. The forest of spaceships thundered up, and up, and out of sight without untoward incident. Billions envied the Angelenos, cramped and on short rations though they were.

Wreckers from San Francisco, whose capsule came up second, moved immediately into the city of the angels for the scrap steel their own flight would require. Senator Hull-Mendoza's constituents could do no less.

The president of Mexico, hypnotically alarmed at this extension of *yanqui imperialismo* beyond the stratosphere, launched his own Venus-colony program.

Across the water it was England versus Ireland, France versus Germany, China versus Russia, India versus Indonesia. Ancient hatreds grew into the flames that were rocket ships assailing the air by hundreds daily.

Dear Ed, how are you? Sam and I are fine and hope you are fine. Is it nice up there like they say with food and close grone on trees? I drove by Springfield yesterday and it sure looked funny all the buildings down but of coarse it is worth it we have to keep the greasers in their place. Do you have any truble with them on Venus? Drop me a line some time. Your loving sister, Alma.

Dear Alma, I am fine and hope you are fine. It is a fine place here fine climate and easy living. The doctor told me today that I seem to be ten years younger. He thinks there is something in the air here keeps people young. We do not have much trouble with the greasers here they keep to theirselves it is just a question of us outnumbering them and staking out the best places for the Americans. In South Bay I know a nice little island that I have been saving for you and Sam with lots of blanket trees and ham bushes. Hoping to see you and Sam soon, your loving brother, Ed.

Sam and Alma were on their way shortly.

Poprob got a dividend in every nation after the emigration had passed the halfway mark. The lonesome stay-at-homes were unable to bear the melancholy of a low population density; their conditioning had been to swarms of their kin. After that point it was possible to foist off the crudest stripped-down accommodations on would-be emigrants; they didn't care.

Black-Kupperman did a final job on President Hull-Mendoza, the last job that genius of hypnotics would ever do on any moron, important or otherwise.

Hull-Mendoza, panic stricken by his presidency over an emptying nation, joined his constituents. The *Independence,* aboard which traveled the national government of America, was the most elaborate of all the spaceships—bigger, more comfortable, with a lounge that was handsome, though cramped, and cloakrooms for Senators and Representatives. It went, however, to the same place as the others and Black-Kupperman killed himself, leaving a note that stated he "couldn't live with my conscience."

The day after the American President departed, Barlow flew into a rage. Across his specially built desk were supposed to flow all Poprob high-level documents, and this thing—this outrageous thing—called Poprob*term* apparently had got into the executive stage before he had even had a glimpse of it!

He buzzed for Rogge-Smith, his statistician. Rogge-Smith seemed to be at the bottom of it. Poprobterm seemed to be about first and second and third derivatives, whatever they were. Barlow had a deep distrust of anything more complex than what he called an "average."

While Rogge-Smith was still at the door, Barlow snapped, "What's the meaning of this? Why haven't I been consulted? How far have you people got and why have you been working on something I haven't authorized?"

"Didn't want to bother you, Chief," said Rogge-Smith. "It

was really a technical matter, kind of a final cleanup. Want to come and see the work?"

Mollified, Barlow followed his statistician down the corridor.

"You still shouldn't have gone ahead without my okay," he grumbled. "Where the hell would you people have been without me?"

"That's right, Chief. We couldn't have swung it ourselves; our minds just don't work that way. And all that stuff you knew from Hitler—it wouldn't have occurred to us. Like poor Black-Kupperman."

They were in a fair-sized machine shop at the end of a slight upward incline. It was cold. Rogge-Smith pushed a button that started a motor, and a flood of arctic light poured in as the roof parted slowly. It showed a small spaceship with the door open.

Barlow gaped as Rogge-Smith took him by the elbow and his other boys appeared: Swenson-Swenson, the engineer; Tsutsugimushi-Duncan, his propellants man; Kalb-French, advertising.

"In you go, Chief," said Tsutsugimushi-Duncan. "This is Poprobterm."

"But I'm the world Dictator!"

"You bet, Chief. You'll be in history, all right—but this is necessary, I'm afraid."

The door was closed. Acceleration slammed Barlow cruelly to the metal floor. Something broke, and warm, wet stuff, salty tasting, ran from his mouth to his chin. Arctic sunlight through a port suddenly became a fierce lancet stabbing at his eyes; he was out of the atmosphere.

Lying twisted and broken under the acceleration, Barlow realized that some things had not changed, that Jack Ketch was never asked to dinner however many shillings you paid him to do your dirty work, that murder will out, that crime pays only temporarily.

The last thing he learned was that death is the end of pain.

Fiddler's Green

Fiddler's Green

RICHARD McKENNA

*Here is another story about an idea-obsessed man like Hein-
lein's D. D. Harriman. But where "The Man Who Sold the
Moon" goes up, this story goes sideways, into a doubtful world
that may or may not exist beside our own.*

On the morning of the fifth day Kinross woke knowing that
before the sun went down one of them would be eaten. He wondered what it would be like.

All yesterday the eight dungaree- and khaki-clad seamen had
wrangled about it in thirst-cracked voices. Eight chance-spared
survivors adrift without food or water in a disabled launch, riding the Indian Ocean swells to a sea anchor. The S.S. *Ixion*,
6,000-ton tramp sneaking contraband explosives to the Reds in
Sumatra, had blown up and sunk in ten minutes the night of
23 December, 1959. Fat John Kruger, the radioman, had not
gotten off a distress signal. Four days under the vertical sun of
Capricorn, off the steamer lanes and a thousand miles from
land, no rain and little hope of any, reason enough and time for
dark thinking.

Kinross, lean and wiry in the faded dungarees of an engineer,
looked at the others and wondered how it would go. They were
in the same general positions as yesterday, still sleeping or pretending to sleep. He looked at the stubbled faces, cracked lips
and sunken eyes and he knew how they felt. Skintight and

159

wooden, tongue stuck to teeth and palate, the dry throat a horror of whistling breath and every cell in the body clamoring.

Thirst was worse than pain, he thought. Weber's law for pain. Pain increased as the logarithm of what caused it; a man could keep pace. But thirst was exponential. It went up and up and never stopped. Yesterday they had turned the corner and today something had to give.

Little Fay, of the rat face and bulging forehead, had begun it yesterday. Human flesh boiled in seawater, he had said, took up most of the salt and left a nourishing broth fresh enough to drink. Kinross remembered that false bit of sea lore being whispered among the apprentices on his first cruise long years ago, but now it was no tidbit for the morbid curiosity of youth. It shouldered into the boat like a ninth passenger sitting between him and all the others.

"No leedle sticks, Fay," the giant Swede Kerbeck had growled. "If we haf to eat somebody we yoost eat you."

Kinross looked at Kerbeck now, sitting just to the left on the stern grating with one huge, bronzed arm draped over the useless tiller. He wore a white singlet and khaki pants and Kinross wondered if he was awake. There was no telling about Kruger just across from him either. The radioman had slept that way, with puffy, hairless hands clasped across the ample stomach under the white sweatshirt, for most of the four days. He had not joined in the restless moving about and talking of the others, stirring only to remoisten the handkerchief he kept on top of his almost hairless head.

"You won't eat me!" Fay had squalled. "Nor draw lots, neither. Let's have a volunteer, somebody that's to blame for this fix."

Fay had blamed Kerbeck because the boat was not provisioned. The Swede retorted angrily that he knew it had been so when they had left Mossamedes. Fay blamed Kinross because the launch engine was disabled. Kinross, skin crawling, pointed out mildly enough that the battery had been up and the diesel okay two days before the sinking. Then Fay turned on Kruger for failing to send out a distress signal. Kruger had insisted that the blast had cut him off from the radio shack and that if he had not started at once to swing out the launch possibly none of them would have survived.

Kinross looked forward now at Fay sleeping beside the engine. On the opposite side, also asleep, was Bo Bo, the huge Senegalese stoker, clad only in dungaree shorts. It had seemed to Kinross yesterday that Fay had some sort of understanding with the powerful Negro. Bo Bo had rumbled assent to Fay's accusations and so had the three men in the forward compartment.

Kruger, surprisingly, had resolved the threat. Speaking without heat in his high-pitched, penetrating voice, he told them: touch one of us aft here and all three will fight. Kerbeck had nodded and unshipped the heavy brass tiller.

While they wavered, Kruger went over to the attack. "Single out only one man, why don't you, Fay? Who's had the most life already? Take the oldest."

Silva, the wizened, popeyed Portygee in the bow, creaked an outraged protest. Beside him the thickset Mexican Garcia laughed harshly.

"Okay, then who's going to die soonest? Take the weakest," said Kruger. "Take Whelan."

The kid Whelan, also in the bow, found strength to whimper an agonized plea. Kinross, remembering yesterday, looked at the two men sprawled in the bow. He half thought the Mexican was looking back at him. His stocky, dungaree-clad body seemed braced against the pitch of the boat as it rode the swells, unlike the flaccidity of the old Portygee.

It was Garcia who had said finally, "You lose, Fay. You'll have to take your chance on drawing lots with the rest of us. I'll line up with Kruger."

The three men aft had voted against drawing lots but agreed to go along with the majority. Then Kruger found fault with every method suggested, pointing out how fraud could enter. The day wore out in wrangling. Kinross thought back to the curiously unstrained, liquid quality of Kruger's light voice as contrasted with the harsh croaking of the others. He had seemed in better shape than the rest and somehow in control of things.

Just before sunset, when they had put it off until next day and while Silva was fingering his rosary and praying for rain, the kid Whelan had seen green fields off to port. He shouted his discovery, flailed his body across the gunwale and sank like a stone.

"There you go, Kruger!" Fay had husked bitterly. "Up to now that fat carcass of yours had one chance in eight." Kinross remembered his own twinge of regret.

Kinross felt the rising sun sucking at his dry eyeballs and thirst flamed three dimensionally through him, consuming sense and reason. He knew that today would be the day and that he wanted it so. He glanced forward again and the Mexican was really looking at him out of red-rimmed eyes.

"I know what you're thinking, Kinross," he called aft. His voice roused the others. They began sitting up.

Little Fay led off, head bobbing and jerking, red eyes demanding agreement. "Draw lots," he said. "No more palaver. Right now or none of us will see sunset."

Kruger agreed. He clinked several shillings in his hand and passed them around to be looked at. Only one was a George V. Blindfold Bo Bo, the stupidest one, he proposed, and let him pick coins out of the bailing bucket one by one. Fay would sit back to back with him and as soon as Bo Bo had a coin up, but before anyone had seen it, Fay would call the name of the man who was to get it. Whoever got the beard would be the victim.

It was agreed. Silva asked for time to pray and Fay mocked at him. The little man perched on the engine housing, his back against Bo Bo, and looked around calculatingly. Kinross could feel the malice in his glance.

Law of averages, Kinross was thinking. In the middle of the series. Number three or four. Nonsense, of course.

Apparently Fay thought so too. When the Negro fumbled up the first coin and asked, "Who gets this one?" Fay answered, "I'll take it." It was a queen, and Kinross hated Fay.

The next one Fay awarded to Bo Bo and the giant black was safe. For the next, while Kinross held his breath, Fay named Kerbeck. Also safe. Each time a sigh went through the boat.

Then the fourth trial and Fay called out "Kinross." The engineer blinked his dry eyes and strained to see the coin in the thick black fingers. He knew first from the relief on Silva's face and then he saw it plainly himself. It was the beard.

No one would meet his eyes but Fay and Bo Bo. Kinross hardly knew what he felt. The thought came, An end of torment and then, I'll die clean. But he still dully resented Fay's nasty air of triumph.

Fay opened his clasp knife and slid the bailing bucket next to the engine. "Hold him across the engine housing, Bo Bo," he ordered. "We can't afford to lose any of the blood."

"Damn you, Fay, I'm still alive," Kinross said. His gaunt features worked painfully and his Adam's apple twitched in a futile attempt at swallowing.

"Knock me in the head first, mates," he pleaded. "You, Kerbeck, use the tiller."

"Yah," said the Swede, still not returning his glance. "Now yoost you wait a leedle, Fay."

"All of you listen to me," Kruger said. "I know a way we can get as much fresh water as we can drink, in just a few minutes, and nobody has to die." His light voice was effortless, liquid, trickling the words into their startled ears.

All hands looked at Kruger, suspicious, half hating him for his cool voice and lack of obvious suffering. Kinross felt a thrill of hope.

"I mean it," Kruger said earnestly. "Cold, fresh water is all around us, waiting for us, if we only knew one little thing that we can't quite remember. You felt it all day yesterday. You feel it now."

They stared. Fay ran his thumb back and forth along the edge of the clasp knife. Then Garcia said angrily, "You're nuts, Kruger. Your gyro's tumbled."

"No, Garcia," Kruger said, "I was never saner. I knew this all the time, before the ship blew even, but I had to wait for the right moment. Sleep, not talk, not move, nothing to waste body water, so I could talk when the time came. Now it's here. Now is the time. You feel it, don't you? Listen to me now." Kruger's clear, light voice babbled like water running over stones. He stepped up on the stern grating and looked down at the six men frozen into a tableau around the engine. Kinross noted that his sparse white hair lay smooth and saw a hint of set muscles under the fat face.

"I'll tell you a true story so you can understand easy," Kruger continued. "Long time ago, long ago, in the Tibesti highlands of Africa, some soldiers were lost and dying of thirst, like us now. They went up a valley, a dry wash with bones on the ground, to two big rocks like pillars side by side. They did something there, and when they went between the two big rocks they were in a different world with green trees and running water. All of them lived and afterward some of them came back."

"I heard that story before, somewhere," Kinross said.

Fay jerked toward him. "A lie, Kinross! You're welshing! Kruger, it's a stall!"

"I didn't believe the story," Kinross said mildly. "I don't believe it now."

"I do believe it," Kruger said sharply. "I *know* it's true. I've been there. I've looked into that world. We can do just what those soldiers did."

"Bilge, Kruger!" Garcia growled. "How could there be such a world? How could you get in it?"

"I didn't get in, Garcia. I could see and hear, but when I walked into it everything faded around me."

"Then what good—"

"Wait. Let me finish. I lacked something we have here. I was alone, not half dead with thirst, and I couldn't all the way believe what I saw and heard."

"So what does—"

"Wait. Hear me out. Believe me, Garcia, all of you. There are seven of us here and no other humans in a thousand miles. Our need is more than we can stand. We can believe. We must believe or die. Trust me. I know."

The Mexican scratched the black stubble along his heavy jaw. "Kruger, you know I think you're crazy as Whelan," he said slowly.

"Whelan wasn't crazy," Kruger said. "He was just a kid and couldn't wait. He saw a green meadow. Believe me now, all of you, if we all had seen that meadow *at the same time Whelan saw it* we would be walking in it right this minute!"

"Yah, like Whelan now is walking," Kerbeck put in.

"We *killed* Whelan, do you understand? We killed him because we couldn't believe what he saw and so it wasn't true." The light, bubbling voice splashed with vehemence.

"I think I get you, Kruger," Garcia said slowly.

"I don't," Kinross said, "unless you want us all to die in a mass hallucination."

"I want us to *live* in a mass hallucination. We can. We must or die. Believe me. I *know* this."

"Then you mean go out in a happy dream, not knowing when the end comes?"

"Damn you, Kinross, you've got a little education. That's why it's so hard for you to understand. But let me tell you, this world, this Indian Ocean, is a hallucination too. The whole human race has been a million years building it up, training itself to see and believe, making the world strong enough to stand any kind of shock. It's like a dream we can't wake up from. But believe me, Kinross, you *can* wake up from this nightmare. Trust me. I know the way."

Kinross thought, I'm a fool to argue. It's a delay for me, in any case. But maybe . . . maybe . . . Aloud he said, "What you say . . . Yes, I know the thought . . . but all anyone can do is talk about it. There's no way to *act* on it."

"The more word juggling the less action, *that's* why! But we can act, like the soldiers of Tibesti."

"A myth. A romantic legend."

"A true story. I've been there, seen, heard. I know. It was long ago, before the Romans, when the web of the world was not so closely woven as now. There were fewer men like you in the world then, Kinross."

"Kruger," Kerbeck broke in, "I hear that story one time myself. You been *sure* now, Kruger?"

"Yes, sure, sure, sure. Kerbeck, I *know* this."

"I go along, Kruger," the big Swede said firmly. Garcia said, "I'm trying, Kruger. Keep talking."

The clear, light voice resumed its liquid cadence. "You, Kinross, you're the obstacle. You're the brain, the engineer with a slide rule on the log desk. You're a symbol and you hold back the rest of us. You've got to believe or we'll cut your throat and try with six men. I mean it, Kinross!"

"I want to believe, Kruger. Something in me knows better, but I can feel it slipping. Talk it up. Help me."

"All right. You know all this already. You're not learning something new but remembering something you were trained to forget. But listen. Reality cracks open sometimes. Indians on vision quest, saints in the Theban desert, martyrs in the flame. Always deprivation, pain long-drawn out, like us here, like Whelan yesterday. But always the world heals itself, clanks back together, with the power of the people who will not see, will not believe, because they think they can't believe. Like you helped to kill Whelan yesterday.

"You know something about electricity. Well, it's like a field, strongest where the most people are. No miracles in cities. People hold the world together. They're trained from the cradle up to hold it together. Our language is the skeleton of the world. The words we talk with are bricks and mortar to build a prison in which we turn cannibal and die of thirst. Kinross, do you follow me?"

"Yes, I follow you, but—"

"No buts. Listen. Here we are, 18 south 82 east, seven men in ten million square miles of emptiness. The reality field is weak here. It's a *thin spot* in the world, Kinross, don't you understand? We're at the limit of endurance. We don't care if the public world comes apart in a thousand places if only we can break out of it here, save our lives, drink cool, fresh water . . ."

Kinross felt a shiver of dread run over him. "Hold on," he said. "I think I do care about the public world coming apart . . ."

"Hah! You begin to believe!" The clear, smooth voice fountained in triumph. "It soaks in, under the words and behind the thinking. It scares you. All right. Believe me now, Kinross. I've studied this for half my life. We will not harm the public world when we steal ourselves from it. We will leave a little opening, as in the Tibesti, but who will ever find it?"

The old Portygee waved his skinny arms and croaked. Then he found his voice and said, "I know the story of Tibesti, Kruger. My fathers have lived in Mogador for six hundred years. It is a Berber story and it is unholy."

"But true, Silva," Kruger said softly. "That's all we care about. We all know it's true."

"You want a black miracle, Kruger. God will not let you do it. We will lose our souls."

"We will take personal possession of our souls, Silva. That's what I've been telling Kinross. God is spread pretty thin at 18 south 82 east."

"No, no," the old man wailed. "It is better we pray for a white miracle, a ship, rain to fall . . ."

"Whatever lets me live is a white miracle," Garcia said ex-

plosively. "Kruger's right, Silva. I been sabotaging every prayer
you made the last four days just by being here. It's the only way
for us, Silva."

"You hear, Kinross?" Kruger asked. "They believe. They're
ready. They can't wait on you much longer."

"I believe," Kinross said, swallowing painfully, "but I have to
know *how*. Okay, black magic, but what words, what thoughts,
what acts?"

"No words. No thoughts. They are walls to break through.
One only act. An unnameable, unthinkable act. I know what
bothers you, Kinross. Listen now. I mean group hypnosis, a
shared hallucination, something done every day somewhere in
the world. But here there is a thin spot. Here there is no mass of
people to keep the public world intact. Our hallucination will
become the public world to us, with water and fruit and grass.
We've been feeling it for days, all around us, waiting for us . . ."

The men around Kinross murmured and snuffled. An enormous excitement began to stir in him.

"I believe, Kruger. I feel it now. But how do you know what
kind of world . . . ?"

"Damn it, Kinross, it's not a preexistent world. It's only there
potentially. We'll make it up as we go along, put in what we
want . . . a Fiddler's Green."

"Yah," said Kerbeck. "Fiddler's Green. I hear about that too.
Hurry up, Kinross."

"I'm ready," Kinross said. "For sure, I'm ready."

"All right," Kruger said. "Now we cross over, to our own
world and the fresh, cold water. All of you lie down, stretch out
best way you can, like you wanted to rest."

Kinross lay flat in the after compartment, beside Kerbeck.
Kruger looked down at them with his moon face that now
seemed hewn of granite. He swayed against the taffrail to the
regular pitch and dip of the boat.

"Rest," he said. "Don't try, don't strain, or you'll miss it. You,

Kinross, don't try to watch yourself. Rest. Don't think. Let your bellies sag and your fingers come apart . . .

"Your bodies are heavy, too heavy for you. You are sinking flat against the soft wood. You are letting go, sagging down . . ."

Kinross felt the languor and the heaviness. Kruger's voice sounded more distant but still clear, liquid, never stopping.

". . . resting now. Pain is going. Fear is going . . . further away . . . happy . . . sure of things . . . you believe me because I know . . . you trust me because I know . . ."

Kinross felt a mouth twitch and it was his own. The inert, heavy body was somehow his own also. There was a singsong rise and fall, like swells, in Kruger's pattering, babbling voice.

". . . resting . . . so-o-o relaxed . . . can't blink your eyes . . . try . . . no matter how hard you try . . ."

Kinross felt a tingling in the hands and feet of the body that could not blink its eyes. But of course . . .

". . . jaws are stuck . . . try hard as you can . . . can't open . . . hand coming up . . . up and up and up . . . as a feather . . . up and up . . . try . . . hard as you can . . . *Kinross,* try to put your hand down!"

The hand floated in Kinross' field of view. It had something to do with him. He willed it to drop but it would not obey. His vision was pulsating to the rhythm of the swells and the fading in and out of Kruger's voice. First he saw Kruger far off but clear and distinct, as if through the wrong way of a telescope, and the voice was clear, burbling, like water falling down rocks. Then the fat man rushed closer and closer, looming larger and larger, becoming more hazy and indistinct as he filled the sky, and the voice faded out. Then the back swing . . .

". . . hands going down . . . relaxed on the soft, restful wood . . . all relaxed . . . almost ready now . . . stay relaxed until I give you the signal . . . HEAR THIS NOW: for the signal I will clap my hands twice and say, 'Act.' You will know

what to do and all together you will do it . . . take me with you
. . . each one, reach out a hand and take me along . . . blind
where you see, deaf where you hear . . . must not fail to take
me . . . REMEMBER THAT.

". . . sea is gone, sky is gone, nothing here but the boat and
a gray mist. *Kinross,* what do you see?"

Gray mist swirling, black boat, no color, no detail, a sketch
in a dream . . . no motion . . . no more pulsation of things
. . . the endless plash and murmur of the voice, and then another voice, "I see gray mist all around."

"Gray mist all around, and in the mist now one thing. One
thing you see. Silva, what do you see?"

"A face. I see a face."

"Fay, you see the face. Describe the face."

"A giant's face. Bigger than the boat. It is worried and stern."

"Kerbeck, you see the face. How is it shaped?"

"Round and fat. A leedle fuzz of beard there is."

"Garcia, you see the face. Tell us the colors."

"Eyes blue. Hair almost white. Skin smooth and white. Lips
thin and red."

"Kinross, you see the face. Describe it in detail."

"Thin eyebrows, high arched, white against white. Broad
forehead. Bulging cheeks. Flat nose, large, flaring nostrils. Wide
mouth, thin lips."

"Bo Bo, you see the face. Who is it, Bo Bo? Tell us who it is."

"It is you, Boss Kruger."

"Yes," said the Face, the great lips moving. "Now you are
ready. Now you are close. Remember the signal. You have let
go of yourselves by giving me control. Now I will do for you
what no man can do for himself: I will set you free. Remember
the signal. Remember your orders.

"You are thirsty. Thirst claws in your throats, tears at your
guts. You have to drink. You don't care, don't think. You would
drink the blood of your children and of your fathers and not

care. Water, cold, wet, splashing water, rivers of water, all around you, waiting for you, green trees and grass and water.

"You already know how to get to it. You always knew, from before time you knew, and now you remember and you are ready for the signal. All together and take me with you. You know what to do. Not in words, not in thoughts, not in pictures, deeper, older, far underneath those, you know. Before the word, before the thought, there was the act."

The great mouth gaped on the final word and green light flashed in its inner darkness. The mists swirled closer and Kinross floated there on an intolerable needlepoint of thirst. Great eyes blue-blazing, with dreadful intensity, the Face spoke again.

"IN THE BEGINNING IS THE ACT!"

It shouted the last word tremendously. There was a sharp double clap of thunder and green lightnings played in the cavernous mouth which yawned wide on the word until it filled the field of vision. The green lightnings firmed into trees, mossy rocks, a brawling stream . . . Kinross tugged the heavy body after him by one arm, splash, splash, in the cold, clear water.

Kinross drank greedily. The coolness flowed into him and out along his arteries and the fire died. He could see the others kneeling in or beside the clear stream running smoothly over rounded pebbles and white sand. Then a great weariness came over him. He drank again briefly, lay down on the smooth turf beside the stream and slept.

When he awoke, Garcia was sitting beside him eating bananas and offered him some. Kinross looked around while he was eating. Level ground extended perhaps ten yards on either side of the little stream; then convexly curved banks rose abruptly for a hundred feet. In the diffuse, watery light the land was green with grass and the darker green of trees and bushes. The colors were flat and homogeneous. There were no random irregularities on the land such as gullies or rock outcrops. The trees were blurred masses never quite in direct view. The grass was blurred and vague. It was like the time he had had his eyes dilated for refraction. But he could see Garcia plainly enough.

Kinross shook his head and blinked. Garcia chuckled.

"Don't let it bother you," he said. "Why be curious?"

"Can't help it, I guess," Kinross replied. Then he spied Kruger's supine form to his left and said, "Let's wake Kruger."

"Tried it already," the Mexican said. "He ain't dead and he ain't alive. Go see what you think."

Kinross felt a pang of alarm. Kruger was needed here. He rose, walked over and examined the body. It was warm and pliant but unresponsive. He shook his head again.

Curses broke out behind the indefinite shrubbery on the bank across the stream. Fay's voice. Then the little man came into view beside the huge Negro. They had papayas and guavas.

"Kruger still asleep?" Fay asked. "Damn him and his world. Everything I pick in it is full of worm holes and rotten spots."

"Try some of my bananas here," Garcia said. Fay ate one and muttered reluctant gratification.

"We've got to do something about Kruger," Kinross said. "Let's have a conference."

"Silva! Kerbeck! Come in!" the Mexican shouted.

The two men came down the bank. Kerbeck was eating a large turnip with the aid of his belt knife. Silva fingered his rosary.

"Kruger's in a kind of trance, I think," Kinross said. "We'll have to build a shelter for him."

"There won't be any weather here," Silva said. "No day, no night, no shadows. This place is unholy. It isn't real."

"Nonsense," Kinross objected. "It's real enough." He kicked at the turf, without leaving any mark on it.

"No!" Silva cried. "Nothing's really here. I can't get close to a tree trunk. They slide away from me." Kerbeck and Fay mumbled in agreement.

"Let's catch Silva a tree," Garcia said with a laugh. "That

little one over there. Spread out in a circle around it and keep looking at it so it can't get away."

Kinross suspected from their expressions that the others shared his own fearful excitement, his sense of the forbidden. All but the mocking Garcia. They surrounded the tree and Kinross could see Kerbeck beyond it well enough, but the smooth, green trunk did seem to slide out of the way of a focused glance.

"We got it for you, Silva," Garcia said. "Go in now. Take hold of it and smell it."

Silva approached the tree gingerly. His wrinkled old face had a wary look and his lips were moving. "You're not me, tree," he said softly. "You've got to be yourself by yourself. You're too smooth and too green."

Suddenly the old man embraced the trunk and held his face a foot away, peering intently. His voice rose higher. "Show me spots and cracks and dents and rough places and bumps . . ."

Fear thrilled Kinross. He heard a far-off roaring noise and the luminous overcast descended in gray swirls. The light dimmed and the flat greens of the landscape turned grayish.

"Silva, stop it!" he shouted.

"Knock it off, Silva!" cried the Mexican.

". . . show me whiskers and spines and wrinkles and lines and pits . . ." Silva's voice, unheeding, rose higher in pitch.

The mists swirled closer. There came a light, slapping, rustling sound. Then a voice spoke, clear and silvery, out of the air above them.

"Silva! Stop that, Silva, or I'll blind you!"

"Unholy!" Silva shrieked. "I will look *through* you!"

"Silva! Be blind!" commanded the silvery voice. It seemed almost to sing the words.

Silva choked off and stood erect. Then he clapped his hands to his eyes and screamed, "I'm blind. Shipmates, it's dark! Isn't it dark? The sun went out . . ."

Kinross, trembling, walked over to Silva as the mists dispersed again.

"Easy, Silva. You'll be all right soon," he comforted the sobbing old man.

"That voice," Garcia said softly. "I know that voice."

"Yes," said Bo Bo. "It was Boss Kruger."

Okay, Kinross and Garcia agreed, no looking closely at anything. The awareness of the others seemed already so naturally unfocused that they could hardly understand the meaning of the taboo. Kinross did not try to explain. Fay proposed that he stay to look after Silva and Kruger, provided that the others would bring food, since all that he picked for himself was inedible.

"Kinross, let's go for a walk," Garcia said. "You haven't looked around yet."

They walked downstream. "What happened just now?" Garcia asked.

"I don't know," Kinross said. "It was Kruger's voice, all right. Maybe we're really still back in that boat and Kruger is making us dream this."

"If that's so, I don't want to come out of it," the Mexican said feelingly, "but I don't think so. *I'm* real, if this world isn't. When I pinch myself it hurts. My insides work."

"Me too. But I could sure smell salt water and diesel oil for a few seconds there. Silva almost made us slip back."

"Kruger was right, I guess," the Mexican said slowly, "but it's tough on poor old Silva."

They walked on in silence beside the rippling stream. Then Kinross said, "I've got a hankering for apples. Wonder if there are any here?"

"Sure," said Garcia, "just over here." He crossed the stream and pointed out apples on a low-hanging bough. They were large, bright red and without blemish. Kinross ate several with relish before he noticed that they had no seeds and remarked on it to the Mexican.

"Watch it," warned Garcia. "No looking close."

"Well, they taste good," Kinross said.

"I'll tell you something," the Mexican said abruptly. "There's only one tree here. You find it wherever you look for it and it's always got what you want growing on it. I found that out while you were asleep. I experimented."

Kinross felt the strange dread run over him gently. "That might be dangerous," he warned.

"I didn't try to make it be two trees," the Mexican assured him. "Something already told me I shouldn't look too close.

"There's something else, too," Garcia said, when Kinross did not answer. "I'll let you find it out for yourself. Let's climb this bank and see what's on top."

"Good idea," Kinross agreed, leading off.

The bank was steeply convex, smooth and regular. Kinross climbed at an angle in order to have a gentler grade and suddenly realized that he was nearly down to the stream again. He swore mildly at his inattention and turned back up the slope, more directly this time. After a few minutes he looked back to see how far down the stream was and realized with a shock that he was really looking up the bank. He looked in front of him again and the floodplain of the little stream was almost at his feet. He could not remember which way he had been going and panic fingered at him.

"Give up," Garcia said. "Do you feel it now?"

"I feel something, but what it is . . ."

"Feel *lost*, maybe?" the Mexican asked.

"No, not lost. Camp, or anyway Kruger, is that way." Kinross pointed upstream.

"Sure it isn't downstream?"

"Sure as sure," Kinross insisted.

"Well, go on back and I'll meet you there," the Mexican said, starting off downstream. "Look for landmarks on the way," he called over his shoulder.

Kinross didn't see any landmarks. Nothing stood out in any

large, general way. As he approached the group around Kruger's body he saw Garcia coming along the bank from the opposite direction.

"Garcia, does this damn creek run in a circle?" he called in surprise.

"No," said the Mexican. "You feel it now, don't you? This world is all one place and you can't cut it any finer. Every time you go up the bank it leads you down to the stream bed. Whichever way you walk along the stream, you come to Kruger."

Kinross woke up to see Kerbeck splashing water over his head in the stream. Garcia was sleeping nearby and Kinross woke him.

"What'll we eat this morning?" he asked. "Papayas, d'ye think?"

"Bacon and eggs," the Mexican yawned. "Let's find a bacon and egg tree."

"Don't joke," Kinross said. "Kruger won't like it."

"Oh well, papayas," Garcia said. He walked down to the stream and splashed water in his face. Then the two men walked up the little valley.

"What do you mean, 'this morning,'" Garcia asked suddenly. "I don't remember any night."

The night was pitch black. "Kinross," Garcia called out of the blackness.

"Yes?"

"Remember how it got suddenly dark just now?"

"Yes, but it was a long while back."

"Bet you won't remember it in the morning."

"Will there be a morning?" Kinross asked. "I've been awake forever." Sleep was a defense.

"Wake up, Kinross," Garcia said, shaking him. "It's a fine morning to gather papayas."

"Is it a morning?" Kinross asked. "I don't remember any night."

"We gotta talk," the Mexican grunted. "Unless we want to sing to ourselves like Kerbeck or moan and cry like Silva over there."

"Silva? I thought that was the wind."

"No wind in this world, Kinross."

Kinross bit into papaya pulp. "How long have we been here, do you think?" he asked Garcia.

"It's been a while."

"I can't remember any whole day. Silva was blinded. Was that yesterday? Kerbeck stopped talking and started singing. Was that yesterday?"

"I don't know," the Mexican said. "It seems like everything happened yesterday. My beard grew half an inch yesterday."

Kinross rubbed his own jaw. The brown whiskers were long enough to lie flat and springy.

He was walking alone when a whisper came from just behind his head. "Kinross, this is Kruger. Come and talk to me."

Kinross whirled to face nothing. "Where?" he whispered.

"Just start walking," came the reply, still from behind.

Kinross started up the bank. He climbed steadily, remembering vaguely a previous attempt at doing so, and suddenly looked back. The stream was far below, lost under the convex curve of the bank that was really a valley wall. Miles across the valley was the other wall, curving up in countersymmetry to the slope he was climbing. He pressed on, wondering, to come out on a height of land like a continental divide. Smooth, sweeping curves fell off enormously on either hand into hazy obscurity.

He walked along it to the right. It had the same terrain of vague grass and indefinite shrubs and trees, flat shades of green with nothing standing out. After a while he saw a gently rounded height rising to his left, but the whisper directed him down a long gentle slope to his right and then up a shorter, steeper slope to a high plain. There was a vast curve to it, almost too great to sense, but the horizon on the left seemed lower than that on the right. He walked on steadily.

Kinross seemed tireless to himself. He did not know how long he had been walking. He climbed another abrupt slope and a series of shallow but enormous transverse swales replaced the rounded plain. The land still curved downward to the left. Far ahead was a clear mountain shape.

It, too, was green. He started up a concave slope which turned steeply convex so that he seemed to be defying gravity as he climbed it. Then the slope leveled off considerably and he was approaching a wall of dark forest beyond which a reddish-black rock pinnacle soared into the sky.

He pushed into the forest, to find it only a half-mile belt of woods which gave way to a desert. This was a dull red, gently rising plain over which were scattered huge reddish boulders many times higher than his head. He picked his way between them over ground which seemed hot and vibrating until he came to the base of the rock pinnacle. As he neared it a pattern of intersecting curves on top indicated that it was cratered.

It was a vertical climb, but Kinross made it with the same inexplicable ease as the earlier ones. He descended a little way into the crater and said, "Here I am, Kruger."

Kruger's natural voice spoke out of the air from a point directly ahead. "Sit down, Kinross. Tell me what you think."

Kinross sat cross legged on the rough rock surface. "I think you're running this show, Kruger," he said. "I think maybe you saved my life. Past that, I don't know what to think."

"You're curious about me, aren't you? Well, so am I. Partly I make up the rules and partly I discover them. This is a very primitive world, Kinross."

"It's prehuman," Kinross said. "You took us deep."

"Had to, for people like us."

"You're just a voice in the air to me," Kinross said. "How do you experience yourself?"

"I have a body, but I suppose it's a private hallucination. I can't animate my real body. It must be some result of my not having been in deep trance when we crossed over."

"Is that good or bad, for you?"

"Depends. I have unique powers but also special responsibilities. For instance, I am forced to animate this world and my capacity is limited. That's the reason for the taboo on looking closely or trying to use things."

"Oh. Silva then . . . can you restore his sight?"

"Yes, his blindness is purely functional. But I won't. He'd destroy us all. He'd look and look until our world fell apart. He gave me a bad time, Kinross."

"I was scared too. Tell me, what would have happened if—?"

"Back in the boat, perhaps. Or some kind of limbo."

"Is your existence purely mental now, Kruger?"

"No. I told you, I have an hallucinated body which seems perfectly real to me. But it cannot use the substance of this world the way you and the others do. Kinross, I still have the same thirst I had when we came over. It is like—what you remember. I can't quench it and I can't endure it. This world is a kind of Hell to me . . ."

"Holy Moses, Kruger! That's too bad. Can we do anything?"

"I have one hope. It's why I brought you here."

"Tell me."

"I want to put you into still deeper hypnosis, deep as man can go. I want to set up such a deep rapport between us that I will share with you the animation of your body and you will share with me the animation of this world. Then I will be able to eat and drink."

"Granting it's possible, how would that seem to me?"

"You mean animating the world? I can't describe it to you. A joy beyond words."

"No, I mean you in my body. How do you know I won't have your thirst then? Which of us would be dominant?"

"We could quench the thirst, that's the point. I would grant you dominance in the body and retain my dominance in the world."

Kinross tugged at his shaggy brown hair. "I don't know," he said slowly. "You scare me, Kruger. Why *me?*"

"Because of your mind, Kinross. You're an engineer. We must build natural law into this world if I am ever to have rest. I need intimate access to your world-picture so that it can inform this world."

"Why can't I help you just as I am?"

"You can, but not enough. I need to superimpose your world-picture on mine in complete interaction."

Decision welled up in Kinross. "No," he said. "Take one of the others. Except for Garcia and maybe Silva they hardly seem to know they're alive, but they eat and drink."

"I've taken a large part of them into the world already, and something of you and Garcia too. But I want you intact, as a unity."

"No."

"Think of the power and the joy. It is indescribable, Kinross."

"No."

"Think of what you can lose. I can blind you, paralyze you."

"I'll grant that. But you won't. In a way I can't explain I know you need us, Kruger. You need our eyes and ears and our understanding minds in order to see and appreciate this world of yours. Your sight dimmed when you blinded Silva."

"That isn't wholly true. I needed you absolutely in order to get across, in order to form this world, but not now."

"I'll gamble you're lying, Kruger. You don't have a large enough population to afford playing tyrant."

"Don't underestimate me, Kinross. You don't know me and you never can. I have a fierce will in this matter that must not be denied. From childhood on I have worked toward this culmination with absolute ruthlessness. I deliberately did not send a distress message from the *Ixion* because I wanted the chance I got. Does that impress you?"

"Not in your favor, Kruger. So little Ratface was right . . ."

"I don't want your favor or your pity, Kinross. I want your conviction that you cannot stand out against me. I'll tell you more. I planted the bomb in the *Ixion*'s cargo hold. I dumped the food and water out of the launch. I ran down the battery and jammed the fuel pump. I timed the explosion so that you would be just coming off watch. That convinces you. Now you know that you cannot stand out against such a will as mine."

Kinross stood up and squinted his brown eyes into the emptiness before him. "I'm convinced that you made your own world but now you can't get all the way into it. I'm convinced that you should not. Kruger, to hell with you."

"It is my world and I'll come all the way into it in spite of you," Kruger said. "Look at me!" On the command the voice rang out strong and silvery, a great singing.

"You're not there," Kinross said, standing up.

"Yes I am here. Look at me."

The air before Kinross became half visible, a ghostly streaming upward.

"Look at me!" the chiming, silvery voice repeated.

There came a sound like tearing silk. The hair stood up on Kinross' neck and a coldness raced over his skin. The streaming air thickened and eddied, became a surface whorled and contoured in a third dimension, became vibrantly alive, became the shape of a great face.

"Kinross, look at me!" the Face commanded in a voice like great bells.

Kinross took a deep breath. "I learn my lessons well, Kruger," he said in a trembling voice. "You're not there. I don't see you."

He walked directly into the Face and through it, feeling an electric thrill in his cringing flesh as he did so. Then he was clambering down the sheer face of the pinnacle.

As Kinross crossed the high plain on his way back, rain began to fall from the overcast. Gusts of wind buffeted him. There was no surface runoff of the rain and no clear effect of the wind in the indefinite trees and shrubbery. "Kruger's learning," Kinross said to himself. Then darkness came suddenly and he lay down and slept. When he awoke he was back beside the little stream and Garcia told him he had been gone four days.

"Four days?" Kinross asked in surprise. "Doesn't everything still happen yesterday?"

"Not anymore," the Mexican said. "Where in hell have you been?"

"Outside somehow, arguing with Kruger," Kinross said, looking around. "Damn it, this place feels different. And where's Kruger's body and the others?"

"It is different," Garcia said. "I'll tell you. First, Fay found a cave . . ."

The cave was the source of the stream, which now ran out of it, Garcia explained. Fay and Bo Bo had carried Kruger's body into it and now spent most of their time in there. Fay claimed that Kruger awoke at intervals to eat and drink and that he had made Fay his spokesman. Fay and Bo Bo had piled up a cairn of rocks before the cave mouth and had commanded Kerbeck and Garcia to bring fruit and place it there every morning. Silva now sat beside the cairn, rocking and wailing as before.

"I couldn't make Kerbeck understand," Garcia added. "He roams the hillsides now like a wild man. So I've been supplying them by myself."

"The place is bigger," Kinross commented. The valley floor extended now for several hundred yards on either side of the little stream and the walls rose hundreds of feet. The oppressive regularity of outline was relieved by a hint of weather sculpturing and meaningful groupings of plant life.

"Space is nailed down better too," Garcia said. "There are all kinds of trees now that stay put and can be looked at." He slapped at a fly buzzing around his head.

"Hello!" Kinross exclaimed. "Insects!"

"Yes," Garcia agreed sourly. "Little animals in the brush, too. Rats and lizards, I think. And I got rained on once. It ain't all good, Kinross."

"Let's go see that cave," Kinross proposed. "I'll tell you what happened to me on the way."

They walked half a mile upstream. The valley narrowed and its walls became more vertical. A tangled growth of dark timber trees filled it. The diffuse light from the permanently overcast sky scarcely penetrated its gloom. Then they came into a clearing perhaps a hundred yards across and Kinross could see the darkly wooded slopes rising steeply on three sides. Directly ahead was the cave.

Two relatively narrow basaltic dikes slanted up the slope for more than a hundred feet, coming together at the top to form an inverted V. The stream ran out of the cavernous darkness at its base, bisected the clearing and lost itself in the dark wood. Near where the stream emerged, Kinross could see the cairn like a low stone platform about ten feet across and he could see and hear Silva, who sat wailing beside it.

"I can't talk to Silva no more than Kerbeck," Garcia said. "Silva thinks I'm a devil."

They walked across the clearing. The giant Bo Bo came out of the cave to meet them.

"You have not brought fruit," he said, in words that Kinross knew were never his own. "Go away and return with fruit."

"Okay, Kruger," Kinross said. "That much I'll do for you."

Days passed. To Kinross they seemed interminable, yet curiously void of remembered activity. He and Garcia tried marking off time with stones from the creek, but overnight the stones disappeared. So did banana peels and papaya rinds. The land would not hold a mark. The two men wrangled over what had happened in the preceding days and at last Kinross said, "It's just like before, only now everything happened last week."

"Then my beard grew an inch last week," said Garcia, stroking its blue-blackness. Kinross' beard was crinkled and reddish and more than an inch long.

"What's the end of this?" the Mexican asked once. "Do we just go on in this two-mile-across world forever?"

"I expect we'll get old and die," Kinross said.

"I ain't so sure even of that," Garcia said. "I feel like I'm getting younger. I want a steak and a bottle of beer and a woman."

"So do I," Kinross agreed, "but this is still better than the boat."

"Yes," Garcia said feelingly. "Give Kruger that much, even if he did set the whole thing up."

"I think Kruger is a lot less happy than we are," Kinross said.

"Nobody's happy but Kerbeck," Garcia growled.

They saw Kerbeck often as they gathered fruit or tramped the confines of the little valley seeking relief of boredom. The giant Swede ranged through the land like an elemental spirit. He wore the remnants of his khaki trousers and singlet, and his yellow hair and red beard were long and tangled. He seemed to recognize Garcia and Kinross but made only humming noises in response to their words.

Kinross often felt that it was the unrelieved blackness of the nights which oppressed him most. He wanted stars and a moon. One night he awoke feeling uneasy and saw a scattering of stars in the sky, strangely constellated. He moved to wake Garcia but sleep overcame him again and he dreamed for the first time he could remember in that world. He was back on the rock pinnacle in the desert talking to Kruger. Kruger was wearing Fay's body and he was worried.

"Something's happened, Kinross," he said. "There are stars and I didn't shape them; I couldn't. This world has suddenly received a great increase in animation and not all of it is under my control."

"What can I do about it? Or care?"

"You care, all right. We're in this world together, like in a lifeboat, Kinross. And I'm scared now. There's an alien presence, perhaps a number of them, seeking our world. They may be hostile."

"I doubt it, if they bring stars," Kinross said. "Where are they?"

"I don't know. Wandering outside of our space here, looking for us, I suppose. I want you and Garcia to go and find them."

"Why can't you do that?"

"Your guess was partly right, Kinross. I have my limits and my need for men like you and Garcia. I'm asking, not commanding. We're still in the same boat, remember."

"Yes. Okay, I'll go. But how . . ."

"Just start walking. I'll let you through the reentry barrier again."

Kinross awoke with a start. The stars were still in the sky and a crescent moon hung above the horizon across the little stream. Garcia snored nearby.

"Wake up!" Kinross said, shaking him. The Mexican snorted and sat up.

"Madre de Dios!" he gasped. "Stars and a moon! Kinross, are we back . . . ?"

"No," Kinross said. "Let's go hunting. I've just been talking to Kruger."

"Hunting? At night? Hunting what?"

"Maybe what made the stars. How do I know? Come on, Garcia, my feet are burning."

Kinross strode off, leaping the creek and heading directly toward the crescent moon. The Mexican stumbled after him muttering in Spanish.

Once more Kinross reached the height of land, and the moon, fuller now, hung above the horizon on the right, in the same direction he had gone before. He walked briskly, the Mexican following in silence. Once Garcia exclaimed and pointed down to the right. Kinross looked and saw the cave mouth far below, the dwarfed clearing and the mighty slope curving convexly up from it to his present level. The moonlight touched the dark treetops with silver.

As they walked Kinross told Garcia about his dream. The Mexican did not doubt that it was genuine. Kinross warned him about the peculiar timelessness of experience outside the reentry barrier. "It's like everything happened two minutes ago," he said.

"Yes," said Garcia. "Look at that moon now, three-quarters full. Maybe we've been walking for a month."

"Or a minute," Kinross said.

It was not to be the same trip as before. Once on the high, gently curving plain he remembered, he found they were bearing sharply to the right, going up a gentle rise. Then the land pitched the other way and they began crossing shallow ravines with running water in their bottoms. The land grew rougher and the ravines deeper until, crossing one of them, Kinross saw that it bore directly for the moon. He continued down the stream bed in ankle-deep water instead of climbing out.

The banks were of wet, dark stone and became steeper and higher as they went. The stream narrowed and became knee deep and the current tugged fiercely at them, forcing them to cling to the stones to maintain their footing. The sharp V of the ravine ahead almost cradled the full moon and Kinross could hear a distant roar of falling water.

"Looks rough up ahead, Garcia," he called to the Mexican ten feet behind him. "Watch it."

He moved ahead another hundred yards toward the increasing noise and edged around a rock shoulder against which the water swirled angrily. The force of the current quickened suddenly, almost snatching his legs from under him, so that he flattened himself against the rock and called a warning back to Garcia.

Over the glassily smooth, veined lip of the waterfall twenty feet in front of him, Kinross looked into a vast pit, steeply conical and many miles across. It was beaded around the rim and threaded down the sides with falling water that whispered enormously across the distance. The full moon riding directly above washed the whole with silver. At the bottom of the pit was another moon which, Kinross thought fleetingly, must be a reflecting pond or lake.

Garcia called from behind. "What do you see, Kinross? Why have you stopped?"

"I see one more step and death, I think," Kinross called back. "It's a waterfall. We'll have to climb the bank here if we possibly can."

He made no move to return but stared down into the pit. Abruptly the urge came to him to surrender, to let the water carry him over the brink. It was sudden and overpowering, almost sexual, a savage assault on his spirit. He clung desperately to the rock face and muttered a prayer under his breath, "Mother of God, spare me now."

The compulsion, still powerful, withdrew a little distance. "Garcia," he called, "start climbing, in the name of God. Keep talking to me."

"There's a ledge back here, slanting up," Garcia said from above. "Come back under me and I'll give you a hand up."

Kinross edged back around the rock shoulder and scrambled up to join Garcia. The Mexican led the way up the narrow ledge.

"There's something up ahead that will take your breath away," Kinross warned him. "A pit. Wait till you see it. And when you do, hang on to yourself."

Garcia grunted and kept climbing. The ledge petered out and

the way became more difficult and dangerous. Then they were standing on a rocky headland falling steeply on three sides into the great pit that was all around them.

"Madre de Dios!" breathed Garcia. He repeated it several times, otherwise speechless. Both men stood silently, gazing into the pit. Finally Garcia raised a hand and whispered, "Listen!"

Kinross listened. He heard a crackling of brush and a rattling of dislodged pebbles. It came from the left, seemingly not far off.

"Something's coming up out of the pit," he whispered.

"What's coming? Kinross, we ain't alone in this world!"

"We've got to go closer," Kinross said. "Have to know. Walk easy."

They stalked the sound, retreating from the headland and skirting the edge of the pit. As they neared the source of the noise, the brush became tangled and waist high and they made noises of their own, unavoidably. Then all was silent and Kinross feared their quarry was alarmed until he heard a snuffling, whimpering noise that set his nerves still more on edge. They crept closer. Then Garcia grasped his arm and pulled him to a crouch.

Kinross strained his eyes toward where the Mexican was pointing. Suddenly, taking vague form in the pattern of silvery light and shadow, he saw a human figure not fifty feet away. "We capture him," he told Garcia in dumb show. The Mexican nodded. Both men rose and rushed headlong.

Kinross' longer legs got him there first. The figure rose and fled a step or two before he brought it down with a flying tackle. A split second later the stocky Mexican added his considerable weight to the tangle of arms and legs and then a despairing, agonized scream arose from the captive. Electric surprise jolted Kinross.

"Let go, Garcia," he commanded. "Get up. It's a woman!"

She was Mary Chadwick and she had three strong brothers who could clobber any man in Queensland and Kinross and

Garcia were beasts and savages and they were to take her home immediately or it would be the worse for them. Then she clung to Kinross and cried hysterically.

While Kinross tried awkwardly to comfort her, day came, less abruptly than usual but swiftly enough to remind Kinross how unaccountably time still ran. The light was harsh and bright and he saw the disk of the sun for the first time. The familiar overcast was gone, the sky clear and blue. Sight of the two bearded men did not seem to reassure the woman.

She was quite young and dressed for riding, khaki shirt and trousers, with laced boots, outlining a tall and generous figure. Honey-colored hair hung loose to her shoulders. Her eyes, swollen with crying, were an intense blue verging on violet. Her fair skin was tanned to pale gold and a dusting of freckles lay across the bridge of her strong nose.

She recovered quickly. "Who are you?" she asked in a clear but low-pitched voice. "What is this place? Nothing like it in the Coast Ranges *I* ever heard of."

The men introduced themselves. Kinross failed completely to make her understand the nature of the world around them.

"Ships? Sailors? What rot!" she exclaimed. "You say you don't understand it yourselves, so go along with that nonsense. All we need do is walk until we find a track or see smoke or— you know all that."

"Okay, we're lost then," Kinross agreed. "We're somewhere in Australia, I take it?"

"Yes, Queensland, and somewhere on the south fork of the Herbert River. I was riding along and I must have fallen asleep . . . where my horse is, I'm sure I have no earthly notion."

Kinross and Garcia exchanged glances. "Excuse me, Mary," the Mexican said, his black eyes blazing with excitement. "I just have to talk crazy for a minute to my friend here." Then to Kinross, "How come? According to the soldiers of the Tibesti story the gate should be in the Indian Ocean. Has this world got more than one hole in it, you suppose?"

"That's bothering me, too. The way I've always understood it, without ever believing any of it, mind you, the two worlds are not superimposed. They just have that one small area in common, the gate . . ."

"Well, if it opens on land . . ."

"I know what you're thinking. But we've got to give Kerbeck and Silva a chance. Anyway, those two." Kinross turned to the girl.

"Mary," he asked, "can you remember exactly where in that pit you first found yourself? Did you mark the spot?"

"No, why should I have? I'll not go back down there for all the mad fossickers in the entire North. Take me to your camp or your diggings or whatever. I hope someone there will talk sense to me."

The Mexican laughed suddenly. "I just remembered old Bart Garcia, my first ancestor in Mexico, was a prospector too," he said. "That was a new world and he had a rough time in it. Lead on, Kinross."

"All roads lead to Kruger," said Kinross, striding off.

"All but one," Garcia corrected, looking back at the great pit, shadowed now by slanting sunlight.

The way back was rugged at first, then more gentle. Kinross exclaimed in pleased surprise when a bird fluttered through the brush and Garcia said, "So that's what I been hearing." Then Kinross heard it too, a multitudinous chirping and twittering all around them. But the birds, like the indefinite trees and shrubs, were always annoyingly peripheral to direct vision. They were wing flashes, darting colors at the edge of sight.

"Doesn't it bother you, not being able to look at them?" he asked the girl.

"But I can see them," she said. "You strange men . . ."

Keck-keck-keck-kee-RACK! came a noise from the brush, and Kinross jumped.

"There!" the girl pointed. "It's a coachwhip. Can't you see him now?"

Kinross could not. "There," she insisted, "hopping about in the wattle. Just *look*, won't you!"

Garcia saw it first. Finally Kinross believed he saw the small, dark green thrush shape with white throat, long, perky tail and black crest. But he felt uneasily that he was really seeing a verbal description. Keck-keck-keck-kee-RACK! He jumped again and felt foolish.

As they walked, Kinross questioned the girl. She lived on a small cattle station in the mountains south of Cairns with her father and three brothers. She was twenty-four and unmarried, had spent a year at school in Brisbane, didn't like cities. Her brothers worked part time in the mines. This would be first-rate country for running stock and she couldn't imagine how the land survey had missed it.

"Look at the sun, Kinross," Garcia said once. "We're going west. Feels good to be able to say that."

The sun was low when they reached the height of land above the valley. "Kruger Valley," Kinross called it, since the girl demanded a name. The stupendous wooded slope rising on three sides from the cave mouth was touched with a glory by the declining sun and her pose of matter-of-fact assurance broke once more.

"Nothing like that in the Coast Ranges," she whispered. "I just know it."

When they started down the slope west of the forested area, Kinross was impressed too. Trees stood out in clear view, unique, individual. The coarse grass was plain to see, as well as clumps of flowers in bright colors. Small, brightly varicolored birds flitted ahead of them and Kinross knew that he was really seeing them. The flat sameness of color and the smooth regularity of form were gone from the land. Kinross with rising excitement pointed out to Garcia rock outcrops, gullies and patches of erosion-bared earth.

"Something's happened, Garcia," he said. "Here, inside the reentry barrier, the land sticks backward into time now."

"Looks sure enough real," the Mexican agreed. "Wonder if we could light a fire tonight?"

"Yes, and chop trees," Kinross almost shouted. "Mary will need a shelter."

"Of *course* a fire," the woman said. "We shall want to roast things, I suppose."

"Maybe knock down some birds," Garcia said. "I'm hungry for meat."

"No!" the girl cried in outrage. "You wouldn't dare!"

"Not these pretty little ones," Garcia hastily assured her. "What do you call them, anyway?"

"They're pittas," she said. "Noisy little paint pots, aren't they? They say 'walk-to-WORK, walk-to-WORK.' "

"That's what we're doing, I guess," Garcia chuckled.

They picked their way down the fairly steep hillside, Kinross preparing the girl for what she would find down by the stream, when she interrupted him.

"Who are they?" she asked, pointing to the left.

Kinross and Garcia could see nothing. "What is it you see?" Kinross asked.

"A whole band of blacks, myalls," she whispered, obviously disturbed. "On their knees, in the bush."

"Now I partly see them," the Mexican said. "It's worse than the birds were this morning."

"I can't see a thing," Kinross complained. "Only trees and shrubs."

"Look slantwise," Garcia urged. "Let your eyes go slack. Every kid knows how to do that."

Kinross tried to unfocus his gaze and suddenly he saw them, dozens of them. Dwarfs, black with red eyes. Naked and grotesquely formed, huge hands and feet, knobbed joints, slubber lips, limbs knotted with muscles. They were looking back at him, but without apparent interest. Alarm bit into him.

"My God!" he breathed.

"They're a pack of devils," Garcia muttered. "Kinross, what in hell are they?"

"They're blacks," the girl said. "Back in the earlies they used to spear white men sometimes in the Coast Ranges, but they're tame enough now. We must just walk by and pretend not to see them. They're supposed to be in the spirit world."

"They're dwarfs, pygmies," Kinross objected. "Do you have pygmies in Queensland?"

"They're on their knees," she answered sharply, "hiding from us in one of their spirit places. Come along! Walk by and pretend not to see them."

"Let's try," Kinross assented.

They walked on without incident until they reached the valley floor. As they walked along the level, Garcia began looking sharply to left and right.

"Kinross, something's dogging us, slipping through the brush after us on both sides," he said.

"Those black things?" Kinross asked, stomach muscles knotting.

"No, can't see well, but they're taller and gray like."

"I can see them," the girl said. "They're gins, Binghi women of that mob we passed. They look like ghosts when they smear themselves with wood ashes."

"What are they after?" Kinross asked, half seeing the elusive shapes in the corner of his eye.

"They want to trail us to our camp so they can steal and beg," the girl said. "Mind you send them away straight off when they come in."

Garcia said, "They got nice shapes, now that I know they're women. Kinross, can you see them yet?"

"Just partly," Kinross said.

The flitting shapes left them before they reached the stream. As they stood doubtfully on the bank, distant shouting came from the hillside they had just descended. Kinross saw Kerbeck charging through the scrub, black motes scattering before him.

"God!" he gasped. "Kerbeck's fighting the black things!"

"Winning, too," Garcia commented, less perturbed than Kinross. "Look at 'em run."

"He shouldn't," the girl said. "They'll creep back and spear him tonight. All of us, perhaps." She shuddered.

Kerbeck came plunging down the hill in great leaps. He crossed the quarter mile of valley floor, in and out of sight, looming up bronzed and gigantic. His floating hair and beard were an aureole in the light of the westering sun. He shouldered Kinross aside and grasped the girl by her upper arms, staring fixedly into her eyes. He was humming and buzzing frantically.

Kinross pulled vainly at one of the great arms, protesting. Then the Swede quieted, releasing the girl, smiling and humming placidly.

"It's all right," the girl said. "He wanted to be sure that my eyes had pupils."

Kinross looked blankly from her blue-violet eyes to the flat blue eyes of the huge Norseman.

"He's been chasing the devil-devils," she explained. "He thought I might be one. Their eyes don't have pupils, just black smudges on white eyeballs." Kerbeck hummed happily. Kinross shook his head.

"She's right, Kinross," Garcia said. "I got part of it. It's another one of them things, you got to listen sideways like."

"They turn into trees and rocks when he catches them," the girl added. "He's been up a gum tree for days about them and he's glad you two are back."

"Oh lord!" Kinross groaned. "I feel like a damned infant. So you do agree they're devils now?"

"No more!" she said sharply. "They're abos on a spirit-land walkabout. The whole push of you are mad as snakes."

"Let's make a fire," Kinross said, turning away.

There was plenty of dried grass and fallen branches, unlike before. Garcia had matches, soon had a fire. Kinross borrowed

Kerbeck's belt knife to trim poles from the branches the giant Swede obligingly pulled off the trees, and work on a small hut went forward rapidly. Garcia cut fronds from a palmettolike tree to weave between the upright poles, and the girl gathered brownish wool from the top of it to make herself a bed. "Burrawang," she called it. She pronounced the finished effort a passable "humpy."

Under the darkness they roasted nubbly breadfruit in the coals and peeled bananas. Kerbeck melted into the night. All ate in silence. Finally the girl said, "Where are we? Fair truth, now. Where are we?"

"Like I told you this morning—" Kinross began, but she stopped him.

"I know. I believe it has to seem that way to you. But do you know where I am?"

Both men murmured their question.

"In Alcheringa," she said. "In the Binghi spirit land. I fell into it somehow, riding through one of the old sacred places. There are picture writings all along the South Herbert. Today, when I saw the abos, I knew . . ."

"Mary, they *were* dwarfs," Kinross said. "They were not human."

"When the abos go back to the spirit land they are not human either," she said. "And at the same time something more than human. I've heard mobs of talk about it. But those gins—they shouldn't be here. Nor I. It's frightful bad luck for a woman to enter the spirit land. When I was a little girl I used to think it blanky unfair . . ."

"How do the natives get in and out of . . . Alcheringa?" Kinross asked with quickened interest.

"They dance and sing their way, paint themselves, use churingas—oh, all sorts of rites," she said. "No one must be about, especially no women."

From the darkness overhead a weird, whistling wail floated down. Both men jumped to their feet.

"Sit down," the girl bade them. "At home, on Chadwick Station, I would call that the cry of a stone curlew. They fly about and call in the darkness. The blacks call them the souls of children trying to break out of the spirit world in order to be born. What are they here, I wonder?"

She looked upward. Kinross and Garcia sat down again. Then a slender bird with thin legs and long, curving beak dropped into the firelight to perch on her shoulder.

"Poor little night baby," the girl addressed it, "you'll watch over me, won't you?"

She rose abruptly, said good night and went into the hut. Kinross looked at Garcia.

"We're responsible for her being here," he said. "We've got to get her back to her people."

"Kruger's responsible," Garcia said.

"Us too. If Kruger doesn't come talk to me tonight I'm going in the cave in the morning. Will you come along?"

"Sure," said the Mexican, yawning. "Pleasant dreams."

Red dawn above the great slope up valley woke Kinross from a dreamless sleep. He blew an ember into flame and built up the fire. Charred breadfruit rinds littered the ground and he reflected wryly that this world no longer policed itself. He put the rinds into the fire.

Somewhere on the hillside across the stream, Kerbeck shouted and brush crackled. Garcia got up and the woman peeped out of her hut as Kinross stood irresolute. Then Kerbeck came in view. He carried a stalk of yellow bananas over his left shoulder and with his right hand clutched a small man by the neck. He half pushed, half kicked the little man down the slope.

The huge Norseman hummed excitedly as he approached across the level. Suddenly Kinross, still half asleep, heard words in the humming, as he had sometimes heard wind voices in the singing of telegraph wires when he was a boy on the high plains of Nebraska.

"I catch me a devil," Kerbeck was saying.

The devil was a swarthy, broad-faced little man dressed in baggy gray woolen garments. His eyes were closed, his face screwed up in fear, and he was gabbling under his breath. Garcia listened, suddenly alert, and then spoke sharply to the man in Spanish. He got a torrent of words in reply.

"He's a Peruvian," Garcia interpreted. "He comes from the mountains above Tacna. He's been wandering lost for days. He thinks he's dead and that Kerbeck is the boss devil."

"Seems to be mutual," Kinross said. "Tell him he'll be all right now. I wonder how many more . . ."

Kerbeck went away, humming and buzzing. The little Peruvian, still badly frightened, crouched beyond the fire and ate bananas with them. Then Kinross, explaining his purpose to the woman, proposed to Garcia that they visit the cave.

"Not empty-handed," the Mexican reminded him. "Remember, we got a duty."

Along the way they gathered guavas and papayas into Kinross' shirt, pushed through the grove and laid the fruits on the stone platform. Silva sat beside it, rocking and wailing almost inaudibly. Kinross patted his shoulder.

"Cheer up, Silva, old man," he said. "We're going in to see Kruger now. May have some good news for you."

"Unholy," the old man moaned. "Full of devils. You're a devil."

The two men walked to the cave mouth and stopped. They looked at each other.

"What are we waiting for?" Garcia asked.

"I don't know. I expected Fay or Bo Bo to be on guard, I guess," Kinross said. "Hell with it. In we go."

The cave pinched sharply in to become a nearly round tunnel about fifteen feet high. The stream splashed along the bottom, forcing them to wade. The water shone with a soft light and moisture oozing through cracks in the black rock made luminous patches here and there on the walls. The rock had the blocky, amorphous look of basalt. The air was cool and utterly still except for the murmur of the stream.

The two men waded in silence for a good way before they heard a clear noise of turbulent water somewhere ahead. Then they came into an indefinitely large chamber with the luminous water cascading broadly down its back wall from a blackness above. Fay and Bo Bo were asleep on rough terraces beside the stream.

"What have you come to tell me, Kinross?" Kruger's voice asked out of the dimness. It seemed to shape the noise of the cascading water into its words.

"We found a woman," Kinross said.

"I know. There are many others, both men and women, still making their way here. I have been greatly strengthened. Have you noticed how the world has firmed up and become extended in time?"

"Yes. But how do these people get here? Is there more than one gate?"

"No. It must have shifted."

"To where, then? One is from Australia, one from Peru."

"So?" Surprise rang in the silvery, liquid voice. "Perhaps it moves then."

"But Tibesti—"

"They didn't know a rotating earth. The sun of Tibesti goes around a stationary earth. But when we—I—set up a succession of days here I must have put a spin into this world. Perhaps it is slightly out of phase with our old world. The gate would wander . . ."

"You sound pleased," Kinross said.

"I am. It takes many people to hold a world in place, Kinross. In a few centuries there may be enough here so that I can really rest. They will breed of course, and they will be long-lived here."

"How big do you think the gate is?"

"About the size of the boat, I expect. Perhaps an ellipse thirty feet on the major axis."

"How do people come through, not knowing—?"

"Several ways are possible. Perhaps it sweeps over them at a moment of intense world loathing, those moments a man can't support beyond a second or two. It snatches them up. Or perhaps daydreamers, with their sense of reality unfocused and their mooring lines to their real world slacked or cast loose. They want only to drift a little way out, but the gate comes by and snatches them. I don't really know, Kinross. Maybe this world is going to be populated by poets and self-haters."

"But the gate? Can we get through it the other way?"

"Yes. Some of the soldiers of Tibesti came back—or fled back or were driven back—the old tales are conflicting. But anyone passing back through this gate would risk dropping into an ocean. I suspect the gate sweeps the eighteenth parallel, or near it."

"Kruger, the woman wants to go back. We have to find a way."

"No. No one may go back. Especially not women."

"Kruger, we have no right—"

"We do have right and beyond that a duty. She would not be here if she had not voluntarily, at least for a moment, relinquished or rejected her own world. She belongs to us now, and we need her."

"Kruger, I may not obey that. I—"

"You must obey. You cannot pass the reentry barrier without my aid."

"Let it go, then, for now," Kinross conceded. "I have other questions. What are the black dwarfs and pearly-gray women?"

"Nature spirits, I suppose you could call them. I stripped them from Fay and Bo Bo, husked them off by the millions until only a bare core of nothingness was left. What those two are now I couldn't describe to you. But the world is partially self-operating and my load is eased."

Garcia spoke for the first time. "Tough on Fay, for all I hated the little rat."

"Was that what you wanted to do with me?" Kinross asked, shuddering.

"No," the clear, liquid voice said solemnly, "you are a different kind of man, Kinross. You could have helped me to bear the load, and perhaps together we could have endured it until the help came that is coming now. Do not wash your hands of Fay and Bo Bo, Kinross."

"Kruger," Garcia said hesitantly, "do you mean that all those devils are really Fay and Bo Bo?"

"Most of them are," the silvery voice confirmed, "but many of them are Kerbeck. He is disintegrating without my interference. And some are you, too, Garcia; some are Kinross, the woman, all of you. You are built into this world more than you know."

"I don't like it," Garcia said. "Kruger, I won't give up my devils."

"You can't help it, Garcia. But you have millions to spare, and besides you don't really lose them, you know. You just spread yourself through the world, in a way. Every time you put a compulsion on this world by expecting something, it costs you a devil or two. Do you understand?"

"No!" the Mexican growled.

"I think you do. If you don't, talk to Kinross later. But it's not so bad, Garcia. When you become a loose cloud of devils, instead of a shiny black stone, you will be a poet or a sylvan god."

"Kruger," Kinross broke in, "do you hold it against me, that I denied you my help that time?"

"Do you hold it against me that I initiated all this by blowing up the *Ixion?*"

"I don't know . . . I just don't know . . ."

"Nor do I know, Kinross. Perhaps we're even. And I still have need of you."

"Where is your body, Kruger? Can you animate it yet?"

"It is above the waterfall. I can see dimly now how I will animate it in the distant future and come into this world in a kind of glory. But not yet, not yet . . ."

"Your thirst, Kruger. Are you still thirsty?"

"Yes, Kinross. It still tears at me. I don't know how much longer I will have to endure it."

"Doesn't rapport with Fay—?"

"No one but you, Kinross. And now not even you. You disobeyed me once."

"Kruger, I'm sorry. I wish it didn't have to be. May we go now?"

"Yes. Go and serve our world. Try to be content."

"Let's go, Garcia," Kinross said, turning. The Mexican set off briskly, leading Kinross. When they were passing through the dark grove Kinross halted.

"Let's sit here and talk about devils for a while, Garcia," he proposed. "I'm not ready to face Mary Chadwick just yet."

When the two men returned to the fire, more than a dozen people were standing around it. Several were women. A tall, slender man wearing a leather jacket and gray trousers tucked into heavy boots came out of the group to meet them. He had reddish-blond hair.

"Mr. Kinross?" he asked. "Allow me to introduce myself and to apologize for making free of your fire. My name is Friedrich von Lankenau."

They shook hands. The newcomer had a sinewy grip in his long fingers. His face was gaunt and bony, frozen, with thin lips and a high, narrow beak of a nose. Kinross stared at him quizzically and deep-set gray eyes looked back at him steadily from under shaggy brows. The thin lips smiled slightly.

"Miss Chadwick tells me that you are Mr. Kruger's lieutenant, so to speak," the man said. "We are a group gathered together in chance meetings along the way here. We are anxious to learn a rational, physical explanation of what we are experiencing."

A babble of voices broke from the group. "Silence!" snapped the tall man. "If Mr. Kinross will explain, you may all listen, you who know English. I will then to the others explain." The babble stilled.

Kinross told the story of the soldiers of Tibesti and of the sailors of the *Ixion*. He watched von Lankenau closely as he spoke. The man never lost the rigid composure of his features, but his eyes blazed and he continually nodded his comprehension. When he finished Kinross checked the renewed babble by setting Garcia to telling the story in Spanish. Then he drew von Lankenau to one side.

"Mind telling me where you were when you came through?" he asked.

"I was nearly to the top of Sajama in Bolivia, climbing alone."

"How about the others?"

"From all over. Brazil, the New Hebrides, Mozambique, Australia, Rhodesia . . ."

"I guess Kruger's right and the gate does sweep the eighteenth parallel," Kinross mused.

"We can establish it quite exactly with a little questioning, I have no doubt," von Lankenau said confidently. "But sooner or later, Mr. Kinross, I would like to talk directly to the Herr Kruger if it can be arranged. I am much intrigued—"

"You just go see him, Mr. Lankenau. I'm not his secretary. But I can tell you now, he will permit no one to return to the old world."

"I would not for anything return to the old world!" von Lankenau spoke with feeling that broke through his composure.

"From boyhood I knew the story of the soldiers of Tibesti," he continued. "As a very young man I sought the gate through all of the Tibesti, and perhaps found the spot, but it did not reveal itself to me as it did for the Herr Kruger. So I sought a gate of my own, on mountaintops in winter, such peaks as Sajama. I am not at all sure that I came through your gate, Mr. Kinross, but I am sure that I came to stay."

"Mary—Miss Chadwick—has somewhat the same notion," Kinross said. "I never knew so many people—" His voice trailed off.

"Forgive my outburst," von Lankenau said, composure regained. "For me this is a lost hope suddenly realized, and I am a bit overcome. If you will excuse me, I will visit the Herr Kruger now."

He bowed and strode away springily. Kinross became aware of the Australian woman at his elbow.

"Mary," he said, "did you hear him? But let me tell you, we can get back to your world, although it will be dangerous. I'll work on it and let you know."

She seemed hardly to listen, staring after the retreating figure. "Bonzer!" she said. "There walks a man."

Kinross walked away, slightly irritated. Garcia was talking to a group of Latins including the three women. Kinross sought out the Rhodesian, a stocky, florid man wearing plaid shorts. His name was Peter White.

"What do you think of all this?" he asked.

"You have quite a good thing here," the man replied. "Like being a child again, isn't it rather?"

Kinross grunted and asked him what he thought of Lankenau. White said he admired von Lankenau, that he had felt rather forlorn and drifting until he had joined von Lankenau's group. Kinross fidgeted over commonplaces for a few minutes and finally said, "You know, White, we can go back through that gate if we work it right."

"I wouldn't want to, just yet," White said soberly. "This is rather a lark."

"But in time—when you get tired—"

"Tired? That's as may be. You know, Kinross, the last I remember of the old world was being almost dead of fever in the low veld. Dreams . . . visions . . . I'm not ready to wake back . . ."

"Then you think this is a dream?"

"Yes. A different and a better one."

Kinross excused himself and walked away shaking his head. Garcia was still yapping in Spanish. He walked aimlessly for a while, then lay under a breadfruit tree near the fire and tried to sleep. He felt bored and angry. He saw two newcomers, both women, come down the hillside and left it to Garcia to welcome them.

Hours later von Lankenau strode back from the grove with an exalted look on his lean face. He called his group together and instructed them in their several languages as to their duties. Each must gather a token handful of fruit or berries every morning and place it on the cairn before the cave entrance. Then he spoke of huts and sanitary arrangements. White had a belt ax. One of the Mozambique Negroes had a bush knife and the other a grubbing hoe. When the work was going forward to his satisfaction he joined Kinross under the breadfruit tree. Garcia came with him.

"I talked to the Herr Kruger a long time," von Lankenau said, sitting down and clasping his long arms around his knees. "He told me much, and much of it about you, Mr. Kinross."

"What about me?" Kinross asked, narrowing his eyes.

"The special relation between you. Something about the reciprocal way you and he came into this world. He does not understand it himself. But he knows that you should be his lieutenant among the people."

Kinross said nothing. Von Lankenau regarded him gravely for a moment and continued, "I will cheerfully defer to your authority, Mr. Kinross, and help in any way I can."

"I don't want authority or responsibility," Kinross said. "You go right on taking charge of things, Mr. Lankenau, only leave me out of it."

"If I must, by your default, then I will. But I hope that I can consult with you."

"Oh, by all means," Kinross said. "I'm good at talking."

"Let us talk then. Do you know, Mr. Kinross, this situation is absolutely fascinating. Cannot you feel it set fire to your thoughts?"

"I know what you mean, I suppose. We're tampering with some of the ultimate mysteries. I won't deny I haven't thought about them in my time and read strange books, too. But now I wonder . . ."

"No moral qualms now, please, Mr. Kinross. You will only torment yourself uselessly like that unfortunate Portuguese. We have a world to build and it need not be a copy of the old one. We may be able to simplify the chemistry, systematize the mineralogy . . . does not the thought *intrigue* you, Mr. Kinross?"

"Huh! You can't beat the energy laws, Mr. Lankenau. The more people come in, the more closely they will apply. Kruger told me that himself, and I can see them taking hold already."

"The Herr Kruger has never worshipped the Second Law. Otherwise none of us would be here. And most of the people who come in will not remain persons, you know."

Von Lankenau turned a doubtful look on Garcia and continued, "That is another fascinating thing, to watch the personality elements filter back into external nature until the boundary between subject and object is almost lost. Think of what a power of mass suggestibility we will dispose of then! The very trees and rocks will be amenable to suggestion, each with its indwelling fragment of the human spirit! Oh, Kinross . . . your Second Law . . . your dry, word-smothered world . . . this will be a world of magic for long ages before it becomes a world of science."

Kinross frowned. "What right have we to disintegrate personalities in that way? Or to let it happen? Fay and Bo Bo—"

"Those two are special cases, sacrificed to an emergency that will not occur again. As for the others, we will devise a set of ritual life patterns that will stabilize them at some lower limit. That is what I and the Herr Kruger talked longest about."

"Let me jump into this," Garcia growled. "Do you birds think that's going to happen to me? Suppose I won't come apart for you, what then?"

"You may not be able to help it, Mr. Garcia. And perhaps you will be much happier when you do . . . come apart."

"You sound like Kruger. Kinross, what does he mean?"

"He means the emptiness of this world pulls you apart, like it or not. Like when you put a lump of salt in a cup of fresh water, it will dissolve a little at a time."

"Emptiness? Not in the old world?"

"Only rarely, in places like the Antarctic, on a life raft at sea, empty places."

"I see. Like in most places the old world is already so salty it can't take more?"

"That's the idea. The lumps of salt gain instead of losing."

"Hmmm. Like we talked this morning. We used to push our devils off on each other."

"Devils. That is the Herr Kruger's analogy," von Lankenau interrupted.

"Funny how I know just what he meant by it, without being able to say it any different," Garcia said.

"You have to lose a few devils before you know," Kinross told him.

"Well, I've lost some, okay. But I'm still Joe Garcia and my insides work."

"Name magic is one of the oldest and most powerful means of binding one's devils into a unity, Mr. Garcia," von Lankenau assured him. "We will stabilize the villagers well above the name level, I hope."

"Why do you and Kinross just take it for granted that you're not in line for this . . . this devil losing?"

"We are. We lose devils cheerfully, but it is a selective losing. I, and I suspect Mr. Kinross also, we hold ourselves together under a higher magic."

"It's like this, Garcia," Kinross said, "you can either just plain *be* all your devils, or you can be yourself and carry a spare load of devils around with you."

"Devils, Mr. Garcia," von Lankenau said gravely, "are bits of experience, large or small, gay or mournful."

"The lived experiences, good or bad, we bind in to ourselves," Kinross said. "The unlived experiences, the regrets, the might-have-beens, the just-escaped things, we carry around on our backs. But we *know* it."

"We're really explaining to each other, aren't we, Mr. Kinross?" said von Lankenau. "We lose the devils which ride us and we keep the ones which power us. The villagers must lose both kinds indiscriminately."

"I'm still with you," Garcia said. "Keep talking."

"To draw on your earlier analogy, Mr. Kinross," von Lankenau said, "might I say that devils exert an osmotic pressure? It is strongly outward on mountaintops and in such places I have shrugged off a thousand devils. But in Berlin or Paris . . . back they came in tens of thousands."

"That I savvy," Garcia said. "It's the difference between being on a long cruise and coming ashore for a month. I get a burn on me to ship out."

"I think you're okay, Garcia," Kinross said. "If you weren't, you would've already drifted off like Kerbeck."

"Is not Kerbeck magnificent?" von Lankenau asked. "The end product of devil dispersion, an elemental force, with powers we hardly dare guess at. The Bo Bo thing, too, black and savage. Mr. Kinross, we pay a price for mind. But we must not let it happen to our villagers."

"No, I guess not," Kinross agreed. "You spoke of rituals . . ."

"Yes, a pattern of group rituals to take them through their days and nights, perhaps later through seasons. We will keep

them in a mass, maintain a local concentration of devils by mutual reenforcement or successive recapture . . . I don't know
quite how to phrase it."

"I see. The thought disturbs me, Mr. Lankenau."

"It need not. I find it exhilarating. I hope that you and Mr.
Garcia will help." Von Lankenau stood up and looked toward
the hut-building activity.

"We'll think about it," Kinross said, getting up himself.

"I'll do what I can," the Mexican said. Lankenau excused
himself and went over to the villagers.

"Kinross, something tells me you're still packing a devil as
big as the *Queen Mary,* for all of your brains," Garcia said.

Krugertown, as they called it, was built in a day. Mary had
a large hut of wattle and daub, near the stone-banked communal
fire and a little apart from the village cluster, which lay nearer
to the dark grove and the cave entrance. Kinross and Garcia
built themselves a similar shelter a short way downstream
from the fire. Von Lankenau lived in the village. Every morning
Kinross and Garcia took a few bananas or a breadfruit to the
cairn. Afterward Garcia often helped von Lankenau with the
villagers, but Kinross walked apart with mixed feelings. He
climbed about the hillsides, heedless of the growing number of
black things and gray women that lurked there. Sometimes he
saw Kerbeck, endlessly pursuing the dwarfs and the smoke
women, and tried to talk to him. He tried to tell Kerbeck what
Kruger had done to him in taking away his humanity. The massive Swede buzzed and hummed and Kinross did not know how
much he understood.

Mary walked apart too, always in a flutter of birds. He saw
dainty green and blue sun birds, green and white pittas, green
and bronze drongos and the demure white nutmeg pigeons she
loved most of all. When they met he tried to talk to her and
found her aloof and remote.

"This world is harmful to you, Mary," he urged one day. "It disintegrates you, makes you lose part of yourself. Don't you want to go back to Queensland while you still can? Before it's too late?"

"I send out my birds and I call them back," she replied. "No harm here."

"That's no answer, Mary," he protested. He looked at her untroubled face with the red lips and the smooth brow and laid his arm across her shoulders. She slipped away from him.

"Mary, I'm going to take you back to Queensland," Kinross said sharply. "It's my duty to you."

She hummed like Kerbeck and moved away. Kinross looked after her morosely. Shortly after, he saw her high on the hillside talking to Kerbeck. . . . Or humming with him.

New arrivals came in almost daily, by ones and twos, and melted at once into the village pattern. One day Kinross asked von Lankenau how long he thought it would go on.

"The rate is dropping off," von Lankenau said. "I expect it will decrease asymptotically and never quite stop. But the gate apparently sweeps a quite narrow path and has already caught up most of the susceptibles. And it may be that, as this world fills, its power of attraction lessens also."

"When will it be full?"

"Never, I hope. We want thousands, a large gene pool, a larger world. I estimate our surface is only about five miles in diameter now, Mr. Kinross."

"Can't Kruger make it larger if he likes?"

"Only at the expense of internal definition. He is striking a workable balance. But it is boundless by reentry, and is not that a most fascinating experience, Mr. Kinross?"

"I found it disturbing and then frustrating," Kinross said.

"Ah! The limits, of course. But with more people we can extend our surface to more comfortable limits. In the end, I suppose, we shall make it spherical and remove the reentry barrier to a higher dimension. But I shall be just a bit sorry when we do. Do you take my feeling, Mr. Kinross?"

"Just who are 'we'?" Kinross asked with a sudden edge in his voice. "You and Kruger?"

"Oh no. All of us. The culture, the Herr Kruger . . . you will have a part."

"You are kind, Mr. Lankenau."

The tall man looked at him sharply. "Mr. Kinross," he said solemnly, "any time that you wish to, you may take your rightful position in this world. I urge you to do so. I command by your default, and you know that very well."

"I'll have no part of it," Kinross said. "Damn Kruger and his world, snatching up a young woman like Mary Chadwick . . ."

"The Herr Kruger loves you, Mr. Kinross. You and Mr. Garcia are his sensorium, due to the peculiar circumstances of your coming here. He can be aware of his world only indifferently through the rest of us and through the Kabeiroi on the hillside."

"Well, I don't love the Herr Kruger. I hope he's still mad with thirst."

Von Lankenau raised a cautionary hand. "He does still suffer from thirst," he said in a low voice, "but your words are unworthy of you, Mr. Kinross. Hate me, if you must, but not the Herr Kruger."

"Why in hell do you have to shave every day?" Kinross asked angrily as he turned away.

He looked back from a distance and tugged at his beard. Mary Chadwick was talking to von Lankenau, standing close, looking up at him. Kinross reflected with a twinge that she had never looked up at him in that way. Then he remembered that she was as tall as himself and could not. He walked away swallowing a curse.

That night in their hut Kinross suggested to Garcia that next day they try to break the reentry barrier. The Mexican declined, saying that he and von Lankenau were working out a path-marking ritual with the villagers.

"Well, I will," Kinross said. "I'll go up there and walk right through it by not believing it's there, just like I should have done in the boat."

"Yes, and got your throat cut," Garcia said. "But it's there, all right. You'll find out."

Kinross found out. He fought the barrier all day, knowing its impossibility, striving to locate the exact point of reversal in order to step boldly across it. He came near doing so. Again and again, with the tiny instant of vertigo almost upon him, he saw the leering Kabeiroi drift by him and birds fly over, but each time he was turned back, suddenly half a mile down the hill and headed the wrong way. He came home in the evening disgruntled and exhausted.

Lankenau called it a world of magic, he reflected. Well, magic, then. Birds fly through the barrier. I'm doing this for Mary. If she would only help me—

He decided to try again during the next thunderstorm, when he hoped Kruger would be too busy with his storm devils to guard the barrier. One morning several days later the sky darkened and the queer light lay along the ground and he knew a storm was making. The black things from the hillside invaded the valley in gusts of damp wind, sidling and eddying through the shrubbery just out of eye reach. Poised on rocks, treetops and all pointed things, the gray women strained upward in a tension of half-visible air. With the first drops of rain Kinross set off up the hillside.

As he neared the barrier zone, the storm grew more violent. Thunder boomed and roared at him, rain slashed at him in sheets, jagged lightning flashes gave him glimpses of the storm devils. The Kabeiroi scurried around him with obscene menaces; over his head the gray women streamed by on the gusty wind. Once he saw Kerbeck, head thrown back, great chest bared to the wind.

All day he fought the barrier, spitting curses into the storm, and all day the storm spat and thundered back at him. He fell and rolled and rose again, over and over, straining up the hill with aching chest. Wind-driven twigs and branches lashed his face and body. Smothering rain drilled at him; wind snatched his breath away. At last his pounding heart and trembling knees convinced him that he was beaten. He turned back down the hillside.

"Well, Kruger, I gave you a fight," he gasped aloud. The storm abated as he limped down the slope and he saw downed trees and scattered branches and raw-earth gullies swirling with runoff. The thought came to him that he had at least forced Kruger to wreck von Lankenau's precious village. Then he was on the valley floor and the storm cleared entirely. Half a mile away he could see the village and its trees seemingly intact.

As he neared his hut, Mary came from behind a screen of shrubbery. White nutmeg pigeons perched on her head and shoulders. She smiled at him oddly.

"Regular cockeye bob up there, wasn't it, Allan?"

He looked at her stupidly. "Didn't it rain down here?" he asked.

"Only a sprinkle," she said, smiling. "Go in by the fire and dry your things. You look tired."

He walked on, soaked, mud-stained, limping on a wrenched ankle. She smiled and called me Allan, he thought. No storm here. Called me Allan. Oh, hell . . .

One morning, remote from the village, Kinross heard a pounding noise. In a clearing he found Peter White and two others beating mulberry bark with rounded paddles. The bearded Rhodesian looked tanned and fit and merry-eyed. The three men avoided looking at Kinross, as all the villagers tended to do, but they were aware of him and the rhythm of their pounding faltered.

On impulse Kinross called out, "White! Come over here!"

White paid no attention. Kinross spoke more sharply. White, without looking around, mumbled something about the Herr Kruger.

"I command you by the power of Kruger!" Kinross shouted in sudden anger. "Come over here!"

Reluctantly the man came to the clearing's edge. He looked down, but did not seem afraid. The Bantu and the Kanaka continued pounding.

"White, you were a man once," Kinross said. "How would you like to be a man again?"

"I am a man, Mr. Kinross," White said soberly.

"A man needs a wife. Do you have a wife, White?"

"Soon the Herr Kruger will give me one."

"I mean back home. Do you have a wife there?"

"There is no woman in my hut, but soon the Herr Kruger—"

"Damn your hut. I mean where you came from, in Rhodesia."

"I have always been here."

"No, you have not. You came from another world and if you try you can remember it. Can't you, now?"

The man looked up. "Yes, but I was a lot of different me's then. It was not a good world."

"Remember it. I command you to remember it by the power of Kruger. Remember your wife and your children."

The man twisted his body and his face darkened. "There were many wives and children. It was an underground world. Everyone lived in tunnels that ran in straight lines. They were tumbled together like straws and sometimes they crossed, but none ran side by side. One of my tunnels came through into Krugerworld. I crawled up out of the ground and here I am. That is all I can remember."

"Okay, go back to your work," Kinross said.

White did not move. "First you must lift the name of the Herr Kruger from me," he said.

"All right, I remove the name," Kinross said.

"Once more. Twice you placed it on me."

"Okay, once more I remove it," Kinross snapped. "Go on, now."

He walked away. Behind him a third club took up the pounding and the rhythm steadied.

Alone in his hut he raged instead of sleeping. A magic world . . . what magic, then? Kruger's teachings . . . before the word, before the thought . . . what act would serve him now? What blind, wordless, unthinking act?

He decided he would refuse to place his usual token of fruit on the cairn in the morning and suddenly he could sleep.

Kinross rose early and walked through the various fruit groves, eating as he walked, until his hunger was stayed. His aimless walking had led him to the edge of the dark timber grove screening the cave mouth. On impulse he walked through the grove into the clearing and on the way discovered with surprise that he had a small guava in his pocket. He threw it away. Two villagers, a man and a woman, were placing fruit on the cairn. Kinross wondered whether they were mated.

Silva, as always, sat beside the cairn. Kinross tried to talk to the old man, patting him on the shoulder, but Silva repulsed him with an incoherent wailing about devils. Kinross shrugged and went back down the valley.

It was beautiful early in the day with birds and flowers color-spotting the green through which the clean-limbed, scantily clad villagers moved in twos and threes. Smoke rose above clean, red flame before Mary's hut. The air was perfumed with flowers, musical with birdcalls and spiced with woodsmoke. Kinross tried to feel good, but a restlessness drove him.

He walked back and forth, jerkily, sat down and got up again, driven to random action that he would not shape into the action demanded of him. He picked fruit and threw it away, drifted toward the dark grove and walked resolutely away from it. At last he decided to make the fight in his hut. He went inside and wove burrawang fronds into a barrier across the door.

For hours, pacing or lying prone with clenched fists in the gloom, Kinross strove with his rebellious muscles and reproachful viscera. Finally the familiar silvery voice, long unheard, spoke to him out of the air.

"Kinross, I am hungry and thirsty. Bring me fruit."

"No. You have it from a hundred others."

"I need it from you, Kinross. We have a relation. I gave you back a lost life. You dragged my body here with your own strength. You owe me a duty."

"I deny it. If I ever did, I repudiate it."

"I have power, Kinross. Silva and Kerbeck bring no fruit. Would you be as they?"

"You lie, Kruger. You have not even the lesser power to command my muscles."

"I don't wish to command them directly. I wish to command you, with your consent, in this one small thing."

"No. I have tested your power before now."

"Not to the full, Kinross. Not to the full. I have been reluctant to hurt you."

Silence extended itself into Kinross' abrupt awareness that the tension was gone. He felt as tired as he had on the days he had fought the reentry barrier. He lay back to rest.

Round one is mine, he thought comfortably.

Distant thunder rumbled. Round two? he thought uneasily and unbarred his door. Black clouds were boiling up over the great ridge above the cave mouth. Black storm devils sifted down from the hillsides and gray women danced singly and in groups on the tops of things. Kinross brought wood into his hut, also stones to bank a fire and a brand to kindle it, working rapidly.

The storm built up fast, with tremendous thunder and jagged bolts of lightning. Kinross shielded and tended his fire, unheeding. The drumming rain changed into a drizzle and set in cold. The day became night without a perceptible sunset. Kinross shivered through the long night, burrowed under sweet grass and with his belly pressed against the warm rocks that banked his fire.

Morning was cold and clear. Frost rimed the grass, flower petals drooped and tree leaves twinkled with silver. Kinross was standing in his hut door, shivering and stamping his feet, when he heard the frosty crunch of footsteps. It was von Lankenau, not yet shaven for the day.

"Good morning, Mr. Kinross," von Lankenau greeted him. "Please pardon my more or less forced intrusion on your privacy."

"That's all right. It's not an intrusion."

"Oh? I had thought that you were deliberately keeping to yourself these last weeks. But I would like to discuss this cold . . ."

"If you can't take it, grow a beard like me."

"I am inured to cold, Mr. Kinross. At the moment I entered this world I had been stopped on a ledge at sixteen thousand feet for about thirty hours. My arms and my legs were frozen. The Seeings had begun . . . you touch my pride, Mr. Kinross, excuse me."

Kinross said nothing.

"How long are you prepared to go on with this defiance of the Herr Kruger?" von Lankenau asked.

"Maybe till Hell freezes over." Kinross laughed harshly, adding, "No. Until Kruger agrees to let me through the reentry barrier. Me and Mary Chadwick."

"He will never let you go, Mr. Kinross. And Miss Chadwick does not wish to go."

"The thing this damned Krugerworld has made of her may not so wish. But if Kruger would give her back to herself—"

"She has never ceased to be herself, Mr. Kinross. We talk increasingly of late and I know her well, in time will know her better still. But I do know what you mean . . ."

"Skip what I mean. Did Kruger send you here?"

"Oh no. It is my curiosity, I am afraid. You interest me, Mr. Kinross, and in studying you I learn much about the Herr Kruger. Tell me: you know the villagers are suffering from cold and will soon be hungry; do you feel any responsibility for their sufferings?"

"No. Kruger's responsible. Let him ease off."

"He will not, I am sure. What then?"

"Then we shiver and we starve. When those lobotomies of yours in the village get desperate enough maybe they'll help me break through the reentry barrier and get their minds and their own world back."

"They will not. That I know. But let me congratulate you on your efforts to break the barrier, Mr. Kinross. Did you know that you had pushed it outward a good way and permanently distorted that corner of Krugerworld? You are a strong and resolute man, sir. I wish you would consent to take your rightful position among us."

"I'll take my rightful departure or die trying."

"Mr. Kinross, the villagers also have a right to live. I will not prompt them nor will Mr. Garcia. We have agreed on that. But if the Herr Kruger can reach them directly through dreams and inspired counsels, and if the collective will moves to act upon you, we will stand aside also."

"Fair enough," Kinross grunted.

"One other thing, Mr. Kinross. I fear you may be moving blindly toward a treason of the light. I will say no more."

Kinross did not answer. Von Lankenau half smiled and saluted him, then turned and left in silence. Within a minute other footsteps approached, light and rapid ones.

It was Mary Chadwick and she was in a fury. Her shirt was half unbuttoned and she clasped in her bosom a dozen or more of the white nutmeg pigeons with black wing and tail tips.

"Down with ice on their poor wings. Half frozen. You stringybark jojo—" she stormed, face twisted with pity and anger.

"I'm sorry—" Kinross began.

"Then stop it, you fool! Stop it at once! Take that silly fruit to that stupid altar and put an end to this nonsense!"

"Did Lankenau or Kruger put you up to this?"

She stared a scornful denial. Kinross swallowed and felt his face burn under his beard.

"Why blame me and not Kruger?"

"Because I can't come at the Herr Kruger and I can come at you, of course. Hop, now!"

"All right," Kinross said. "I'll do it for you, Mary. Will you understand that I do it for you and not for Kruger, Mary? Will you accept?" He took hold of her hand among the rustling pigeons and looked into her blue-violet eyes murky with waning anger.

"Of course for me," she said. "That's what I came to tell you, idiot."

"Glory!" Kinross gasped and walked away rapidly. When he came back through the grove the frost had already melted under a warming sun.

"Round two is at least a draw," he thought, "but I kind of think I won it too."

Weeks passed into months and the land smiled. Kinross left fruit at the cairn each morning, whispering under his breath, "For you, Mary." Also each morning he laid flowers on a quartz boulder he had carried up from the creek and placed by Mary's hut. The flowers always disappeared, although he never saw her take them.

Stragglers continued coming into Krugerworld by ones or twos every few days and the population of Krugertown approached three hundred. Kinross talked amicably with Garcia and von Lankenau from time to time. Von Lankenau discussed the expansion of Krugerworld with an increasing population. He thought that at some critical point it would expand enough to accommodate another village and perhaps be dumbbell-shaped rather than elliptical. Garcia told Kinross pridefully that Pilar was carrying a child, he hoped a son.

Sometimes Kinross talked with the villagers. They had lost all memory of their origin. They believed they had come from underground, shaped of earth's substance at the bottom of a great pit, and that sometime they might go back there to sleep again. They had no clear notion of death.

Kinross no longer wandered aimlessly. At a site a mile down valley from the village, he built a stone hut. He built it massively, bedding large stones from the creek in clay and rammed earth, giving it several rooms beamed with ironwood and heavily thatched with nipa fronds. He built a stone fireplace and crude furniture.

Mary passed by several times a day, taking little interest in his work. When the house was complete she would not come in to look at it.

"It is a waste of strength and good living time," she said, laughing. "Allan, Allan, walk under the trees again."

"Will you walk with me?" he asked.

She laughed and turned away.

Kinross built a walled garden around the hut. He brought water into it with a raised ditch, pierced for drainage, taking off from above a low dam he built in the creek. It fed a bathing pool and turned a small waterwheel. He threshed out grass seeds and spread them and berries on the flagstones of his garden. Birds came and ate, but Mary would not come in.

"You don't paddock me with anything cold as stone, not by half," she said.

He saw her more often with von Lankenau and gradually tended to avoid them both, nagged by a question he dared not ask for fear of an answer. The black moods came back and he neglected his house to roam the hillsides as of old. Sometimes he met Kerbeck, vacant-eyed and enormous, wild and shaggy as a bear, and cursed Kruger bitterly while Kerbeck buzzed and hummed. He did not fail to leave his token of fruit each morning on the cairn.

Then one day, leaving Kerbeck and the Kabeiroi on the hillside, he came into the valley and saw a village woman tending grapevines alone at the foot of the hill. She was young, supple and brown and wore only a short paperbark skirt. She stopped working and bowed her head, waiting for him to pass. He stopped and searched in his mind for his limited Spanish.

"*Cómo te llamas?*"

"*Milagros, señor.*" Her voice was very low and she would not look at him.

"*Bueno. Tu estás muy bonita, Milagros.*"

"*Por favor, tengo que trabajar . . . el Señor Kruger . . .*"

"*Ven conmigo, Milagros. Yo te mando por el nombre del Señor Kruger.*"

She flushed darkly, then paled. She looked up at him with beseeching eyes shiny with tears.

"*Por favor, por gran favor, no me mande usted . . .*"

"*Quién te manda?*" asked a new voice from behind the screen of vines, and then, "Oh. You, Kinross?"

Garcia came into view around the vines. Like Kinross, he was barefooted and wore only stagged-off dungarees.

"What's it all about?" he asked.

"I was trying to talk to her . . ."

Garcia spoke rapidly in Spanish and the woman answered in a fearful voice. The thickset Mexican turned back to Kinross, fists knuckling hipbones.

"Take the name of Kruger back off of her, Kinross!"

"I remove the name, Milagros," Kinross said. "Garcia, I—"

"Take it off in Spanish," Garcia interrupted. "You put it on in Spanish."

Kinross garbled out a sentence in Spanish. Garcia was still angry. He sent the woman away.

"Kinross, I can't take away your power to use the name of
Kruger. But if you use it wrong, I can beat you half to death.
Maybe all the way to death. You get me?"

"Don't judge me so damned offhand. How do you know what
I intended?"

"Milagros knew. She knew, all right. I believe her."

"Believe what you like, then."

"Listen, Kinross, stay away from the villagers. I command
you in the name of Garcia and his two fists. You can outtalk
me and outthink me, but—" The stocky Mexican struck his
right fist into his left biceps with a solid thump.

Kinross clenched his teeth and breathed deeply through flaring nostrils. Then he said, "Okay, Garcia. I appreciate your
position. The only man I really want to fight doesn't have a
body."

"Good," the Mexican said. "No hard feelings, then. But you
still stay clear of the villagers, a kind of agreement between you
and me. Okay?"

"Okay," Kinross said and walked away.

When he came into his walled garden he saw nutmeg pigeons
pecking at overripe mangoes he had placed there for them.
Fearless, they hardly made way for his suddenly slowed feet.
The two fluttered briefly when he, unthinking, bent and seized
them. They quieted in his hands and he carried them inside,
wondering why.

For hours after nightfall he sat before his fire and stared into
the red coals. So he could outthink and outtalk Garcia, could
he? Well, yes, he could. But the act? How act? How get at a
man without a body?

Where was Kruger vulnerable? What force could he align
against Kruger? He had touched Kruger once only, and that
was by a refusal to act. That was negative. Now what was the
positive side? What act, what unthinking, nameless act . . .
and the fit stole over him and he took up the pigeons and left

the house and walked through the dark grove to the cairn where
Silva moaned in sleep and did what there was to do and returned and slept, to wake unremembering.

Day was advanced when Kinross came out of his house. He
walked up the valley, crossing over the little stream to avoid the
village, and picked two overripe mangoes, which he carried
through the grove to the cairn. Silva was rocking and wailing
thinly in an extremity of woe. To the right a knot of silent villagers clustered.

On the cairn he saw the headless pigeons with blood-dabbled
feathers and the black, sticky blood on the stones. Fingers
tugged at his memory and he frowned, refusing to think what
this strange thing might mean. He flung down his mangoes into
the blood spots with force enough to burst them and said aloud,
"For you, Mary." Then he stared arrogantly at the knot of villagers and strode away. But he was reluctant to emerge from
the grove, prowling its tangled shades far from path and stream
for upwards of an hour. Then he walked back toward the
village.

A strange silence held the land. No air moved. The villagers
were drifting toward the grove in small groups, without the customary singing and talking. He heard no birdcalls. Then, as he
neared the village, he heard a woman's voice strident with grief
and anger. It was Mary.

"What kind of Kelly rules do you keep here, you and your
Kruger, you smooth-faced blood drinker?"

Then von Lankenau's voice, soothing and indistinct behind
the huts, and then Mary again, agonized, "Oh, my lovely white
sea pigeons! Poor dears, poor dears, I'll take them all away with
me. You'll pay! You'll pay!"

She broke into a loud humming and came into view, running
toward the hillside. Her long hair streamed behind her and her
once lovely face was frightfully twisted and gaping with menace. Kinross noticed with another start that the black grotesques

from the hillside had invaded the valley floor and were all about the village. They gave way before the infuriated woman and all at once the birds became vocal, deafeningly so, clouds of them swooping at the black things with squawks and screeches.

Kinross stood in vagueness, looking around. Never had he seen the sun of Krugerworld more warm and smiling, the flowers more voluptuous, the trees more heavily laden with bright fruit. At his feet earth tilted and crumbled and a red-capped mushroom emerged, visibly rising and unfolding. Von Lankenau, his shaven face set in grave lines, came toward Kinross from out of the cluster of huts. Before he could speak, Garcia shouted from the direction of the grove and they saw him running toward them.

"Something's haywire with the villagers," he told von Lankenau, panting. "They won't follow ritual. They won't obey me."

"What are they doing?" von Lankenau asked.

"Nothing. Just standing still. But I don't like the feeling of things in there, don't ask me why."

"Something of truly enormous significance has happened, Joe. I do not know what . . . I was about to ask Mr. Kinross for his ideas. Those pigeons . . . but you are right, we must get the villagers back to their huts and to the fruit groves. Perhaps Mr. Kinross will help us."

"How do you know I won't play Pied Piper and lead them clear out of Krugerworld?" Kinross asked, his thoughts beginning to mesh again.

"Perhaps, now, that would be merciful. I truly do not know, Mr. Kinross. But let us see what may be done."

A distant scream came out of the dark grove, repeated, a volley of screams.

"Silva's voice!" Garcia exclaimed. *"Por Dios,* what now?"

He started running back toward the grove. Kinross and von Lankenau ran after him. The screaming ceased abruptly.

In the clearing, villagers stood in silent groups on either side of the stone platform and in small groups elsewhere. On the

cairn lay the body of the old Portygee, looking fragile and collapsed. His head was crushed horribly.

Garcia swore softly in Spanish. Von Lankenau said mus-
ingly, "Now, for as long as Krugerworld shall last . . . I must
manage to understand. I must!" A dark memory itched in Kinross' fingers.

"Kinross," came a whisper from close behind their heads.
The men whirled as one, to see nothing.

The whisper continued, still behind their heads so that they
whirled again, vainly. "Thank you, Kinross, for teaching me
how to relieve my thirst. My terrible thirst. I will purge my
world of thirst, Kinross, with your service."

Von Lankenau gripped Kinross' arm with iron fingers.
"What have you done, Kinross?" he pleaded. "Tell me. I must
know. *What have you done?*"

"You'll never know," Kinross said harshly. "Look behind
us."

The three men turned around again. The villagers had com-
pacted into a mob with a concave front that was slowly closing
in on them. Von Lankenau ordered them back in whiplash
tones, to no effect. He turned to Kinross, his face pale and grim.

"Command them under the name of the Herr Kruger, if you
can, Mr. Kinross. We have no other chance."

"Stop, damn you, in the name of Kruger!" Kinross shouted.
His hands were sweating and his heart was in his throat.

They did not stop. The horns of the crescent met on the far
side of the cairn. The solid front of the villagers, coming on in
a slow amoeboid shuffle of hundreds of feet, was ten yards
away. Kinross saw the girl Milagros, teeth bared. They had seconds only before, as Kinross somehow knew, they would join
Silva on the bloody stones.

"Quickly, Kinross," von Lankenau said. "Tell me while there
is time. *What have you done?*"

"Heart's truth," Kinross whispered, "I don't know. *I don't
know!*"

"Let's give 'em a fight," Garcia growled, then, "Hey! They've stopped!"

A cloud of birds came over the clearing, flashing in many colors, circling and shrieking. Brush crackled and water splashed in the dark grove. Then something went wrong at the back of the mob of villagers. It shuddered and broke into fragments which crept rapidly to either side, opening an aisle through its midst.

It was Kerbeck, floating hair and beard ablaze with sunlight. Rags of clothing fluttered on the great, bronzed limbs. Sweeps of his massive arms knocked villagers a dozen feet through the air. Booming and buzzing, wide blue eyes two-dimensional and unknowing, he passed the three wonder-stricken men. In his wake ran Mary Chadwick, birds about her head.

"He's going in to kill Kruger's body," she told them, coming to a halt. The frightful malevolence still rode in her features and Kinross' fear was not wholly relieved.

"Madre de Dios!" Garcia gasped.

They watched the giant Swede round the stone platform and head for the cave. From the darkness floated a gobbling howl that sent a hair-bristling shudder down Kinross' back. The great form of Bo Bo emerged to block the entrance.

Kerbeck ran forward with a shout. The Negro ran to meet him with his bubbling squall. The two massive figures shocked together and the world seemed to tremble. They swayed, stumbling back and forth, locked in furious embrace, and a great sighing moan went up from the fragmented mob of villagers. Kinross felt a hand on his arm and glimpsed von Lankenau's white, rapt face beside him.

Black giant with white strove and roared and howled and stumbled. They cannoned into the cairn and destroyed it, scattering and treading the stones underfoot like pebbles. They splashed into the creek and out of it, roiling the clear water to dark turbidity. Both giants were increasing in stature, to Kinross' eyes, clearly superhuman now. The force of their roaring and howling beat down on him with physical pressure. He saw Mary Chadwick on his right, blue-violet fire blazing in her eyes, fierce red lips parted eagerly.

First one giant and then the other was forced to his knees, only to rise again in thunderous shouting and howling. The fight drifted nearer to the cave mouth, entered and swirled out again, entered and stayed. Kerbeck's hair and beard seemed to shine with a light of their own, dwindling sparklike into the depths. The gigantic battle shouts became a continuous hollow roaring under the earth. Kinross felt a hand shaking him insistently. It was von Lankenau.

"Go now," he was saying. "For certain, the barrier will be down momentarily. I begin to understand. I almost—I do salute you, Mr. Kinross. Take the woman, if she will go."

Kinross collected his thoughts. "Mary, will you go?" he asked.

"Too bloody right I will," she said, "and take my birds off with me!"

Kinross looked at Garcia and held out his hand. "Part friends, Joe?" he asked.

"I don't savvy this, Kinross," the Mexican said, "but good luck and get out of here."

Kinross shook hands with the two men. Then he and Mary Chadwick, their arms linked, walked rapidly back toward the village.

The dark grove swarmed with Kabeiroi, but no more than a scattering of the ugly shapes could be seen on the open valley floor. The sky was overcast and the diffuse, watery light of the early days lay again on the valley. The old indefinite quality was back, nothing quite in full view.

"Mary," Kinross said, "I do believe we're already through the barrier. Space has drawn in around the cave mouth."

"Good-oh!"

Kinross led her up the hillside, talking feverishly. They would

marry, he said. He was quite well off, had a good job doing confidential work for the U.S. government. He had lots of back pay
coming for his last job and a bonus, too, when he told them
about it. They would live in California, it was a lot like Queensland. Trips, the theater, music, a fine home, gracious living.

Mary said little. Birds kept fluttering in to land on her head
and shoulders, but the number around her did not seem to increase. The light grew weaker as they climbed and the land
more indefinite. When they reached the height of land and Kinross knew for sure that they had escaped, it was almost dark.
From time to time a rippling quiver ran over the ground sending them sprawling, but they rose and pressed onward. As before, progress seemed timeless and effortless. There was no
moon.

Mary lagged behind him and Kinross kept turning to wait for
her. By degrees in the fading light he saw the strained malevolence of her expression give way to a vague and remote sorrow.
The wide brow was smooth again, red lips dreaming. Once she
said, "My birds. I can't get back all my birds."

Suddenly the wailing cry of a stone curlew reached down
from the darkness. Mary stopped and looked up. Kinross turned
back to watch. The forlorn, throbbing cry repeated. Mary
raised her arms to the black sky and crooned. Nothing happened.

She looked at Kinross, both of them vague in shadow. "It
won't come down to me," she whispered plaintively.

A third time the call floated downward. Mary dropped her
arms.

"I'm going back," she said. "You go on alone, Allan."

"No!" he protested. "You must come with me. I won't let you
go back!"

He seized her shoulders. She came stiffly erect and a light
gleamed from her eyes. A touch, a twinge only, of the old feeling hit him and his knees turned to water. He collapsed, kneeling, clasping her around the thighs, pleading, "No, no, Mary!
Don't leave me alone here in the dark!"

"I must," she said calmly. Then, with a touch of pity, "Be brave and go along now, Allan. It is all you can do."

She raised him and kissed his forehead. He stumbled away, not daring to look back for fear of a renewed weakness. The sky rifted with silver as the overcast broke up and presently a full moon rode high ahead. He looked back then, but she was nowhere.

On to the great pit under the moon, leg over leg unthinking. It was all he could do now. He found the ravine and waded down it, outrunning the current. He heard the roar of falling water and saw the last rock shoulder that interposed itself between him and the brink. For just a heartbeat he clung to the rock and stared into the pit with all its silver beauty and its reflecting pool in the bottom. Then, not letting the water take him only, but rushing, pitching his body forward, he went over the edge.

It was not a sheer drop but rather a series of stages. Plunge and strike and roll, plunge and strike and roll, rhythmically, painlessly, with intolerable excitement of the spirit, down and down he went until the circle of sky above him smalled with distance and the silvery pool below waxed enormous. It was as if the great pit were reversing its dimensions, flexing through itself, turning inside out, as if he were falling into the moon. Then, on the very point of an unbearable instant, the waters closed over him.

Down, down through the water, pain and darkness and fear vise-clamping his chest, kicking and waving his arms and there was a dry crackling and a pain in his toe and he sat in the thorn scrub gasping. His skin was dry.

It was daylight. A stream ran nearby and above it reared a yellowish sandstone ledge with figures of paunchy kangaroos and stick men done in faded red and black. He picked up a handful of earth and looked at it. There it was, hard and sharp and clear in all of its minute particulars, deep as any microscope might probe, solidly there beyond all tampering forever.

It was the old world. His world. Kinross stood up, feeling an overpowering thirst.

He went down to the creek and drank deeply and was as thirsty as before. He buried his face in the water and drank until he was near bursting and rose, wavering on his feet, thirst tearing at him unbearably. He tugged at his beard and wondered.

Sounds came, a jingle of metal and splashing. Then the creak of leather and low voices. Riders were coming up the creek. Suddenly he sensed them directly, horses and men, radiant with life, red, living blood pumping through veins and arteries. His thirst became a cloud of madness enfolding him, and he knew who and what he was.

He waited, wondering if they would be able to see him . . .

The Saliva Tree

The Saliva Tree

BRIAN W. ALDISS

Brian Aldiss, who has enlivened science fiction with his mordant wit for the last thirteen years, now says he is beginning to think science fiction is as obsolete as 1840 church novels. In this story he takes a nostalgic look at another obsolete world, and incidentally suggests a new source for the extraordinary ideas of Mr. H. G. Wells.

> *There is neither speech nor language;*
> *but their voices are heard among them.*
> PSALM XIX

You know, I'm really much exercised about the Fourth Dimension," said the fair-haired young man, with a suitable earnestness in his voice.

"Um," said his companion, staring up at the night sky.

"It seems very much in evidence these days. Do you not think you catch a glimpse of it in the drawings of Aubrey Beardsley?"

"Um," said his companion.

They stood together on a low rise to the east of the sleepy East Anglian town of Cottersall, watching the stars shivering a little in the chill February air. They are both young men in their early twenties. The one who is occupied with the Fourth Dimension is called Bruce Fox; he is tall and fair and works as

233

junior clerk in the Norwich firm of lawyers, Prendergast and Tout. The other, who has so far vouchsafed us only an *um* or two, although he is to figure largely as the hero of our account, is by name Gregory Rolles. He is tall and dark, with gray eyes set in his handsome and intelligent face. He and Fox have sworn to Think Large, thus distinguishing themselves, at least in their own minds, from all the rest of the occupants of Cottersall in these last years of the nineteenth century.

"There's another!" exclaimed Gregory, breaking at last from the realm of monosyllables. He pointed a gloved finger up at the constellation of Auriga the Charioteer. A meteor streaked across the sky like a runaway flake of the Milky Way, and died in midair.

"Beautiful!" they said together.

"It's funny," Fox said, prefacing his words with an oft-used phrase, "the stars and men's minds are so linked together and always have been, even in the centuries of ignorance before Charles Darwin. They always seem to play an ill-defined role in man's affairs. They help me think large too, don't they you, Greg?"

"You know what I think—I think that some of those stars may be occupied. By people, I mean." He breathed heavily, overcome by what he was saying. "People who—perhaps they are better than us, live in a just society, wonderful people. . . ."

"I know, socialists to a man!" Fox exclaimed. This was one point on which he did not share his friend's advanced thinking. He had listened to Mr. Tout talking in the office, and thought he knew better than his rich friend how these socialists, of which one heard so much these days, were undermining society. "Stars full of socialists!"

"Better than stars full of Christians! Why, if the stars were full of Christians, no doubt they would already have sent missionaries down here to preach their Gospel."

"I wonder if there ever will be planetary journeys as predicted by Nunsowe Greene and Monsieur Jules Verne—" Fox said, when the appearance of a fresh meteor stopped him in mid sentence.

Like the last, this meteor seemed to come from the general direction of Auriga. It traveled slowly, and it glowed red, and it sailed grandly toward them. They both exclaimed at once and gripped each other by the arm. The magnificent spark burned in the sky, larger now, so that its red aura appeared to encase a brighter orange glow. It passed overhead (afterward, they argued whether it had not made a slight noise as it passed) and disappeared below a clump of willow. They knew it had been near. For an instant, the land had shone with its light.

Gregory was the first to speak.

"Bruce, Bruce, did you see that? That was no ordinary fireball!"

"It was so big! What was it?"

"Perhaps our heavenly visitor has come at last!"

"Hey, Greg, it must have landed by your friends' farm—the Grendon place—mustn't it?"

"You're right! I must pay old Mr. Grendon a visit tomorrow and see if he or his family saw anything of this."

They talked excitedly, stamping their feet as they exercised their lungs. Their conversation was the conversation of optimistic young men and included much speculative matter that began "Wouldn't it be wonderful if—" or "Just supposing—" Then they stopped and laughed at their own absurd beliefs.

Fox said slyly, "So you'll be seeing all the Grendon family tomorrow?"

"It seems probable, unless that red hot planetary ship has already borne them off to a better world."

"Tell us true, Greg—you really go to see that pretty Nancy Grendon, don't you?"

Gregory struck his friend playfully on the shoulder.

"No need for your jealousy, Bruce! I go to see the father, not the daughter. Though the one is female, the other is progressive, and that must interest me more just yet. Nancy has beauty, true, but her father—ah, her father has electricity!"

Laughing, they cheerfully shook hands and parted for the night.

On Grendon's farm, things were a deal less tranquil, as Gregory was to discover.

Gregory Rolles rose before seven next morning as was his custom. It was while he was lighting his gas mantle, and wishing Mr. Fenn (the baker in whose house Gregory lodged) would install electricity, that a swift train of thought led him to reflect again on the phenomenal thing in the previous night's sky. He let his mind wander luxuriously over all the possibilities that the "meteor" illuminated. He decided that he would ride out to see Mr. Grendon within the hour.

He was lucky in being able, at this stage of his life, to please himself largely as to how his days were spent, for his father was a person of some substance. Edward Rolles had had the fortune, at the time of the Crimean War, to meet Escoffier, and with some help from the great chef had brought on to the market a baking powder, "Eugenol," that, being slightly more palatable and less deleterious to the human system than its rivals, had achieved great commercial success. As a result, Gregory had attended one of the Cambridge colleges.

Now, having gained a degree, he was poised on the verge of a career. But which career? He had acquired—more as result of his intercourse with other students than with those officially delegated to instruct him—some understanding of the sciences; his essays had been praised and some of his poetry published, so that he inclined toward literature; and an uneasy sense that life for everyone outside the privileged classes contained too large a proportion of misery led him to think seriously of a political career. In Divinity, too, he was well grounded; but at least the idea of Holy Orders did not tempt him.

While he wrestled with his future, he undertook to live away from home, since his relations with his father were never smooth. By rusticating himself in the heart of East Anglia, he hoped to gather material for a volume tentatively entitled "Wanderings with a Socialist Naturalist," which would assuage all sides of his ambitions. Nancy Grendon, who had a pretty hand with a pencil, might even execute a little emblem for the title page. . . . Perhaps he might be permitted to dedicate it to his author friend, Mr. Herbert George Wells. . . .

He dressed himself warmly, for the morning was cold as well as dull, and went down to the baker's stables. When he had saddled his mare, Daisy, he swung himself up and set out along a road that the horse knew well.

The land rose slightly toward the farm, the area about the house forming something of a little island amid marshy ground and irregular stretches of water that gave back to the sky its own dun tone. The gate over the little bridge was, as always, open wide; Daisy picked her way through the mud to the stables, where Gregory left her to champ oats contentedly. Cuff and her pup, Lardie, barked loudly about Gregory's heels as usual, and he patted their heads on his way over to the house.

Nancy came hurrying out to meet him before he got to the front door.

"We had some excitement last night, Gregory," she said. He noted with pleasure she had at last brought herself to use his first name.

"Something bright, and glaring!" she said. "I was retiring, when this noise come and then this light, and I rush to look out through the curtains, and there's this here great thing like an egg sinking into our pond." In her speech, and particularly when she was excited, she carried the lilting accent of Norfolk.

"The meteor!" Gregory exclaimed. "Bruce Fox and I were out last night, as we were the night before, watching for the lovely Aurigids that arrive every February, when we saw an extra big one. I said then it was coming over very near here."

"Why, it almost landed on our house," Nancy said. She looked very pleasing this morning, with her lips red, her cheeks shining, and her chestnut curls all astray. As she spoke, her mother appeared in apron and cap, with a wrap hurriedly thrown over her shoulders.

"Nancy, you come in, standing freezing like that! You ent daft, girl, are you? Hello, Gregory, how be going on? I didn't reckon as we'd see you today. Come in and warm yourself."

"Good day to you, Mrs. Grendon. I'm hearing about your wonderful meteor of last night."

"It was a falling star, according to Bert Neckland. I ent sure what it was, but it certainly stirred up the animals, that I *do* know."

"Can you see anything of it in the pond?" Gregory asked.

"Let me show you," Nancy said.

Mrs. Grendon returned indoors. She went slowly and grandly, her back very straight and an unaccustomed load before her. Nancy was her only daughter; there was a younger son, Archie, a stubborn lad who had fallen at odds with his father and now was apprenticed to a blacksmith in Norwich; and no other children living. Three infants had not survived the mixture of fogs alternating with bitter east winds that comprised the typical Cottersall winter. But now the farmer's wife was unexpectedly gravid again and would bear her husband another baby when the spring came in.

As Nancy led Gregory over to the pond, he saw Grendon with his two laborers working in the West Field, but they did not wave.

"Was your father not excited by the arrival last night?"

"That he was—when it happened! He went out with his shotgun, and Bert Neckland with him. But there was nothing to see but bubbles in the pond and steam over it, and this morning he wouldn't discuss it and said that work must go on whatever happen."

They stood beside the pond, a dark and extensive slab of

water with rushes on the farther bank and open country beyond. As they looked at its ruffled surface, they stood with the windmill black and bulky on their left hand. It was to this that Nancy now pointed.

Mud had been splashed across the boards high up the sides of the mill; some was to be seen even on the top of the nearest white sail. Gregory surveyed it all with interest. Nancy, however, was still pursuing her own line of thought.

"Don't you reckon Father works too hard, Gregory? When he ent outside doing jobs, he's in reading his pamphlets and his electricity manuals. He never rests but when he sleeps."

"Um. Whatever went into the pond went in with a great smack! There's no sign of anything there now, is there? Not that you can see an inch below the surface."

"You being a friend of his, Mum thought perhaps as you'd say something to him. He don't go to bed till ever so late— sometimes it's near midnight, and then he's up again at three and a half o'clock. Would you speak to him? You know Mother dassent."

"Nancy, we ought to see whatever it was that went in the pond. It can't have dissolved. How deep is the water? Is it very deep?"

"Oh, you aren't listening, Gregory Rolles! Bother the old meteor!"

"This is a matter of science, Nancy. Don't you see—"

"Oh, rotten old science, is it? Then I don't want to hear. I'm cold, standing out here. You can have a good look if you like but I'm going in before I gets froze. It was only an old stone out of the sky, because I heard father and Bert Neckland agree to it."

"Fat lot Bert Neckland knows about such things!" he called to her departing back.

He looked down at the dark water. Whatever it *was* that had arrived last night, it was here, only a few feet from him. He longed to discover what remained of it. Vivid pictures entered his mind: his name in headlines in *The Morning Post,* the Royal Society making him an honorary member, his father embracing him and pressing him to return home.

Thoughtfully, he walked over to the barn. Hens ran clucking out of his way as he entered and stood looking up, waiting for his eyes to adjust to the dim light. There, as he remembered it, was a little rowing boat. Perhaps in his courting days old Mr. Grendon had taken his prospective wife out for excursions on the Oast in it. Surely it had not been used in years. He dragged the boat from the barn and launched it in the shallows of the pond. It floated. The boards had dried, and water leaked through a couple of seams, but not nearly enough to deter him.

Climbing delicately in among the straw and filth, he pushed off.

When he was over the approximate center of the pond, he shipped his oars and peered over the side. There was an agitation in the water, and nothing could be seen, although he imagined much.

As he stared over the one side, the boat unexpectedly tipped to the other. Gregory swung around. The boat listed heavily to the left, so that the oars rolled over that way. He could see nothing. Yet—he heard something. It was a sound much like a hound slowly panting. And whatever made it was about to capsize the boat.

"What is it?" he said, as all the skin prickled up his back and skull.

The boat lurched, for all the world as if someone invisible were trying to get into it. Frightened, he grasped the oar, and, without thinking, swept it over that side of the rowing boat.

It struck something solid where there was only air.

Dropping the oar in surprise, he put out his hand. It touched something yielding. At the same time, his arm was violently struck.

His actions were then entirely governed by instinct. Thought did not enter the matter. He picked up the oar again and smote the thin air with it. It hit something. There was a splash, and the boat righted itself so suddenly he was almost pitched into the water. Even while it still rocked he was rowing frantically for the shallows, dragging the boat from the water and running for the safety of the farmhouse.

Only at the door did he pause. His reason returned, his heart began gradually to stop stammering its fright. He stood looking at the seamed wood of the porch, trying to evaluate what he had seen and what had actually happened. But what had happened?

Forcing himself to go back to the pond, he stood by the boat and looked across the sullen face of the water. It lay undisturbed, except by surface ripples. He looked at the boat. A quantity of water lay in the bottom of it. He thought, All that happened was that I nearly capsized, and let my idiot fears run away with me. Shaking his head, he pulled the boat back to the barn.

Gregory, as he often did, stayed to eat lunch at the farm, but he saw nothing of the farmer till milking time.

Joseph Grendon was in his late forties, and a few years older than his wife. He had a gaunt solemn face and a heavy beard that made him look older than he was. For all his seriousness, he greeted Gregory civilly enough. They stood together in the gathering dusk as the cows swung behind them into their regular stalls. Together they walked into the machine house next door, and Grendon lit the oil burners that started the steam engine into motion that would turn the generator that would supply the vital spark.

"I smell the future in here," Gregory said, smiling. By now, he had forgotten the shock of the morning.

"The future will have to get on without me. I shall be dead by then." The farmer spoke as he walked, putting each word reliably before the next.

"That is what you always say. You're wrong—the future is rushing upon us."

"You ent far wrong there, Master Gregory, but I won't have no part of it, I reckon. I'm an old man now. Here she come!"

This last exclamation was directed at a flicker of light in the pilot bulb overhead. They stood there contemplating with satisfaction the wonderful machinery. As steam pressure rose, the great leather belt turned faster and faster, and the flicker in the pilot bulb grew stronger. Although Gregory was used to a home lit by both gas and electricity, he never felt the excitement of it as he did here, out in the wilds, where the nearest incandescent bulb was probably in Norwich, a great part of a day's journey away.

Now a pale flickering radiance illuminated the room. By contrast, everything outside looked black. Grendon nodded in satisfaction, made some adjustments to the burners, and they went outside.

Free from the bustle of the steam engine, they could hear the noise the cows were making. At milking time, the animals were usually quiet; something had upset them. The farmer ran quickly into the milking shed, with Gregory on his heels.

The new light, radiating from a bulb hanging above the stalls, showed the beasts of restless demeanor and rolling eye. Bert Neckland stood as far away from the door as possible, grasping his stick and letting his mouth hang open.

"What in blazes you staring at, bor?" Grendon asked.

Neckland slowly shut his mouth.

"We had a scare," he said. "Something come in here."

"Did you see what it was?" Gregory asked.

"No, there weren't nothing to see. It was a ghost, that's what it was. It came right in here and touched the cows. It touched me too. It was a ghost."

The farmer snorted. "A tramp more like. You couldn't see because the light wasn't on."

His man shook his head emphatically. "Light weren't that

bad. I tell you, whatever it was, it come right up to me and touched me." He stopped, and pointed to the edge of the stall. "Look there! See, I weren't telling you no lie, master. It was a ghost, and there's its wet hand print."

They crowded around and examined the worn and chewed timber at the corner of the partition between two stalls. An indefinite patch of moisture darkened the wood. Gregory's thoughts went back to his experience on the pond, and again he felt the prickle of unease along his spine. But the farmer said stoutly, "Nonsense, it's a bit of cowslime. Now you get on with the milking, Bert, and let's have no more hossing about, because I want my tea. Where's Cuff?"

Bert looked defiant.

"If you don't believe me, maybe you'll believe the bitch. She saw whatever it was and went for it. It kicked her over, but she ran it out of here."

"I'll see if I can see her," Gregory said.

He ran outside and began calling the bitch. By now it was almost entirely dark. He could see nothing moving in the wide space of the front yard, and so set off in the other direction, down the path toward the pigsties and the fields, calling Cuff as he went. He paused. Low and savage growls sounded ahead, under the elm trees. It was Cuff. He went slowly forward. At this moment, he cursed that electric light meant lack of lanterns and wished too that he had a weapon.

"Who's there?" he called.

The farmer came up by his side. "Let's charge 'em!"

They ran forward. The trunks of the four great elms were clear against the western sky, with water glinting leadenly behind them. The dog became visible. As Gregory saw Cuff, she sailed into the air, whirled around, and flew at the farmer. He flung up his arms and warded off the body. At the same time, Gregory felt a rush of air as if someone unseen had run past him, and a stale muddy smell filled his nostrils. Staggering, he looked behind him. The wan light from the cow sheds spread across the path between the outhouses and the farmhouse. Beyond the light, more distantly, was the silent countryside behind the grain store. Nothing untoward could be seen.

"They killed my old Cuff," said the farmer.

Gregory knelt down beside him to look at the bitch. There was no mark of injury on her, but she was dead, her fine head lying limp.

"She knew there was something there," Gregory said. "She went to attack whatever it was and it got her first. What was it? Whatever in the world was it?"

"They killed my old Cuff," said the farmer again, unhearing. He picked the body up in his arms, turned, and carried it toward the house. Gregory stood where he was, mind and heart equally uneasy.

He jumped violently when a step sounded nearby. It was Bert Neckland.

"What, did that there ghost kill the old bitch?" he asked.

"It killed the bitch certainly, but it was something more terrible than a ghost."

"That's one of them ghosts, bor. I seen plenty in my time. I ent afraid of ghosts, are you?"

"You looked fairly sick in the cow shed a minute ago."

The farmhand put his fists on his hips. He was no more than a couple of years older than Gregory, a stocky young man with a spotty complexion and a snub nose that gave him at once an air of comedy and menace. "Is that so, Master Gregory? Well, you looks pretty funky standing there now."

"I am scared. I don't mind admitting it. But only because we have something here a lot nastier than any specter."

Neckland came a little closer.

"Then if you are so blooming windy, perhaps you'll be staying away from the farm in future."

"Certainly not." He tried to edge back into the light, but the laborer got in his way.

"If I was you, I should stay away." He emphasized his point by digging an elbow into Gregory's coat. "And just remember that Nancy was interested in me long afore you come along, bor."

"Oh, that's it, is it! I think Nancy can decide for herself in whom she is interested, don't you?"

"I'm *telling* you who she's interested in, see? And mind you don't forget, see?" He emphasized the words with another nudge. Gregory pushed his arm away angrily. Neckland shrugged his shoulders and walked off. As he went, he said, "You're going to get worse than ghosts if you keep hanging round here."

Gregory was shaken. The suppressed violence in the man's voice suggested that he had been harboring malice for some time. Unsuspectingly, Gregory had always gone out of his way to be cordial, had regarded the sullenness as mere slow-wittedness and done his socialist best to overcome the barrier between them. He thought of following Neckland and trying to make it up with him; but that would look too feeble. Instead, he followed the way the farmer had gone with his dead bitch and made for the house.

Gregory Rolles was too late back to Cottersall that night to meet his friend Fox. The next night the weather became exceedingly chill and Gabriel Woodcock, the oldest inhabitant, was prophesying snow before the winter was out (a not very venturesome prophecy to be fulfilled within forty-eight hours, thus impressing most of the inhabitants of the village, for they took pleasure in being impressed and exclaiming and saying "Well I never!" to each other). The two friends met in The Wayfarer, where the fires were bigger, though the ale was weaker, than in The Three Poachers at the other end of the village.

Seeing to it that nothing dramatic was missed from his account, Gregory related the affairs of the previous day, omitting any reference to Neckland's pugnacity. Fox listened fascinated, neglecting both his pipe and his ale.

"So you see how it is, Bruce," Gregory concluded. "In that deep pond by the mill lurks a vehicle of some sort, the very one we saw in the sky, and in it lives an invisible being of evil intent. You see how I fear for my friends there. Should I tell the police about it, do you think?"

"I'm sure it would not help the Grendons to have old Farrish bumping out there on his pennyfarthing," Fox said, referring to the local representative of the law. He took a long draw first on the pipe and then on the glass. "But I'm not sure you have your conclusions quite right, Greg. Understand, I don't doubt the facts, amazing though they are. I mean, we were more or less expecting celestial visitants. The world's recent blossoming with gas and electric lighting in its cities at night must have been a signal to half the nations of space that we are now civilized down here. But have our visitants done any deliberate harm to anyone?"

"They nearly drowned me and they killed poor Cuff. I don't see what you're getting at. They haven't begun in a very friendly fashion, have they now?"

"Think what the situation must seem like to them. Suppose they come from Mars or the Moon—we know their world must be absolutely different from Earth. They may be terrified. And it can hardly be called an unfriendly act to try and get into your rowing boat. The first unfriendly act was yours, when you struck out with the oar."

Gregory bit his lip. His friend had a point. "I was scared."

"It may have been because they were scared that they killed Cuff. The dog attacked them, after all, didn't she? I feel sorry for these creatures, alone in an unfriendly world."

"You keep saying 'these'! As far as we know, there is only one of them."

"My point is this, Greg. You have completely gone back on

your previous enlightened attitude. You are all for killing these poor things instead of trying to speak to them. Remember what you were saying about other worlds being full of socialists? Try thinking of these chaps as invisible socialists and see if that doesn't make them easier to deal with."

Gregory fell to stroking his chin. Inwardly, he acknowledged that Bruce Fox's words made a great impression on him. He had allowed panic to prejudice his judgment; as a result, he had behaved as immoderately as a savage in some remote corner of the Empire, confronted by his first steam locomotive.

"I'd better get back to the farm and sort things out as soon as possible," he said. "If these things really do need help, I'll help them."

"That's it. But try not to think of them as 'things.' Think of them as—as—I know, as The Aurigans."

"Aurigans it is. But don't be so smug, Bruce. If you'd been in that boat—"

"I know, old friend. I'd have died of fright." To this monument of tact, Fox added, "Do as you say, go back and sort things out as soon as possible. I'm longing for the next installment of this mystery. It's quite the jolliest thing since Sherlock Holmes."

Gregory Rolles went back to the farm. But the sorting out of which Bruce had spoken took longer than he expected. This was chiefly because the Aurigans seemed to have settled quietly into their new home after the initial day's troubles.

They came forth no more from the pond, as far he could discover; at least they caused no more disturbance. The young graduate particularly regretted this since he had taken his friend's words much to heart and wanted to prove how enlightened and benevolent he was toward this strange form of life. After some days, he came to believe the Aurigans must have left as unexpectedly as they arrived. Then a minor incident convinced him otherwise; and that same night, in his snug room over the baker's shop, he described it to his correspondent in Worcester Park, Surrey.

Dear Mr. Wells,

I must apologise for my failure to write earlier, owing to lack of news concerning the Grendon Farm affair.

Only today, the Aurigans showed themselves again!— if indeed "showed" is the right word for invisible creatures.

Nancy Grendon and I were in the orchard feeding the hens. There is still much snow lying about, and everywhere is very white. As the poultry came running to Nancy's tub, I saw a disturbance further down the orchard—merely some snow dropping from an apple bough, but the movement caught my eye, and I then saw a *procession* of falling snow proceed towards us from tree to tree. The grass is long there, and I soon noted the stalks being thrust aside by *an unknown agency!* I directed Nancy's attention to the phenomenon. The motion in the grass stopped only a few yards from us.

Nancy was startled, but I determined to acquit myself more like a Briton than I had previously. Accordingly, I advanced and said, "Who are you? What do you want? We are your friends if you are friendly."

No answer came. I stepped forward again, and now the grass again fell back, and I could see by the way it was pressed down that the creature must have large feet. By the movement of the grasses, I could see he was running. I cried to him and ran too. He went round the side of the house and then over the frozen mud in the farmyard. I could see no further trace of him. But instinct led me forward, past the barn to the pond.

Surely enough, I then saw the cold, muddy water rise and heave, as if engulfing a body that slid quietly in. Shards of broken ice were thrust aside, and by an outward motion I could see where the strange being went. In a flurry and a small whirlpool he was gone, and I have no doubt dived down to the mysterious vehicle.

These things—people—I know not what to call them—must be aquatic; perhaps they live in the canals of the Red Planet. But imagine, Sir—an invisible mankind! The idea is almost as wonderful and fantastic as something from your novel, *The Time Machine*.

Pray give me your comment, and trust in my sanity and accuracy as a reporter!

Yours in friendship,
Gregory Rolles

What he did not tell was the way Nancy had clung to him after, in the warmth of the parlor, and confessed her fear. And he had scorned the idea that these beings could be hostile, and had seen the admiration in her eyes, and had thought that she was, after all, a dashed pretty girl, and perhaps worth braving the wrath of those two very different people for: Edward Rolles, his father, and Bert Neckland, the farm laborer.

It was at lunch a week later, when Gregory was again at the farm, taking with him an article on electricity as a pretext for his visit, that the subject of the stinking dew was first discussed.

Grubby was the first to mention it in Gregory's hearing. Grubby, with Bert Neckland, formed the whole strength of Joseph Grendon's labor force; but whereas Neckland was considered couth enough to board in the farmhouse (he had a gaunt room in the attic), Grubby was fit only to sleep in a little flint-and-chalk hut well away from the farm buildings. His "house," as he dignified the miserable hut, stood below the orchard and near the sties, the occupants of which lulled Grubby to sleep with their snorts.

"Reckon we ent ever had a dew like that before, Mr. Grendon," he said, his manner suggesting to Gregory that he had made this observation already this morning; Grubby never ventured to say anything original.

"Heavy as an autumn dew," said the farmer firmly, as if there had been an argument on that point.

Silence fell, broken only by a general munching and, from Grubby, a particular guzzling, as they all made their way through huge platefuls of stewed rabbit and dumplings.

"It weren't no ordinary dew, that I do know," Grubby said after a while.

"It stank of toadstools," Neckland said. "Or rotten pond water."

More munching.

"It may be something to do with the pond," Gregory said. "Some sort of freak evaporation."

Neckland snorted. From his position at the top of the table, the farmer halted his shoveling operations to point a fork at Gregory.

"You may well be right there. Because I tell you what, that there dew only come down on our land and property. A yard the other side of the gate, the road was dry. Bone dry it was."

"Right you are there, master," Neckland agreed. "And while the West Field was dripping with the stuff, I saw for myself that the bracken over the hedge weren't wet at all. Ah, it's a rum go!"

"Say what you like, we ent ever had a dew like it," Grubby said. He appeared to be summing up the feeling of the company.

The strange dew did not fall again. As a topic of conversation, it was limited, and even on the farm, where there was little new to talk about, it was forgotten in a few days. The February passed, being neither much worse nor much better than most Februaries, and ended in heavy rainstorms. March came, letting in a chilly spring over the land. The animals on the farm began to bring forth their young.

They brought them forth in amazing numbers, as if to over-turn all the farmer's beliefs in the unproductiveness of his land.

"I never seen anything like it!" Grendon said to Gregory. Nor had Gregory seen the taciturn farmer so excited. He took the young man by the arm and marched him into the barn.

There lay Trix, the nanny goat. Against her flank huddled three little brown and white kids, while a fourth stood nearby, wobbling on its spindly legs.

"Four on 'em! Have you ever heard of a goat throwing off *four* kids? You better write to the papers in London about this, Gregory! But just you come down to the pigsties."

The squealing from the sties was louder than usual. As they marched down the path toward them, Gregory looked up at the great elms, their outlines dusted in green, and thought he detected something sinister in the noises, something hysterical that was perhaps matched by an element in Grendon's own bearing.

The Grendon pigs were mixed breeds, with a preponderance of Large Blacks. They usually gave litters of something like ten piglets. Now there was not a litter without fourteen in it; one enormous black sow had eighteen small pigs swarming about her. The noise was tremendous and, standing looking down on this swarming life, Gregory told himself that he was foolish to imagine anything uncanny in it; he knew so little about farm life. After he had eaten with Grendon and the men—Mrs. Grendon and Nancy had driven to town in the trap—Gregory went by himself to look about the farm, still with a deep and (he told himself) unreasoning sense of disturbance inside him.

A pale sunshine filled the afternoon. It could not penetrate far down into the water of the pond. But as Gregory stood by the horse trough staring at the expanse of water, he saw that it teemed with young tadpoles and frogs. He went closer. What he had regarded as a sheet of rather stagnant water was alive with small swimming things. As he looked, a great beetle surged out of the depths and seized a tadpole. The tadpoles were also providing food for two ducks that, with their young, were swimming by the reeds on the far side of the pond. And how many young did the ducks have? An armada of chicks was there, parading in and out of the rushes.

For a minute, he stood uncertainly, then began to walk

slowly back the way he had come. Crossing the yard, Gregory
went over to the stable and saddled Daisy. He swung himself
up and rode away without bidding goodbye to anyone.

Riding into Cottersall, he went straight to the marketplace.
He saw the Grendon trap, with Nancy's little pony, Hetty, between the shafts, standing outside the grocer's shop. Mrs. Grendon and Nancy were just coming out. Jumping to the ground,
Gregory led Daisy over to them and bid them good day.

"We are going to call on my friend Mrs. Edwards and her
daughters," Mrs. Grendon said.

"If you would be so kind, Mrs. Grendon, I would be very
obliged if I might speak privately with Nancy. My landlady,
Mrs. Fenn, has a little downstairs parlor at the back of the shop,
and I know she would let us speak there. It would be quite
respectable."

"Drat respectable! Let people think what they will, I say."
All the same, she stood for some time in meditation. Nancy remained by her mother with her eyes on the ground. Gregory
looked at her and seemed to see her anew. Under her blue coat,
fur trimmed, she wore her orange-and-brown-squared gingham
dress; she had a bonnet on her head. Her complexion was pure
and blemishless, her skin as firm and delicate as a plum, and
her dark eyes were hidden under long lashes. Her lips were
steady, pale, and clearly defined, with appealing tucks at each
corner. He felt almost like a thief, stealing a sight of her beauty
while she was not regarding him.

"I'm going on to Mrs. Edwards," Marjorie Grendon declared
at last. "I don't care what you two do so long as you behave—
but I shall, mind, if you aren't with me in a half hour, Nancy,
do you hear?"

"Yes, Mother."

The baker's shop was in the next street. Gregory and Nancy
walked there in silence. Gregory shut Daisy in the stable and
they went together into the parlor through the back door. At

this time of day, Mr. Fenn was resting upstairs, with his wife looking after the shop, so the little room was empty.

Nancy sat upright in a chair and said, "Well, Gregory, what's all this about? Fancy dragging me off from my mother like that in the middle of town!"

"Nancy, don't be cross. I had to see you."

She pouted. "You come out to the old farm often enough and don't show any particular wish to see me there."

"That's nonsense. I always come to see you—lately in particular. Besides, you're more interested in Bert Neckland, aren't you?"

"Bert Neckland, indeed! Why should I be interested in him? Not that it's any of your business if I am."

"It is my business, Nancy. I love you, Nancy!"

He had not meant to blurt it out in quite that fashion, but now it was out, it was out, and he pressed home his disadvantage by crossing the room, kneeling at her feet, and taking her hands in his. "Nancy, darling Nancy, say that you like me just a little. Encourage me somewhat."

"You are a very fine gentleman, Gregory, and I feel very kind towards you, to be sure, but . . ."

"But?"

She gave him the benefit of her downcast eyes again.

"Your station in life is very different from mine, and besides —well, you don't *do* anything."

He was shocked into silence. With the natural egotism of youth, he had not seriously thought that she could have any firm objection to him; but in her words he suddenly saw the truth of his position, at least as it was revealed to her.

"Nancy—I—well, it's true I do not seem to you to be working at present. But I do a lot of reading and studying here, and I write to several important people in the world. And all the time I am coming to a great decision about what my career will be. I do assure you I am no loafer, if that's what you think."

"No, I don't think that. But Bert says you often spend a convivial evening in that there Wayfarer."

"Oh, he does, does he? And what business is it of his if I do —or of yours, come to that? What damned cheek!"

She stood up. "If you have nothing left to say but a lot of swearing, I'll be off to join my mother, if you don't mind."

"Oh, by Jove, I'm making a mess of this!" He caught her wrist. "Listen, my sweet thing. I ask you only this, that you try and look on me favorably. And also that you let me say a word about the farm. Some strange things are happening there, and I seriously don't like to think of you being there at night. All these young things being born, all these little pigs—it's uncanny!"

"I don't see what's uncanny no more than my father does. I know how hard he works, and he's done a good job rearing his animals, that's all. He's the best farmer around Cottersall by a long chalk."

"Oh, certainly. He's a wonderful man. But he didn't put seven or eight eggs into a hedge sparrow's nest, did he? He didn't fill the pond with tadpoles and newts till it looks like a broth, did he? Something strange is happening on your farm this year, Nancy, and I want to protect you if I can."

The earnestness with which he spoke, coupled perhaps with his proximity and the ardent way he pressed her hand, went a good way toward mollifying Nancy.

"Dear Gregory, you don't know anything about farm life, I don't reckon, for all your books. But you're very sweet to be concerned."

"I shall always be concerned about you, Nancy, you beautiful creature."

"You'll make me blush!"

"Please do, for then you look even lovelier than usual!" He put an arm around her. When she looked up at him, he caught her up close to his chest and kissed her fervently.

She gasped and broke away, but not with too great haste.
"Oh, Gregory! Oh, Gregory! I must go to Mother now!"
"Another kiss first! I can't let you go until I get another."
He took it, and stood by the door trembling with excitement
as she left. "Come and see us again soon," she whispered.
"With dearest pleasure," he said. But the next visit held more
dread than pleasure.

The big cart was standing in the yard full of squealing piglets
when Gregory arrived. The farmer and Neckland were bustling
about it. The former greeted Gregory cheerfully.
"I've a chance to make a good quick profit on these little
chaps. Old sows can't feed them, but suckling pig fetches its
price in Norwich, so Bert and me are going to drive over to
Heigham and put them on the train."
"They've grown since I last saw them!"
"Ah, they put on over two pounds a day. Bert, we'd better
get a net and spread over this lot, or they'll be diving out.
They're that lively!"
The two men made their way over to the barn, clomping
through the mud. Mud squelched behind Gregory. He turned.
In the muck between the stables and the cart, footprints appeared, two parallel tracks. They seemed to imprint themselves
with no agency but their own. A cold flow of acute supernatural
terror overcame Gregory, so that he could not move. The scene
seemed to go gray and palsied as he watched the tracks come
toward him.
The cart horse neighed uneasily, the prints reached the cart,
the cart creaked, as if something had climbed aboard. The piglets squealed with terror. One dived clear over the wooden
sides. Then a terrible silence fell.
Gregory still could not move. He heard an unaccountable
sucking noise in the cart, but his eyes remained rooted on the
muddy tracks. Those impressions were of something other than

a man: something with dragging feet that were in outline something like a seal's flippers. Suddenly he found his voice. *"Mr. Grendon!"* he cried.

Only as the farmer and Bert came running from the barn with the net did Gregory dare look into the cart.

One last piglet, even as he looked, seemed to be deflating rapidly, like a rubber balloon collapsing. It went limp and lay silent among the other little empty bags of pig skin. The cart creaked. Something splashed heavily off across the farmyard in the direction of the pond.

Grendon did not see. He had run to the cart and was staring like Gregory in dismay at the deflated corpses. Neckland stared, too, and was the first to find his voice.

"Some sort of disease got 'em all, just like that! Must be one of them there new diseases from the Continent of Europe!"

"It's no disease," Gregory said. He could hardly speak, for his mind had just registered the fact that there were no bones left in or amid the deflated pig bodies. "It's no disease—look, the pig that got away is still alive."

He pointed to the animal that had jumped from the cart. It had injured its leg in the process, and now lay in the ditch some feet away, panting. The farmer went over to it and lifted it out.

"It escaped the disease by jumping out," Neckland said. "Master, we better go and see how the rest of them is down in the sties."

"Ah, that we had," Grendon said. He handed the pig over to Gregory, his face set. "No good taking one alone to market. I'll get Grubby to unharness the horse. Meanwhile, perhaps you'd be good enough to take this little chap in to Marjorie. At least we can all eat a bit of roast pig for dinner tomorrow."

"Mr. Grendon, this is no disease. Have the veterinarian over from Heigham and let him examine these bodies."

"Don't you tell me how to run my farm, young man. I've got trouble enough."

Despite this rebuff, Gregory could not keep away. He had to

see Nancy, and he had to see what occurred at the farm. The morning after the horrible thing happened to the pigs, he received a letter from his most admired correspondent, Mr. H. G. Wells, one paragraph of which read: "At bottom, I think I am neither optimist nor pessimist. I tend to believe both that we stand on the threshold of an epoch of magnificent progress— certainly such an epoch is within our grasp—and that we may have reached the *fin du globe* prophesied by our gloomier fin de siècle prophets. I am not at all surprised to hear that such a vast issue may be resolving itself on a remote farm near Cottersall, Norfolk—all unknown to anyone but the two of us. Do not think that I am in other than a state of terror, even when I cannot help exclaiming 'What a lark!' "

Too preoccupied to be as excited over such a letter as he would ordinarily have been, Gregory tucked it away in his jacket pocket and went to saddle up Daisy.

Before lunch, he stole a kiss from Nancy and planted another on her overheated left cheek as she stood by the vast range in the kitchen. Apart from that, there was little pleasure in the day. Grendon was reassured to find that none of the other piglets had fallen ill of the strange shrinking disease, but he remained alert against the possibility of its striking again. Meanwhile, another miracle had occurred. In the lower pasture, in a tumbledown shed, he had a cow that had given birth to four calves during the night. He did not expect the animal to live, but the calves were well enough and being bottle-fed by Nancy.

The farmer's face was dull, for he had been up all night with the laboring cow, and he sat down thankfully at the head of the table as the roast pig arrived on its platter.

It proved uneatable. In no time, they were all flinging down their implements in disgust. The flesh had a bitter taste for which Neckland was the first to account.

"It's diseased!" he growled. "This here animal had the disease all the time. We didn't ought to eat this here meat or we may all be dead ourselves inside of a week."

They were forced to make a snack on cold salted beef and cheese and pickled onions, none of which Mrs. Grendon could face in her condition. She retreated upstairs in tears at the thought of the failure of her carefully prepared dish, and Nancy ran after her to comfort her.

After the dismal meal, Gregory spoke to Grendon.

"I have decided I must go to Norwich tomorrow for a few days, Mr. Grendon," he said. "You are in trouble here, I believe. Is there anything, any business, I can transact for you in the city? Can I find you a veterinary surgeon there?"

Grendon clapped his shoulder. "I know you mean well, and I thank 'ee for it, but you don't seem to realize that veterinaries cost a lot of money and aren't always too helpful when they do come."

"Then let me do something for you, Joseph, in return for all your kindness to me. Let me bring a vet back from Norwich at my own expense, just to have a look round, nothing more."

"Blow me if you aren't stubborn as they come. I'm telling you, same as my dad used to say, if I finds any person on my land as I didn't ask here, I'm getting that there shotgun of mine down and I'm peppering him with buckshot, same as I did with them two old tramps last year. Fair enough?"

"I suppose so."

"Then I must go and see to the cow. And stop worrying about what you don't understand."

The visit to Norwich (an uncle had a house in that city) took up the better part of Gregory's next week. Consequently, apprehension stirred in him when he again approached the Grendon farm along the rough road from Cottersall. He was surprised to see how the countryside had altered since he was last this way. New foliage gleamed everywhere, and even the heath looked a happier place. But as he came up to the farm, he saw how overgrown it was. Great ragged elder and towering cow parsley had shot up, so that at first they hid all the buildings.

He fancied the farm had been spirited away until, spurring Daisy on, he saw the black mill emerge from behind a clump of nearby growth. The South Meadows were deep in rank grass. Even the elms seemed much shaggier than before and loomed threateningly over the house.

As he clattered over the flat wooden bridge and through the open gate into the yard, Gregory noted huge hairy nettles craning out of the adjoining ditches. Birds fluttered everywhere. Yet the impression he received was one of death rather than life. A great quiet lay over the place, as if it were under a curse that eliminated noise and hope.

He realized this effect was partly because Lardie, the young bitch collie who had taken the place of Cuff, was not running up barking as she generally did with visitors. The yard was deserted. Even the customary fowls had gone. As he led Daisy into the stables, he saw a heavy piebald in the first stall and recognized it as Dr. Crouchorn's. His anxieties took more definite shape.

Since the stable was now full, he led his mare across to the stone trough by the pond and hitched her there before walking over to the house. The front door was open. Great ragged dandelions grew against the porch. The creeper, hitherto somewhat sparse, pressed into the lower windows. A movement in the rank grass caught his eye and he looked down, drawing back his riding boot. An enormous toad crouched under weed, the head of a still-writhing grass snake in its mouth. The toad seemed to eye Gregory fixedly, as if trying to determine whether the man envied it its gluttony. Shuddering in disgust, he hurried into the house.

Muffled sounds came from upstairs. The stairs curled around the massive chimneypiece and were shut from the lower rooms by a latched door. Gregory had never been invited upstairs, but he did not hesitate. Throwing the door open, he started up the dark stairwell and almost at once ran into a body.

Its softness told him that this was Nancy; she stood in the

dark weeping. Even as he caught her and breathed her name, she broke from his grasp and ran from him up the stairs. He could hear the noises more clearly now, and the sound of crying —though at the moment he was not listening. Nancy ran to a door on the landing nearest to the top of the stairs, burst into the room beyond, and closed it. When Gregory tried the latch, he heard the bolt slide to on the other side.

"Nancy!" he called. "Don't hide from me! What is it? What's happening?"

She made no answer. As he stood there baffled against the door, the next door along the passage opened and Dr. Crouchorn emerged, clutching his little black bag. He was a tall, somber man, with deep lines on his face that inspired such fear into his patients that a remarkable percentage of them did as he bid and recovered. Even here, he wore the top hat that, simply by remaining constantly in position, contributed to the doctor's fame in the neighborhood.

"What's the trouble, Dr. Crouchorn?" Gregory asked, as the medical man shut the door behind him and started down the stairs. "Has the plague struck this house, or something equally terrible?"

"Plague, young man, plague? No, it is something much more unnatural than that."

He stared at Gregory unsmilingly, as if promising himself inwardly not to move a muscle again until Gregory asked the obvious.

"What did you call for, doctor?"

"The hour of Mrs. Grendon's confinement struck during the night," he said.

A wave of relief swept over Gregory. He had forgotten Nancy's mother! "She's had her baby? Was it a boy?"

The doctor nodded in slow motion. "She bore two boys, young man." He hesitated, and then a muscle in his face twitched and he said in a rush, "She also bore seven daughters. Nine children! And they all—they all live."

Gregory found Grendon round the corner of the house. The farmer had a pitchfork full of hay which he was carrying over his shoulder into the cow sheds. Gregory stood in his way but he pushed past.

"I want to speak to you, Joseph."

"There's work to be done. Pity you can't see that."

"I want to speak about your wife."

Grendon made no reply. He worked like a demon, tossing the hay down, turning for more. In any case, it was difficult to talk. The cows and calves, closely confined, seemed to set up a perpetual uneasy noise of lowing and uncowlike grunts. Gregory followed the farmer around to the hayrick, but the man walked like one possessed. His eyes seemed sunk into his head, his mouth was puckered until his lips were invisible. When Gregory laid a hand on his arm, he shook it off. Stabbing up another great load of hay, he swung back toward the sheds so violently that Gregory had to jump out of his way.

Gregory lost his temper. Following Grendon back into the cow shed, he swung the bottom of the two-part door shut, and bolted it on the outside. When Grendon came back, he did not budge.

"Joseph, what's got into you? Why are you suddenly so heartless? Surely your wife needs you by her?"

His eyes had a curious blind look as he turned them at Gregory. He held the pitchfork before him in both hands almost like a weapon as he said, "I been with her all night, bor, while she brought forth her increase."

"But now—"

"She got a nursing woman from Dereham Cottages with her now. I been with her all night. Now I got to see to the farm— things keep growing, you know."

"They're growing too much, Joseph. Stop and think—"

"I've no time for talking." Dropping the pitchfork, he elbowed Gregory out of the way, unbolted the door, and flung it open. Grasping Gregory firmly by the biceps of one arm, he began to propel him to the vegetable beds by South Meadows. The early lettuce were gigantic here. Everything bristled out of the ground. Recklessly, Grendon ran among the lines of new green, pulling up fistfuls of young radishes, carrots, spring onions, scattering them over his shoulder as fast as he plucked them from the ground.

"See, Gregory—all bigger than you ever seen 'em, and weeks early! The harvest is going to be a bumper. Look at the fields! Look at the orchard!" With wide gesture, he swept a hand toward the lines of trees, buried in the mounds of snow and pink of their blossom. "Whatever happens, we got to take advantage of it. It may not happen another year. Why—it's like a fairy story!"

He said no more. Turning, he seemed already to have forgotten Gregory. Eyes down at the ground that had suddenly achieved such abundance, he marched back toward the sheds.

Nancy was in the kitchen. Neckland had brought her in a stoup of fresh milk, and she was supping it wearily from a ladle.

"Oh, Greg, I'm sorry I ran from you. I was so upset." She came to him, still holding the ladle but dangling her arms over his shoulders in a familiar way she had not used before. "Poor Mother, I fear her mind is unhinged with—with bearing so many children. She's talking such strange stuff as I never heard before, and I do believe she fancies as she's a child again."

"Is it to be wondered at?" he said, smoothing her hair with his hand. "She'll be better once she's recovered from the shock."

They kissed each other, and after a minute she passed him a ladleful of milk. He drank and then spat it out in disgust.

"Ugh! What's got into the milk? Is Neckland trying to poison you or something? Have you tasted it? It's as bitter as sloes!"

She pulled a puzzled face. "I thought it tasted rather strange, but not unpleasant. Here, let me try again."

"No, it's too horrible. Some Sloane's Liniment must have got mixed in it."

Despite his warning, she put her lips to the metal spoon and sipped, then shook her head. "You're imagining things, Greg. It does taste a bit different, 'tis true, but there's nothing wrong with it. You'll stay to take a bite with us, I hope?"

"No, Nancy, I'm off now. I have a letter awaiting me that I must answer; it arrived when I was in Norwich. Listen, my lovely Nancy, this letter is from a Dr. Hudson-Ward, an old acquaintance of my father's. He is headmaster of a school in Gloucester, and he wishes me to join the staff there as teacher on most favorable terms. So you see I may not be idle much longer!"

Laughing, she clung to him. "That's wonderful, my darling! What a handsome schoolmaster you will make. But Gloucester —that's over the other side of the country. I suppose we shan't be seeing you again once you get there."

"Nothing's settled yet, Nancy."

"You'll be gone in a week and we shan't never see you again. Once you get to that there old school, you will never think of your Nancy no more."

He cupped her face in his hands. "Are you my Nancy? Do you care for me?"

Her eyelashes came over her dark eyes. "Greg, things are so muddled here—I mean—yes, I do care, I dread to think I'd not see you again."

Recalling her saying that, he rode away a quarter of an hour later very content at heart—and entirely neglectful of the dangers to which he left her exposed.

Rain fell lightly as Gregory Rolles made his way that evening to The Wayfarer Inn. His friend Bruce Fox was already there, ensconced in one of the snug seats by the inglenook.

On this occasion, Fox was more interested in purveying details of his sister's forthcoming wedding than in listening to what Gregory had to tell, and since some of his future brother-in-law's friends soon arrived and had to buy and be bought libations, the evening became a merry and thoughtless one. And in a short while, the ale having its good effect, Gregory also forgot what he wanted to say and began wholeheartedly to enjoy the company.

Next morning, he awoke with a heavy head and in a dismal state of mind. The day was too wet for him to go out and take exercise. He sat moodily in a chair by the window, delaying an answer to Dr. Hudson-Ward, the headmaster. Lethargically, he returned to a small leather-bound volume on serpents that he had acquired in Norwich a few days earlier. After a while, a passage caught his particular attention:

"Most serpents of the venomous variety, with the exception of the opisthoglyphs, release their victims from their fangs after striking. The victims die in some cases in but a few seconds, while in other cases the onset of moribundity may be delayed by hours or days. The saliva of some serpents contains not only venom but a special digestive virtue. The deadly coral snake of Brazil, though attaining no more than a foot in length, has this virtue in abundance. Accordingly, when it bites an animal or a human being, the victim not only dies in profound agony in a matter of seconds, but his interior parts are then dissolved, so that even the bones become no more than jelly. Then may the little serpent suck all of the victim out as a kind of soup or broth from the original wound in its skin, which latter alone remains intact."

For a long while, Gregory sat where he was in the window, with the book open in his lap, thinking about the Grendon farm, and about Nancy. He reproached himself for having done so little for his friends there and gradually resolved on a plan of action the next time he rode out, but his visit was to be delayed for some days; the wet weather had set in with more determination than the end of April and the beginning of May generally allowed.

Gregory tried to concentrate on a letter to the worthy Dr. Hudson-Ward in the county of Gloucestershire. He knew he should take the job, indeed he felt inclined to do so; but first he knew he had to see Nancy safe. The indecisions he felt caused him to delay answering the doctor until the next day, when he feebly wrote that he would be glad to accept the post offered at the price offered, but begged to have a week to think about it. When he took the letter down to the postwoman in The Three Poachers, the rain still fell.

One morning, the rains were suddenly vanished, the blue and wide East Anglian skies were back and Gregory saddled up Daisy and rode out along the miry track he had so often taken. As he arrived at the farm, Grubby and Neckland were at work in the ditch, unblocking it with shovels. He saluted them and rode in. As he was about to put the mare into the stables, he saw Grendon and Nancy standing on the patch of waste ground under the windowless east side of the house. He went slowly to join them, noting as he walked how dry the ground was here, as if no rain had fallen in a fortnight. But this observation was drowned in shock as he saw the nine little crosses Grendon was sticking into nine freshly turned mounds of earth.

Nancy stood weeping. They both looked up as Gregory approached, but Grendon went stubbornly on with his task.

"Oh, Nancy, Joseph, I'm so sorry about this!" Gregory exclaimed. "To think that they've all—but where's the parson? Where's the parson, Joseph? Why are *you* burying them, without a proper service or anything?"

"I told Father, but he took no heed!" Nancy exclaimed.

Grendon had reached the last grave. He seized the last crude wooden cross, lifted it above his head and stabbed it down into the ground as if he would pierce the heart of what lay under it. Only then did he straighten and speak.

"We don't need a parson here. I've no time to waste with parsons. I have work to do if you ent."

"But these are your children, Joseph! What has got into you?"

"They are part of the farm now, as they always was." He

turned, rolling his shirt sleeves further up his brawny arms, and strode off in the direction of the ditching activities.

Gregory took Nancy in his arms and looked at her tear-stained face. "What a time you must have been having these last few days!"

"I—I thought you'd gone to Gloucester, Greg! Why didn't you come? Every day I waited for you to come!"

"It was so wet and flooded."

"It's been lovely weather since you were last here. Look how everything has grown!"

"It poured with rain every single day in Cottersall."

"Well, I never! That explains why there is so much water flowing in the Oast and in the ditches. But we've had only a few light showers."

"Nancy, tell me, how did these poor little mites die?"

"I'd rather not say, if you don't mind."

"Why didn't your father get in Parson Landon? How could he be so lacking in feeling?"

"Because he didn't want anyone from the outside world to know. You see—oh, I must tell you, my dear—it's Mother. She has gone completely off her head, completely! It was the evening before last, when she took her first turn outside the back door."

"You don't mean to say she—"

"Ow, Greg, you're hurting my arms! She—she crept upstairs when we weren't noticing and she—stifled each of the babies in turn, Greg, under the best goose feather pillow."

He could feel the color leaving his cheeks. Solicitously, she led him to the back of the house. They sat together on the orchard railings while he digested the words in silence.

"How is your mother now, Nancy?"

"She's silent. Father had to bar her in her room for safety. Last night she screamed a lot. But this morning she's quiet."

He looked dazedly about him. The appearance of everything was speckled, as if the return of his blood to his head somehow infected it with a rash. The blossom had gone almost entirely from the fruit trees in the orchard and already the embryo apples showed signs of swelling. Nearby, broad beans bowed under enormous pods. Seeing his glance, Nancy dipped into her apron pocket and produced a bunch of shining crimson radishes as big as tangerines.

"Have one of these. They're crisp and wet and hot, just as they should be."

Indifferently, he accepted and bit the tempting globe. At once he had to spit the portion out. There again was that vile bitter flavor!

"Oh, but they're lovely!" Nancy protested.

"Not even 'rather strange' now—simply 'lovely'? Nancy, don't you see, something uncanny and awful is taking place here. I'm sorry, but I can't see otherwise. You and your father should leave here at once."

"*Leave* here, Greg? Just because you don't like the taste of these lovely radishes? How can we leave here? Where should we go? See this here house? My granddad died here, and his father before him. It's our *place*. We can't just up and off, not even after this bit of trouble. Try another radish."

"For heaven's sake, Nancy, they taste as if the flavor was intended for creatures with a palate completely different from ours . . . Oh . . . " He stared at her. "And perhaps they are. Nancy, I tell you—"

He broke off, sliding from the railing. Neckland had come up from one side, still plastered in mud from his work in the ditch, his collarless shirt flapping open. In his hand, he grasped an ancient and military-looking pistol.

"I'll fire this if you come nearer," he said. "It goes okay, never worry, and it's loaded, Master Gregory. Now you're a-going to listen to me!"

"Bert, put that thing away!" Nancy exclaimed. She moved forward to him, but Gregory pulled her back and stood before her.

"Don't be a bloody idiot, Neckland. Put it away!"

"I'll shoot you, bor, I'll shoot you, I swear, if you mucks about." His eyes were glaring, and the look on his dark face left no doubt that he meant what he said. "You're going to swear to me that you're going to clear off of this farm on that nag of yours and never come back again."

"I'm going straight to tell my father, Bert," Nancy warned. The pistol twitched.

"If you move, Nancy, I warn you I'll shoot this fine chap of yours in the leg. Besides, your father don't care about Master Gregory any more—he's got better things to worry him."

"Like finding out what's happening here?" Gregory said. "Listen, Neckland, we're all in trouble. This farm is being run by a group of nasty little monsters. You can't see them because they're invisible—"

The gun exploded. As he spoke, Nancy had attempted to run off. Without hesitating, Neckland fired down at Gregory's knees. Gregory felt the shot pluck his trouser leg and knew himself unharmed. With knowledge came rage. He flung himself at Neckland and hit him hard over the heart. Falling back, Neckland dropped the pistol and swung his fist wildly. Gregory struck him again. As he did so, the other grabbed him and they began furiously hitting each other. When Gregory broke free, Neckland grappled with him again. There was more pummeling of ribs.

"Let me go, you swine!" Gregory shouted. He hooked his foot behind Neckland's ankle, and they both rolled over on to the grass. At this point, a sort of flood bank had been raised long ago between the house and low-lying orchard. Down this the two men rolled, fetching up sharply against the stone wall of the kitchen. Neckland got the worst of it, catching his head on the corner, and lay there stunned. Gregory found himself looking at two feet encased in ludicrous stockings. Slowly, he rose to his feet and confronted Mrs. Grendon at less than a yard's distance. She was smiling.

He stood there and gradually straightened his back, looking at her anxiously.

"So there you are, Jackie, my Jackalums," she said. The smile was wider now and less like a smile. "I wanted to talk to you. You are the one who knows about the things that walk on the lines, aren't you?"

"I don't understand, Mrs. Grendon."

"Don't call me that there daft old name, sonnie. You know all about the little gray things that aren't supposed to be there, don't you?"

"Oh, those . . . Suppose I said I did know?"

"The other naughty children will pretend they don't know what I mean, but you know, don't you? You know about the little gray things."

The sweat stood out on his brow. She had moved nearer. She stood close, staring into his eyes, not touching him; but he was acutely conscious that she could touch him at any moment. From the corner of his eye, he saw Neckland stir and crawl away from the house, but there were other things to occupy him.

"These little gray things," he said. "Did you save the nine babies from them?"

"The gray things wanted to kiss them, you see, but I couldn't let them. I was clever. I hid them under the good feather pillow and now even *I* can't find them!" She began to laugh, making a horrible low whirring sound in her throat.

"They're small and gray and wet, aren't they?" Gregory said sharply. "They've got big feet, webbed like frogs, but they're heavy and short, aren't they, and they have fangs like a snake, haven't they?"

She looked doubtful. Then her eye seemed to catch a movement. She looked fixedly to one side. "Here comes one now, the female one," she said.

Gregory turned to look where she did. Nothing was visible. His mouth was dry. "How many are there, Mrs. Grendon?"

Then he saw the short grass stir, flatten, and raise near at hand, and let out a cry of alarm. Wrenching off his riding boot, he swung it in an arc, low above the ground. It struck something concealed in thin air. Almost at once, he received a terrific kick in the thigh, and fell backward. Despite the hurt, fear made him jump up almost at once.

Mrs. Grendon was changing. Her mouth collapsed as if it would run off one corner of her face. Her head sagged to one side. Her shoulders fell. A deep crimson blush momentarily suffused her features, then drained, and as it drained she dwindled like a deflating rubber balloon. Gregory sank to his knees, whimpering, buried his face in his hands and pressed his hands to the grass. Darkness overcame him.

His senses must have left him only for a moment. When he pulled himself up again, the almost empty bag of women's clothes was still settling slowly to the ground.

"Joseph! Joseph!" he yelled. Nancy had fled. In a distracted mixture of panic and fury, he dragged his boot on again and rushed around the house toward the cow sheds.

Neckland stood halfway between barn and mill, rubbing his skull. In his rattled state, the sight of Gregory apparently in full pursuit made him run away.

"Neckland!" Gregory shouted. He ran like mad for the other. Neckland bolted for the mill, jumped inside, tried to pull the door to, lost his nerve, and ran up the wooden stairs. Gregory bellowed after him.

The pursuit took them right up to the top of the mill. Neckland had lost enough wit even to kick over the bolt of the trapdoor. Gregory burst it up and climbed out panting. Thoroughly cowed, Neckland backed toward the opening until he was almost out on the little platform above the sails.

"You'll fall out, you idiot," Gregory warned. "Listen, Neckland, you have no reason to fear me. I want no enmity between us. There's a bigger enemy we must fight. Look!"

He came toward the low door and looked down at the dark surface of the pond. Neckland grabbed the overhead pulley for security and said nothing.

"Look down at the pond," Gregory said. "There's where the Aurigans live. My God—Bert, look, there one goes!"

The urgency in his voice made the farmhand look down where he pointed. Together, the two men watched as a depression slid over the black water; an overlapping chain of ripples swung back from it. At approximately the middle of the pond, the depression became a commotion. A small whirlpool formed and died, and the ripples began to settle.

"There's your ghost, Bert," Gregory gasped. "That must have been the one that got poor Mrs. Grendon. Now do you believe?"

"I never heard of a ghost as lived under water," Neckland gasped.

"A ghost never harmed anyone—we've already had a sample of what these terrifying things can do. Come on, Bert, shake hands, understand I bear you no hard feelings. Oh, come on, man! I know how you feel about Nancy, but she must be free to make her own choice in life."

They shook hands and grinned rather foolishly at each other.

"We better go and tell the farmer what we seen," Neckland said. "I reckon that thing done what happened to Lardie last evening."

"Lardie? What's happened to her? I thought I hadn't seen her today."

"Same as happened to the little pigs. I found her just inside the barn. Just her coat was left, that's all. No insides! Like she'd been sucked dry."

It took Gregory twenty minutes to summon the council of war on which he had set his mind. The party gathered in the farmhouse, in the parlor. By this time, Nancy had somewhat recovered from the shock of her mother's death and sat in an armchair with a shawl about her shoulders. Her father stood nearby with his arms folded, looking impatient, while Bert Neckland lounged by the door. Only Grubby was not present. He had been told to get on with the ditching.

"I'm going to have another attempt to convince you all that you are in very grave danger," Gregory said. "You won't see it for yourselves. The situation is that we're all animals together at present. Do you remember that strange meteor that fell out of the sky last winter, Joseph? And do you remember that ill-smelling dew early in the spring? They were not unconnected, and they are connected with all that's happening now. That meteor was a space machine of some sort, I firmly believe, and it brought in it a kind of life that—that is not so much hostile to terrestrial life as *indifferent to its quality*. The creatures from that machine—I call them Aurigans—spread the dew over the farm. It was a growth accelerator, a manure or fertilizer, that speeds growth in plants and animals."

"So much better for us!" Grendon said.

"But it's not better. The things grow wildly, yes, but the taste is altered to suit the palates of those things out there. You've seen what happened. You can't sell anything. People won't touch your eggs or milk or meat—they taste too foul."

"But that's a lot of nonsense. We'll sell in Norwich. Our produce is better than it ever was. We eat it, don't we?"

"Yes, Joseph, *you* eat it. But anyone who eats at your table is doomed. Don't you understand—you are all 'fertilized' just as surely as the pigs and chickens. Your place has been turned into a superfarm, and you are all meat to the Aurigans."

That set a silence in the room, until Nancy said in a small voice, "You don't believe such a terrible thing."

"I suppose these unseen creatures told you all this?" Grendon said truculently.

"Judge by the evidence, as I do. Your wife—I must be brutal, Joseph—your wife was eaten, like the dog and the pigs. As everything else will be in time. The Aurigans aren't even cannibals. They aren't like us. They don't care whether we have souls or intelligence, any more than we really care whether the bullocks have."

"No one's going to eat me," Neckland said, looking decidedly white about the gills.

"How can you stop them? They're invisible, and I think they can strike like snakes. They're aquatic and I think they may be only two feet tall. How can you protect yourself?" He turned to the farmer. "Joseph, the danger is very great, and not only to us here. At first, they may have offered us no harm while they got the measure of us—otherwise I'd have died in your rowing boat. Now there's no longer doubt of their hostile intent. I beg you to let me go to Heigham and telephone to the chief of police in Norwich, or at least to the local militia, to get them to come and help us."

The farmer shook his head slowly, and pointed a finger at Gregory.

"You soon forgot them talks we had, bor, all about the coming age of socialism and how the powers of the state was going to wither away. Directly we get a bit of trouble, you want to call in the authorities. There's no harm here a few savage dogs like my old Cuff can't handle, and I don't say as I ent going to get a couple of dogs, but you'm a fule if you reckon I'm getting the authorities down here. Fine old socialist you turn out to be!"

"You have no room to talk about that!" Gregory exclaimed. "Why didn't you let Grubby come here? If you were a socialist, you'd treat the men as you treat yourself. Instead, you leave him out in the ditch. I wanted him to hear this discussion."

The farmer leaned threateningly across the table at him.

"Oh, you did, did you? Since when was this your farm? And Grubby can come and go as he likes when it's his, so put that in your pipe and smoke it, bor! Who do you just think you are?" He moved closer to Gregory, apparently happy to work off his fears as anger. "You're trying to scare us all off this here little old bit of ground, ent you? Well, the Grendons ent a scaring sort, see! Now I'll tell you something. See that shotgun there on the wall? That be loaded. And if you ent off this farm by midday, that shotgun ont be on that wall no more. It'll be here, bor, right here in my two hands, and I'll be letting you have it right where you'll feel it most."

"You can't do that, Father," Nancy said. "You know Gregory is a friend of ours."

"For God's sake, Joseph," Gregory said, "see where your enemy lies. Bert, tell Mr. Grendon what we saw on the pond, go on!"

Neckland was far from keen to be dragged into this argument. He scratched his head, drew a red-and-white spotted kerchief from around his neck to wipe his face, and muttered, "We saw a sort of ripple on the water, but I didn't see nothing really, Master Gregory. I mean, it could have been the wind, couldn't it?"

"Now you be warned, Gregory," the farmer repeated. "You be off my land by noon by the sun, and that mare of yours, or I ont answer for it." He marched out into the pale sunshine, and Neckland followed.

Nancy and Gregory stood staring at each other. He took her hands, and they were cold.

"You believe what I was saying, Nancy?"

"Is that why the food did at one point taste bad to us, and then soon tasted well enough again?"

"It can only have been that at that time your systems were not fully adjusted to the poison. Now they are. You're being fed up, Nancy, just like the livestock—I'm sure of it! I fear for you, darling love, I fear so much. What are we to do? Come back to Cottersall with me! Mrs. Fenn has another fine little drawing room upstairs that I'm sure she would rent."

"Now you're talking nonsense, Greg! How can I? What would people say? No, you go away for now and let the tempest of Father's wrath abate, and if you could come back tomorrow, you will find he will be milder for sure, because I plan to wait on him tonight and talk to him about you. Why, he's half daft with grief and doesn't know what he says."

"All right, my darling. But stay inside as much as you can. The Aurigans have not come indoors yet, as far as we know, and it may be safer here. And lock all the doors and put the shutter over the windows before you go to bed. And get your father to take that shotgun of his upstairs with him."

The evenings were lengthening with confidence toward summer now, and Bruce Fox arrived home before sunset. As he jumped from his bicycle this evening, he found his friend Gregory impatiently awaiting him.

They went indoors together, and while Fox ate a large tea, Gregory told him what had been happening at the farm that day.

"You're in trouble," Fox said. "Look, tomorrow's Sunday. I'll skip church and come out with you. You need help."

"Joseph may shoot me. He'll be certain to if I bring along a stranger. You can help me tonight by telling me where I can purchase a young dog straightaway to protect Nancy."

"Nonsense, I'm coming with you. I can't bear hearing all this at secondhand anyhow. We'll pick up a pup in any event—the blacksmith has a litter to be rid of. Have you got any plan of action?"

"Plan? No, not really."

"You must have a plan. Grendon doesn't scare too easily, does he?"

"I imagine he's scared well enough. Nancy says he's scared. He just isn't imaginative enough to see what he can do but carry on working as hard as possible."

"Look, I know these farmers. They won't believe anything till you rub their noses in it. What we must do is *show* him an Aurigan."

"Oh, splendid, Bruce! And how do you catch one?"

"You trap one."

"Don't forget they're invisible—hey, Bruce, yes, by Jove, you're right! I've the very idea! Look, we've nothing more to worry about if we can trap one. We can trap the lot, however many there are, and we can kill the little horrors when we have trapped them."

Fox grinned over the top of a chunk of cherry cake. "We're agreed, I suppose, that these Aurigans aren't socialist utopians any longer?"

It helped a great deal, Gregory thought, to be able to visualize roughly what the alien life form looked like. The volume on serpents had been a happy find, for not only did it give an idea of how the Aurigans must be able to digest their prey so rapidly—"a kind of soup or broth"—but presumably it gave a clue to their appearance. To live in a space machine, they would probably be fairly small, and they seemed to be semi-aquatic. It all went to make up a picture of a strange being: skin perhaps scaled like a fish, great flipper feet like a frog, barrel-like diminutive stature, and a tiny head with two great fangs in the jaw. There was no doubt but that the invisibility cloaked a really ugly-looking dwarf!

As the macabre image passed through his head, Gregory and Bruce Fox were preparing their trap. Fortunately, Grendon had offered no resistance to their entering the farm; Nancy had evidently spoken to good effect. And he had suffered another shock. Five fowls had been reduced to little but feathers and skin that morning almost before his eyes, and he was as a result sullen and indifferent of what went on. Now he was out in a distant field, working, and the two young men were allowed to carry out their plans unmolested—though not without an occasional anxious glance at the pond—while a worried Nancy looked on from the farmhouse window.

She had with her a sturdy young mongrel dog of eight months, which Gregory and Bruce had brought along, called Gyp. Grendon had obtained two ferocious hounds from a distant neighbor. These wide-mouthed brutes were secured on long running chains that enabled them to patrol from the horse trough by the pond, down the west side of the house, almost to the elms and the bridge leading over to West Field. They barked stridently most of the time and seemed to cause a general unease among the other animals, all of which gave voice restlessly this forenoon.

The dogs would be a difficulty, Nancy had said, for they refused to touch any of the food the farm could provide. It was hoped they would take it when they became hungry enough.

Grendon had planted a great board by the farm gate and on the board had painted a notice telling everyone to keep away.

Armed with pitchforks, the two young men carried flour sacks out from the mill and placed them at strategic positions across the yard as far as the gate. Gregory went to the cow sheds and led out one of the calves there on a length of binder twine under the very teeth of the barking dogs—he only hoped they would prove as hostile to the Aurigans as they seemed to be to human life.

As he was pulling the calf across the yard, Grubby appeared.

"You'd better stay away from us, Grubby. We're trying to trap one of the ghosts."

"Master, if I catch one, I shall strangle him, straight I will."

"A pitchfork is a better weapon. These ghosts are dangerous little beasts at close quarters."

"I'm strong, bor, I tell 'ee! I'd strangle un!"

To prove his point, Grubby rolled his striped and tattered sleeve even further up his arm and exposed to Gregory and Fox his enormous biceps. At the same time, he wagged his great heavy head and lolled his tongue out of his mouth, perhaps to demonstrate some of the effects of strangulation.

"It's a very fine arm," Gregory agreed. "But, look, Grubby, we have a better idea. We are going to do this ghost to death with pitchforks. If you want to join in, you'd better get a spare one from the stable."

Grubby looked at him with a sly-shy expression and stroked his throat. "I'd be better at strangling, bor. I've always wanted to strangle someone."

"Why should you want to do that, Grubby?"

The laborer lowered his voice. "I always wanted to see how difficult it would be. I'm strong, you see. I got my strength up as a lad by doing some of this here strangling—but never men, you know, just cattle."

Backing away a pace, Gregory said, "This time, Grubby, it's pitchforks for us." To settle the issue, he went into the stables, got a pitchfork, and returned to thrust it into Grubby's hand.

"Let's get on with it," Fox said.

They were all ready to start. Fox and Grubby crouched down in the ditch on either side of the gate, weapons at the ready. Gregory emptied one of the bags of flour over the yard in a patch just before the gate, so that anyone leaving the farm would have to walk through it. Then he led the calf toward the pond.

The young animal set up an uneasy mooing, and most of the beasts nearby seemed to answer. The chickens and hens scattered about the yard in the pale sunshine as if demented. Gregory felt the sweat trickle down his back, although his skin was cold with the chemistries of suspense. With a slap on its rump, he forced the calf into the water of the pond. It stood there unhappily, until he led it out again and slowly back across the yard, past the mill and the grain store on his right, past Mrs. Grendon's neglected flowerbed on his left, toward the gate where his allies waited. And for all his determination not to do so, he could not stop himself looking backward at the leaden surface of the pond to see if anything followed him. He led the calf through the gate and stopped. No tracks but his and the calf's showed in the strewn flour.

"Try it again," Fox advised. "Perhaps they are taking a nap down there."

Gregory went through the routine again, and a third and

fourth time, on each occasion smoothing the flour after he had been through it. Each time, he saw Nancy watching helplessly from the house. Each time, he felt a little more sick with tension.

Yet when it happened, it took him by surprise. He had got the calf to the gate for a fifth time when Fox's shout joined the chorus of animal noises. The pond had shown no special ripple, so the Aurigan had come from some dark-purposed prowl of the farm—suddenly, its finned footsteps were marking the flour.

Yelling with excitement, Gregory dropped the rope that led the calf and ducked to one side. Seizing up an opened bag of flour by the gatepost, he flung its contents before the advancing figure.

The bomb of flour exploded all over the Aurigan. Now it was revealed in chalky outline. Despite himself, Gregory found himself screaming in sheer fright as the ghastliness was revealed in whirling white. It was especially the size that frightened: this dread thing, remote from human form, was too big for earthly nature—ten feet high, perhaps twelve! Invincible, and horribly quick, it came rushing at him with unnumbered arms striking out toward him.

Next morning, Dr. Crouchorn and his silk hat appeared at Gregory's bedside, thanked Mrs. Fenn for some hot water, and dressed Gregory's leg wound.

"You got off lightly, considering," the old man said. "But if you will take a piece of advice from me, Mr. Rolles, you will cease to visit the Grendon farm. It's an evil place and you'll come to no good there."

Gregory nodded. He had told the doctor nothing, except that Grendon had run up and shot him in the leg; which was true enough, but that it omitted most of the story.

"When will I be up again, doctor?"

"Oh, young flesh heals soon enough, or undertakers would be rich men and doctors paupers. A few days should see you right as rain. But I'll be visiting you again tomorrow, until then you are to stay flat on your back and keep that leg motionless."

"I suppose I may write a letter, doctor?"

"I suppose you may, young man."

Directly Dr. Crouchorn had gone, Gregory took pen and paper and addressed some urgent lines to Nancy. They told her that he loved her very much and could not bear to think of her remaining on the farm; that he could not get to see her for a few days because of his leg wound; and that she must immediately come away on Hetty wtih a bag full of her things and stay at The Wayfarer, where there was a capital room for which he would pay. That if she thought anything of him, she must put the simple plan into action this very day and send him word around from the inn when she was established there.

With some satisfaction, Gregory read this through twice, signed it and added kisses, and summoned Mrs. Fenn with the aid of a small bell she had provided for that purpose.

He told her that the delivery of the letter was a matter of extreme urgency. He would entrust it to Tommy, the baker's boy, to deliver when his morning round was over, and would give him a shilling for his efforts. Mrs. Fenn was not enthusiastic about this, but with a little flattery was persuaded to speak to Tommy; she left the bedroom clutching both letter and shilling.

At once, Gregory began another letter, this one to Mr. H. G. Wells. It was some while since he had last addressed his correspondent, and so he had to make a somewhat lengthy report; but eventually he came to the events of the previous day.

So horrified was I by the sight of the Aurigan [he wrote], that I stood where I was, unable to move, while the flour blew about us. And how can I now convey to you— who are perhaps the most interested person in this vital subject in all the British Isles—what the monster looked like, outlined in white? My impressions were, of course, both brief and indefinite, but the main handicap is that there is nothing on Earth to liken this weird being to!

It appeared, I suppose, most like some horrendous goose, but the neck must be imagined as almost as thick as the body—indeed, it was almost all body, or all neck, whichever way you look at it. And on top of this neck was no head but a terrible array of various sorts of arms, a nest of writhing cilia, antennae, and whips, for all the world as if an octopus were entangled with a Portuguese man-of-war as big as itself, with a few shrimp and starfish legs thrown in. Does this sound ludicrous? I can only swear to you that as it bore down on me, perhaps twice my own height or more, I found it something almost too terrifying for human eyes to look on—and yet I did not see it, but merely the flour that adhered to it!

That repulsive sight would have been the last my eyes ever dwelt on had it not been for Grubby, the simple farmhand I have had occasion to mention before.

As I threw the flour, Grubby gave a great cry and rushed forward, dropping the pitchfork. He jumped at the creature as it turned on me. This put out our plan, which was that he and Bruce Fox should pitchfork the creature to death. Instead, he grasped it as high as he possibly might and commenced to squeeze with the full force of his mighty muscles. What a terrifying contest! What a fear-fraught combat!

Collecting his wits, Bruce charged forward and attacked with his pitchfork. It was his battle cry that brought me back from my paralysis into action. I ran and seized Grubby's pitchfork and also charged. That thing had arms for us all! It struck out, and I have no doubt now that several arms held poisoned needle teeth, for I saw one come toward me gaping like a snake's mouth. Need I stress the danger—particularly when you recall that the effect of the flour cloud was only partial, and there were still invisible arms flailing round us!

Our saving was that the Aurigan was cowardly. I saw Bruce jab it hard, and a second later, I rammed my pitchfork right through its foot. At once it had had enough. Grubby fell to the ground as it retreated. It moved at amazing speed, back towards the pool. We were in pursuit! And all the beasts of the barnyard uttered their cries to it.

As it launched itself into the water, we both flung our pitchforks at its form. But it swam out strongly and then dived below the surface, leaving only ripples and a scummy trail of flour.

We stood staring at the water for an instant, and then with common accord ran back to Grubby. He was dead. He lay face up and was no longer recognisable. The Aurigan must have struck him with its poisoned fangs as soon as he attacked. Grubby's skin was stretched tight and glistened oddly. He had turned a dull crimson. No longer was he more than a caricature of human shape. All his internal substance had been transformed to liquid by the rapid-working venoms of the Aurigan; he was like a sort of giant man-shaped rotten haggis.

There were wound marks across his neck and throat and what had been his face, and from these wounds his substance drained, so that he slowly deflated into his trampled bed of flour and dust. Perhaps the sight of fabled Medusa's head, that turned men to stone, was no worse than this, for we stood there utterly paralysed. It was a blast from Farmer Grendon's shotgun that brought us back to life.

He had threatened to shoot me. Now, seeing us despoiling his flour stocks and apparently about to make off with a calf, he fired at us. We had no choice but to run for it. Grendon was in no explaining mood. Good Nancy came running out to stop him, but Neckland was charging up too with the pair of savage dogs growling at the end of their chains.

Bruce and I had ridden up on my Daisy. I had left her

saddled. Bringing her out of the stable at a trot, I heaved Bruce up into the saddle and was about to climb on myself when the gun went off again and I felt a burning pain in my leg. Bruce dragged me into the saddle and we were off —I half unconscious.

Here I lie now in bed, and should be about again in a couple of days. Fortunately, the shot did not harm any bones.

So you see how the farm is now a place of the damned! Once, I thought it might even become a new Eden, growing the food of the gods for men like gods. Instead—alas! the first meeting between humanity and beings from another world has proved disastrous, and the Eden is become a battleground for a war of worlds. How can our anticipations for the future be anything other than gloomy?

Before I close this overlong account, I must answer a query in your letter and pose another to you, more personal than yours to me.

First, you question if the Aurigans are entirely invisible and say—if I may quote your letter—"Any alteration in the refractive index of the eye lenses would make vision impossible, but without such alteration the eyes would be visible as glassy globules. And for vision it is also necessary that there should be visual purple behind the retina and an opaque cornea. How then do your Aurigans manage for vision?" The answer must be that they do without eyesight as we know it, for I think they naturally maintain a complete invisibility. How they "see" I know not, but whatever sense they use, it is effective. How they communicate I know not—our fellow made not the slightest sound when I speared his foot!—yet it is apparent they must communicate effectively. Perhaps they tried originally to communicate with us through a mysterious sense we do not possess and, on receiving no answer, assumed us to be as dumb as our dumb animals. If so, what a tragedy!

Now to my personal enquiry. I know, sir, that you must grow more busy as you grow more famous; but I feel that what transpires here in this remote corner of East Anglia is of momentous import to the world and the future. Could you not take it upon yourself to pay us a visit here? You would be comfortable at one of our two inns, and the journey here by railway is efficient if tedious—you can easily get a regular waggon from Heigham station here, a distance of only eight miles. You could then view Grendon's farm for yourself, and perhaps one of these interstellar beings too. I feel you are as much amused as concerned by the accounts you receive from the undersigned, but I swear not one detail is exaggerated. Say you can come!

If you need persuasion, reflect on how much delight it will give to

Your sincere admirer,

Gregory Rolles

Reading this long letter through, scratching out two superfluous adjectives, Gregory lay back in some satisfaction. He had the feeling he was still involved in the struggle although temporarily out of action.

But the later afternoon brought him disquieting news. Tommy, the baker's boy, had gone out as far as the Grendon farm. Then the ugly legends circulating in the village about the place had risen in his mind, and he had stood wondering whether he should go on. An unnatural babble of animal noise came from the farm, mixed with hammering, and when Tommy crept forward and saw the farmer himself looking as black as a puddle and building a great thing like a gibbet in the yard, he had lost his nerve and rushed back the way he came, the letter to Nancy undelivered.

Gregory lay on the bed worrying about Nancy until Mrs. Fenn brought up supper on a tray. At least it was clear now why the Aurigans had not entered the farmhouse; they were

far too large to do so. She was safe as long as she kept indoors
—as far as anyone on that doomed plot was safe.

He fell asleep early that night. In the early hours of the
morning, nightmare visited him. He was in a strange city where
all the buildings were new and the people wore shining clothes.
In one square grew a tree. The Gregory in the dream stood in
a special relationship to the tree: he fed it. It was his job to
push people who were passing by the tree against its surface.
The tree was a saliva tree. Down its smooth bark ran quantities
of saliva from red lips like leaves up in the boughs. It grew
enormous on the people on which it fed. As they were thrown
against it, they passed into the substance of the tree. Some of
the saliva splashed on to Gregory. But instead of dissolving him,
it caused everything he touched to be dissolved. He put his arms
about the girl he loved, and as his mouth went toward hers, her
skin peeled away from her face.

He awoke weeping desperately and fumbling blindly for the
ring of the gas mantle.

Dr. Crouchorn came late next morning and told Gregory he
should have at least three more days' complete rest for the re-
covery of the muscles of his leg. Gregory lay there in a state of
acute dissatisfaction with himself. Recalling the vile dream, he
thought how negligent he had been toward Nancy, the girl he
loved. His letter to her still lay undelivered by his bedside. After
Mrs. Fenn had brought up his dinner, he determined that he
must see Nancy for himself. Leaving the food, he pulled himself out of bed and dressed slowly.

The leg was more painful than he had expected, but he got
himself downstairs and out to the stable without too much
trouble. Daisy seemed pleased to see him. He rubbed her nose
and rested his head against her long cheek in sheer pleasure at
being with her again.

"This may be the last time you have to undertake this particular journey, my girl," he said.

Saddling her was comparatively easy. Getting into the saddle involved much bodily anguish. But eventually he was comfortable and they turned along the familiar and desolate road to the domain of the Aurigans. His leg was worse than he had bargained for. More than once, he had to get the mare to stop while he let the throbbing subside. He saw he was losing blood plentifully.

As he approached the farm, he observed what the baker's boy had meant by saying Grendon was building a gibbet. A pole had been set up in the middle of the yard. A cable ran to the top of it, and a light was rigged there, so that the expanse of the yard could be illuminated by night.

Another change had taken place. A wooden fence had been built behind the horse trough, cutting off the pond from the farm. But at one point, ominously, a section of it had been broken down and splintered and crushed, as if some monstrous thing had walked through the barrier unheeding.

A ferocious dog was chained just inside the gate, and barking its head off, to the consternation of the poultry. Gregory dared not enter. As he stood wondering the best way to tackle this fresh problem, the door of the farmhouse opened fractionally and Nancy peeped out. He called and signaled frantically to her.

Timidly, she ran across and let him in, dragging the dog back. Gregory kissed her cheek, soothed by the feel of her sturdy body in his arms.

"Where's your father?"

"My dearest, your leg, your poor leg! It's bleeding yet!"

"Never mind my leg. Where's your father?"

"He's down in South Meadow, I think."

"Good! I'm going to speak with him. Nancy, I want you to go indoors and pack some belongings. I'm taking you away with me."

"I can't leave Father!"

"You must. I'm going to tell him now." As he limped across

the yard, she called fearfully, "He has that there gun of his'n with him all the time—do be careful!"

The two dogs on a running chain followed him all the way down the side of the house, nearly choking in their efforts to get at him, their teeth flashing uncomfortably close to his ankles. He noticed Neckland below Grubby's little hut, busy sawing wood; the farmer was not with him. On impulse, Gregory turned into the sties.

It was gloomy there. In the gloom, Grendon worked. He dropped his bucket when he saw Gregory there and came forward threateningly.

"You came back? Why don't you stay away? Can't you see the notice by the gate? I don't want you here no more, bor. I know you mean well, and I intend you no harm, but I'll kill 'ee, understand, kill 'ee if you ever come here again. I've plenty of worries without you to add to them. Now then, get you going!"

Gregory stood his ground.

"Mr. Grendon, are you as mad as your wife was before she died? Do you understand that you may meet Grubby's fate at any moment? Do you realize what you are harboring in your pond?"

"I ent a fule. But suppose them there things do eat everything, humans included? Suppose this is now their farm? They still got to have someone tend it. So I reckon they ent going to harm me. So long as they sees me work hard, they ent going to harm me."

"You're being fattened, do you understand? For all the hard work you do, you must have put on a stone this last month. Doesn't that scare you?"

Something of the farmer's pose broke for a moment. He cast a wild look around. "I ent saying I ent scared. I'm saying I'm doing what I have to do. We don't own our lives. Now do me a favor and get out of here."

Instinctively, Gregory's glance had followed Grendon's. For the first time, he saw in the dimness the size of the pigs. Their great broad black backs were visible over the top of the sties. They were the size of young oxen.

"This is a farm of death," he said.

"Death's always the end of all of us, pig or cow or man alike."

"Right-ho, Mr. Grendon, you can think like that if you like. It's not my way of thinking, nor am I going to see your dependents suffer from your madness. Mr. Grendon, sir, I wish to ask for your daughter's hand in marriage."

For the first three days that she was away from her home, Nancy Grendon lay in her room in The Wayfarer near to death. It seemed as if all ordinary food poisoned her. But gradually under Dr. Crouchorn's ministration—terrified perhaps by the rage she suspected he would vent upon her should she fail to get better—she recovered her strength.

"You look so much better today," Gregory said, clasping her hand. "You'll soon be up and about again, once your system is free of all the evil nourishment of the farm."

"Greg, dearest, promise me you will not go to the farm again. You have no need to go now I'm not there."

He cast his eyes down and said, "Then you don't have to get me to promise, do you?"

"I just want to be sure we neither of us go there again. Father, I feel sure, bears a charmed life. It's as if I was now coming to my senses again—but I don't want it to be as if you were losing yours! Supposing those things followed us here to Cottersall, those Aurigans?"

"You know, Nancy, I've wondered several times why they remain on the farm as they do. You would think that once they found they could so easily defeat human beings, they would attack everyone, or send for more of their own kind and try to invade us. Yet they seem perfectly content to remain in that one small space."

She smiled. "I may not be very clever compared with you,

but I can tell 'ee the answer to that one. They ent interested in going anywhere. I think there's just two of them, and they come to our little old world for a holiday in their space machine, same as we might go to Great Yarmouth for a couple of days for our honeymoon. Perhaps they're on their honeymoon."

"On honeymoon! What a ghastly idea!"

"Well, on holiday then. That was Father's idea—he says as there's just two of them, treating Earth as a quiet place to stay. People like to eat well when they're on holiday, don't they?"

He stared at Nancy aghast.

"But that's horrible! You're trying to make the Aurigans out to be *pleasant!*"

"Of course I ent, you silly ha'p'orth! But I expect they seem pleasant to each other."

"Well, I prefer to think of them as menaces."

"All the more reason for you to keep away from them!"

But to be out of sight was not to be out of mind's reach. Gregory received another letter from Dr. Hudson-Ward, a kind and encouraging one, but he made no attempt to answer it. He felt he could not bear to take up any work that would remove him from the neighborhood, although the need to work, in view of his matrimonial plans, was now pressing; the modest allowance his father made him would not support two in any comfort. Yet he could not bring his thoughts to grapple with such practical problems. It was another letter he looked for and the horrors of the farm that obsessed him. And the next night, he dreamed of the saliva tree again.

In the evening, he plucked up enough courage to tell Fox and Nancy about it. They met in the little snug at the back of The Wayfarer's public bar, a discreet and private place with red plush on the seats. Nancy was her usual self again and had been out for a brief walk in the afternoon sunshine.

"People wanted to give themselves to the saliva tree. And although I didn't see this for myself, I had the distinct feeling that perhaps they weren't actually killed so much as changed into something else—something less human maybe. And this time, I saw the tree was made of metal of some kind and was growing bigger and bigger by pumps—you could see through the saliva to big armatures and pistons, and out of the branches steam was pouring."

Fox laughed, a little unsympathetically. "Sounds to me like the shape of things to come, when even plants are grown by machinery. Events are preying on your mind, Greg! Listen, my sister is going to Norwich tomorrow, driving in her uncle's trap. Why don't the two of you go with her? She's going to buy some adornments for her bridal gown, so that should interest you, Nancy. Then you could stay with Greg's uncle for a couple of days. I assure you I will let you know immediately the Aurigans invade Cottersall, so you won't miss anything."

Nancy seized Gregory's arm. "Can we please, Gregory, can we? I ent been to Norwich for long enough and it's a fine city."

"It would be a good idea," he said doubtfully.

Both of them pressed him until he was forced to yield. He broke up the little party as soon as he decently could, kissed Nancy good night, and walked hurriedly back down the street to the baker's. Of one thing he was certain: if he must leave the district even for a short while, he had to have a look to see what was happening at the farm before he went.

The farm looked in the summer's dusk as it had never done before. Massive wooden screens nine feet high had been erected and hastily creosoted. They stood about in forlorn fashion, intended to keep the public gaze from the farm, but lending it unmeaning. They stood not only in the yard but at irregular intervals along the boundaries of the land, inappropriately among fruit trees, desolately amid bracken, irrelevantly in swamp. A sound of furious hammering, punctuated by the unwearying animal noises, indicated that more screens were still being built.

But what lent the place its unearthly look was the lighting.

The solitary pole supporting an electric light now had five companions: one by the gate, one by the pond, one behind the house, one outside the engine house, one down by the pigsties. Their hideous yellow glare reduced the scene to the sort of unlikely picture that might be found and puzzled over in the eternal midnight of an Egyptian tomb.

Gregory was too wise to try and enter by the gate. He hitched Daisy to the low branches of a thorn tree and set off over wasteland, entering Grendon's property by the South Meadow. As he walked stealthily toward the distant outhouses, he could see how the farmland differed from the territory about it. The corn was already so high it seemed in the dark almost to threaten by its ceaseless whisper of movement. The fruits had ripened fast. In the strawberry beds were great strawberries like pears. The marrows lay on their dunghill like bloated bolsters, gleaming from a distant shaft of light. In the orchard, the trees creaked, weighed down by distorted footballs that passed for apples; with a heavy autumnal thud one fell overripe to the ground. Everywhere on the farm, there seemed to be slight movement and noise, so much so that Gregory stopped to listen.

A wind was rising. The sails of the old mill shrieked like a gull's cry as they began to turn. In the engine house, the steam engine pumped out its double unfaltering note as it generated power. The dogs still raged, the animals added their uneasy chorus. He recalled the saliva tree; here as in the dream, it was as if agriculture had become industry and the impulses of nature swallowed by the new god of Science. In the bark of the trees rose the dark steam of novel and unknown forces.

He talked himself into pressing forward again. He moved carefully through the baffling slices of shadow and illumination created by the screens and lights and arrived near the back door of the farmhouse. A lantern burned in the kitchen window. As Gregory hesitated, the crunch of broken glass came from within.

Cautiously, he edged himself past the window and peered

in through the doorway. From the parlor, he heard the voice of Grendon. It held a curious muffled tone, as if the man spoke to himself.

"Lie there! You're no use to me. This is a trial of strength. Oh God, preserve me, to let me prove myself! Thou has made my land barren till now—now let me harvest it! I don't know what You're doing. I didn't mean to presume, but this here farm is my life. Curse 'em, curse 'em all! They're all enemies." There was more of it; the man was muttering like one drunk. With a horrid fascination, Gregory was drawn forward till he had crossed the kitchen flags and stood on the verge of the larger room. He peered around the half-open door until he could see the farmer, standing obscurely in the middle of the room.

A candle stood in the neglected hearth, its flickering flame glassily reflected in the cases of maladroit animals. Evidently the house electricity had been cut off to give additional power to the new lights outside.

Grendon's back was to Gregory. One gaunt and unshaven cheek was lit by candlelight. His back seemed a little bent by the weight of what he imagined his duties, yet looking at that leather-clad back now Gregory experienced a sort of reverence for the independence of the man and for the mystery that lay under his plainness. He watched as Grendon moved out through the front door, leaving it hanging wide, and passed into the yard, still muttering to himself. He walked around the side of the house and was hidden from view as the sound of his tread was lost amid the renewed barking of dogs.

The tumult did not drown a groan from near at hand. Peering into the shadows, Gregory saw a body lying under the table. It rolled over, crunching broken glass as it did so, and exclaimed in a dazed way. Without being able to see clearly, Gregory knew it was Neckland. He climbed over to the man and propped his head up, kicking away a stuffed fish as he did so.

"Don't kill me, bor! I only want to get away from here."

"Bert? It's Greg here. Bert, are you badly hurt?"

He could see some wounds. The fellow's shirt had been practically torn from his back, and the flesh on his side and back
was cut from where he had rolled in the glass. More serious was
a great weal over one shoulder, changing to a deeper color as
Gregory looked at it.

Wiping his face and speaking in a more rational voice, Neckland said, "Gregory? I thought as you was down Cottersall?
What are you doing here? He'll kill you proper if he finds you
here!"

"What happened to you, Bert? Can you get up?"

The laborer was again in possession of his faculties. He
grabbed Gregory's forearm and said imploringly, "Keep your
voice down, for Christ's sake, or he'll hear us and come back
and settle my hash for once for all! He's gone clean off his head,
says as these pond things are having a holiday here. He nearly
knocked my head off my shoulder with that stick of his! Lucky
I got a thick head!"

"What was the quarrel about?"

"I tell you straight, bor, I have got the wind up proper about
this here farm. They things as live in the pond will eat me and
suck me up like they done Grubby if I stay here any more. So
I run off when Joe Grendon weren't looking, and I come in here
to gather up my traps and my bits and leave here at once. This
whole place is evil, a bed of evil, and it ought to be destroyed.
Hell can't be worse than this here farm!"

As he spoke, he pulled himself to his feet and stood, keeping
his balance with Gregory's aid. Grunting, he made his way over
to the staircase.

"Bert," Gregory said, "supposing we rush Grendon and lay
him out. We can then get him in the cart and all leave together."

Neckland turned to stare at him, his face hidden in shadows,
nursing his shoulder with one hand.

"You try it!" he said, and then he turned and went steadily
up the stairs.

Gregory stood where he was, keeping one eye on the window. He had come to the farm without any clear notion in his head, but now that the idea had been formulated, he saw that it was up to him to try and remove Grendon from his farm. He felt obliged to do it; for although he had lost his former regard for Grendon, a sort of fascination for the man held him, and he was incapable of leaving any human being, however perverse, to face alone the alien horrors of the farm. It occurred to him that he might get help from the distant houses, Dereham Cottages, if only the farmer were rendered in one way or another unable to pepper the intruders with shot.

The machine house possessed only one high window, and that was barred. It was built of brick and had a stout door which could be barred and locked from the outside. Perhaps it would be possible to lure Grendon into there; outside aid could then be obtained.

Not without apprehension, Gregory went to the open door and peered out into the confused dark. He stared anxiously at the ground for sight of a footstep more sinister than the farmer's, but there was no indication that the Aurigans were active. He stepped into the yard.

He had not gone two yards before a woman's screams rang out. The sound seemed to clamp an icy grip about Gregory's ribs, and into his mind came a picture of poor mad Mrs. Grendon. Then he recognized the voice, in its few shouted words, as Nancy's. Even before the sound cut off, he began to pelt down the dark side of the house as fast as he could run.

Only later did he realize how he seemed to be running against a great army of animal cries. Loudest was the babel of the pigs; every swine seemed to have some message deep and nervous and indecipherable to deliver to an unknown source; and it was to the sties that Gregory ran, swerving past the giant screens under the high and sickly light.

The noise in the sties was deafening. Every animal was attacking its pen with its sharp hooves. One light swung over the middle pen. With its help, Gregory saw immediately how terrible was the change that had come over the farm since his last visit. The sows had swollen enormously and their great ears clattered against their cheeks like boards. Their hirsute backs curved almost to the rafters of their prison.

Grendon was at the far entrance. In his arms he held the unconscious form of his daughter. A sack of pig feed lay scattered by his feet. He had one pen gate half open and was trying to thrust his way in against the flank of a pig whose mighty shoulder came almost level with his. He turned and stared at Gregory with a face whose blankness was more terrifying than any expression of rage.

There was another presence in the place. A pen gate near Gregory swung open. The two sows wedged in the narrow sty gave out a terrible falsetto squealing, clearly scenting the presence of an unappeasable hunger. They kicked out blindly, and all the other animals plunged with a sympathetic fear. Struggle was useless. An Aurigan was there; the figure of Death itself, with its unwearying scythe and unaltering smile of bone, was as easily avoided as this poisoned and unseen presence. A rosy flush spread over the back of one of the sows. Almost at once, her great bulk began to collapse; in a moment, her substance had been ingested.

Gregory did not stay to watch the sickening action. He was running forward, for the farmer was again on the move. And now it was clear what he was going to do. He pushed into the end sty and dropped his daughter down into the metal food trough. At once, the sows turned with smacking jaws to deal with this new fodder. His hands free, Grendon moved to a bracket set in the wall. There lay his gun.

Now the uproar in the sties had reached its loudest. The sow whose companion had been so rapidly ingested broke free and burst into the central aisle. For a moment she stood—mercifully, for otherwise Gregory would have been trampled—as if dazed by the possibility of liberty. The place shook and the other swine fought to get to her. Brick crumbled, pen gates buckled. Gregory jumped aside as the second pig lumbered free, and next moment the place was full of grotesque fighting bodies, fighting their way to liberty.

He had reached Grendon, but the stampede caught them even as they confronted each other. A hoof stabbed down on Grendon's instep. Groaning, he bent forward and was at once swept underfoot by his creatures. Gregory barely had time to vault into the nearest pen before they thundered by. Nancy was trying pitifully to climb out of the trough as the two beasts to which she had been offered fought to kick their way free. With a ferocious strength—without reason—almost without consciousness—Gregory hauled her up, jumped until he swung up on one of the overhead beams, wrapped a leg around the beam, hung down till he grasped Nancy, pulled her up with him.

They were safe, but the safety was not permanent. Through the din and dust, they could see that the gigantic beasts were wedged tightly in both entrances. In the middle was a sort of battlefield, where the animals fought to reach the opposite end of the building; they were gradually tearing each other to pieces —but the sties too were threatened with demolition.

"I had to follow you," Nancy gasped. "But Father—I don't think he even recognized me!"

At least, Gregory thought, she had not seen her father trampled underfoot. Involuntarily glancing in that direction, he saw the shotgun that Grendon had never managed to reach still lying across a bracket on the wall. By crawling along a traverse beam, he could reach it easily. Bidding Nancy sit where she was, he wriggled along the beam, only a foot or two above the heaving backs of the swine. At least the gun should afford them some protection: the Aurigan, despite all its ghastly differences from humanity, would hardly be immune to lead.

As he grasped the old-fashioned weapon and pulled it up, Gregory was suddenly filled with an intense desire to kill one of the invisible monsters. In that instant, he recalled an earlier hope he had had of them: that they might be superior beings, beings of wisdom and enlightened power, coming from a better society where higher moral codes directed the activities of its citizens. He had thought that only to such a civilization would the divine gift of traveling through interplanetary space be granted. But perhaps the opposite held true: perhaps such a great objective could be gained only by species ruthless enough to disregard more humane ends. As soon as he thought it, his mind was overpowered with a vast diseased vision of the universe, where such races as dealt in love and kindness and intellect cowered forever on their little globes, while all about them went the slayers of the universe, sailing where they would to satisfy their cruelties and their endless appetites.

He heaved his way back to Nancy above the bloody porcine fray.

She pointed mutely. At the far end the entrance had crumbled away, and the sows were bursting forth into the night. But one sow fell and turned crimson as it fell, sagging over the floor like a shapeless bag. Another, passing the same spot, suffered the same fate.

Was the Aurigan moved by anger? Had the pigs, in their blind charging, injured it? Gregory raised the gun and aimed. As he did so, he saw a giant hallucinatory column in the air; enough dirt and mud and blood had been thrown up to spot the Aurigan and render him partly visible. Gregory fired.

The recoil nearly knocked him off his perch. He shut his eyes, dazed by the noise, and was dimly aware of Nancy clinging to him, shouting, "Oh, you marvelous man, you marvelous man! You hit that old bor right smack on target!"

He opened his eyes and peered through the smoke and dust. The shade that represented the Aurigan was tottering. It fell. It fell among the distorted shapes of the two sows it had killed, and corrupt fluids splattered over the paving. Then it rose again. They saw its progress to the broken door, and then it had gone.

For a minute, they sat there, staring at each other, triumph and speculation mingling on both their faces. Apart from one badly injured beast, the building was clear of pigs now. Gregory climbed to the floor and helped Nancy down beside him. They skirted the loathsome messes as best they could and staggered into the fresh air.

Up beyond the orchard, strange lights showed in the rear windows of the farmhouse.

"It's on fire! Oh, Greg, our poor home is afire! Quick, we must gather what we can! All Father's lovely cases—"

He held her fiercely, bent so that he spoke straight into her face. "Bert Neckland did this! He did it! He told me the place ought to be destroyed and that's what he did."

"Let's go, then—"

"No, no, Nancy, we must let it burn! Listen! There's a wounded Aurigan loose here somewhere. We didn't kill him. If those things feel rage, anger, spite, they'll be set to kill us now —don't forget there's more than one of 'em! We aren't going that way if we want to live. Daisy's just across the meadow here, and she'll bear us both safe home."

"Greg, dearest, this is my home!" she cried in her despair.

The flames were leaping higher. The kitchen windows broke in a shower of glass. He was running with her in the opposite direction, shouting wildly, "I'm your home now! I'm your home now!"

Now she was running with him, no longer protesting, and they plunged together through the high rank grass.

When they gained the track and the restive mare, they paused to take breath and look back.

The house was well ablaze now. Clearly nothing could save it. Sparks had carried to the windmill, and one of the sails was ablaze. About the scene, the electric lights shone spectral and pale on the tops of their poles. An occasional running figure of a gigantic animal dived about its own purposes. Suddenly, there was a flash as of lightning and all the electric lights went out.

One of the stampeding animals had knocked down a pole; crashing into the pond, it short-circuited the system.

"Let's get away," Gregory said, and he helped Nancy on to the mare. As he climbed up behind her, a roaring sound developed, grew in volume and altered in pitch. Abruptly it died again. A thick cloud of steam billowed above the pond. From it rose the space machine, rising, rising, rising, suddenly a sight to take the heart in awe. It moved up into the soft night sky, was lost for a moment, began dully to glow, was seen to be already tremendously far away.

Desperately, Gregory looked for it, but it had gone, already beyond the frail confines of the terrestrial atmosphere. An awful desolation settled on him, the more awful for being irrational, and then he thought, and cried his thought aloud, "Perhaps they were only holiday-makers here! Perhaps they enjoyed themselves here, and will tell their friends of this little globe! Perhaps Earth has a future only as a resort for millions of the Aurigan kind!"

The church clock was striking midnight as they passed the first cottages of Cottersall.

"We'll go first to the inn," Gregory said. "I can't well disturb Mrs. Fenn at this late hour, but your landlord will fetch us food and hot water and see that your cuts are bandaged."

"I'm right as rain, love, but I'd be glad of your company."

"I warn you, you shall have too much of it from now on!"

The door of the inn was locked, but a light burned inside, and in a moment the landlord himself opened to them, all eager to hear a bit of gossip he could pass on to his custom.

"So happens as there's a gentleman up in Number Three wishes to speak with you in the morning," he told Gregory. "Very nice gentleman came on the night train, only got in here an hour past, off the wagon."

Gregory made a wry face.

"My father, no doubt."

"Oh, no, sir. His name is a Mr. Wills or Wells or Walls—his signature was a mite difficult to make out."

"Wells! Mr. Wells! So he's come!" He caught Nancy's hands, shaking them in his excitement. "Nancy, one of the greatest men in England is here! There's no one more profitable for such a tale as ours! I'm going up to speak with him right away."

Kissing her lightly on the cheek, he hurried up the stairs and knocked on the door of Number Three.

The Ugly Little Boy

The Ugly Little Boy

ISAAC ASIMOV

*The central idea of this story derives from an unlikely source,
A. E. van Vogt's "The Seesaw." I call this unlikely because if
I were going to pick two writers to represent the most conserva-
tive and the most radical thinking in American science fiction,
Asimov would be the one and van Vogt the other.*

*"The Ugly Little Boy" is unusual in another way: it is a sci-
ence fiction story about love. Such stories are rare, partly because so many of our best-known writers—Asimov included—
grew up in what I might call the locker-room school of science
fiction. But it is clear that Asimov is not a writer who can be
confined to a category. This story is neither Old Wave nor
New: it is a work of fiction, as honest and as durable as "Nightfall" and "The Martian Way."*

Edith Fellowes smoothed her working smock as she always
did before opening the elaborately locked door and stepping
across the invisible dividing line between the *is* and the *is not*.
She carried her notebook and her pen although she no longer
took notes except when she felt the absolute need for some
report.

This time she also carried a suitcase. ("Games for the boy,"
she had said, smiling, to the guard—who had long since
stopped even thinking of questioning her and who waved her
on.)

And, as always, the ugly little boy knew that she had entered and came running to her, crying, "Miss Fellowes—Miss Fellowes—" in his soft, slurring way.

"Timmie," she said, and passed her hand over the shaggy, brown hair on his misshapen little head. "What's wrong?"

He said, "Will Jerry be back to play again? I'm sorry about what happened."

"Never mind that now, Timmie. Is that why you've been crying?"

He looked away. "Not just about that, Miss Fellowes. I dreamed again."

"The same dream?" Miss Fellowes' lips set. Of course, the Jerry affair would bring back the dream.

He nodded. His too-large teeth showed as he tried to smile and the lips of his forward-thrusting mouth stretched wide. "When will I be big enough to go out there, Miss Fellowes?"

"Soon," she said softly, feeling her heart break. "Soon."

Miss Fellowes let him take her hand and enjoyed the warm touch of the thick dry skin of his palm. He led her through the three rooms that made up the whole of Stasis Section One— comfortable enough, yes, but an eternal prison for the ugly little boy all the seven (was it seven?) years of his life.

He led her to the one window, looking out onto a scrubby woodland section of the world of *is* (now hidden by night), where a fence and painted instructions allowed no men to wander without permission.

He pressed his nose against the window. "Out there, Miss Fellowes?"

"Better places. Nicer places," she said sadly as she looked at his poor little imprisoned face outlined in profile against the window. The forehead retreated flatly and his hair lay down in tufts upon it. The back of his skull bulged and seemed to make the head overheavy so that it sagged and bent forward, forcing the whole body into a stoop. Already, bony ridges were beginning to bulge the skin above his eyes. His wide mouth thrust forward more prominently than did his wide and flattened nose and he had no chin to speak of, only a jawbone that curved smoothly down and back. He was small for his years and his stumpy legs were bowed.

He was a very ugly little boy and Edith Fellowes loved him dearly.

Her own face was behind his line of vision, so she allowed her lips the luxury of a tremor.

They would *not* kill him. She would do anything to prevent it. Anything. She opened the suitcase and began taking out the clothes it contained.

Edith Fellowes had crossed the threshold of Stasis, Inc., for the first time just a little over three years before. She hadn't, at that time, the slightest idea as to what Stasis meant or what the place did. No one did then, except those who worked there. In fact, it was only the day after she arrived that the news broke upon the world.

At the time, it was just that they had advertised for a woman with knowledge of physiology, experience with clinical chemistry, and a love for children. Edith Fellowes had been a nurse in a maternity ward and believed she fulfilled those qualifications.

Gerald Hoskins, whose nameplate on the desk included a Ph.D. after the name, scratched his cheek with his thumb and looked at her steadily.

Miss Fellowes automatically stiffened and felt her face (with its slightly asymmetric nose and its a-trifle-too-heavy eyebrows) twitch.

He's no dreamboat himself, she thought resentfully. He's getting fat and bald and he's got a sullen mouth. But the salary mentioned had been considerably higher than she expected, so she waited.

Hoskins said, "Now do you really love children?"

"I wouldn't say I did if I didn't."

"Or do you just love pretty children? Nice chubby children with cute little button noses and gurgly ways?"

Miss Fellowes said, "Children are children, Dr. Hoskins, and the ones that aren't pretty are just the ones who may happen to need help most."

"Then suppose we take you on—"

"You mean you're offering me the job now?"

He smiled briefly, and, for a moment, his broad face had an absentminded charm about it. He said, "I make quick decisions. So far the offer is tentative, however. I may make as quick a decision to let you go. Are you ready to take the chance?"

Miss Fellowes clutched at her purse and calculated just as swiftly as she could, then ignored calculations and followed impulse. "All right."

"Fine. We're going to form the Stasis tonight and I think you had better be there to take over at once. That will be at eight P.M. and I'd appreciate it if you could be here at seven-thirty."

"But what—"

"Fine. Fine. That will be all now." On signal, a smiling secretary came in to usher her out.

Miss Fellowes stared back at Dr. Hoskins' closed door for a moment. What was Stasis? What had this large barn of a building—with its badged employees, its makeshift corridors, and its unmistakable air of engineering—to do with children?

She wondered if she should go back that evening or stay away and teach that arrogant man a lesson. But she knew she would be back if only out of sheer frustration. She would have to find out about the children.

She came back at seven-thirty and did not have to announce herself. One after another, men and women seemed to know her and to know her function. She found herself all but placed on skids as she was moved inward.

Dr. Hoskins was there, but he only looked at her distantly and murmured, "Miss Fellowes."

He did not even suggest that she take a seat, but she drew one calmly up to the railing and sat down.

They were on a balcony, looking down into a large pit filled with instruments that looked like a cross between the control panel of a spaceship and the working face of a computer. On one side were partitions that seemed to make up an unceilinged apartment, a giant doll house into the rooms of which she could look from above.

She could see an electronic cooker and a freeze-space unit in one room and a washroom arrangement off another. And surely the object she made out in another room could only be part of a bed, a small bed.

Hoskins was speaking to another man and, with Miss Fellowes, they made up the total occupancy of the balcony. Hoskins did not offer to introduce the other man, and Miss Fellowes eyed him surreptitiously. He was thin and quite fine looking in a middle-aged way. He had a small mustache and keen eyes that seemed to busy themselves with everything.

He was saying, "I won't pretend for one moment that I understand all this, Dr. Hoskins; I mean, except as a layman, a reasonably intelligent layman, may be expected to understand it. Still, if there's one part I understand less than another, it's this matter of selectivity. You can only reach out so far; that seems sensible; things get dimmer the further you go; it takes more energy. But then, you can only reach out so near. That's the puzzling part."

"I can make it seem less paradoxical, Deveney, if you will allow me to use an analogy."

(Miss Fellowes placed the new man the moment she heard his name, and despite herself was impressed. This was obviously Candide Deveney, the science writer of the Telenews, who was notoriously at the scene of every major scientific breakthrough. She even recognized his face as one she saw on the news plate when the landing on Mars had been announced. So Dr. Hoskins must have something important here.)

"By all means use an analogy," said Deveney ruefully, "if you think it will help."

"Well, then, you can't read a book with ordinary-sized print if it is held six feet from your eyes, but you can read it if you hold it one foot from your eyes. So far, the closer the better. If you bring the book to within one inch of your eyes, however, you've lost it again. There is such a thing as being too close, you see."

"Hmm," said Deveney.

"Or take another example. Your right shoulder is about thirty inches from the tip of your right forefinger and you can place your right forefinger on your right shoulder. Your right elbow is only half the distance from the tip of your right forefinger; it should by all ordinary logic be easier to reach, and yet you cannot place your right finger on your right elbow. Again, there is such a thing as being too close."

Deveney said, "May I use these analogies in my story?"

"Well, of course. Only too glad. I've been waiting long enough for someone like you to have a story. I'll give you anything else you want. It is time, finally, that we want the world looking over our shoulder. They'll see something."

(Miss Fellowes found herself admiring his calm certainty despite herself. There was strength there.)

Deveney said, "How far out will you reach?"

"Forty thousand years."

Miss Fellowes drew in her breath sharply.

Years?

There was tension in the air. The men at the controls scarcely moved. One man at a microphone spoke into it in a soft monotone, in short phrases that made no sense to Miss Fellowes.

Deveney, leaning over the balcony railing with an intent stare, said, "Will we see anything, Dr. Hoskins?"

"What? No. Nothing till the job is done. We detect indirectly, something on the principle of radar, except that we use

mesons rather than radiation. Mesons reach backward under
the proper conditions. Some are reflected and we must analyze
the reflections."

"That sounds difficult."

Hoskins smiled again, briefly as always. "It is the end product of fifty years of research; forty years of it before I entered
the field. Yes, it's difficult."

The man at the microphone raised one hand.

Hoskins said, "We've had the fix on one particular moment
in time for weeks; breaking it, remaking it after calculating our
own movements in time; making certain that we could handle
time flow with sufficient precision. This must work now."

But his forehead glistened.

Edith Fellowes found herself out of her seat and at the balcony railing, but there was nothing to see.

The man at the microphone said quietly, "Now."

There was a space of silence sufficient for one breath and
then the sound of a terrified little boy's scream from the doll-
house rooms. Terror! Piercing terror!

Miss Fellowes' head twisted in the direction of the cry. A
child was involved. She had forgotten.

And Hoskins' fist pounded on the railing and he said in a
tight voice, trembling with triumph, *"Did* it."

Miss Fellowes was urged down the short, spiral flight of steps
by the hard press of Hoskins' palm between her shoulder blades.
He did not speak to her.

The men who had been at the controls were standing about
now, smiling, smoking, watching the three as they entered on
the main floor. A very soft buzz sounded from the direction of
the doll house.

Hoskins said to Deveney, "It's perfectly safe to enter Stasis.
I've done it a thousand times. There's a queer sensation which
is momentary and means nothing."

He stepped through an open door in mute demonstration,

and Deveney, smiling stiffly and drawing an obviously deep breath, followed him.

Hoskins said, "Miss Fellowes! Please!" He crooked his forefinger impatiently.

Miss Fellowes nodded and stepped stiffly through. It was as though a ripple went through her, an internal tickle.

But once inside all seemed normal. There was the smell of the fresh wood of the doll house and—of—of soil somehow.

There was silence now, no voice at least, but there was the dry shuffling of feet, a scrabbling as of a hand over wood—then a low moan.

"Where is it?" asked Miss Fellowes in distress. Didn't these fool men *care?*

The boy was in the bedroom; at least the room with the bed in it.

It was standing naked, with its small, dirt-smeared chest heaving raggedly. A bushel of dirt and coarse grass spread over the floor at its bare brown feet. The smell of soil came from it and a touch of something fetid.

Hoskins followed her horrified glance and said with annoyance, "You can't pluck a boy cleanly out of time, Miss Fellowes. We had to take some of the surroundings with it for safety. Or would you have preferred to have it arrive here minus a leg or with only half a head?"

"Please!" said Miss Fellowes, in an agony of revulsion. "Are we just to stand here? The poor child is frightened. And it's *filthy.*"

She was quite correct. It was smeared with encrusted dirt and grease and had a scratch on its thigh that looked red and sore.

As Hoskins approached him, the boy, who seemed to be something over three years in age, hunched low and backed away rapidly. He lifted his upper lip and snarled in a hissing fashion like a cat. With a rapid gesture, Hoskins seized the boy's arms and lifted him, writhing and screaming, from the floor.

Miss Fellowes said, "Hold him, now. He needs a warm bath first. He needs to be cleaned. Have you the equipment? If so, have it brought here, and I'll need to have help in handling him just at first. Then, too, for heaven's sake, have all this trash and filth removed."

She was giving the orders now and she felt perfectly good about that. And because now she was an efficient nurse, rather than a confused spectator, she looked at the child with a clinical eye—and hesitated for one shocked moment. She saw past the dirt and shrieking, past the thrashing of limbs and useless twisting. She saw the boy himself.

It was the ugliest little boy she had ever seen. It was horribly ugly from misshapen head to bandy legs.

She got the boy cleaned with three men helping her and with others milling about in their efforts to clean the room. She worked in silence and with a sense of outrage, annoyed by the continued strugglings and outcries of the boy and by the undignified drenchings of soapy water to which she was subjected.

Dr. Hoskins had hinted that the child would not be pretty, but that was far from stating that it would be repulsively deformed. And there was a stench about the boy that soap and water was only alleviating little by little.

She had the strong desire to thrust the boy, soaped as he was, into Hoskins' arms and walk out; but there was the pride of profession. She had accepted an assignment after all. —And there would be the look in his eyes. A cold look that would read: Only pretty children, Miss Fellowes?

He was standing apart from them, watching coolly from a distance with a half smile on his face, when he caught her eyes, as though amused at her outrage.

She decided she would wait a while before quitting. To do so now would only demean her.

Then, when the boy was a bearable pink and smelled of scented soap, she felt better anyway. His cries changed to whimpers of exhaustion as he watched carefully, eyes moving in quick frightened suspicion from one to another of those in the room. His cleanness accentuated his thin nakedness as he shivered with cold after the bath.

Miss Fellowes said sharply, "Bring me a nightgown for the child!"

A nightgown appeared at once. It was as though everything were ready and yet nothing were ready unless she gave orders; as though they were deliberately leaving this in her charge without help, to test her.

The newsman, Deveney, approached and said, "I'll hold him, Miss. You won't get it on yourself."

"Thank you," said Miss Fellowes. And it was a battle indeed, but the nightgown went on, and when the boy made as though to rip it off, she slapped his hand sharply.

The boy reddened, but did not cry. He stared at her and the splayed fingers of one hand moved slowly across the flannel of the nightgown, feeling the strangeness of it.

Miss Fellowes thought desperately, Well, what next?

Everyone seemed in suspended animation, waiting for her—even the ugly little boy.

Miss Fellowes said sharply, "Have you provided food? Milk?"

They had. A mobile unit was wheeled in, with its refrigeration compartment containing three quarts of milk, with a warming unit and a supply of fortifications in the form of vitamin drops, copper-cobalt-iron syrup and others she had no time to be concerned with. There was a variety of canned self-warming junior foods.

She used milk, simply milk, to begin with. The radar unit heated the milk to a set temperature in a matter of ten seconds and clicked off, and she put some in a saucer. She had a certainty about the boy's savagery. He wouldn't know how to handle a cup.

Miss Fellowes nodded and said to the boy, "Drink. Drink."

She made a gesture as though to raise the milk to her mouth. The boy's eyes followed, but he made no move.

Suddenly, the nurse resorted to direct measures. She seized the boy's upper arm in one hand and dipped the other in the milk. She dashed the milk across his lips, so that it dripped down cheeks and receding chin.

For a moment, the child uttered a high-pitched cry, then his tongue moved over his wetted lips. Miss Fellowes stepped back.

The boy approached the saucer, bent toward it, then looked up and behind sharply as though expecting a crouching enemy; bent again and licked at the milk eagerly, like a cat. He made a slurping noise. He did not use his hands to lift the saucer.

Miss Fellowes allowed a bit of the revulsion she felt to show on her face. She couldn't help it.

Deveney caught that, perhaps. He said, "Does the nurse know, Dr. Hoskins?"

"Know what?" demanded Miss Fellowes.

Deveney hesitated, but Hoskins (again that look of detached amusement on his face) said, "Well, tell her."

Deveney addressed Miss Fellowes. "You may not suspect it, Miss, but you happen to be the first civilized woman in history ever to be taking care of a Neanderthal youngster."

She turned on Hoskins with a kind of controlled ferocity. "You might have told me, Doctor."

"Why? What difference does it make?"

"You said a child."

"Isn't that a child? Have you ever had a puppy or a kitten, Miss Fellowes? Are those closer to the human? If that were a baby chimpanzee, would you be repelled? You're a nurse, Miss Fellowes. Your record places you in a maternity ward for three years. Have you ever refused to take care of a deformed infant?"

Miss Fellowes felt her case slipping away. She said, with much less decision, "You might have told me."

"And you would have refused the position? Well, do you refuse it now?" He gazed at her coolly, while Deveney watched
from the other side of the room, and the Neanderthal child,
having finished the milk and licked the plate, looked up at her
with a wet face and wide, longing eyes.

The boy pointed to the milk and suddenly burst out in a short
series of sounds repeated over and over; sounds made up of
gutturals and elaborate tongue clickings.

Miss Fellowes said, in surprise, "Why, he talks."

"Of course," said Hoskins. "Homo neanderthalensis is not a
truly separate species, but rather a subspecies of Homo sapiens.
Why shouldn't he talk? He's probably asking for more milk."

Automatically, Miss Fellowes reached for the bottle of milk,
but Hoskins seized her wrist. "Now, Miss Fellowes, before we
go any further, are you staying on the job?"

Miss Fellowes shook free in annoyance, "Won't you feed him
if I don't? I'll stay with him—for a while."

She poured the milk.

Hoskins said, "We are going to leave you with the boy, Miss
Fellowes. This is the only door to Stasis Section One and it is
elaborately locked and guarded. I'll want you to learn the details of the lock which will, of course, be keyed to your finger-
prints as they are already keyed to mine. The spaces overhead"
—he looked upward to the open ceilings of the doll house—
"are also guarded and we will be warned if anything untoward
takes place in here."

Miss Fellowes said indignantly, "You mean I'll be under
view." She thought suddenly of her own survey of the room in-
teriors from the balcony.

"No, no," said Hoskins seriously, "your privacy will be re-
spected completely. The view will consist of electronic symbol-
ism only, which only a computer will deal with. Now you will
stay with him tonight, Miss Fellowes, and every night until further notice. You will be relieved during the day according to

some schedule you will find convenient. We will allow you to arrange that."

Miss Fellowes looked about the doll house with a puzzled expression. "But why all this, Dr. Hoskins? Is the boy dangerous?"

"It's a matter of energy, Miss Fellowes. He must never be allowed to leave these rooms. Never. Not for an instant. Not for any reason. Not to save his life. Not even to save *your* life, Miss Fellowes. Is that clear?"

Miss Fellowes raised her chin. "I understand the orders, Dr. Hoskins, and the nursing profession is accustomed to placing its duties ahead of self-preservation."

"Good. You can always signal if you need anyone." And the two men left.

Miss Fellowes turned to the boy. He was watching her and there was still milk in the saucer. Laboriously she tried to show him how to lift the saucer and place it to his lips. He resisted, but let her touch him without crying out.

Always, his frightened eyes were on her, watching, watching for the one false move. She found herself soothing him, trying to move her hand very slowly toward his hair, letting him see it every inch of the way, see there was no harm in it.

And she succeeded in stroking his hair for an instant.

She said, "I'm going to have to show you how to use the bathroom. Do you think you can learn?"

She spoke quietly, kindly, knowing he would not understand the words but hoping he would respond to the calmness of the tone.

The boy launched into a clicking phrase again.

She said, "May I take your hand?"

She held out hers and the boy looked at it. She left it outstretched and waited. The boy's own hand crept forward toward hers.

"That's right," she said.

It approached within an inch of hers and then the boy's courage failed him. He snatched it back.

"Well," said Miss Fellowes calmly, "we'll try again later. Would you like to sit down here?" She patted the mattress of the bed.

The hours passed slowly and progress was minute. She did not succeed either with bathroom or with the bed. In fact, after the child had given unmistakable signs of sleepiness he lay down on the bare ground and then, with a quick movement, rolled beneath the bed.

She bent to look at him and his eyes gleamed out at her as he tongue-clicked at her.

"All right," she said, "if you feel safer there, you sleep there."

She closed the door to the bedroom and retired to the cot that had been placed for her use in the largest room. At her insistence, a makeshift canopy had been stretched over it. She thought, Those stupid men will have to place a mirror in this room and a larger chest of drawers and a separate washroom if they expect me to spend nights here.

It was difficult to sleep. She found herself straining to hear possible sounds in the next room. He couldn't get out, could he? The walls were sheer and impossibly high but suppose the child could climb like a monkey? Well, Hoskins said there were observational devices watching through the ceiling.

Suddenly she thought, Can he be dangerous? Physically dangerous?

Surely Hoskins couldn't have meant that. Surely he would not have left her here alone, if—

She tried to laugh at herself. He was only a three- or four-year-old child. Still, she had not succeeded in cutting his nails. If he should attack her with nails and teeth while she slept—

Her breath came quickly. Oh, ridiculous, and yet—

She listened with painful attentiveness, and this time she heard the sound.

The boy was crying.

Not shrieking in fear or anger; not yelling or screaming. It was crying softly, and the cry was the heartbroken sobbing of a lonely, lonely child.

For the first time, Miss Fellowes thought with a pang, Poor thing!

Of course, it was a child; what did the shape of its head matter? It was a child that had been orphaned as no child had ever been orphaned before. Not only its mother and father were gone, but all its species. Snatched callously out of time, it was now the only creature of its kind in the world. The last. The only.

She felt pity for it strengthen, and with it shame at her own callousness. Tucking her own nightgown carefully about her calves (incongruously, she thought, Tomorrow I'll have to bring in a bathrobe) she got out of bed and went into the boy's room.

"Little boy," she called in a whisper. "Little boy."

She was about to reach under the bed, but she thought of a possible bite and did not. Instead, she turned on the night light and moved the bed.

The poor thing was huddled in the corner, knees up against his chin, looking up at her with blurred and apprehensive eyes.

In the dim light, she was not aware of his repulsiveness.

"Poor boy," she said, "poor boy." She felt him stiffen as she stroked his hair, then relax. "Poor boy. May I hold you?"

She sat down on the floor next to him and slowly and rhythmically stroked his hair, his cheek, his arm. Softly she began to sing a slow and gentle song.

He lifted his head at that, staring at her mouth in the dimness, as though wondering at the sound.

She maneuvered him closer while he listened to her. Slowly, she pressed gently against the side of his head, until it rested on her shoulder. She put her arm under his thighs and with a smooth and unhurried motion lifted him into her lap.

She continued singing, the same simple verse over and over, while she rocked back and forth, back and forth.

He stopped crying, and after a while the smooth burr of his breathing showed he was asleep.

With infinite care, she pushed his bed back against the wall and laid him down. She covered him and stared down. His face looked so peaceful and little-boy as he slept. It didn't matter so much that it was so ugly. Really.

She began to tiptoe out, then thought, If he wakes up?

She came back, battled irresolutely with herself, then sighed and slowly got into bed with the child.

It was too small for her. She was cramped and uneasy at the lack of canopy, but the child's hand crept into hers and, somehow, she fell asleep in that position.

She awoke with a start and a wild impulse to scream. The latter she just managed to suppress into a gurgle. The boy was looking at her, wide-eyed. It took her a long moment to remember getting into bed with him, and now, slowly, without unfixing her eyes from his, she stretched one leg carefully and let it touch the floor, then the other one.

She cast a quick and apprehensive glance toward the open ceiling, then tensed her muscles for quick disengagement.

But at that moment, the boy's stubby fingers reached out and touched her lips. He said something.

She shrank at the touch. He was terribly ugly in the light of day.

The boy spoke again. He opened his own mouth and gestured with his hands as though something were coming out.

Miss Fellowes guessed at the meaning and said tremulously, "Do you want me to sing?"

The boy said nothing but stared at her mouth.

In a voice slightly off key with tension, Miss Fellowes began the little song she had sung the night before and the ugly little boy smiled. He swayed clumsily in rough time to the music and made a little gurgly sound that might have been the beginnings of a laugh.

Miss Fellowes sighed inwardly. Music hath charms to soothe the savage breast. It might help . . .

She said, "You wait. Let me get myself fixed up. It will just take a minute. Then I'll make breakfast for you."

She worked rapidly, conscious of the lack of ceiling at all times. The boy remained in bed, watching her when she was in view. She smiled at him at those times and waved. At the end, he waved back, and she found herself being charmed by that.

Finally she said, "Would you like oatmeal with milk?" It took a moment to prepare, and then she beckoned to him.

Whether he understood the gesture or followed the aroma, Miss Fellowes did not know, but he got out of bed.

She tried to show him how to use a spoon but he shrank away from it in fright. (Time enough, she thought.) She compromised on insisting that he lift the bowl in his hands. He did it clumsily enough and it was incredibly messy, but most of it did get into him.

She tried the drinking milk in a glass this time, and the little boy whined when he found the opening too small for him to get his face into conveniently. She held his hand, forcing it around the glass, making him tip it, forcing his mouth to the rim.

Again a mess but again most went into him, and she was used to messes.

The washroom, to her surprise and relief, was a less frustrating matter. He understood what it was she expected him to do.

She found herself patting his head, saying, "Good boy. Smart boy."

And to Miss Fellowes' exceeding pleasure, the boy smiled at that.

She thought, When he smiles, he's quite bearable. Really.

Later in the day, the gentlemen of the press arrived.

She held the boy in her arms and he clung to her wildly while across the open door they set cameras to work. The commotion frightened the boy and he began to cry, but it was ten minutes before Miss Fellowes was allowed to retreat and put the boy in the next room.

She emerged again, flushed with indignation, walked out of the apartment (for the first time in eighteen hours) and closed the door behind her. "I think you've had enough. It will take me a while to quiet him. Go away."

"Sure, sure," said the gentleman from the *Times-Herald.* "But is that really a Neanderthal kid or is this some kind of gag?"

"I assure you," said Hoskins' voice, suddenly, from the background, "that this is no gag. The child is authentic Homo neanderthalensis."

"Is it a boy or a girl?"

"Boy," said Miss Fellowes briefly.

"Ape-boy," said the gentleman from the *News.* "That's what we've got here. Ape-boy. How does he act, Nurse?"

"He acts exactly like a little boy," snapped Miss Fellowes, annoyed into the defensive, "and he is not an ape–boy. His name is—is Timothy, Timmie—and he is perfectly normal in his behavior."

She had chosen the name Timothy at a venture. It was the first that had occurred to her.

"Timmie the Ape-boy," said the gentleman from the *News* and, as it turned out, Timmie the Ape-boy was the name under which the child became known to the world.

The gentleman from the *Globe* turned to Hoskins and said, "Doc, what do you expect to do with the ape-boy?"

Hoskins shrugged. "My original plan was completed when I proved it possible to bring him here. However, the anthropologists will be very interested, I imagine, and the physiologists. We have here, after all, a creature which is at the edge of being

human. We should learn a great deal about ourselves and our
ancestry from him."

"How long will you keep him?"

"Until such a time as we need the space more than we need
him. Quite a while, perhaps."

The gentleman from the *News* said, "Can you bring it out
into the open so we can set up sub-etheric equipment and put
on a real show?"

"I'm sorry, but the child cannot be removed from Stasis."

"Exactly what is Stasis?"

"Ah." Hoskins permitted himself one of his short smiles.
"That would take a great deal of explanation, gentlemen. In
Stasis, time as we know it doesn't exist. Those rooms are in-
side an invisible bubble that is not exactly part of our Universe.
That is why the child could be plucked out of time as it was."

"Well, wait now," said the gentleman from the *News* dis-
contentedly, "what are you giving us? The nurse goes into the
room and out of it."

"And so can any of you," said Hoskins matter of factly.
"You would be moving parallel to the lines of temporal force
and no great energy gain or loss would be involved. The child,
however, was taken from the far past. It moved across the lines
and gained temporal potential. To move it into the Universe
and into our own time would absorb enough energy to burn out
every line in the place and probably blank out all power in the
city of Washington. We had to store trash brought with him on
the premises and will have to remove it little by little."

The newsmen were writing down sentences busily as Hoskins
spoke to them. They did not understand and they were sure
their readers would not, but it sounded scientific and that was
what counted.

The gentleman from the *Times-Herald* said, "Would you be
available for an all-circuit interview tonight?"

"I think so," said Hoskins at once, and they all moved off.

Miss Fellowes looked after them. She understood all this

about Stasis and temporal force as little as the newsmen but she managed to get this much. Timmie's imprisonment (she found herself suddenly thinking of the little boy as Timmie) was a real one and not one imposed by the arbitrary fiat of Hoskins. Apparently it was impossible to let him out of Stasis at all, ever.

Poor child. Poor child.

She was suddenly aware of his crying and she hastened in to console him.

Miss Fellowes did not have a chance to see Hoskins on the all-circuit hookup, and though his interview was beamed to every part of the world and even to the outposts on the Moon, it did not penetrate the apartment in which Miss Fellowes and the ugly little boy lived.

But he was down the next morning, radiant and joyful.

Miss Fellowes said, "Did the interview go well?"

"Extremely. And how is—Timmie?"

Miss Fellowes found herself pleased at the use of the name. "Doing quite well. Now come out here, Timmie, the nice gentleman will not hurt you."

But Timmie stayed in the other room, with a lock of his matted hair showing behind the barrier of the door and, occasionally, the corner of an eye.

"Actually," said Miss Fellowes, "he is settling down amazingly. He is quite intelligent."

"Are you surprised?"

She hesitated just a moment, then said, "Yes, I am. I suppose I thought he was an ape-boy."

"Well, ape-boy or not, he's done a great deal for us. He's put Stasis, Inc., on the map. We're in, Miss Fellowes, we're in." It was as though he had to express his triumph to someone, even if only to Miss Fellowes.

"Oh?" She let him talk.

He put his hands in his pockets and said, "We've been work-

ing on a shoestring for ten years, scrounging funds a penny at
a time wherever we could. We had to shoot the works on one
big show. It was everything, or nothing. And when I say the
works, I mean it. This attempt to bring in a Neanderthal took
every cent we could borrow or steal, and some of it *was* stolen
—funds for other projects, used for this one without permission. If that experiment hadn't succeeded, I'd have been
through."

Miss Fellowes said abruptly, "Is that why there are no
ceilings?"

"Eh?" Hoskins looked up.

"Was there no money for ceilings?"

"Oh. Well, that wasn't the only reason. We didn't really
know in advance how old the Neanderthal might be exactly.
We can detect only dimly in time, and he might have been large
and savage. It was possible we might have had to deal with him
from a distance, like a caged animal."

"But since that hasn't turned out to be so, I suppose you can
build a ceiling now."

"Now, yes. We have plenty of money, now. Funds have been
promised from every source. This is all wonderful, Miss Fellowes." His broad face gleamed with a smile that lasted and
when he left, even his back seemed to be smiling.

Miss Fellowes thought, He's quite a nice man when he's off
guard and forgets about being scientific.

She wondered for an idle moment if he were married, then
dismissed the thought in self-embarrassment.

"Timmie," she called. "Come here, Timmie."

In the months that passed, Miss Fellowes felt herself grow to
be an integral part of Stasis, Inc. She was given a small office
of her own with her name on the door, an office quite close to
the doll house—as she never stopped calling Timmie's Stasis
bubble. She was given a substantial raise. The doll house was
covered by a ceiling; its furnishings were elaborated and im-

proved; a second washroom was added—and even so, she
gained an apartment of her own on the institute grounds and,
on occasion, did not stay with Timmie during the night. An
intercom was set up between the doll house and her apartment
and Timmie learned how to use it.

Miss Fellowes got used to Timmie. She even grew less con-
scious of his ugliness. One day she found herself staring at an
ordinary boy in the street and finding something bulgy and un-
attractive in his high domed forehead and jutting chin. She had
to shake herself to break the spell.

It was more pleasant to grow used to Hoskins' occasional
visits. It was obvious he welcomed escape from his increasingly
harried role as head of Stasis, Inc., and that he took a sentimental interest in the child who had started it all, but it seemed
to Miss Fellowes that he also enjoyed talking to her.

(She had learned some facts about Hoskins, too. He had invented the method of analyzing the reflection of the past-pene-
trating mesonic beam; he had invented the method of estab-
lishing Stasis; his coldness was only an effort to hide a kindly
nature; and, oh yes, he *was* married.)

What Miss Fellowes could *not* get used to was the fact that
she was engaged in a scientific experiment. Despite all she could
do, she found herself getting personally involved to the point of
quarreling with the physiologists.

On one occasion Hoskins came down and found her in the
midst of a hot urge to kill. They had no right; they had no *right*
— Even if he *was* a Neanderthal, he still wasn't an animal.

She was staring after them in a blind fury, staring out the
open door and listening to Timmie's sobbing, when she noticed
Hoskins standing there. He might have been there for minutes.

He said, "May I come in?"

She nodded curtly, then hurried to Timmie, who clung to
her, curling his little bandy legs—still thin, so thin—about her.

Hoskins watched, then said gravely, "He seems quite un-
happy."

Miss Fellowes said, "I don't blame him. They're at him every day now with their blood samples and their probings. They keep him on synthetic diets that I wouldn't feed a pig."

"It's the sort of thing they can't try on a human, you know."

"And they can't try it on Timmie, either. Dr. Hoskins, I insist. You told me it was Timmie's coming that put Stasis, Inc., on the map. If you have any gratitude for that at all, you've *got* to keep them away from the poor thing at least until he's old enough to understand a little more. After he's had a bad session with them, he has nightmares, he can't sleep. Now I warn you"—she reached a sudden peak of fury—"I'm not letting them in here any more."

(She realized that she had screamed that, but she couldn't help it.)

She said more quietly, "I know he's Neanderthal, but there's a great deal we don't appreciate about Neanderthals. I've read up on them. They had a culture of their own. Some of the greatest human inventions arose in Neanderthal times. The domestication of animals, for instance; the wheel; various techniques in grinding stone. They even had spiritual yearnings. They buried their dead and buried possessions with the body, showing they believed in a life after death. It amounts to the fact that they invented religion. Doesn't that mean Timmie has a right to human treatment?"

She patted the little boy gently on his buttocks and sent him off into his playroom. As the door was opened, Hoskins smiled briefly at the display of toys that could be seen.

Miss Fellowes said defensively, "The poor child deserves his toys. It's all he has and he earns them with what he goes through."

"No, no. No objections, I assure you. I was just thinking how you've changed since the first day, when you were quite angry I had foisted a Neanderthal on you."

Miss Fellowes said in a low voice, "I suppose I didn't . . ." and faded off.

Hoskins changed the subject. "How old would you say he is, Miss Fellowes?"

She said, "I can't say, since we don't know how Neanderthals develop. In size he'd only be three but Neanderthals are smaller generally and with all the tampering they do with him, he probably isn't growing. The way he's learning English, though, I'd say he was well over four."

"Really? I haven't noticed anything about learning English in the reports."

"He won't speak to anyone but me. For now, anyway. He's terribly afraid of others, and no wonder. But he can ask for an article of food; he can indicate any need practically; and he understands almost anything I say. Of course"—she watched him shrewdly, trying to estimate if this was the time—"his development may not continue."

"Why not?"

"Any child needs stimulation and this one lives a life of solitary confinement. I do what I can, but I'm not with him all the time and I'm not all he needs. What I mean, Dr. Hoskins, is that he needs another boy to play with."

Hoskins nodded slowly. "Unfortunately, there's only one of him, isn't there? Poor child."

Miss Fellowes warmed to him at once. She said, "You do like Timmie, don't you?" It was so nice to have someone else feel like that.

"Oh, yes," said Hoskins, and with his guard down, she could see the weariness in his eyes.

Miss Fellowes dropped her plans to push the matter at once. She said, with real concern, "You look worn out, Dr. Hoskins."

"Do I, Miss Fellowes? I'll have to practice looking more life-like then."

"I suppose Stasis, Inc., is very busy and that that keeps you very busy."

Hoskins shrugged. "You suppose right. It's a matter of ani-

mal, vegetable, and mineral in equal parts, Miss Fellowes. But
then, I suppose you haven't ever seen our displays."

"Actually, I haven't. But it's not because I'm not interested.
It's just that I've been so busy."

"Well, you're not all that busy right now," he said with im-
pulsive decision. "I'll call for you tomorrow at eleven and give
you a personal tour. How's that?"

She smiled happily. "I'd love it."

He nodded and smiled in his turn and left.

Miss Fellowes hummed at intervals for the rest of the day.
Really—to think so was ridiculous, of course—but really, it was
almost like—like making a date.

He was quite on time the next day, smiling and pleasant. She
had replaced her nurse's uniform with a dress. One of conservative cut, to be sure, but she hadn't felt so feminine in years.

He complimented her on her appearance with staid formality
and she accepted with equally formal grace. It was really a perfect prelude, she thought. And then the additional thought came,
prelude to what?

She shut that off by hastening to say goodbye to Timmie and
to assure him she would be back soon. She made sure he knew
all about what and where lunch was.

Hoskins took her into the new wing, into which she had never
yet gone. It still had the odor of newness about it and the sound
of construction, softly heard, was indication enough that it was
still being extended.

"Animal, vegetable, and mineral," said Hoskins, as he had
the day before. "Animal right there; our most spectacular ex-
hibits."

The space was divided into many rooms, each a separate
Stasis bubble. Hoskins brought her to the view glass of one and
she looked in. What she saw impressed her first as a scaled,
tailed chicken. Skittering on two thin legs it ran from wall to

wall with its delicate birdlike head, surmounted by a bony keel like the comb of a rooster, looking this way and that. The paws on its small forelimbs clenched and unclenched constantly.

Hoskins said, "It's our dinosaur. We've had it for months. I don't know when we'll be able to let go of it."

"Dinosaur?"

"Did you expect a giant?"

She dimpled. "One does, I suppose. I know some of them are small."

"A small one is all we aimed for, believe me. Generally, it's under investigation, but this seems to be an open hour. Some interesting things have been discovered. For instance, it is not entirely cold blooded. It has an imperfect method of maintaining internal temperatures higher than that of its environment. Unfortunately it's a male. Ever since we brought it in we've been trying to get a fix on another that may be female, but we've had no luck yet."

"Why female?"

He looked at her quizzically. "So that we might have a fighting chance to obtain fertile eggs, and baby dinosaurs."

"Of course."

He led her to the trilobite section. "That's Professor Dwayne of Washington University," he said. "He's a nuclear chemist. If I recall correctly, he's taking an isotope ratio on the oxygen of the water."

"Why?"

"It's primeval water; at least half a billion years old. The isotope ratio gives the temperature of the ocean at that time. He himself happens to ignore the trilobites, but others are chiefly concerned in dissecting them. They're the lucky ones because all they need are scalpels and microscopes. Dwayne has to set up a mass spectrograph each time he conducts an experiment."

"Why's that? Can't he—"

"No, he can't. He can't take anything out of the room as far as can be helped."

There were samples of primordial plant life too and chunks of rock formations. Those were the vegetable and mineral. And every specimen had its investigator. It was like a museum, a museum brought to life and serving as a superactive center of research.

"And you have to supervise all of this, Dr. Hoskins?"

"Only indirectly, Miss Fellowes. I have subordinates, thank heaven. My own interest is entirely in the theoretical aspects of the matter: the nature of Time, the technique of mesonic intertemporal detection and so on. I would exchange all this for a method of detecting objects closer in Time than ten thousand years ago. If we could get into historical times—"

He was interrupted by a commotion at one of the distant booths, a thin voice raised querulously. He frowned, muttered hastily, "Excuse me," and hastened off.

Miss Fellowes followed as best she could without actually running.

An elderly man, thinly bearded and red faced, was saying, "I had vital aspects of my investigations to complete. Don't you understand that?"

A uniformed technician with the interwoven SI monogram— for Stasis, Inc.—on his lab coat, said, "Dr. Hoskins, it was arranged with Professor Ademewski at the beginning that the specimen could only remain here two weeks."

"I did not know then how long my investigations would take. I'm not a prophet," said Ademewski heatedly.

Dr. Hoskins said, "You understand, Professor, we have limited space; we must keep specimens rotating. That piece of chalcopyrite must go back; there are men waiting for the next specimen."

"Why can't I have it for myself, then? Let me take it out of there."

"You know you can't have it."

"A piece of chalcopyrite, a miserable five-kilogram piece? Why not?"

"We can't afford the energy expense!" said Hoskins brusquely. "You know that."

The technician interrupted. "The point is, Dr. Hoskins, that he tried to remove the rock against the rules and I almost punctured Stasis while he was in there, not knowing he was in there."

There was a short silence and Dr. Hoskins turned on the investigator with a cold formality. "Is that so, Professor?"

Professor Ademewski coughed. "I saw no harm . . ."

Hoskins reached up to a hand pull dangling just within reach, outside the specimen room in question. He pulled it.

Miss Fellowes, who had been peering in, looking at the totally undistinguished sample of rock that occasioned the dispute, drew in her breath sharply as its existence flickered out. The room was empty.

Hoskins said, "Professor, your permit to investigate matters in Stasis will be permanently voided. I am sorry."

"But wait—"

"I am sorry. You have violated one of the stringent rules."

"I will appeal to the International Association . . ."

"Appeal away. In a case like this, you will find I can't be overruled."

He turned away deliberately, leaving the professor still protesting, and said to Miss Fellowes, his face still white with anger, "Would you care to have lunch with me, Miss Fellowes?"

He took her into the small administration alcove of the cafeteria. He greeted others and introduced Miss Fellowes with complete ease, although she herself felt painfully self-conscious.

What must they think, she thought, and tried desperately to appear businesslike.

She said, "Do you have that kind of trouble often, Dr. Hoskins? I mean like that you just had with the professor?" She took her fork in hand and began eating.

"No," said Hoskins forcefully. "That was the first time. Of course I'm always having to argue men out of removing specimens but this is the first time one actually tried to *do* it."

"I remember you once talked about the energy it would consume."

"That's right. Of course, we've tried to take it into account. Accidents will happen and so we've got special power sources designed to stand the drain of accidental removal from Stasis, but that doesn't mean we want to see a year's supply of energy gone in half a second, or can afford to without having our plans of expansion delayed for years. Besides, imagine the professor's being in the room while Stasis was about to be punctured."

"What would have happened to him if it had been?"

"Well, we've experimented with inanimate objects and with mice and they've disappeared. Presumably they've traveled back in Time; carried along, so to speak, by the pull of the object simultaneously snapping back into its natural time. For that reason, we have to anchor objects within Stasis that we don't want to move and that's a complicated procedure. The professor would not have been anchored and he would have gone back to the Pliocene at the moment when we abstracted the rock—plus, of course, the two weeks it had remained here in the present."

"How dreadful it would have been."

"Not on account of the professor, I assure you. If he were fool enough to do what he did, it would serve him right. But imagine the effect it would have on the public if the fact came out. All people would need is to become aware of the dangers involved and funds could be choked off like that." He snapped his fingers and played moodily with his food.

Miss Fellowes said, "Couldn't you get him back? The way you got the rock in the first place?"

"No, because once an object is returned, the original fix is lost unless we deliberately plan to retain it and there was no reason to do that in this case. There never is. Finding the professor again would mean relocating a specific fix and that would be like dropping a line into the oceanic abyss for the purpose of dredging up a particular fish. My God, when I think of the precautions we take to prevent accidents, it makes me mad. We have every individual Stasis unit set up with its own puncturing device. We have to, since each unit has its separate fix and must be collapsible independently. The point is, though, none of the puncturing devices is ever activated until the last minute. And then we deliberately make activation impossible except by the pull of a rope carefully led outside the Stasis. The pull is a gross mechanical motion that requires a strong effort, not something that is likely to be done accidentally."

Miss Fellowes said, "But doesn't it—change history to move something in and out of Time?"

Hoskins shrugged. "Theoretically, yes; actually, except in unusual cases, no. We move objects out of Stasis all the time. Air molecules. Bacteria. Dust. About ten percent of our energy consumption goes to make up micro-losses of that nature. But moving even large objects in Time sets up changes that damp out. Take that chalcopyrite from the Pliocene. Because of its absence for two weeks some insect didn't find the shelter it might have found and is killed. That could initiate a whole series of changes, but the mathematics of Stasis indicates that this is a converging series. The amount of change diminishes with time and then things are as before."

"You mean, reality heals itself?"

"In a manner of speaking. Abstract a human from Time or send one back, and you make a larger wound. If the individual is an ordinary one, that wound still heals itself. Of course, there are a great many people who write to us each day and want us to bring Abraham Lincoln into the present, or Mohammed, or Lenin. *That* can't be done, of course. Even if we could find them, the change in reality in moving one of the history molders would be too great to be healed. There are ways of calculating when a change is likely to be too great and we avoid even approaching that limit."

Miss Fellowes said, "Then, Timmie—"

"No, he presents no problem in that direction. Reality is safe.

But"—he gave her a quick, sharp glance, then went on—"But never mind. Yesterday you said he needed companionship."

"Yes." Miss Fellowes smiled her delight. "I didn't think you paid that any attention."

"Of course I did. I'm fond of the child. I appreciate your feelings for him and I was concerned enough to want to explain to you. Now I have; you've seen what we do; you've gotten some insight into the difficulties involved; so you know why, with the best will in the world, we can't supply companionship for Timmie."

"You can't?" said Miss Fellowes, with sudden dismay.

"But I've just explained. We couldn't possibly expect to find another Neanderthal his age without incredible luck, and if we could, it wouldn't be fair to multiply risks by having another human being in Stasis."

Miss Fellowes put down her spoon and said energetically, "But, Dr. Hoskins, that is not at all what I meant. I don't want you to bring another Neanderthal into the present. I know that's impossible. But it isn't impossible to bring another child to play with Timmie."

Hoskins stared at her in concern. "A *human* child?"

"*Another* child," said Miss Fellowes, completely hostile now. "Timmie is human."

"I couldn't dream of such a thing."

"Why not? Why couldn't you? What is wrong with the notion? You pulled that child out of Time and made him an eternal prisoner. Don't you owe him something? Dr. Hoskins, if there is any man who, in this world, is that child's father in every sense but the biological, it is you. Why can't you do this little thing for him?"

Hoskins said, "His *father?*" He rose, somewhat unsteadily, to his feet. "Miss Fellowes, I think I'll take you back now, if you don't mind."

They returned to the doll house in a complete silence that neither broke.

It was a long time after that before she saw Hoskins again, except for an occasional glimpse in passing. She was sorry about that at times; then, at other times, when Timmie was more than usually woebegone or when he spent silent hours at the window with its prospect of little more than nothing, she thought, fiercely, Stupid man.

Timmie's speech grew better and more precise each day. It never entirely lost a certain soft slurriness that Miss Fellowes found rather endearing. In times of excitement, he fell back into tongue clicking, but those times were becoming fewer. He must be forgetting the days before he came into the present, except for dreams.

As he grew older, the physiologists grew less interested and the psychologists more so. Miss Fellowes was not sure that she did not like the new group even less than the first. The needles were gone; the injections and withdrawals of fluid; the special diets. But now Timmie was made to overcome barriers to reach food and water. He had to lift panels, move bars, reach for cords. And the mild electric shocks made him cry and drove Miss Fellowes to distraction.

She did not wish to appeal to Hoskins; she did not wish to have to go to him; for each time she thought of him, she thought of his face over the luncheon table that last time. Her eyes moistened and she thought, Stupid, *stupid* man.

And then one day Hoskins' voice sounded unexpectedly, calling into the doll house, "Miss Fellowes."

She came out coldly, smoothing her nurse's uniform, then stopped in confusion at finding herself in the presence of a pale woman, slender and of middle height. The woman's fair hair and complexion gave her an appearance of fragility. Standing behind her and clutching at her skirt was a round-faced, large-eyed child of four.

Hoskins said, "Dear, this is Miss Fellowes, the nurse in charge of the boy. Miss Fellowes, this is my wife."

(Was this his wife? She was not as Miss Fellowes had imagined her to be. But then, why not? A man like Hoskins would choose a weak thing to be his foil. If that was what he wanted . . .)

She forced a matter-of-fact greeting. "Good afternoon, Mrs. Hoskins. Is this your—your little boy?"

(*That* was a surprise. She had thought of Hoskins as a husband, but not as a father, except, of course . . . She suddenly caught Hoskins' grave eyes and flushed.)

Hoskins said, "Yes, this is my boy, Jerry. Say hello to Miss Fellowes, Jerry."

(Had he stressed the word "this" just a bit? Was he saying *this* was his son and not—)

Jerry receded a bit further into the folds of the maternal skirt and muttered his hello. Mrs. Hoskins' eyes were searching over Miss Fellowes' shoulders, peering into the room, looking for something.

Hoskins said, "Well, let's go in. Come, dear. There's a trifling discomfort at the threshold, but it passes."

Miss Fellowes said, "Do you want Jerry to come in too?"

"Of course. He is to be Timmie's playmate. You said that Timmie needed a playmate. Or have you forgotten?"

"But—" She looked at him with a colossal, surprised wonder. "*Your* boy?"

He said peevishly, "Well, whose boy, then? Isn't this what you want? Come on in, dear. Come on in."

Mrs. Hoskins lifted Jerry into her arms with a distinct effort and, hesitantly, stepped over the threshold. Jerry squirmed as she did so, disliking the sensation.

Mrs. Hoskins said in a thin voice, "Is the creature here? I don't see him."

Miss Fellowes called, "Timmie. Come out."

Timmie peered around the edge of the door, staring up at the little boy who was visiting him. The muscles in Mrs. Hoskins' arms tensed visibly.

She said to her husband, "Gerald, are you sure it's safe?"

Miss Fellowes said at once, "If you mean is Timmie safe, why, of course he is. He's a gentle little boy."

"But he's a sa—savage."

(The ape-boy stories in the newspapers!) Miss Fellowes said emphatically, "He is not a savage. He is just as quiet and reasonable as you can possibly expect a five-and-a-half-year-old to be. It is very generous of you, Mrs. Hoskins, to agree to allow your boy to play with Timmie, but please have no fears about it."

Mrs. Hoskins said with mild heat, "I'm not sure that I agree."

"We've had it out, dear," said Hoskins. "Let's not bring up the matter for new argument. Put Jerry down."

Mrs. Hoskins did so and the boy backed against her, staring at the pair of eyes which were staring back at him from the next room.

"Come here, Timmie," said Miss Fellowes. "Don't be afraid."

Slowly, Timmie stepped into the room. Hoskins bent to disengage Jerry's fingers from his mother's skirt. "Step back, dear. Give the children a chance."

The youngsters faced one another. Although the younger, Jerry was nevertheless an inch taller, and in the presence of his straightness and his high-held, well-proportioned head, Timmie's grotesqueries were suddenly almost as pronounced as they had been in the first days.

Miss Fellowes' lips quivered.

It was the little Neanderthal who spoke first, in childish treble. "What's your name?" And Timmie thrust his face suddenly forward as though to inspect the other's features more closely.

Startled, Jerry responded with a vigorous shove that sent Timmie tumbling. Both began crying loudly and Mrs. Hoskins snatched up her child, while Miss Fellowes, flushed with repressed anger, lifted Timmie and comforted him.

Mrs. Hoskins said, "They just instinctively don't like one another."

"No more instinctively," said her husband wearily, "than any two children dislike each other. Now put Jerry down and let him get used to the situation. In fact, we had better leave. Miss Fellowes can bring Jerry to my office after a while and I'll have him taken home."

The two children spent the next hour very aware of each other. Jerry cried for his mother, struck out at Miss Fellowes and, finally, allowed himself to be comforted with a lollipop. Timmie sucked at another, and at the end of an hour, Miss Fellowes had them playing with the same set of blocks, though at opposite ends of the room.

She found herself almost maudlinly grateful to Hoskins when she brought Jerry to him.

She searched for ways to thank him but his very formality was a rebuff. Perhaps he could not forgive her for making him feel like a cruel father. Perhaps the bringing of his own child was an attempt, after all, to prove himself both a kind father to Timmie and, also, not his father at all. Both at the same time!

So all she could say was, "Thank you. Thank you very much."

And all he could say was, "It's all right. Don't mention it."

It became a settled routine. Twice a week, Jerry was brought in for an hour's play, later extended to two hours' play. The children learned each other's names and ways and played together.

And yet, after the first rush of gratitude, Miss Fellowes found herself disliking Jerry. He was larger and heavier and in all things dominant, forcing Timmie into a completely secondary role. All that reconciled her to the situation was the fact that, despite difficulties, Timmie looked forward with more and more delight to the periodic appearances of his playfellow.

It was all he had, she mourned to herself.

And once, as she watched them, she thought, Hoskins' two children, one by his wife and one by Stasis.

While she herself . . .

Heavens, she thought, putting her fists to her temples and feeling ashamed: I'm jealous!

"Miss Fellowes," said Timmie (carefully, she had never allowed him to call her anything else), "when will I go to school?"

She looked down at those eager brown eyes turned up to hers and passed her hand softly through his thick, curly hair. It was the most disheveled portion of his appearance, for she cut his hair herself while he sat restlessly under the scissors. She did not ask for professional help, for the very clumsiness of the cut served to mask the retreating forepart of the skull and the bulging hinder part.

She said, "Where did you hear about school?"

"Jerry goes to school. Kin-der-gar-ten." He said it carefully. "There are lots of places he goes. Outside. When can I go outside, Miss Fellowes?"

A small pain centered in Miss Fellowes' heart. Of course, she saw, there would be no way of avoiding the inevitability of Timmie's hearing more and more of the outer world he could never enter.

She said, with an attempt at gaiety, "Why, whatever would you do in kindergarten, Timmie?"

"Jerry says they play games, they have picture tapes. He says there are lots of children. He says—he says—" A thought, then a triumphant upholding of both small hands with the fingers splayed apart. "He says this many."

Miss Fellowes said, "Would you like picture tapes? I can get you picture tapes. Very nice ones. And music tapes, too."

So that Timmie was temporarily comforted.

He pored over the picture tapes in Jerry's absence and Miss Fellowes read to him out of ordinary books by the hour.

There was so much to explain in even the simplest story, so much that was outside the perspective of his three rooms. Tim-

mie took to having his dreams more often now that the outside
was being introduced to him.

They were always the same, about the outside. He tried halt-
ingly to describe them to Miss Fellowes. In his dreams, he was
outside, an empty outside, but very large, with children and
queer indescribable objects half digested in his thought out of
bookish descriptions half understood, or out of distant Neanderthal memories half recalled.

But the children and objects ignored him and though he was
in the world, he was never part of it but was as alone as though
he were in his own room—and would wake up crying.

Miss Fellowes tried to laugh at the dreams, but there were
nights in her own apartment when she cried, too.

One day, as Miss Fellowes read, Timmie put his hand under
her chin and lifted it gently so that her eyes left the book and
met his.

He said, "How do you know what to say, Miss Fellowes?"

She said, "You see these marks? They tell me what to say.
These marks make words."

He stared at them long and curiously, taking the book out of
her hands. "Some of these marks are the same."

She laughed with pleasure at this sign of his shrewdness and
said, "So they are. Would you like to have me show you how to
make the marks?"

"All right. That would be a nice game."

It did not occur to her that he could learn to read. Up to the
very moment that he read a book to her, it did not occur to her
that he could learn to read.

Then, weeks later, the enormity of what had been done struck
her. Timmie sat in her lap, following word by word the printing
in a child's book, reading to her. He was reading to her!

She struggled to her feet in amazement and said, "Now Timmie, I'll be back later. I want to see Dr. Hoskins."

Excited nearly to frenzy, it seemed to her she might have an answer to Timmie's unhappiness. If Timmie could not leave to enter the world, the world must be brought into those three rooms to Timmie—the whole world in books and film and sound. He must be educated to his full capacity. So much the world owed him.

She found Hoskins in a mood that was oddly analogous to her own: a kind of triumph and glory. His offices were unusually busy, and for a moment she thought she would not get to see him, as she stood abashed in the anteroom.

But he saw her, and a smile spread over his broad face. "Miss Fellowes, come here."

He spoke rapidly into the intercom, then shut it off. "Have you heard? No, of course, you couldn't have. We've done it. We've actually done it. We have intertemporal detection at close range."

"You mean," she tried to detach her thought from her own good news for a moment, "that you can get a person from historical times into the present?"

"That's just what I mean. We have a fix on a fourteenth-century individual right now. Imagine. *Imagine!* If you could only know how glad I'll be to shift from the eternal concentration on the Mesozoic, replace the paleontologists with the historians— But there's something you wish to say to me, eh? Well, go ahead; go ahead. You find me in a good mood. Anything you want you can have."

Miss Fellowes smiled. "I'm glad. Because I wonder if we might not establish a system of instruction for Timmie?"

"Instruction? In what?"

"Well, in everything. A school. So that he might learn."

"But *can* he learn?"

"Certainly, he *is* learning. He can read. I've taught him so much myself."

Hoskins sat there, seeming suddenly depressed. "I don't know, Miss Fellowes."

She said, "You just said that anything I wanted—"

"I know and I should not have. You see, Miss Fellowes, I'm sure you must realize that we cannot maintain the Timmie experiment forever."

She stared at him with sudden horror, not really understanding what he had said. How did he mean "cannot maintain"? With an agonizing flash of recollection, she recalled Professor Ademewski and his mineral specimen that was taken away after two weeks. She said, "But you're talking about a boy. Not about a rock . . ."

Dr. Hoskins said uneasily, "Even a boy can't be given undue importance, Miss Fellowes. Now that we expect individuals out of historical time, we will need Stasis space, all we can get."

She didn't grasp it. "But you can't. Timmie—Timmie—"

"Now, Miss Fellowes, please don't upset yourself. Timmie won't go right away; perhaps not for months. Meanwhile we'll do what we can."

She was still staring at him.

"Let me get you something, Miss Fellowes."

"No," she whispered. "I don't need anything." She arose in a kind of nightmare and left.

Timmie, she thought, you will *not* die. You will *not* die.

It was all very well to hold tensely to the thought that Timmie must not die, but how was that to be arranged? In the first weeks Miss Fellowes clung only to the hope that the attempt to bring forward a man from the fourteenth century would fail completely. Hoskins' theories might be wrong or his practice defective. Then things could go on as before.

Certainly that was not the hope of the rest of the world and, irrationally, Miss Fellowes hated the world for it. "Project Middle Ages" reached a climax of white-hot publicity. The press and the public had hungered for something like this. Stasis, Inc., had lacked the necessary sensation for a long time now. A new rock or another ancient fish failed to stir them. But *this* was *it*.

A historical human; an adult speaking a known language; someone who could open a new page of history to the scholar.

Zero-time was coming and this time it was not a question of three onlookers from a balcony. This time there would be a world-wide audience. This time the technicians of Stasis, Inc., would play their role before nearly all of mankind.

Miss Fellowes was herself all but savage with waiting. When young Jerry Hoskins showed up for his scheduled playtime with Timmie, she scarcely recognized him. He was not the one she was waiting for.

(The secretary who brought him left hurriedly after the barest nod for Miss Fellowes. She was rushing for a good place from which to watch the climax of Project Middle Ages. And so ought Miss Fellowes with far better reason, she thought bitterly, if only that stupid girl would arrive.)

Jerry Hoskins sidled toward her, embarrassed. "Miss Fellowes?" He took the reproduction of a news strip out of his pocket.

"Yes? What is it, Jerry?"

"Is this a picture of Timmie?"

Miss Fellowes stared at him, then snatched the strip from Jerry's hand. The excitement of Project Middle Ages had brought about a pale revival of interest in Timmie on the part of the press.

Jerry watched her narrowly, then said, "It says Timmie is an ape-boy. What does that mean?"

Miss Fellowes caught the youngster's wrist and repressed the impulse to shake him. "Never say that, Jerry. Never, do you understand? It is a nasty word and you mustn't use it."

Jerry struggled out of her grip, frightened.

Miss Fellowes tore up the news strip with a vicious twist of the wrist. "Now go inside and play with Timmie. He's got a new book to show you."

And then, finally, the girl appeared. Miss Fellowes did not know her. None of the usual stand-ins she had used when business took her elsewhere was available now, not with Project Middle Ages at climax, but Hoskins' secretary had promised to find *someone,* and this must be the girl.

Miss Fellowes tried to keep querulousness out of her voice. "Are you the girl assigned to Stasis Section One?"

"Yes, I'm Mandy Terris. You're Miss Fellowes, aren't you?"

"That's right."

"I'm sorry I'm late. There's just so much excitement."

"I know. Now I want you—"

Mandy said, "You'll be watching, I suppose." Her thin, vacuously pretty face filled with envy.

"Never mind that. Now I want you to come inside and meet Timmie and Jerry. They will be playing for the next two hours so they'll be giving you no trouble. They've got milk handy and plenty of toys. In fact, it will be better if you leave them alone as much as possible. Now I'll show you where everything is located and—"

"Is it Timmie that's the ape-b—"

"Timmie is the Stasis subject," said Miss Fellowes firmly.

"I mean, he's the one who's not supposed to get out, is that right?"

"Yes. Now, come in. There isn't much time."

And when she finally left, Mandy Terris called after her shrilly, "I hope you get a good seat and, golly, I sure hope it works."

Miss Fellowes did not trust herself to make a reasonable response. She hurried on without looking back.

But the delay meant she did *not* get a good seat. She got no nearer than the wall-viewing-plate in the assembly hall. Bitterly she regretted that. If she could have been on the spot; if she could somehow have reached out for some sensitive portion of the instrumentation; if she were in some way able to wreck the experiment—

She found the strength to beat down her madness. Simple destruction would have done no good. They would have rebuilt and reconstructed and made the effort again. And she would never be allowed to return to Timmie.

Nothing would help. Nothing but that the experiment itself fail; that it break down irretrievably.

So she waited through the countdown, watching every move on the giant screen, scanning the faces of the technicians as the focus shifted from one to the other, watching for the look of worry and uncertainty that would mark something going unexpectedly wrong; watching, watching—

There was no such look. The count reached zero, and very quietly, very unassumingly, the experiment succeeded!

In the new Stasis that had been established there stood a bearded, stoop-shouldered peasant of indeterminate age, in ragged dirty clothing and wooden shoes, staring in dull horror at the sudden mad change that had flung itself over him.

And while the world went mad with jubilation, Miss Fellowes stood frozen in sorrow, jostled and pushed, all but trampled; surrounded by triumph while bowed down with defeat.

And when the loudspeaker called her name with strident force, it sounded it three times before she responded.

"Miss Fellowes. Miss Fellowes. You are wanted in Stasis Section One immediately. Miss Fellowes. Miss Fell—"

"Let me through!" she cried breathlessly, while the loudspeaker continued its repetitions without pause. She forced her way through the crowd with wild energy, beating at it, striking out with closed fists, flailing, moving toward the door in a nightmare slowness.

Mandy Terris was in tears. "I don't know how it happened. I just went down to the edge of the corridor to watch a pocket-viewing-plate they had put up. Just for a minute. And then before I could move or do anything—" She cried out in sudden accusation, "You said they would make no trouble; you *said* to leave them alone—"

Miss Fellowes, disheveled and trembling uncontrollably, glared at her. "Where's Timmie?"

A nurse was swabbing the arm of a wailing Jerry with disinfectant and another was preparing an antitetanus shot. There was blood on Jerry's clothes.

"He bit me, Miss Fellowes," Jerry cried in rage. "He *bit* me."

But Miss Fellowes didn't even see him.

"What did you do with Timmie?" she cried out.

"I locked him in the bathroom," said Mandy. "I just threw the little monster in there and locked him in."

Miss Fellowes ran into the doll house. She fumbled at the bathroom door. It took an eternity to get it open and to find the ugly little boy cowering in the corner.

"Don't whip me, Miss Fellowes," he whispered. His eyes were red. His lips were quivering. "I didn't mean to do it."

"Oh, Timmie, who told you about whips?" She caught him to her, hugging him wildly.

He said tremulously, "She said, with a long rope. She said you would hit me and hit me."

"You won't be. She was wicked to say so. But what happened? What happened?"

"He called me an ape-boy. He said I wasn't a real boy. He said I was an animal." Timmie dissolved in a flood of tears. "He said he wasn't going to play with a monkey any more. I said I wasn't a monkey; I *wasn't* a monkey. He said I was all funny looking. He said I was horrible ugly. He kept saying and saying and I bit him."

They were both crying now. Miss Fellowes sobbed, "But it isn't true. You know that, Timmie. You're a real boy. You're a dear real boy and the best boy in the world. And no one, *no* one will ever take you away from me."

It was easy to make up her mind, now; easy to know what to do. Only it had to be done quickly. Hoskins wouldn't wait much longer, with his own son mangled—

No, it would have to be done this night, *this* night; with the place four-fifths asleep and the remaining fifth intellectually drunk over Project Middle Ages.

It would be an unusual time for her to return but not an unheard-of one. The guard knew her well and would not dream of questioning her. He would think nothing of her carrying a suitcase. She rehearsed the noncommittal phrase, "Games for the boy," and the calm smile.

Why shouldn't he believe that?

He did. When she entered the doll house again, Timmie was still awake, and she maintained a desperate normality to avoid frightening him. She talked about his dreams with him and listened to him ask wistfully after Jerry.

There would be few to see her afterward, none to question the bundle she would be carrying. Timmie would be very quiet and then it would be a fait accompli. It would be done and what would be the use of trying to undo it. They would leave her be. They would leave them both be.

She opened the suitcase, took out the overcoat, the woolen cap with the ear flaps and the rest.

Timmie said, with the beginning of alarm, "Why are you putting all these clothes on me, Miss Fellowes?"

She said, "I am going to take you outside, Timmie. To where your dreams are."

"My dreams?" His face twisted in sudden yearning, yet fear was there, too.

"You won't be afraid. You'll be with me. You won't be afraid if you're with me, will you, Timmie?"

"No, Miss Fellowes." He buried his little misshapen head against her side, and under her enclosing arm she could feel his small heart thud.

It was midnight and she lifted him into her arms. She disconnected the alarm and opened the door softly.

And she screamed, for facing her across the open door was Hoskins!

There were two men with him and he stared at her, as astonished as she.

Miss Fellowes recovered first by a second and made a quick attempt to push past him; but even with the second's delay he had time. He caught her roughly and hurled her back against a chest of drawers. He waved the men in and confronted her, blocking the door.

"I didn't expect this. Are you completely insane?"

She had managed to interpose her shoulder so that it, rather than Timmie, had struck the chest. She said pleadingly, "What harm can it do if I take him, Dr. Hoskins? You can't put energy loss ahead of a human life?"

Firmly, Hoskins took Timmie out of her arms. "An energy loss this size would mean millions of dollars lost out of the pockets of investors. It would mean a terrible setback for Stasis, Inc. It would mean eventual publicity about a sentimental nurse destroying all that for the sake of an ape-boy."

"*Ape-boy!*" said Miss Fellowes in helpless fury.

"That's what the reporters would call him," said Hoskins.

One of the men emerged now, looping a nylon rope through eyelets along the upper portion of the wall.

Miss Fellowes remembered the rope that Hoskins had pulled outside the room containing Professor Ademewski's rock specimen so long ago.

She cried out, "No!"

But Hoskins put Timmie down and gently removed the overcoat he was wearing. "You stay here, Timmie. Nothing will happen to you. We're just going outside for a moment. All right?"

Timmie, white and wordless, managed to nod.

Hoskins steered Miss Fellowes out of the doll house ahead of himself. For the moment Miss Fellowes was beyond resistance. Dully she noticed the hand pull being adjusted outside the doll house.

"I'm sorry, Miss Fellowes," said Hoskins. "I would have spared you this. I planned it for the night so that you would know only when it was over."

She said in a weary whisper, "Because your son was hurt. Because he tormented this child into striking out at him."

"No. Believe me. I understand about the incident today and I know it was Jerry's fault. But the story has leaked out. It would have to with the press surrounding us on this day of all days. I can't risk having a distorted story about negligence and savage Neanderthalers, so-called, distract from the success of Project Middle Ages. Timmie has to go soon anyway; he might as well go now and give the sensationalists as small a peg as possible on which to hang their trash."

"It's not like sending a rock back. You'll be killing a human being."

"Not killing. There'll be no sensation. He'll simply be a Neanderthal boy in a Neanderthal world. He will no longer be a prisoner and alien. He will have a chance at a free life."

"What chance? He's only seven years old, used to being taken care of, fed, clothed, sheltered. He will be alone. His tribe may not be at the point where he left them now that four years have passed. And if they were, they would not recognize him. He will have to take care of himself. How will he know how?"

Hoskins shook his head in hopeless negative. "Lord, Miss Fellowes, do you think we haven't thought of that? Do you think we would have brought in a child if it weren't that it was the first successful fix of a human or near human we made and that we did not dare to take the chance of unfixing him and finding another fix as good? Why do you suppose we kept Timmie as long as we did, if it were not for our reluctance to send a child back into the past. It's just"—his voice took on a desperate urgency—"that we can wait no longer. Timmie stands in the way of expansion! Timmie is a source of possible bad publicity; we are on the threshold of great things, and I'm sorry, Miss Fellowes, but we can't let Timmie block us. We cannot. We cannot. I'm sorry, Miss Fellowes."

"Well, then," said Miss Fellowes sadly. "Let me say goodbye. Give me five minutes to say goodbye. Spare me that much."

Hoskins hesitated. "Go ahead."

Timmie ran to her. For the last time he ran to her and for the last time Miss Fellowes clasped him in her arms.

For a moment she hugged him blindly. She caught at a chair with the toe of one foot, moved it against the wall, sat down.

"Don't be afraid, Timmie."

"I'm not afraid if you're here, Miss Fellowes. Is that man mad at me, the man out there?"

"No, he isn't. He just doesn't understand about us. Timmie, do you know what a mother is?"

"Like Jerry's mother?"

"Did he tell you about his mother?"

"Sometimes. I think maybe a mother is a lady who takes care of you and who's very nice to you and who does good things."

"That's right. Have you ever wanted a mother, Timmie?"

Timmie pulled his head away from her so that he could look into her face. Slowly, he put his hand to her cheek and hair and stroked her, as long, long ago she had stroked him. He said, "Aren't you my mother?"

"Oh, Timmie."

"Are you angry because I asked?"

"No. Of course not."

"Because I know your name is Miss Fellowes, but—but sometimes, I call you 'Mother' inside. Is that all right?"

"Yes. Yes, it's all right. And I won't leave you any more and nothing will hurt you. I'll be with you to care for you always. Call me Mother, so I can hear you."

"Mother," said Timmie contentedly, leaning his cheek against hers.

She rose, and, still holding him, stepped up on the chair. The sudden beginning of a shout from outside went unheard and, with her free hand, she yanked with all her weight at the cord where it hung suspended between two eyelets.

And Stasis was punctured and the room was empty.

SUGGESTIONS FOR FURTHER READING

Aldiss, Brian. *Who Can Replace a Man?* (Fourteen stories). Harcourt, Brace & World, 1965.

Asimov, Isaac. "The Martian Way," in *Worlds to Come,* edited by Damon Knight. Harper & Row, 1967.

————. "Nightfall," in *Beyond Tomorrow,* edited by Damon Knight. Harper & Row, 1965.

Heinlein, Robert A. *The Past Through Tomorrow* (Twenty-one stories). Putnam, 1967.

Kornbluth, C. M. "The Little Black Bag," in *Time Probe,* edited by Arthur C. Clarke. Delacorte, 1966.

McKenna, Richard. "The Secret Place," in *Orbit 1,* edited by Damon Knight. Putnam, 1966.

————. "Bramble Bush," in *Orbit 3,* edited by Damon Knight. Putnam, 1968.

van Vogt, A. E. "The Seesaw," in *Beyond Tomorrow,* edited by Damon Knight. Harper & Row, 1965.